Regency Surrender

Wicked Deception
Christine Merrill
August 2018

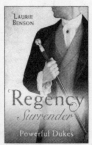
Powerful Dukes
Laurie Benson
September 2018

Scandalous Return
Janice Preston
October 2018

Forbidden Pasts
Elizabeth Beacon
November 2018

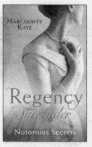
Notorious Secrets
Marguerite Kaye
December 2018

Infamous Reputations
Sarah Mallory
January 2019

Rebellious Debutantes
Annie Burrows
February 2019

Defiant Lords
Annie Herries
March 2019

Passionate Marriages
Sophia James
April 2019

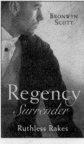
Ruthless Rakes
Bronwyn Scott
May 2019

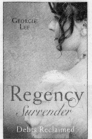
Debts Reclaimed
Georgie Lee
June 2019

Sinful Conquests
Louise Allen
July 2019

Regency Surrender:
Sinful Conquests

LOUISE ALLEN

FSC
FSC C007454

This book is produced from independently certified FSC™ paper
to ensure responsible forest management.

For more information visit: www.harpercollins.co.uk/green

Printed and bound in Great Britain
by CPI Group (UK) Ltd, Croydon, CR0 4YY

MILLS & BOON

First Published in Great Britain 2019
By Mills & Boon, an imprint of HarperCollinsPublishers
1 London Bridge Street, London, SE1 9GF

REGENCY SURRENDER: SINFUL CONQUESTS © 2019 Harlequin Books
S.A.

The Many Sins of Cris de Feaux © 2016 Melanie Hilton
The Unexpected Marriage of Gabriel Stone © 2016 Melanie Hilton

ISBN: 978-0-263-26798-3

52-0719

MIX
Paper from

THE MANY SINS OF
CRIS DE FEAUX

For the Quayistas, in memory of a very cheerful week's research.

Chapter One

Cris de Feaux was drowning. And he was angry. The realisation of both came with the slap of a wave of icy salt water in the face and he shook it out of his eyes, cursing, while he came to terms with the fact that he had swum out from the little cove without thinking, without stopping to do anything but shed his clothes on the rocks and plunge into the breakers.

It had felt good to cut through the surf out into deep water, to push his body hard while his mind became mercifully blank of anything except the co-ordination of arms and legs, the stretch of muscles, the power of a kick. It had felt good, for once in his life, not to consider consequences, not to plan with care and forethought. And now that indulgence was going to kill him.

Was that what he had wanted? Eyes wide with shock, Cris went under, into a watery blue-green world, and kicked up to the surface, spitting and furious. He had fallen in love, unsuitably, impossibly, against all sense and honour. He knew it could never be, he had walked away before any more damage could be done and now his aimless wanderings across England had brought him here, to the edge of North Devon and the ocean.

Which was about to kill him, unless he was very lucky indeed. No, he did not want to die, however much he ached for what could never be, but he had swum too far, beyond the limits of his strength and what he could ask of his hard-exercised horseman's body.

Use your head, he snarled at himself. *You got yourself into this mess, now get yourself out of it. You will not give up. I am* not *killing myself for love.*

He studied the shore between sore, salt-crusted lids. High cliffs, toothed at their base with jagged surf-lashed rocks, mocked him, dared him to try to land and be dashed to bloody death. But there were little coves between the headlands, he knew that. The current was carrying him south-west along the line of the shore so he would go with it, conserve his strength until he saw a point to aim at. Even in those few minutes as he hung in the water it had already carried him onwards, but he dared not risk just lying there, a passive piece of flotsam on the flow. It might be the first day of June, but the sea was strength-sappingly cold. He could hardly feel his legs, except for the white-hot pain of over-extended muscles and tendons. His shoulders and arms felt no better.

The wind shifted, slapping the water into his face from a different angle. *There.* Above the nearest towering headland, a drift of something against the blue of the perfect sky. Smoke. Which meant a house, a beach or perhaps a jetty. *Swim.* Ignore the pain. Dig down to every last ounce of strength and then find some more. Whatever it was that eventually killed the fifth Marquess of Avenmore, it was not going to be a hopeless love and a lack of guts.

Time passed, became simply a blur of pain and effort. He was conscious, somewhere in the back of what was left of his consciousness, that he could not stay afloat much longer. He lifted his head, a lead weight, and saw land, close. A beach, breakers. It seemed the scent of wood smoke and wild garlic cut through the salt for a second. Not a mirage.

But that is. In the moment of clarity he thought he saw a woman, waist-deep in the water, thick brown hair curling loose on her shoulders, calling to him, 'Hold on!'

Mermaid... And then his body gave up, his legs sank, he went under and staggered as his feet hit sand. Somehow he found the strength to stand and the mermaid was coming towards him, her hands held out. The water dragged at him, forcing his legs to move with the frustrating slowness of dream running. The sand shifted beneath his feet as the undertow from the retreating wave sucked at him, but he struggled on. One step towards her, then another and, staggering, four more.

She reached for him as he took one more lurching step and stumbled into her, his hands grasping her shoulders for balance. Under his numb hands her skin was hot, burning, her eyes were brown, like her hair. There were freckles on her nose and her lips were parted.

This was not a mermaid. This was a real, naked, woman. This was life and he was alive. He bent his head and kissed her, her mouth hot, his hands shaking as he pulled her against him.

She kissed him back, unresisting. There was the taste of woman and life and hope through the cold and the taste of salt and the hammering of the blood where his hands rested against her throat.

The wave broke against his back, pushing them both over. She scrabbled free, got to her feet and reached for him, but he was on his feet now, some last reserve of strength coming with that kiss and with hope. He put his arm around her waist and lifted her against him.

'I do not require holding up—you do,' she protested as they gained the hard sand of the beach, but he held on, stumbling across the sand, over stones he could not feel against his numbed soles. Then, when they reached the grass, his legs finally gave way, and he went down again, hardly conscious that he was falling on to rough grass and into oblivion.

Tamsyn stared down at the man at her feet, Adam-naked, pale, tall, beautifully muscled, his hair slicked tight to his head, his face a mask of exhaustion and sheer determination even in unconsciousness. *A sea god, thrown out of his element.*

You could not live on this coast for long without knowing what to do when someone was near drowned. Tamsyn did not hesitate, for all that her head was spinning and an inner voice was demanding to know what she thought she had been doing just then in his arms. She threw all the towels she had over the still body, then her cloak, dragged her shift over her head and set off at a run up the lane that sloped up past the front lawn of her aunts' house on the left and the steep flank of Stib's Head on the right, shouting for help.

'Mizz Tamsyn?' Johnny, the gardener, came out from the woodshed, dropping the armful of logs when he saw her. 'What's amiss?'

She clung to the gatepost, gasping for breath. 'Get Michael and a hurdle. There's a man down at the shore, half-drowned and freezing cold. Bring him back here and keep the cloak over him. Hurry!'

Her aunts' cook just stared as she burst into the

kitchen. 'Get Mrs Tape, tell her we need blankets and hot bricks for the couch in the bathing room.'

She made herself stop in her headlong dash and open the door into the bathing room more slowly so as not to alarm her aunts. They were there already; Aunt Rosie, tight-lipped with pain, had just reached her armchair after the slow walk from her bedchamber, supported between Aunt Izzy and Harris, her maid. Steam was rising from the big tub, where she took the two long soaks a day that were the only remedy that eased her crippled joints. All three women looked up.

'Tamsyn, dear, your clothes…' Izzy began.

'They are bringing a man up from the beach, he needs to get warm.' Tamsyn plunged her hands into the water, winced. 'Too hot, it will be agony, I'll let some out and run in cold.' She moved as she talked, yanking out the plug, turning on the tap. 'I'm sorry, Aunt Rosie, but I think he will die if we don't do something drastic. I've never felt anyone so frozen.' *Except for his mouth.* 'I've sent Cook for Mrs Tape and blankets, we'll have to use the couch in here for him.'

'Yes, of course. Izzy, Harris, never mind me—help Miss Tamsyn.' Rosie was all practicality as usual. 'Hot bricks, do you think? And lots of towels. Warm them by the range and then they can go on the bed to wrap him in, you must keep replacing them as they cool.' The urgency animated Rosie's face, even as she frowned in anxious thought. 'Poor creature, a fisherman, I suppose.'

'I'm heating that beef broth.' Cook bustled in and held the door open. 'Here they come. There's a lot of him, that's for sure.'

Johnny and Michael had clearly sent for help, for along with them Jason, the groom, had one corner of the hurdle while Molly, the maid of all work, and skinny little Peter, the odd-job boy, struggled with the other.

Over six foot of solid, unconscious man was indeed a lot, Tamsyn realised, as they lowered their burden to the floor. She checked the water—warm, but not hot— and pulled the cloak and towels from him. Aunt Izzy gave a squeak, Cook sucked in her breath and Molly murmured, 'Oh, *my...*'

'For goodness' sake, stop having the vapours, all of you. Haven't you seen a naked man before?' As she spoke she realised that the aunts probably hadn't, even if Cook and Molly had quite *active* social lives and she... *Never mind that now.* 'Lift him up and lower him into the water.'

That brought him round. Cursing, the stranger flailed at the men's hands as he was lowered into the big tub until only his head was above the surface. 'What the hell?' His eyes opened, red-rimmed from the salt. 'Damn, that hurts.' Tamsyn saw him focus on her, then his hands moved convulsively under the water to cover himself.

'Not you, too,' she scolded, dropping a large towel strategically into the tub. 'It doesn't matter in the slightest that you are stark naked. No one is looking and we need to get you warm.'

'I apologise for my language.' The words came out in a mumble through chapped lips that set into a tight line as he closed his eyes.

'That is of no account either. I know this is painful, but we need to warm you.' A sharp nod was his only answer, so Tamsyn reached into the water, took his right hand and began to chafe it. 'Molly, you rub his other hand. And, Harris, could you help Miss Pritchard back to her room? You had best go, too, Aunt Izzy.'

'Nonsense, we will stay right here.' Aunt Rosie was as brisk in her manner as she was slow in her movements. 'Johnny, ride for Dr Tregarth.'

'Don't need a...' Cris began.

'You be quiet, young man. Do as you are told and stop wasting your energy.'

Across the tub Tamsyn met Molly's amused gaze. She doubted whether the man under their hands, who must be about thirty, had been addressed like a stubborn schoolboy for quite some time. He was exceedingly handsome in a severe way and very blond now that his hair was drying patchily. She shuffled along on her knees, dipped her hands into the water and felt for his feet, which recoiled at the touch, bringing his knees above the water and a small tidal wave slopping over the edge.

'I'm sorry if you are ticklish. Can you bear it if we add more hot water?'

'Yes. And not ticklish,' he muttered. 'Taken by surprise.'

And aren't you cross about that, my merman? He was not used to being at a disadvantage, Tamsyn suspected. Certainly he was unused to his body not being under his complete control. She stood up to reach for the hot tap, hoping the supply of hot water would last. As she leaned across him he opened his eyes and looked directly at her.

Tamsyn realised she was wearing nothing but a linen shift that clung to her wet body in a manner that was barely decent and was probably thoroughly unflattering into the bargain. And not only was the stranger looking at her, but the room was full of male staff and a lad who certainly shouldn't be exposed to the sight of the youngest lady of the house in such a state. She topped up the hot water and picked up the cloak from the floor with an assumption of ease. 'I'll just go and put on something…warmer. Keep chafing his hands and feet. Oh, there you are, Mrs Tape—can you make up the couch as a bed and get it warm, please? I'll be back in a minute.' She fled.

It was a perfectly calm and collected exit, on the outside. But it was flight nevertheless. Her hands were shaking as she stripped off the shift, sponged the salt from her skin as rapidly as she could, heedless of drips and splashes. Her hair, curly and wayward at the best of times, was resistant to having the salty tangles combed out, but the pain as the comb snagged and pulled was a welcome distraction.

The stranger surely wouldn't recall that they had kissed in that hot, open-mouthed exchange of life and… well, *desire* on her part, she might as well face it. She couldn't pretend it had been shock and that she had been merely passive. She had kissed him back, she knew she had. Goodness only knew what had made him kiss her. Delirium, maybe?

He probably wouldn't recall being dumped stark naked into a large vat of warm water with an interested audience of most of their household, male and female, either. He would be lucky to survive this without catching an inflammation of the lungs, and that was what she ought to be worrying about, not wondering what had come over her to feel a visceral, dizzying stab of lust for a total stranger.

He had a beautiful body and she had seen it, all of it, and she was not made of stone. She was, after all, the notorious Tamsyn Perowne of Barbary Combe House and she might as well live up to it, once in a while.

But that was quite enough scandal for one day. The

gown she pulled from the clothes press was an ordinary workaday one with sleeves to the elbow and a neckline that touched her collarbone. She twisted up her plait, stabbed a few hairpins into it and topped it with a cap. *There, perfect.* She gave her reflection a brisk nod in the mirror. No one in history ever had inappropriate thoughts while wearing a cap, surely?

When she re-entered the bathing chamber the couch was heaped with pillows, towels and blankets. Mrs Tape was wrapping bricks in flannel and the aunts had retreated behind the screen. Molly was up to her elbows in the tub, rubbing the stranger's feet with what Tamsyn decided was unnecessary enthusiasm.

'That will do, Molly. I think we had best transfer the gentleman to the couch.'

'We?' It came out as a croak. He opened his eyes, narrow slits of winter-sea blue. Perhaps she had over-estimated the likelihood of him forgetting anything.

'Jason and Michael, help the gentleman out and to the couch. Come, Molly, behind the screen with you.' She shooed the maid along in front of her and grimaced at her aunts. Aunt Izzy was looking interested, although anything from the mating habits of snails to the making of damson jam interested her. Aunt Rosie wore an expression of mixed amusement and concern.

'Did he say anything while I was changing?' Tamsyn whispered while splashing, grunting and muffled curses marked the unseen progress from tub to couch.

'Nothing,' Aunt Izzy whispered back. 'Except, when we added more hot water, some words in a foreign tongue we do not know. They sounded...forceful.'

'Perhaps he is a foreigner.'

'I do not think so.' Aunt Rosie pushed her spectacles

further up her nose. 'He looks English to me and definitely a gentleman, not a fisherman, so goodness knows what he was doing in our bay. He reminds me of a very cross archangel. So very blond and severe.'

'Are you acquainted with many archangels, dear?' Aunt Izzy teased. 'And are they all English?'

'He is how I have always imagined them, although I have to confess, he does require a pair of wings, shimmering raiment and a fiery sword to complete the picture and I do not think he is looking quite at his best, just at the moment.'

'Excuse me, ladies, but the gentleman is in bed now.' Michael, their footman, stepped round the screen, his hands full of damp towels. 'I brought one of my own nightshirts down for him. It's not what he's used to, I'll be bound, but it's a clean one.'

'Excellent. Thank you, Michael. Now, if you could just drain the tub and refill it for Miss Pritchard I'll set the screen around the bed and everyone can be private.'

'All the hot water's gone, Miss Tamsyn. Jason's gone to stoke up the boiler.'

'In that case, if you'll help me through to the front parlour, Michael, I'll rest in there.' Aunt Rosie put one twisted hand on the footman's arm. 'I have no doubt our visitor would appreciate some peace and quiet.'

Tamsyn left Aunt Izzy and Molly to accompany Rosie on her painful way to the front of the house, straightened her cap, and, hopefully, her emotions, and went to see how her patient was.

He opened his eyes as she approached the bed. 'Thank you.' They had propped him up against the pillows, the covers pulled right up under his armpits, but his arms were free. His words were polite, but the blue eyes were furious.

'Do not try to speak, it is obviously painful. Have they given you anything to drink yet? Just nod.'

He inclined his head and she saw the beaker on the edge of the tub and fetched it over, sniffed the contents and identified watered brandy. 'Cook will bring you some broth when you feel a little stronger. Sip this. Can you hold it?' He did not look like a man who was taking kindly to being treated like an invalid, whether he was one or not. His long fingers closed around the beaker, brushing hers. The touch was cold still, but not with the deadly chill his skin had held before.

Tamsyn went to fuss with the screen, pulling it around the bed so he wouldn't feel she was staring at him if he fumbled with the drink. She would find some warm water in a moment so he could bathe his sore eyes.

The beaker was empty when she turned back and she took it from his hand, disconcerted to find those reddened eyes watching her with a curious intentness. *Surely he does not remember that kiss?* She willed away both the blush and the urge to press her lips to his again. 'What is your name, sir? I am Tamsyn Perowne and the two other ladies are Miss Pritchard and Miss Isobel Holt.'

'Cri... De...'

She leaned closer to catch the horse whisper. 'Christopher Defoe? Are you a connection of the writer? I love *Robinson Crusoe.*' He shook his head, a sharp, definitive denial. 'No? Never mind. Whoever you are, you are very welcome here at Barbary Combe House. Rest a little and when the doctor has been in I will fetch the broth. In fact, that sounds like him now.' The sound of raised voices in the entrance hall penetrated even the heavy door. 'And someone else. What on earth is going on?' She had barely reached the other side of the screen when the door opened and Dr Tregarth strode in, speaking angrily over his shoulder to the man who pushed through after him.

'Don't be a fool, Penwith. Of course this isn't Jory Perowne. The man went over Barbary Head on to the rocks two years ago, right in front of six dragoons and the Revenue's Riding Officer. He was dead before you could get a noose around his neck and he certainly hasn't walked out of the sea now!'

'That's as may be, but he was a tricky bastard, was Perowne, and I wouldn't put it past him to play some disappearing game. And I'm the magistrate for these parts and I'll not take any chances.'

Squire Penwith. *Will he never give up?* Tamsyn stopped dead in front of the man, hands on hips, chin up so he could not see how much his words distressed her. *Stupid, vindictive, blustering old goat.* She managed not to actually say so. 'Mr Penwith, if you can tell me how a man can go over a two-hundred-foot cliff on to rocks and survive the experience I would be most interested to hear.' That glimpse of the shattered, limp body in the second before the waves took it… She hardened her voice against the shake that threatened it. 'My husband was certainly a tricky bastard, but I have yet to hear he could fly.'

Chapter Two

So, his mermaid in a dowdy cap was a widow, was she? Cris winced as the cracked corner of his mouth kicked up in an involuntary smile at the sharp defiance in her voice, then the amusement faded as the other man, the magistrate, began to bluster at her.

'He wasn't the only tricky one in this household. I wouldn't put it past the pair of you to have rigged up some conjuror's illusion—and don't open those big brown eyes at me, all innocent-like. I know the smuggling's still going on, so who is running it if your husband's dead. Eh? Tell me that.'

'Smuggling's been a way of life on this coast since man could paddle a raft, you foolish man.' Cris liked the combination of logic and acid in the clear voice. 'Long before Jory Perowne was born, and for long after, I'll be bound.' Mrs Perowne spoke as though to a somewhat stupid scholar.

'Don't you call me a fool, you—'

'Penwith, you must not speak to Mrs Perowne in that intemperate manner.' That was the doctor, he assumed.

The magistrate swore and Cris threw back the covers, swung his legs off the couch and realised he was clad only in a nightshirt that came to mid-thigh. With a grimace he draped the top sheet around himself, flung one end over his shoulder like a toga and stalked around the screen, which, mercifully, was sturdy enough not to fall over when he grabbed its frame for support after two strides.

His mermaid—*Tamsyn*—swung round. 'Mr Defoe, kindly get back to your bed.' She sounded completely exasperated, presumably with the entire male sex, him included. He couldn't say he blamed her.

'In a moment, ma'am.' The two men stared at him. One, young, lanky, with a leather bag in his hand, lifted dark eyebrows at the sight of him. That must be the doctor. The other had the face of an irritable middle-aged schoolmaster complete with jowls and topped with an old-fashioned brown wig. 'You, sir, used foul language in the presence of this lady. You will apologise and leave. I imagine even you do not require the doctor to explain the difference between me and a man two years dead?' His voice might be hoarse and cracked, his eyes might be swollen, but he could still look down his nose with the hauteur of a marquess confronted with a muck heap when he wanted to.

Predictably the magistrate went red and made gobbling sounds. 'You cannot speak to me like that, sir. I'll see you—'

'At dawn in some convenient field, your worship?' He raised his left eyebrow in a manner that he knew was infuriatingly superior. His friends told him so often enough. The anger with his own stupidity still burned in his veins and dealing with this bully was as good a way to vent it as any.

'Mr Penwith, my husband was five feet and ten inches tall, he had black hair and brown eyes and his right earlobe was missing. Now, as you can quite clearly see, Mr Defoe is taller, of completely different colouring and is in possession of both his ears in their entirety. Now, perhaps you would like to leave before you make even more of an ass of yourself?' Tamsyn Perowne, pink in the face with the steam from the bath, her brown curls coming down beneath that ludicrous cap, was an unlikely Boudicca, but she was magnificent, none the less.

Cris locked his knees and hung on grimly until the magistrate banged out of the room, then let the doctor take his arm and help him back to the couch. Somehow his muscles had been replaced by wet flannel, his joints were being prodded with red-hot needles and he wanted nothing more than a bottle of brandy and a month's sleep.

'You stay that side of the screen, Mrs Perowne,' the doctor said. 'I'll just check your shipwrecked sailor for broken bones.' He began to manipulate Cris's legs, blandly unconcerned by the muttered curses he provoked.

'Nothing is broken. I swam out too far, got caught by the current and almost drowned. That is all that is wrong with me. Idiocy, not shipwreck.'

'Where did you go in?' Tregarth pushed up one of Cris's eyelids, then the other.

'Hartland Quay.'

'You swam from there and then got yourself out of the current and into this bay? By Neptune, sir, you're a strong swimmer, I'll say that for you.' He produced a conical wooden instrument from his bag, pressed the wide end to Cris's chest and applied his ear to the other. 'Your lungs are clear. You'll feel like a bag of unravelled knitting for a day or so, I've no doubt, and those muscles will give you hell from overwork, but there's no harm done.' He pulled up the bedding. 'You may come round now, Mrs Perowne. Keep him in bed tomorrow, if you can. Feed him up, keep him warm, let him sleep and send for me if he throws a fever. Good day to you, Mr Defoe.'

'I'm not—' *Not Mr Defoe. I'm Anthony Maxim Charles St Crispin de Feaux, Marquess of Avenmore*. With no calling card, no money—and no breeches, come to that, which left him precious little aristocratic dignity. Tamsyn, *Mrs Perowne*, had misheard his mumbled words. The family always used the French pronunciation of their name, but apparently that did not survive gargling with half the Atlantic.

The doctor had gone and Tamsyn was standing at the foot of the bed, hands crossed neatly at her waist, cap perched on her curls, looking for all the world as though butter would not melt in her mouth and not at all like a woman who would call a magistrate an ass or kiss a naked stranger in the surf. He could tell her that kiss might have saved his life, but he suspected that would not be welcome.

'The broth is coming, Mr Defoe.'

Yes, he'd stay a commoner for a while, it was simpler and he had no intention of broadcasting his recklessness to the world. He nodded his thanks.

'Where should we send to inform someone of your safety? I imagine your acquaintance will be very anxious.' She took a tray from the cook and laid it across his thighs. 'Try to swallow the broth slowly, it will soothe your throat as well as strengthen you.'

In his experience women tended to fuss at sickbeds and he had been braced against attempts to spoon-feed him. Mrs Perowne appeared to trust him to manage, despite the evidence of his shaking hand. His arm muscles felt as though he had been racked. 'Traveller,' he managed between mouthfuls. 'My valet is at Hartland Quay with my carriage.'

'And he can bring you some clothes.' She caught his eye and smiled, a sudden, wicked little quirk of the lips that sent messages straight to his groin. *One muscle still in full working order.* 'Magnificent as you look in a toga, sir, it is not a costume best suited to the Devon winds.'

Had he really kissed her in the sea, or was that a hallucination? No, it was real. He could conjure up the heat of her body pressed to his, the feminine softness and curves as their naked flesh met. He could remember, too, the heat of her mouth, open under his, the sweet glide of her tongue. Hell, that made him feel doubly guilty, firstly for forcing himself on a complete stranger and secondly for even thinking about anyone but Katerina. *Who can never be mine.* He focused on the guilt, a novel enough emotion, to prevent him thinking about that body, now covered in layers of sensible cotton.

'You will stay in bed and rest, as the doctor said?'

Cris nodded. He had no desire to make a fool of himself, fetching his length on the floor in front of her when his legs gave out on him. Tomorrow he would be better. Tomorrow he might even be able to think rationally.

'Good.' She lifted the tray and he saw the strength in the slim arms, the curve of sleek feminine muscle where her sleeves were rolled up to the elbow. She swam well enough to take to the sea by herself and he'd wager that she rode, too. 'We know you are stubborn from the way you tried to get up the lane by yourself instead of waiting where I left you. I've just spoken to them and the lads said you were crawling.'

'I was getting there. If I hadn't been weakened by

that…encounter in the sea, I could have walked.' Even as he said it, he could have bitten his tongue. So much for apologising, something that Lord Avenmore rarely had to do. Apparently Mr Defoe was more apt to blunder than the marquess was. He certainly had an unexpectedly bawdy sense of humour.

'An encounter, you call it?' There was a definite spark in the brown eyes and the colour was up over her cheekbones. Indignation seemed to make those brown curls fight free of the cap, too. His one functioning muscle stirred again, complaining that it was in need of exercise. 'That, you poor man, was the resuscitation of the half-drowned. We do it a lot in these parts. I'll fetch you pen and paper.'

And that apparently dealt with the apology. Mrs Perowne was not in the common run of gentry ladies, it seemed. Nor did her late husband seem to have been the kind of man he would have expected to be the owner of this elegant old house, not if the local magistrate was after him with a noose and his widow referred to him as a *tricky bastard.* That clod of a squire had spoken with unfeeling bluntness about her husband's death and yet she had stood up to him, covering her emotions with defiance and pride.

The puzzling Mrs Perowne returned with a writing slope under one arm and a small bowl in the other. 'I'll just bathe your eyes, they look exceedingly sore.'

Cris thought he probably looked an exceeding mess, all over. His hair had dried anyhow, his skin felt as though he'd been sandpapered and doubtless his eyes were both red and squinty. And he needed a shave. What his friends would say if they saw him now, he shuddered to think. Collins, when he arrived, would express himself even more strongly. He regarded the

Marquess of Avenmore as a walking testimonial to his own skills as a valet and did not take kindly to seeing his master looking less than perfect.

'If you would give me the bowl I will bathe them myself.' He had his pride and being tended to while he looked like this did nothing for his filthy mood.

'Very well.' She set the writing slope on the chair beside the couch, handed him the bowl and dragged the screen around the bed. 'My aunt, who suffers from severe arthritic pain, will be taking one of her regular hot soaks shortly. We will try not to disturb you.'

'Mrs Perowne?'

She looked around the edge of the screen. 'Mr Defoe?'

'I am in your aunt's bathing chamber, occupying her couch. I must remove myself to another room.'

'If you do, you will agitate her. She is worried enough about you as it is.' She smiled suddenly, a wide, unguarded smile, so unlike the carefully controlled expressions of the diplomatic ladies he had spent so much time with recently. 'Rest here for the moment, control your misplaced chivalrous impulses and we will find you another chamber at some point.'

Misguided chivalrous impulses. Little cat. She was obviously unused to men who actually acted like gentlemen. Cris twisted the water out of the cloth in the basin and sponged his eyes until the worst of the stinging subsided, then put the bowl aside and reached for the writing slope. Beyond the screen people were moving about, water was pouring into the tub, steam rose. This might be the edge of the country and manners might be earthy, but they certainly possessed plumbing that surpassed that in any of his houses.

He focused on the letter to shut out the sounds of either Miss Prichard or Miss Holt being helped into the bath. Collins was rather more than a valet, more of a confidential assistant, and he could be relied upon to use his discretion.

…pay the reckoning and bring everything to…

'Mrs Perowne, if I might trouble you for a moment?'

'Sir?' She was decidedly flushed from the steam now. Her pink cheeks and the damp tendrils of hair on her brow suited her.

He recalled her leaning over him to turn on the tap as he lay in the bath and forced his croak of a voice into indifferent politeness. 'Could you tell me how I should direct my man to find this house?'

'Barbary Combe House, Stibworthy. If he asks in the village, anyone will direct him.'

'Thank you.'

Barbary Combe House, Stibworthy. Do not enquire in the village for Mr Defoe as I am not known there, having come by sea. Ensure you bring an appropriate vehicle.
C. Defoe

Collins would not fail to pick up on that. The interior of Cris's travelling coach with its ingenious additions and luxurious upholstery might go unnoticed, but not if the crests on the door panels were left uncovered. It had caused enough of a stir at Hartland Quay to have a marquess descend on a waterside inn, but with any luck the gossip would be fairly localised.

He folded the letter, wrote the address and found a wafer in the box to seal it with, then forced himself to relax. The doctor's advice had been sound, but despite it, when Collins arrived tomorrow he would be out of here and away from the curiously distracting

Mrs Perowne. Back to London, to the normality he had fled from.

Eyes closed, he willed himself to sleep. The room was quiet now, with only the sounds of someone moving about as they tidied up. He was exhausted and yet his eyes would not stay closed. Cris stared at the ceiling. He could *always* sleep when he needed to, it was simply a matter of self-discipline.

He seemed to be somewhat short of any kind of control just at the moment. He hadn't had enough focus to notice when he was in danger of drowning himself and he couldn't even manage to fall flat on his face on a beach without kissing the local widow before he did so. And he was the man the government relied on to settle diplomatic contretemps discreetly, and, if necessary, unconventionally. Just now he wouldn't trust himself to defuse an argument between two drovers in the local public house, let alone one between a brace of ambassadors over a vital treaty clause.

It had all begun when he had first set eyes on Katerina, Countess von Stadenburg, the wife of a Prussian diplomat at the Danish court. Tiny, blonde, blue-eyed, exquisite and intelligent. His perfect match. And she wanted him, too, he could see it in her eyes, in the almost imperceptible, perfectly controlled gestures she made when he was close, the brush of fingertips on his cuff, the touch of a shoe against his under the dinner table, the flutter of a fan. That one kiss.

But she was married and he was the representative of the British Crown. To have indulged in an *affaire*, even if Katerina had been willing, was not only to dishonour her, but to risk a diplomatic incident. And he did not want an *affaire*, he had wanted to marry her. Which was impossible. Honour, duty, respect gave him only one logical course of action. He concluded his business as fast as possible and then he left, taking his leave of her under the jealous eye of her husband as casually as though she was just another, barely noticed, diplomatic wife, a pretty adjunct to her husband's social life.

Her control had been complete, her polite, formulaic responses perfect in their indifference. Only her eyes, dark with hurt and resignation, had told him the truth. He wished, for the thousandth time, he had not looked, had not seen, and that he could carry away with him only the memory of her cool, accented, voice. 'You are leaving the court, Lord Avenmore? Do have a safe journey, my lord. Heinrich, come, we will be late for the start of the concert.'

Finally he felt his lids drift closed, sensed the soft sounds of the house blur and fade. Strangely the eyes that he imagined watching him, just as it all slipped away, were brown, not blue.

'Michael, take this and give it to Jason, please. Tell him to ride to Hartland Quay at once and find Mr Defoe's man.'

'Is he sleeping, dear?' Aunt Izzy looked up from the vase of flowers she was arranging.

'Yes. So soundly I thought for an awful moment that he had stopped breathing.' Tamsyn closed the drawing-room door behind her and went to straighten the bookstand that kept Aunt Rosie's novel propped at just the right angle for her. 'He must be exhausted. I am certain it was only sheer cussedness that kept him going. It would be exhausting enough to swim that distance when the sea is warm, but it is still so cold, and with that current it is a miracle he survived.' She picked up the cut flower stems for Aunt Izzy, then twitched a leaf spray.

'He must be very fit, which is not surprising with that physique. You are fidgeting, Tamsyn.' Aunt Rosie looked up from her book. 'Did wretched Squire Penwith upset you, talking about dear Jory like that?'

'The man is a fool. *Dear Jory* was a tricky—er… devil, but even he could not fly.' She flung herself down on the window seat with more energy than elegance. 'Yes, the squire upset me, with his blustering and his utter lack of imagination. And, yes, I still hate to think about that afternoon.' She stared out over the sloping lawn at the sea, placid and blue in the sunlight, hiding its wicked currents and sharp fangs under a mask of serenity. Jory had lived with its dangers and its beauty and he had chosen it to end his life, which meant she could never look at it the same way again.

She lifted her feet up and hugged her knees. 'And it worries me that Mr Penwith is of no use to us whatsoever with the troubles we've been having. I cannot decide whether he thinks we should suffer as payment for my husband's sins, regardless of what crimes are committed against us, or whether he simply hates me.'

'Or whether he is a lazy fool,' Aunt Rosie said tartly. 'A hayrick on fire—must be small boys up to mischief. Our stock escaping through the hedge—must be the fault of the hedger. Every single lobster pot being empty for a week—must be the incompetence of our fishermen. Really, does he think we are idiots?'

'He thinks we are women, Rosie dear,' Aunt Izzy said, hacking at a blameless fern frond with her shears. 'And not only that, women who choose to live without male protection, which proves we are either reckless or soft in the head.'

'Perhaps he is being bribed to look the other way,' Tamsyn said. She had not mentioned it before because she did not want to upset Aunt Izzy. Even now she did not mention a name.

'Bribed? By my nephew Franklin, I presume.' Izzy might be vague, but there was nothing amiss with her wits.

'He does want us out of here.'

'Out of here and into that poky dower house on his estate where we will be *safe* and where he can *look after us* as though we were a trio of children or lunatics. The boy's a vulture, Isobel,' Rosie snapped, her fierceness alarming in one so frail. 'He wants to get his hands on this house, this estate. He wants Barbary.'

'Well, he can't have it. Papa left it to me for my lifetime and I've a good thirty years left in me, so he will have to learn patience.' Izzy picked up the vase and placed it on the sideboard. 'His foolish little games won't scare me out.'

So long as they stay foolish little games, Tamsyn thought, even as she smiled approval of her aunt's defiance. She rested her chin on her knees and let her gaze rest, unfocused, on the sea. But why would Lord Chelford trouble himself over this one small estate, other than through pique at not being left the entirety of his great-uncle's holdings when he inherited the title? Franklin was spoilt and greedy and he would soon get tired of this game and go back to his life of leisure and pleasure in London.

It was strange, though, that he should have made that offer to rehouse his aunt and her companion now. After all, Aunt Izzy had inherited the life interest in the Barbary Combe estate, the house and the contents when her father, the previous Lord Chelford, died five years ago and she had lived there for ten years before that.

It must be a sudden whim. Or perhaps she was

misjudging Franklin, perhaps his intentions were good and the series of mishaps just after Izzy had refused his offer were nothing but coincidence and bad luck. *Or perhaps the moon's made of green cheese.*

Chapter Three

There was something in the quality of the soft sounds around his bed that was very familiar. Cris kept his eyes closed and inhaled a discreet hint of bay-rum cologne and leather polish. 'Collins?'

'Yes, sir?' Typically there was no hesitation over the correct way to address him.

Cris opened his eyes and turned over on to his back. Collins did not so much as raise an eyebrow at the sudden violence of the swear word.

'Muscle strain, sir?'

'The pain you get when you over-exercise.' Cris levered himself up against the pillow. 'The kind that makes you think your muscles are full of ground glass.'

'Massage,' Collins pronounced, blandly ignoring the reaction that threat of torture provoked. 'I have unpacked your possessions in an upstairs room and the bed is made up, sir. I thought you would wish to transfer there before nightfall. It is five o'clock and the ladies are all in the front room just at the moment.'

Collins was considerably more than a valet. He numbered code breaking, five languages and lethally accurate knife-throwing amongst his less public skills, although he was also more than capable of turning out the Marquess of Avenmore in a state of perfection for any social occasion.

Now he shook out Cris's heavy silk banyan and waited patiently while, swearing under his breath, Cris got out of bed. Collins did, however, wince at the sight of the borrowed nightshirt.

'I've already been carried through the house and dumped in the bath stark naked in front of every female in the place.' Cris eased his arms into the sleeves of the robe and allowed Collins to tie the sash. 'I thought it courteous to cover myself.' The more he thought about it, the more embarrassing it became. He had no reticence about his own body, but being dropped nude and dripping like a half-stunned fish, in front of a gaggle of single ladies was…not good form.

The other man muttered something about stable doors and bolted horses and dropped a pair of backless leather slippers on the floor for him to shuffle his feet into.

'I feel as though I'm a hundred and four,' Cris grumbled as he made his way across to the door.

'If you came ashore here, I would suggest that you had not been swimming like a centenarian.' Collins opened the door and tactfully did not offer his arm. 'Top of the stairs, first on the right, sir.'

'I was swimming like a damn fool, I know that.' Cris walked straight up the stairs without stopping. Swearing in Russian certainly helped. 'You must have assumed I had drowned.'

'I saw no signs of a struggle on the beach when I found your clothes, sir.' Collins followed him into the bedchamber and shut the door. 'I therefore concluded you had entered the sea of your own volition. I confess to a degree of anxiety, especially as you had gone out so early and I had not thought to look for you for some time. I questioned the local fishermen, but they had seen nothing. They did, however, inform me of the direction of the currents and I was about to ride along the clifftops in the hope of sighting you when the message arrived.'

'I was distracted.' Cris ignored the tactful murmur of *Quite, sir.* However discreet he had been, and, in fact, there was nothing to be discreet about, it was close to impossible to keep secrets from Collins. Ominously, the bed was covered with towels and the man was pouring oil into his palm. With grim resignation Cris stripped off and lay face down. 'If you could stop short of actually making me scream I would be obliged. There are ladies around.'

Collins took hold of his right calf and started doing hideous things to the muscles with his thumbs. 'Yes, sir. An interesting household.'

'Mrs Perowne is the widow of a man who leapt off a cliff rather than be arrested and hanged for smuggling and associated crimes.'

'Indeed, sir? Very novel. If you could just bend your knee… Miss Holt, the owner, seems a kindly lady.'

'Is she the owner? I assumed Mrs Perowne was.' *Brown eyes, hot, sweet mouth, the promise of oblivion for a while.* He stirred, uncomfortably aware of how arousing that thought was. 'Ow! Damn it, man—are you attempting to plait those muscles?'

'No, to unplait them, sir.' Collins moved to the other leg. 'Miss Holt welcomed me to her home. That was how she worded it.'

A ruthless massage was certainly an effective antidote to inappropriate erotic thoughts that made him feel unfaithful to Katerina. Which was a pointless emotion.

An indulgence he was not going to wallow in, making himself feel like some tragic victim. They had not been lovers, they had not even spoken of that feeling between them, let alone exchanged protestations of love. There had just been those silent exchanges amidst crowds of others and that one, snatched, burning kiss when they had found themselves alone, passing in a corridor at the Danish royal palace. No words, no hesitation, only her body trembling between his hands, only her mouth sealed to his, her hands on his shoulders, and then her little sob as they tore themselves apart and, without a word, turned and walked away.

It was a relationship that could never be, not without the sacrifice of her reputation, his honour. Cris set his jaw, as much against the pain in his heart as the agony in his overstretched joints. He was a man, he was not going to become a monk because of how he felt for an unattainable woman. Next season he must find himself a bride, get married, assume the responsibilities of his title. He would be faithful to his wife, but not to a phantom—that way lay madness.

Tamsyn Perowne had kissed him back. He smiled into the pillow. It had probably been shock. Doubtless she would box his ears if he took any further liberties. Any fantasies about a willing widow to make him forget his ghosts were just that, fantasies. She was a respectable lady in a small community, not some society sophisticate. He'd be gone tomorrow, out of her life.

There was a tap of knuckles on wood, the creak of hinges and a sudden flap of linen as Collins swirled the sheet over his prone body.

'Oh, I beg your pardon, I had assumed Mr Defoe would be in bed by now, not...' Tamsyn put down the tray on the small table in the window embrasure and tried to forget the brief glimpse of elegant, sharp-boned bare feet as the sheet had settled over the man on the bed. She had seen all of him today, in the sea, in the bath, so what was there to discomfort her so in one pair of bare feet?

'I have brought some more broth.' *Long toes, high arches, the line of the tendon at his heel...* She was prattling now, looking anywhere but at the bed. But it was a small room and a big bed and there wasn't anywhere else to look, except at the ceiling or the fireplace or the soberly dressed man who stood beside the bed in his shirtsleeves, hands glistening with oil. 'It isn't much, and dinner will not be long, but the doctor said to keep his strength up and it will help Mr Defoe's throat.'

'Thank you, ma'am,' the valet said. 'I will see that Mr Defoe drinks the soup while it is hot.'

'Mr Defoe is present, and conscious, and capable of speech, Collins.' The husky voice from the bed brought her head round with a jerk. His eyes were closed, his head resting on his crossed arms, his expression as austere as that of an effigy on a tomb.

'Are you warm enough? Perhaps I should light the fire.' She moved without thinking, touched her fingers to the exposed six inches of shoulder above the sheet, just as she would if it had been one of the aunts in the bed. But this was not one of the aunts and his eyes opened, heavy-lidded, watchful, and she did not seem able to move her fingers from the smooth, chill, skin. When they had kissed, those beautiful, unreadable blue eyes had been open, too. Now she tried not to show any recollection of that moment.

'Yes, I will light the fire.' The words came out in

a coherent sentence, which was a surprise. Her hand was still refusing to obey her. 'You seem a trifle cool.'

'Cool? You think so?' The question had a mocking edge that seemed directed more at himself than at her.

'I will deal with the fire, ma'am.' The manservant's words jerked her back into some sort of reality, mercifully before her hand could trail down below the edge of the sheet.

'Thank you.' Tamsyn twitched the cover up over Mr Defoe's shoulders. 'I'll just…' The blue eyes were still open, still watching her. 'You should drink that soup while it is hot.'

She retreated with what dignity she could muster and did her best to close the door firmly, but quietly, behind her and not bang it shut and run. What was the matter with her? He was an attractive man. A very attractive man, and she had seen the whole of him, so was in an excellent position to judge, and she had been foolish enough to kiss him and she had saved his life. No, probably not. He was determined enough, and strong enough, to have kept going up the lane if he'd had to. He would have walked in through the kitchen door, in all his naked glory—and that would have made for a nasty accident if Cook had her hands full of something hot at the time. The thought made her smile.

'How is Mr Defoe, dear?' asked Aunt Izzy. 'You look very cheerful.'

'Alive, a little warmer and, I suspect, in considerable pain, but his manservant seems highly competent and I am sure he is not going to succumb to a fever.'

'That is good news. I suppose we may rely on his man to contact his wife, let her know he is safe.'

'His *what*?'

'Wife.' Aunt Izzy stopped with her hand on the door into the drawing room.

'Whose wife?'

'Mr Defoe's. He is more likely to be married than not, don't you think? He is very personable, I am sure he is most respectable when he has some clothes on and, if he can afford such a superior manservant, he is obviously in funds.' She cocked her head on one side, thinking. 'And he is probably thirty, wouldn't you say?'

'About that, yes. Not more.' His body was that of a fit young man, but there was something about him that spoke of maturity and responsibility. Doubtless marriage would give him that. It had not made Jory any more dependable, let alone respectable, but the man had been wild from a boy and his sense of duty and accountability was not one that most decent men would recognise.

She had no desire to smile now, which was only right and proper. A woman might look at an attractive man and allow her imagination to wander a little…*a lot.* But a respectable woman did not look at a *married* man and think anything at all, nor see him as anything other than a fellow human being in need of succour.

'Mizz Tamsyn, is it convenient for you to review the list of linen for the order I was going to send off tomorrow?' She looked up to find Mrs Tape at the door, inventory in hand. 'Only you said you wanted to look it over it with me, but if you're busy I can leave it.'

'Certainly. I will come now, Mrs Tape.' She turned and followed the housekeeper. Linen cupboards full of darned sheets were exactly what she should be concentrating on. And then the accounts and a decision about which of the sheep to send to market would keep her busy until dinner time.

All the humdrum duties of everyday life for an almost respectable country widow who should be very grateful for a calm, uneventful life.

'Do you think Mr Defoe will find our dinner time unfashionably early?' Aunt Izzy sipped her evening glass of sherry and fixed her gaze on Tamsyn.

'I am sure I do not know. I suppose seven o'clock is neither an old-fashioned country hour nor a fashionably late town one. But as he is either asleep, or will be having his meal on a tray at his bedside, I do not think we need concern ourselves too much with whether his modish sensibilities are likely to be offended.'

'Mr Defoe strikes me as an adaptable man,' Aunt Rosie remarked. 'Although how I can tell that from the brief glimpses I have had of him—'

'Excuse me, Miss Holt.' It was Jason, hat in hand, at the drawing-room door. 'Only there's a message from Willie Tremayne—a dozen of the sheep have gone over the cliff at Striding's Cove.'

'*A dozen?*' Tamsyn realised she was on her feet, halfway across the room. 'How can that be? The pastures are all fenced, Willie was with them, wasn't he? Is he all right?'

'Aye, Willie's safe enough, though by all accounts he's proper upset. A rogue dog got in with them and the hurdle was broken down in the far corner, though the lad Willie sent says he's no idea how that happened, because it was all right and tight yesterday.'

'Whose dog?' Tamsyn yanked at the bell pull. 'There aren't any around these parts that aren't chained or are working dogs, good with stock.'

'Don't rightly know, Mizz Tamsyn. The lad says Willie shot it and it doesn't seem to have been mad, by all accounts. Not frothing at the mouth nor anything like that. Just vicious.'

'Oh, Michael, there you are. Find Molly, tell her to put out my riding habit and boots. Jason, saddle my mare.'

'I don't think there's rightly anything you can do, Mizz Tamsyn, not at this time in the evening. Some of the men from the village helped Willie barricade the fence and one of the boats has gone down to the foot of the cliffs to see if there's anything to salvage.' Jason shrugged. 'By the time you get there it'll all be done.' He looked past her to the fireside and lowered his voice. 'I think the ladies are a mite upset, perhaps you'd be best biding here. I'll send the lad back with the message that you'll be along in the morning, shall I?'

She wanted to go, to stand on the clifftop and rage, but it would achieve nothing. She had to think. 'Yes, do that if you please, Jason.'

When she turned back into the room she was glad she had listened to him. Aunt Izzy was pale, a lace handkerchief pressed to her lips. Rosie was white-faced also, but hers was the pallor of anger. 'That was no accident. That was Chelford up to his nasty tricks again. Izzy, that boy is becoming a serious nuisance.'

'He is no boy,' Tamsyn snapped. 'He is thirty years old with an over-developed sense of what is owed to his consequence and no scruples about the methods he uses to get what he wants. If this is down to him, then he is becoming more than a nuisance. I think he is becoming dangerous.'

'Who is becoming dangerous, if I might ask?'

Mr Defoe stood in the doorway, dressed, shaved and very much awake. His eyes were fully open, the flexible voice had lost almost all of the painful huskiness, and the long, lean body was clad in what she could only assume was fashionable evening wear for a dinner on the wilder coasts of Devon—slim-fitting pantaloons, a swallowtail coat, immaculate white linen and a neck-cloth of intricate folds fixed with a simple sapphire pin that matched the subtle embroidery of his waistcoat.

'What are you doing out of bed. Mr Defoe? The doctor said you should rest and not get up until tomorrow.' Tamsyn knew she was staring, which did not help her find any sort of poise. And, faced with this man, she discovered that she wanted poise above everything.

'I am warm, rested and I need to keep my muscles moving,' he said mildly as he moved past her into the room. 'Good evening, Miss Holt, Miss Pritchard. Thank you for the invitation to dine with you.'

Invitation? What invitation? One glance at them had Tamsyn seething inwardly. They had invited him without telling her, for some nefarious reason of their own. They should have left the poor man to sleep. She eyed the *poor man* as he made his way slowly, but steadily, to the fireside and made his elegant bow to the aunts.

Predictably Aunt Izzy beamed at him and Aunt Rosie sent him a shrewd, slanting smile. 'Do sit down, Mr Defoe. I can well appreciate your desire to leave your room. Tamsyn, dear, perhaps Mr Defoe would care for a glass of sherry or Madeira?'

'Thank you, sherry would be very welcome.'

Tamsyn poured the rich brown wine into one of Aunt Izzy's best glasses. At least their tableware would not disgrace them. The house was full of small treasures that Izzy treated with casual enjoyment. She was as likely to put wildflowers into the exquisite glasses as fine wine and, if one of the others protested, she would shrug and say, *Oh, Papa let me take all sorts of things down here. I'm sure none of them are very valuable and I like to use nice objects.*

Mr Defoe stood beside the wing chair, waiting until Tamsyn had completed her task. 'Thank you.' He took the glass, then when she perched on the sofa next to Izzy he sat down with grace, and, to an observant eye, some caution. She suspected his overstretched muscles were giving him hell and he was more exhausted than he would allow himself to show. His features were naturally fine cut, she guessed, but even allowing for that, she detected strain hidden by force of will.

'Again, I have to ask you—who is dangerous? I apologise for my inadvertent eavesdropping, but having heard, I do not know how to ignore the fact that you seem to be in need of protection.'

In the silence that fell the three women eyed each other, then Tamsyn said, 'A rogue dog chased some of our flock of Devon Longwools over the cliff.'

'And moved a hurdle, I gather.' He rotated the glass between his fingertips, his attention apparently on the wine. 'A talented hound.'

He had sharp ears, or he had lingered on the stairs, listening. Probably both. 'That must be coincidence and it is simply a sorry chapter of accidents,' Tamsyn said. 'Tell me, Mr Defoe, do you come from an agricultural area?'

'I own some land,' he conceded. The amusement in his eyes was, she supposed, for her heavy-handed attempt at steering the subject away from the sheep. 'But I do not have sheep. Arable, cattle and horses in the south. This must be challenging country for agriculture, so close to the sea and the wild weather.'

'Everyone mixes farming and fishing,' Aunt Rosie said. 'And we have land that is much more sheltered than the sheep pastures on top of the cliffs, so we keep some dairy cattle and grow our own wheat and hay.' Aunt Izzy opened her mouth as though to bewail the burnt hayricks again, then closed her lips tight at the look from Rosie. 'We own some of the fishing boats that operate out of Stib's Landing, which is the next, much larger cove, just around Barbary Head to the south.'

'A complex business, but no doubt you have a competent farm manager. I am often away, so I rely heavily on mine.'

'Oh, no, dear Tamsyn does it all,' Izzy said cheerfully. Tamsyn wondered why Rosie rolled her eyes at her—it was, after all, only the truth.

'I have to earn my keep,' she said with a smile. 'And I like to keep busy. Are you travelling for pleasure, Mr Defoe? We are beginning to quite rival the south-coast resorts in this part of the world. Ilfracombe, for example, is positively fashionable.'

'Perfect for sea bathing,' Izzy said vaguely, then blushed. 'Oh, I didn't mean…'

'I am sure I would have done much better with a genteel bathing machine—I might have remembered to swim back when my time was up and not go ploughing off into the ocean while I thought of other things.' He smiled, but there was a bitter twist to it.

'Is that what you were doing? I did wonder, for the beach—if you can call it that—at Hartland Quay is hardly the kind of place you find people taking the saltwater cure.' Not, that Mr Defoe needed curing of anything, Tamsyn considered. He looked as though he would be indecently healthy, once rested.

'I was seized with an attack of acute boredom with the Great North Road, down which I was travelling, so, when I got to Newark, I turned south-west and just kept going, looking for somewhere completely wild and unspoilt.'

'And then attempted to swim to America?' What on earth prompted a man to strip off all his clothes, plunge into a cold sea and swim out so far that the current took him?

'I needed the exercise and I wanted to clear my mind. I certainly achieved the first, if not the second.' He stopped turning the glass between his fingers and took a long sip. 'This is very fine wine, I commend you on your supplier.'

'Probably smuggled,' Rosie said, accepting the abrupt change of subject. 'Things turn up on the doorstep. I suppose the correct thing to do is to knock a hole in the cask and drain it away, but that seems a wanton waste and one can hardly turn up at the excise office to pay duty without very awkward questions being asked.'

'There is much smuggling hereabouts?' Mr Defoe took another appreciative sip.

'It is the other main source of income,' Izzy, incorrigibly chatty and enthusiastic, confided. 'And of course dear Jory led the gang around here.'

'Jory?'

'My late husband,' Tamsyn said it reluctantly.

'Such a dear boy. I took him in when he was just a lad, he came from over the border in Cornwall, but his father found him…difficult and he ran away from home.'

'Dear Isobel is a great collector of lost lambs,' Rosie said drily.

'Such as me.' Even as she said it Tamsyn knew it sounded bitter and that had never been how she felt. She managed to lighten her voice as she added, 'My mother was Aunt Isobel's cousin and when she died when I was ten I came to live with her. Jory arrived the next year.'

'How romantic. Childhood sweethearts.' The word romantic emerged like a word barely understood in a foreign language.

'I married my best friend,' Tamsyn said stiffly. She was not going to elaborate on that one jot and have yet another person wonder why on earth she had married that scapegrace Jory Perowne when she could have had the eligible Franklin Holt, Viscount Chelford.

'And speaking of marriage,' Aunt Izzy said with her usual blithe disregard for atmosphere, 'has your manservant notified your family of your whereabouts? Because, if not, the carrier's wagon will be leaving the village at nine tomorrow morning and will take letters into the Barnstaple receiving office.'

'Thank you, ma'am, but there is no one expecting my return. Now I have set Collins's mind at rest, my conscience can be clear on that front.'

'Excellent,' Tamsyn said briskly. It was nothing of the kind. Either he had a wife he could leave in ignorance with impunity, or he did not have one, and she would very much like to know which it was. Not that she was going to explore why she was so curious. 'Now, tell me, Mr Defoe, are you able to eat rabbit? I do hope you do not despise it, for we have a glut of the little menaces and I feel certain it will feature in tonight's dinner.'

Chapter Four

'What have you gleaned from your flirtation with Cook?' Cris asked as Collins took his discarded coat. The bed was looking devilishly tempting so he sat down on a hard upright chair instead and bent to take off his shoes. The doctor had been quite right, damn him. He should have stayed in bed for the whole of the day and not tried to get up until tomorrow, but everything in him rebelled against succumbing to weakness.

'Flirtation, sir? The lady is amiable enough, but her charms are rather on the mature side for my taste.' Cris lifted his head to glare at him and he relented. 'Cook, and Molly the maid, are both all of a flutter over a personable gentleman landing on Mrs Perowne's doorstep, as it were. That lady is the main force in the household, that's for certain, although Miss Holt owns the property. Very active and well liked in the local community is Mrs Perowne, even though she married the local, how shall I put it—?'

'Bad boy?' Cris enquired drily as he stood up and began to unbutton his waistcoat, resisting the temptation to pitch face down on the bed and go to sleep. It had been a long, long day.

'Precisely, sir. A charismatic young man, by all account, and a complete scoundrel, reading between the lines. But a sort of protégé of the two older ladies, who seem to have regarded him as a lovable rogue.'

'A substitute son, perhaps?'

'I wondered if that was the case.' Collins began to turn down the bed. 'And Molly did say something about it being a good thing he married Miss Tamsyn because otherwise *that little toad* Franklin Holt would have pestered her to distraction. Which I thought interesting, but Cook soon silenced Molly on that topic.'

'Franklin Holt? He is Viscount Chelford, I believe. I think I have seen him around. About my age, black hair, dark eyes, thinks a lot of himself.' Cris put his sapphire stickpin on the dresser and unwound his neckcloth. 'A gamester. I have no knowledge about his amphibious qualities.'

'That is the man, sir.' Collins's knowledge of the peerage was encyclopedic and almost as good as his comprehension of the underworld. 'He has a reputation as someone who plunges deep in all matters of sport and play and he is Miss Holt's nephew. He inherited her father's lands and titles.'

'And he was annoying Miss Tamsyn, was he?' And was more than annoying her now, by the sound of it. But why the ladies should imagine he was responsible for sending their sheep over a cliff, he could not imagine.

Cris pulled off his shirt, shed his trousers and sank gratefully into the enfolding goose-feather bed. 'You know, Collins, I think I may have overdone things this evening. I feel extraordinarily weak suddenly.'

'That is very worrying, sir.' The other man's face was perfectly expressionless. 'I fear you may have to presume on Miss Holt's hospitality for several days in that case. I would diagnose a severely pulled muscle in your back and a possible threat to your weak chest.'

Cris, who could not recall ever having had a wheeze, let alone a bad chest, tried out a pathetic cough. 'I do fear that travelling would be unwise, but I am reluctant to impose further upon the ladies.'

'I understand your scruples, sir. I will find a cane so you may hobble more comfortably. However, it will be agony for you to travel over these roads with such an injury and I confess myself most anxious that you might insist on doing so. I will probably be so concerned that I will let my tongue run away with me and say so in front of the servants.'

Cris closed his eyes. 'Thank you, Collins. You know, you almost convince me of how weak I am. I am certain that if you confide your fears to Cook the intelligence will reach Miss Holt before the morning.'

'Good night, sir.' The door closed softly behind the valet and when Cris opened his eyes the room was dark. He smiled, thinking, not for the first time, that it was a good thing that Collins chose to employ his dubious talents on the side of the government and law and order.

Correct behaviour would be to take himself off the next morning, relieving his kind hostesses of the presence of a strange man in their house. But something was wrong her. Tamsyn Perowne was tense, the vague and cheerful Miss Holt was hiding anxiety and the much sharper Miss Pritchard was on the point of direct accusations. But why would they think that Chelford was behind the agricultural slaughter? The man would have to be deranged and, although Cris had seen nothing in their brief encounters to like about the viscount, neither had he any reason to think him insane.

It was a mystery and Cris liked mysteries. What was

more, there were three ladies in distress, who had, between them, possibly saved his life. He owed them his
assistance. If he was searching for something to take
his mind off love lost in the past, and a marriage of duty
in the future, then surely this was it? There was, after
all, nothing else he felt like doing.

Come the morning Cris was not certain that he
needed any acting skills to convince his hostesses that
he was unable to travel. His exhausted muscles, eased
the day before by the hot bath and Collins's manipula-
tion, had stiffened overnight into red-hot agony. After
another painful massage session he swore his way out
of bed and through the process of dressing. He negotiated the stairs with the assistance of the cane Collins had produced from somewhere and had no trouble
sounding irritable when he and the other man took
up their carefully calculated positions in the hall in
order to have a *sotto voce* argument. He pitched both
his voice and his tone to tempt even the best-behaved
person to approach the other side of the door to listen
to what was going on.

'Of course we are going to leave after breakfast.
How many more times do I have to tell you, Collins?
I cannot presume upon the hospitality of three single
ladies in this way.'

'But, sir, with the risk of your bronchitis returning, I
cannot like it,' Collins protested. 'And the pain to your
back with the jolting over these roads—why, you might
be incapacitated for weeks afterwards.'

'That does not matter. I am sure I can find a halfway
acceptable inn soon enough.'

'In this area? And we do not have our own sheets
with us, sir!' Collins's dismay was so well-acted that

Cris was hard put to it not to laugh. 'Please, I beg you to reconsider.'

'No, my mind is made up. I am going—'

'Nowhere, Mr Defoe.' The door to the drawing room opened to reveal Mrs Perowne, her ridiculous cap slightly askew as it slid from the pins skewering it to her brown hair. Her hands were on her hips, those lush lips firmly compressed.

The thought intruded that he would like to see them firmly compressed around— *No.*

His thoughts could not have been visible on his face, given that she did not slap it. 'The doctor said you were to stay in bed yesterday and you ignored him, so no wonder you are not feeling quite the thing this morning. If you have a tendency to bronchitis it is completely foolish to risk aggravating it and what is this about a painful back?'

Cris discovered that he did not like to be thought of as weak, or an invalid, or, for that matter, prone to bronchitis, which should be of no importance whatsoever beside the necessity of convincing Mrs Perowne that he should stay put in this house. His pride was, he realised, thoroughly affronted. That was absurd—was he so insecure that he needed to show off his strength in front of some country widow? 'The merest twinge, and Collins exaggerates. It is only that I had a severe cold last winter.'

'Oh, sir.' The reproach in Collins's voice would have not been out of place in a Drury Lane melodrama. 'After what the doctor said last year. Madam, I could tell you tales—'

'But not if you wish to remain in my employ,' Cris snapped and they both turned reproachful, anxious looks on him.

'Mr Defoe, please, I implore you to stay. My aunts would worry so if you left before you were quite recovered, and besides, we are most grateful for your company.' There was something in the warm brown eyes that was certainly not pity for an invalid, a flicker of recognition of him as a man that touched his wounded pride and soothed it, even as he told himself not to be such a coxcomb as to set any store by what a virtual stranger thought of him. Before now he had played whatever role his duties as a not-quite-official diplomat required and it had never given him the slightest qualm to appear over-cautious, or indiscreet, or naïve, in some foreign court. He knew he was none of those things, so that was all that mattered.

But this woman, who should mean nothing to him, had him wanting to parade his courage and his endurance and his fitness like some preening peacock flaunting his tail in front of his mate. He swallowed what was left of his pride. 'If it would not be an imposition, Mrs Perowne, I confess I would be grateful for a few days' respite.'

'Excellent. My aunts will be very relieved to hear it.'

'They are not within earshot, then?' he enquired, perversely wanting to provoke her.

He was rewarded with the tinge of colour that stained her cheekbones. 'You reprove me for eavesdropping, Mr Defoe? I plead guilty to it, but I was concerned for you and suspected you would attempt to leave today, however you felt.'

Now he felt guilty on top of everything else and it was an unfamiliar emotion. He did not do things that offended his own sense of honour, therefore there was never anything to feel guilty about. 'I apologise, Mrs

Perowne. That was ungracious of me when you show such concern for an uninvited guest.'

'You are forgiven, and to show to what extent, let me lead you through to the breakfast room and you may tell me what you think of our own sausages and bacon.'

Cris, ignoring Collins's faint smile, which, in a lesser man, would have been a smirk, followed her into a sunny room with yellow chintz curtains and a view down the sloping lawn to the sea. 'Should we not wait for your aunts?'

'They always breakfast in their room.' Mrs Perowne gestured to a seat and sat opposite. The centre of the table had platters of bread and ham, a bowl of butter and a covered dish. 'Let me serve you, you will not want to be stretching to lift dishes.' As she spoke she raised the dome and a tantalising aroma of bacon and sausage wafted out.

'Thank you.' He meekly accepted a laden plate and tried to work out the enigma that was Mrs Tamsyn Perowne. She was well spoken, confident, competent and a lady, even if she was decidedly out of the ordinary. She was distantly related to a viscount, but she had married a local man who had died one leap ahead of the noose.

'That is a charming portrait on the wall behind you,' he remarked. 'Your aunts do not resemble each other greatly. Are they your mother's relations or your father's, if I might ask?'

'Aunt Isobel is my mother's cousin. Aunt Rosie is not a relation.' Mrs Perowne shot him a very direct glance as though measuring his reaction. 'They left home to set up house together when they were in their late twenties. It was—is—a passionate friendship, as close as a marriage.'

'Like the famous Ladies of Llangollen?'

'Yes, just like that. It was their inspiration, I believe. Are you shocked?'

'No, not at all. Why should they not be happy together?' Lucky women, able to turn their backs on the demands of society and its expectations. But daughters did not bear the same weight of expectation that sons did, especially elder sons, with the requirements of duty to make a good match, bring wealth and connections into the family, provide an heir to title and estates.

'And you?' he asked when she gave him an approving nod and turned her attention to a dish of eggs in cream. 'What led you to make your life here?'

'My father was a naval man and I cannot even recall his face. He was killed at sea when I was scarcely toddling. Mama found things very difficult without him. I think she was not a strong character.'

'So you had to be strong for both of you?' he suggested.

'Yes. How did you know?' The quick look of pleasure at his understanding made Cris smile back. She really was a charming woman with her expressive face and healthy colour. And young still, not much above twenty-five, he would estimate.

'You have natural authority, yet you wear it lightly. I doubt you learned it recently. What happened to your mother?'

'She succumbed to one of the cholera epidemics. We lived in Portsmouth and like all ports many kinds of infection are rife.'

'And then you came here?' He tried to imagine the feelings of the orphaned girl, leaving the place that she knew, mourning for her mother. He had lost his own mother when he was four, bearing the sibling he never knew. His father, a remote, chilly figure, had died when he was barely ten, leaving Cris a very young, very frightened marquess. Rigorously hiding his feelings behind a mask of frigid reserve had got him through that ordeal. It still served him well.

'Do your duty,' was his father's dying command and the only advice he ever gave his son on holding one of the premier titles in the land. But he had found it covered every difficulty he encountered. *Do your duty* usually meant *do what you least want to do* because it was hard, or painful, or meant he must use his head, not his heart, to solve a problem, but he had persevered. *It even stood me in good stead to prevent me sacrificing honour for love*, he thought bitterly.

'Aunt Izzy is a maternal creature,' Tamsyn said. 'She adopted Jory, she took me in.' She slanted a teasing smile at Cris. 'I think she sees you as her next good cause.'

'Do I appear to need mothering?'

'From my point of view?' She studied him, head on one side, a wicked glint in her eyes, apparently not at all chilled by his frigid tone. 'No, I feel absolutely no inclination to mother you, Mr Defoe. But you could have died, you are still recovering, and that is quite enough for Aunt Izzy.' Having silenced him, she added, 'Will you be resting today?'

'I will walk. My muscles will seize up if I rest. I thought I would go along the lane for a while.'

'It is uphill all the way for a mile until the combe joins Stib Valley, but there are several places to rest—fallen trees, rocks.' Mrs Perowne was showing not the slightest desire to fuss over him, which was soothing to his male pride and a setback for his scheme to draw her out.

'Will you not come with me? Show me the way?'

'There is absolutely no opportunity for you to get lost, Mr Defoe. If you manage to reach the lane to Stibworthy, then by turning right you will descend to Stib's Landing. Left will take you to the village and the tracks to either side will lead you to the clifftops.'

'I was hoping for your company, not your guidance.' Cris tried to look wistful, which, he knew, was not an expression that sat well on his austere features.

Tamsyn took the top off a boiled egg with a sharp swipe of her knife. 'Lonely, Mr Defoe?' she enquired sweetly.

Cris did not rise to the mockery. 'It is a while since I had the opportunity to walk in such unspoiled countryside and have a conversation with a young lady at the same time.'

She pursed her mouth, although whether to suppress a smile or a wry expression of resignation he could not tell. 'I have to go and see our shepherd about the… incident yesterday. I am intending to ride, but I will walk with you up the combe until you tire, then ride on from there. There is no particular hurry, the damage has been done.'

Cris wondered whether she was as cool and crisp with everyone or whether she did not like him. Possibly it was a cover for embarrassment. After all, he had come lurching out of the sea, stark naked, seized hold of her and then kissed her, neither of which were the actions of a gentleman. But Tamsyn Perowne did not strike him as a woman who was easily embarrassed. She had an earthy quality about her, which was not at all coarse but rather made him think of pagan goddesses—Primavera, perhaps, bringing growing things and springtime in her wake.

It was refreshing after the artificiality of London society or the Danish court. There, ladies wore expressions of careful neutrality and regarded showing their feelings as a sign of weakness, or ill breeding. Even Katerina had hidden behind a façade of indifferent politeness. *And thank heavens, for that*, Cris thought. Self-control and the ability to disguise their feelings had been all that stood between them and a major scandal. Mrs Perowne could keep secrets, he was sure of that, but she would find it hard to suppress her emotions. He thought of her spirited response to the magistrate, the anger so openly expressed. Would her lovemaking be so passionate, so frank?

It was an inappropriate thought and, from her suddenly arrested expression, this time something of it had shown on his face. 'Mr Defoe?' There was a touch of ice behind the question.

'I was thinking of how magnificently you routed that boor of a magistrate yesterday,' he said.

'I dislike incompetence, laziness and foolishness,' she said. 'Mr Penwith possesses all three in abundance.'

'Doubtless you consider me foolish, almost getting myself drowned yesterday.' If she thought him an idiot she was not going to confide in him, and unless she did, it was going to be more difficult to discover what was threatening the ladies Combe. Not impossible, just more time consuming and, for all he knew, there wasn't the luxury of time.

'Reckless, certainly.' She was cutting into her toast with the same attack that she had applied to beheading the egg. 'I suspect you had something on your mind.'

'Yes,' he agreed. 'That must be my excuse.'

'Mr Defoe.' She laid down her knife and looked directly at him across the breakfast table. 'It is easy to become...distracted when we are hurting. It would be a mistake to allow that distraction to become fatal. There is always hope. Everything passes.'

She thinks I was trying to kill myself. The realisation hit him as he saw there was no smile, no teasing, in those brown eyes. Then he saw the ghost of something besides concern. *Pain. She is speaking of herself. When her husband died did she want to die, too?*

'I know. And there are responsibilities and duties to keep one going, are there not? I was angry with myself for my lack of focus, Tamsyn. I have no desire to find myself in a lethal predicament again because I have lost concentration.'

Cris realised he had called her by her first name as her eyebrows lifted, giving her tanned, pleasant face a sudden look of haughty elegance. She was not a conventional beauty, but he was reminded again what a very feminine creature she was, for all her practicality. 'I apologise for the familiarity, but your concern disarmed me. May we not be friends? I do feel we have been very thoroughly introduced.'

Tamsyn laughed, a sudden rich chuckle that held surprise and wickedness and warmth even though she blushed, just a little. 'Indeed we have… That moment in the sea. I do not normally…'

'Kiss strange men?' Now she was pink from the collarbone upwards. 'If it is any consolation, I do not normally kiss mermaids.' That made her laugh. 'It felt like touching life when I thought I was dying.'

'It was an extraordinary moment, like something from a myth. You thought I was a mermaid, I thought you were a merman, Christopher.'

'Cris,' he corrected. 'St Crispin, if we are to be exact.'

"And Crispin Crispian shall ne'er go by, from this

*day to the ending of the world, but we in it shall be
remember'd,"'* she quoted, visibly recovering her composure. 'Your parents were Shakespearian enthusiasts?
Or is your birthday October the twenty-fifth?'

'Both. My father was much given to quoting Henry V.
"Once more unto the breach, dear friends." He would
mutter it before anything he did not want to do, such
as attending social gatherings.'

'How infuriating for your mother.'

'She died many years ago, in childbirth. My father
was shot in the shoulder in a hunting accident and developed blood poisoning.' He stopped to calculate. 'It
was nineteen years ago, the day before my tenth birthday.' He would not normally speak so openly about their
deaths, but he wanted Tamsyn to talk of her husband's
fatal plunge from the cliff and his frankness might encourage hers.

'I am so sorry. You poor little boy, you must have
been so alone. I was ten when I lost my mother to that
epidemic, but at least I had the aunts.'

'There were many people to look after me.' Four
trustees, one hundred servants, indoor and outdoor.
There had been three tutors, a riding master, a fencing
master, an art master, a dancing master—all dedicated
to turning out the young Marquess of Avenmore in as
perfect a form as possible.

'I am glad of that,' Tamsyn murmured. 'Now, some
more coffee before we take our walk?' She passed him
the pot, a fine old silver one. 'I cannot delay much longer or Willie Tremayne will think I have forgotten him.
I will meet you at the garden gate.'

Cris sat with his coffee cooling in the cup for several minutes after she had gone from the room. This
household, and its inhabitants, were unlike any he had

encountered before. He supposed it was because, used as he was to palaces, government offices, great houses or bachelor lodgings, he had never before experienced the world of the gentry. Were they all so warm, so un-affected? He gave himself a shake and swallowed the cold coffee as a penance for daydreaming. He had to get his reluctant limbs moving and find a coat or he would be keeping Tamsyn Perowne waiting.

Chapter Five

The garden gate was as good a perch as it had been when she had first come to Barbary, but now it did not seem like a mountain to climb. Tamsyn hooked the toes of her riding boots over a rail and kept her weight at the hinge end, as a proper countrywoman knew to do. The breeze from the sea blew up the lane, stirring the curls that kept escaping from under the old-fashioned tricorn she had jammed over her hair and flipping the ends of her stock until she caught them and stuffed them into the neck of her jacket. She felt almost frivolous, and if that was the result of looking forward to a very slow walk up the lane with an ailing gentleman, then it was obvious that she was not getting out enough.

Mr Defoe—*Cris*—emerged from the door just as Jason led out Foxy, her big chestnut gelding, and she bit her lip rather than smile at her own whimsy. He might think she was laughing at his cane.

'Leg up, Mrs Tamsyn?'

'I'm walking for a little while, thank you, Jason.' She jumped down from the gate and pulled the reins over the gelding's head to lead him and he butted her with his nose, confused about why she was not mounting.

'That's a big beast.' Cris was walking slowly, using the cane, but without limping or leaning on it. She did her best not to stare. He would experience enough of that if he walked as far as Stibworthy and the locals had a good look at his pale tan buckskins and beautiful boots. He might as well have dressed for a ball, as donned that dark brown riding coat and the low-crowned beaver. He clicked his tongue at Foxy and the horse turned his head to look at him. 'Powerful hocks and a good neck on him. Is he a puller?'

'No, he's a pussy cat with lovely manners and a soft mouth, aren't you, my handsome red fox?' She was rewarded with a slobbery nuzzle at her shoulder. 'But I wish you were a tidier kisser.'

That provoked a snort of amusement from the man holding the gate open for her. Possibly references to kissing were not such a good idea. She could still feel the heat of his mouth on hers, in shocking contrast to the cold of his skin. And despite any amount of effort with the tooth powder, she imagined she could still taste him, salty and male.

Two years without kisses had been a long time, and this was a man who seemed to have been created to tempt women. *He probably has several in keeping and has to beat off the rest with his fine leather gloves.* Intimacy with a man to whom she was not married had never occurred to her before now. Was it simply that the passage of time had left her yearning for the lovemaking that she had learned to enjoy? Or was it this man?

She had never seriously considered remarrying, although sometimes she wondered if, given any encouragement, Dr Tregarth might have declared an interest. But it would be unfair to any man when she… *With my past*, she substituted before she let herself follow that train of thought.

Thoughts of illicit intimacy were certainly occurring to her now and the fact that Cris Defoe was walking with a cane and complaining of a bad back and weak chest did absolutely nothing to suppress some very naughty thoughts. They turned up the lane and she wandered along, letting Cris set the pace. The sound of their feet and the horse's hooves were muffled by the sand that filled the ruts in the pebbly turf, and the music of the sea behind them and the song of the skylark high above filled the silence between them.

'Salt from the sea, vanilla from the gorse and wild garlic,' he said after a few minutes. 'The air around here is almost painfully clear after the smoke of towns or the heat of inland countryside, don't you think?'

Cris was not breathing heavily, despite the increasing slope of the lane as it rose up the combe. He was certainly very fit. She remembered the muscles strapping his chest and his flat stomach, the hard strength as she had gripped his bare shoulders in the sea. Unless he developed the chest infection his valet seemed to fear, his recovery should be rapid. 'I do not know about towns— I hardly recall Portsmouth and our local ones, Barnstaple, Bideford and Bude, are small and they are not the kind I think you have in mind. How is your back?'

'My… Oh, yes. Amazingly the exercise has already straightened the knots out of it. You have never been to London, then?'

'No, never.'

And I'll wager you have never had bronchitis in your life and your back hurts you no more than the rest of you does. So what is this nonsense about being unable to endure a coach ride over rough roads?

The track turned as they came out from the trees on to the pastureland. 'There's a fallen tree.' Cris stopped, made a show of flexing his shoulders. 'Shall we sit a while? The view looks good from here.'

And you need a rest? He was a good actor, she would give him that. But she suspected that this man would no more willingly admit weakness than he would ride a donkey, so he must have a good reason other than exhaustion or sore muscles for wanting to stop. 'Certainly,' she agreed, and tossed Foxy's reins over a handy branch. 'Don't mind me, you sit down,' she added over her shoulder. As she turned back to the tree trunk she was treated to a fine display of bravely controlled wincing and the sight of Cris's long legs being folded painfully down to the low seat.

She could go along with it and let him fish for whatever it was he wanted, or she could stop this nonsense now. Jory had been a man who was constitutionally incapable of giving a straight answer, a husband who could keep virtually his entire life, and certainly his thoughts, secret from his wife, and she was weary of mysteries.

'Mr Defoe.' His head came up at her tone and his eyes narrowed for an instant before he was all amiable attention. No, he was doing a good job of it, but she was not at all convinced by this harmless exterior.

'Why so formal all of a sudden, Tamsyn?'

Now he was trying to unsettle her because he knew she was not entirely comfortable with first names. Tamsyn sat down. 'Because I have a bone to pick with you, sir. You are no more in need of a rest than I am. I can believe that you are sore and your muscles are giving you hell, but if you are so sickly that you are about to succumb to a chest infection and you are incapable of riding in a coach over rough ground, then I am the Queen of the May.'

'You are flattening to a man's self-esteem, Mrs Perowne.'

'Why flattening? I imagine you hate being thought less than invincible. Most men do.'

'Ouch. Now *that* hurts. I mean that I dislike being so transparent.'

'You are not. But I saw you stripped to the core yesterday—and I do not mean stripped of clothes,' she added as that infuriating eyebrow rose. She did so wish she could do that… 'You would have kept on going until you dropped dead rather than lie there passively on the beach and be fetched. You hated being weak and in need of help. If your man with your coach had been anywhere in the neighbourhood, you would have crawled a mile to him on your hands and knees rather than admit to needing three women to help you. So why so unwilling to travel now and leave here?'

Cris leaned back against a sapling, folded his hands over the head of his cane and looked at her. It was a long, considering stare with no humour and no flirtation in it. If she was a parlour maid being interviewed, she suspected she would not get the position. If she was a horse for sale, he was obviously doubtful about her bloodlines. When he spoke she almost jumped.

'You may well have saved my life. I am in your debt. There is something very wrong here and if it is in my power, I will remedy it.' From another man there would have been a note of boasting, of masculine superiority over the poor, helpless females. But this sounded like a simple declaration of fact. Something was wrong. Crispin Defoe would fix it.

It had been so long since there had been anyone from

outside the household to confide in, or to lean on, just a little. Even Jory could be relied on only to do what suited his interests. They had been fortunate that he had adored Aunt Izzy and had been fond of Tamsyn. But this man would be leaving, very soon. He did not belong here, he had drifted to Barbary Combe House, borne on the current of a whim that had brought him across England. Soon he would return and to rely on him for anything—other than to disturb her dreams—was dangerous.

'Nonsense. You do not owe us anything, we would have done the same for anyone who needed help. And there is absolutely nothing wrong except for a rogue dog and some valuable sheep lost.'

'You see?' The austere face was disapproving. 'That is precisely why I felt it necessary to have an excuse for lingering here. You are going to be stubborn.'

'I am not stubborn—if anyone is, it is you. You find three women living alone and assume they are incapable of dealing with life and its problems.' She walked away across the grass, spun round and marched back, temper fraying over her moment of weakness. 'We are managing very well by ourselves, Mr Defoe, and I am rather tired of gentlemen telling me that we are not.'

'Who else has the nerve to do that?'

'It takes no particular nerve, merely impertinence.' She took Foxy's reins, led him to the far end of the tree trunk and used it as a mounting block. 'I am sure you can manage the path back.' Cris stood up and took the reins just above the bit. 'Let go at once!'

'Tamsyn, I am not an idiot and neither are you. Something is wrong, your aunts are distressed and who is the other interfering gentleman?'

'Aunt Izzy's nephew considers we would do better

living in a house on his estate. He seems over-protective all of a sudden.'

'Lord Chelford.'

'You have been *eavesdropping*.' Foxy's ears twitched back as her voice rose. 'Hardly the action of a gentleman.'

'Neither is ignoring ladies in distress.' He stood there looking up at her, his hand firm on Foxy's bridle. 'I wish you would get down off your high horse, Tamsyn. Literally. You are giving me a crick in my neck. I happened to overhear something completely accidentally. Collins heard more because he likes to gossip. Now, of course, you may simply be a trio of hysterical females, leaping to conclusions and making a crisis out of a series of accidents—'

'How dare you?' Tamsyn twisted in the saddle to face him, lost her balance and grabbed for the reins. Cris reached up, took her by the waist and lifted her, sliding and protesting, down to the ground. Trapped between Foxy's bulk and Cris's body, she clenched her fist and thumped him square in the centre of the chest. 'You are no gentleman!'

'Yes, I am. The problem is that you do not appear to have any others in your life with whom to compare me. Now, stop jumping up and down on my toes, which is doing nothing for the state of my boots, and come and sit on the tree trunk and tell me all about it.' She opened her mouth to speak. 'And I am the soul of discretion, you need have no fear this will go any further.'

'If you would allow me to get a word in edgeways, Mr Defoe, I would point out to you that I am unable to get off your toes, or move in any direction, because you still have your hands on my person.' In fact they seemed to be encircling her waist, which was impossible, she was not that slim.

'I have?' He did not move, although she could have sworn that the pressure on her waist increased. 'It must be a reflex. I was anxious that you were going to fall off.' He still managed to maintain that austere, almost haughty, expression, except for a wicked glint in those blue eyes that should have looked innocent and instead held a wealth of knowledge and deep wells of experience. *Thank goodness. He is going to kiss me.*

And then he…didn't. Cris stepped back, released her and gestured to the tree trunk. 'Shall we sit down and try this again? I will tie up your horse again, he is becoming confused.'

'He is not the only one,' Tamsyn muttered. Of course he was not going to kiss her. Whoever got kissed wearing a dreadful old hat like hers? Certainly no one being held by an elegant gentleman whose boots would probably have cost more than her entire wardrobe for the past five years.

Cris came back to the tree and she noticed his cane was lying forgotten on the grass. 'What else has happened besides the accident to the sheep yesterday?' he asked as he sat beside her.

'You will doubtless say we are simply imagining things.'

'Try me. I can be remarkably imaginative myself when I want to be.'

'A hayrick caught fire two weeks ago. Our little dairy herd got through a fence last week and strayed all over the parish before we caught them. All our lobster pots keep coming up empty. And now the sheep.'

'All this in the span of two weeks?' When she nodded he scrubbed his hand across his chin and frowned at the now-scuffed toes of his boots. 'Even my imagination is baulking at that as a series of coincidences.' His frown deepened and Tamsyn fought the urge to apologise for the state of his boots. 'May I ask how your aunts are supported financially?'

She saw no harm in telling him, none of it was a secret, after all. 'Aunt Izzy has the use of Barbary Combe House and its estate for her lifetime, along with all the income to spend as she wishes. She also has the use of everything in the house for her lifetime. Anything she buys with the income is hers to dispose of as she wishes, as are the stock and movable assets of the estate. Aunt Rosie has a very respectable competence inherited from her father and other relatives. She has high expenses, of course, because of her health—she paid for the bathing room, which uses a lot of fuel, and she also consults a number of medical men. Both of them live well within their incomes.'

'And you?' Cris said it quite without inflection, as though he were her banker or her lawyer gathering the facts before advising on an investment. And there was no reason why she should not tell him. After all, establishing her non-existent pride was simply another fact for his calculations.

'I have a small inheritance from my parents. Aunt Izzy makes me an allowance and in return I act as her land steward.'

'And your husband?'

The cool, impersonal voice left her no room for manoeuvre. Tamsyn shrugged. 'Jory left me nothing. Or, rather, he had a fishing smack, a small house, nets, gear, firearms… All used in the commission of criminal offences, all seized by the Excise after his death. To have laid claim to anything would have been to admit I was a partner in his activities.'

'And were you?'

'I knew what he was doing, of course I did, even though he kept all the actual details secret. Everyone on this coast knew and I was married to the man, after all. He led a gang of smugglers.'

If she had thought for a moment that she would fob off Cris Defoe with that as an explanation, then she was mistaken, it seemed. 'Smuggling covers everything from bringing in the odd cask of brandy under a load of herring, to a cover for spying, by way of full-scale organised crime accompanied by murder, extortion and blackmail. Where on that spectrum was Jory Perowne?'

'You know a lot about it. Perhaps you are a magistrate yourself and I would be well advised not to compound my indiscretion.' She smiled, lowered her lashes, wondered if she could remember how to flirt. *If I ever knew.*

'No, I am not a magistrate.' That was a surprise. He had said he was a landowner and most landowners of any standing were justices. 'I have been crossing the Channel, back and forth, for ten years and one cannot do that without hearing about smugglers.'

There was a little nugget of information to tuck away and muse upon in that comment. Mr Defoe had been crossing the Channel at a time when England was at war with France, even if it was now five years since Waterloo had brought peace again. Had he been in the army? But the way that he spoke made it sound as though he was still crossing over to the Continent on a regular basis. He could hardly be a merchant, not with his clothes and the indefinable air of *ton*nishness that even a country mouse like her could recognise. And *ton*nish gentlemen did not engage in trade.

Perhaps he is a spy himself and he ended up in the sea after being thrown overboard by an arch enemy in a life-and-death struggle—

'Mrs Perowne? Am I boring you?'

'Not at all, Mr Defoe. I was merely contemplating the perils of the sea for a moment.'

And wondering why your voice sends little shivers up and down my back when you drawl like that when really I ought to give you a sharp set-down for sarcasm.

Just to prove she had been paying attention she added coolly, 'Jory was in about the middle of your spectrum. He ran a highly organised smuggling ring with high-value goods and he was not averse to violence when his business was threatened by rivals or the Excise. But he protected the aunts fiercely, the people hereabouts worshipped him and he looked after them. You probably think me shocking for not condemning him, but he was loyal and courageous and looked after his men, and smuggling is a way of life around these coasts.'

'The Excise must have given you a very difficult time after his death when they were looking for the profits of his activities.'

'They could not have been looking as hard as I was.' The villagers had needed the money when their main local industry collapsed overnight with Jory's death. 'They bullied me and threatened me and finally allowed that I was just a poor feeble woman led astray by a wicked rogue.'

'Could Chelford be searching for hidden treasure on the assumption that Jory Perowne hid his ill-gotten gains somewhere on the estate?' She must have been staring at him with her mouth agape because he enquired, dry as a bone, 'Is that such a ridiculous idea?'

Chapter Six

Despite herself, Tamsyn laughed. 'Ridiculous? No. It is brilliant and I am just amazed that I am such a ninnyhammer that I did not think of it for myself. It is precisely the kind of thing that Franklin would think of—that there must be treasure and therefore a chance to grab it for himself.'

'Then I suggest we search, locate the hoard and thwart Chelford.' The thought of hunting for buried treasure seemed to appeal to Cris.

All men are such boys, even the most impressive specimens. 'Unfortunately, whatever fantasies Franklin might have, I do not believe there is any treasure to be found. The idea that he would think it exists is a good one, but I suspect Jory would have done something truly infuriating with his profits, like putting it in a bank in Exeter under a false name and then forgetting to tell me.'

'Are you certain there is not?' Cris's question had a hopeful note to it.

Yes, he is definitely disappointed. 'There are no secret caves or tunnels. Or, rather, none that I or the villagers don't know about. And Jory had more sense than to bury money in the churchyard in a nice fresh grave or any of the other tricks. He would want it earning interest and to be safe, not where someone might stumble across it.'

'*A nice fresh grave?*' Cris sounded incredulous. 'You shock me.'

'It is the best way to hide newly turned earth, of course. You wait for someone in the village to be buried, come along that night and do the reverse of grave robbing.' The question was in his eyes and she thought of teasing him some more, but relented. 'And, no, I have never taken part in such a thing. I have more respect for my fellow parishioners, although I suspect none of them would be very surprised or distressed if it happened.' He still looked unconvinced. 'It is difficult for city dwellers to shake off their preconceptions about us rustics who live on the very edge of the country. We are not neatly divided into dyed-in-the-wool rogues and happy pastoral innocents.'

'No, I suspect you are all rather more complex than that.' He watched her from beneath lowered lids, an unsettling appraisal that made her feel anything but complicated.

'I must go.' It was far too comfortable sitting here in the sunshine exchanging ideas, teasing and being teased. Tamsyn stood up and Cris followed her. 'I must see Willie Tremayne and make certain the remainder of the flock are safe.'

'Of course.' He made no move to detain her. But why should he? That moment when he had held her so close as she slid from the saddle and she had thought he was about to kiss her had been nothing more than her imagination. Just because he had kissed her once was no reason to suppose he had any desire to do it again.

'Let me give you a leg up.'

'No need.' She was on the log, and from there to the saddle, as she spoke, chiding herself as she did it.

You have no idea how to flirt, do you? You should have let him help you mount, let his hands linger on your foot or perhaps your ankle. You should have thanked him prettily, as a lady should, not gone scrambling on to Foxy like a tomboy.

'I will see you at luncheon, perhaps.' She waved her free hand as she urged the horse into a canter along the path that led to the clifftop pastures and did not look back.

When she knew she was out of sight she slowed, reined Foxy back to a walk, which was quite fast enough on the rabbit-burrowed turf, and turned her face into the breeze to cool the colour that she guessed was staining her cheeks. Cris Defoe had done nothing at all, other than look at her with warmth in his eyes and hold her a little too close when she dismounted, and yet she was all aflutter and expecting more. A great deal more.

She had no excuse, she told herself as she reached the stone and turf bank and turned along it towards the gate. Nor was there any reason not to be honest with herself. For the first time since Jory had died she had been jolted out of her hard-working, pleasant routine by a man. A handsome—*oh, very well, beautiful*—man. A man of sophistication and education. Someone who could discuss more than the price of herring and the demand for beef cattle in Barnstaple.

He had kissed her in the sea and now she had woken up from her trance, a rather soggy Sleeping Beauty. *Not much of a beauty... But I want him.* To be exact, and to look the thing squarely in the face, she wanted to go to bed with him, get her hands on that lean body, make

love with him. She should be shocked with herself, she
supposed. But weren't widows allowed more freedom?
Couldn't she be a little daring, a trifle dashing? 'I'm my
own mistress,' she informed Foxy, who politely swivelled an ear back to listen. 'And I would rather like to
be Cris Defoe's mistress, just for a while.'

He was a man who knew about these things, she
was sure. Elegant, sophisticated widows probably indicated their availability to him on a daily basis when
he was not stuck in the wilds of Devon. And there was
the rub. *Sophisticated.* Tamsyn hooked the latch with
her riding crop and let Foxy push the gate open, then
reined back to hook it closed again. She could attend
the local assemblies at Barnstaple or Bideford looking
perfectly respectable and well dressed. She would receive a gratifying number of requests for dances, she
was never short of a supper partner, but none of those
gentlemen had one-tenth of the poise or *finish* that Cris
Defoe possessed. And while she entertained with confidence and knew she had nothing to be ashamed of in
her education or her manners, her social skills had never
been tested in a London drawing room.

Which was not really the problem, Tamsyn told herself as she urged Foxy into a canter across the level
ground of the headland. Put her in a drawing room
with a duchess and she was sure courtesy and imagination would see her through. But how did one go about
indicating one's availability to a man, other than by
coming right out and stating one's desires? Or dressing immodestly?

She'd had to do neither with Jory. One day she
had bumped into him as she came running across the
meadow, late for tea because of a difficult encounter
with Franklin. They had clung together, breathless. He

had been laughing until he saw the tears she was fighting not to show. They had been old friends, comfortable together. And then their eyes had met and the laughter in his had died, and the comfort was replaced by something that was not at all cosy or familiar, and the next thing his mouth was on hers and...

'Mizz Tamsyn!' It was Willie, hailing her from the far gate, his battered old hat pushed far back so his weathered face was clear to see. He looked grim, but he raised a smile for her as she drew close. Behind him he had the sheep penned under the watchful eye of his black and white Border collie, Thorn.

'A bad business, Willie.' She stayed where she was, not wanting to disturb the remains of the flock any more than she had to.

'Aye, it is that. And deliberate, too. The hurdle was dragged out of the gap and thrown aside. There's no way it could have been pushed out by the sheep, or blown by the wind.'

'I know, you always wire it back into the gap when it isn't being used to move the flock.' She saw him relax a little. 'Does anyone recognise the dog?'

'No, it's not from round here. Scrawny, mean-looking beast, but not mad, I reckon.'

'Someone brought it in, especially?'

'Aye, that'll be it. Someone got a grudge, Mizz Tamsyn? Folks is starting to talk, what with the ricks and all that. Isn't anyone local—you know that. We all owe too much to you and the ladies, and no one forgets Jory Perowne, not round here.'

'No, it isn't a grudge, Willie. I think someone is out to scare us, though. Tell people to look out for strangers, will you?'

'We will that.' He grinned suddenly, exposing his

tobacco-stained teeth. 'Not likely to be yon merman you fished out, that's for sure.'

'He's no merman, Willie. Just a gentleman who got caught in the current when he was swimming.'

'Ha! Fool thing to be doing, that swimming lark. They do say that folks are visiting Ilfracombe specially to get in the sea in wooden huts on wheels and they pay to be ducked by hefty great females. Pay good money! What they be wanting to do that for, Mizz Tamsyn? 'Tis foolishness.'

'Some doctors say seawater is good for you, Willie.'

'Huh! Good for drowning in, more like.'

'Well, they must find something good about it, given how hard it is to get to Ilfracombe with the roads like they are.'

'That what yon gentleman was doing, then? Sea bathing for his health?' He nodded, obviously pleased that he had solved the mystery. 'He'll be some weedy invalid then, all spindleshanks and a cough.'

'Not *quite*.' Tamsyn managed not to smile. There was absolutely nothing spindly about Cris Defoe. 'But he will be staying with us for a while longer. For his health.'

'Will he now?'

Tamsyn knew the tone. It could be roughly interpreted as, *Some of us will take a look at him and we'll sort him out proper if he's up to anything with Jory Perowne's widow.* She appreciated their loyalty, but there were times when the fact that the whole close-knit community knew everyone's business made her want to scream with frustration.

'Yes, he will. Now, do you think we ought to pay some of the lads to watch the animals at night for a while?'

'Good idea.' Willie, distracted from the thought of a strange man under the Barbary Combe House roof, leaned his elbows on the gate and settled down to a discussion of who was reliable and whether one lad alone was more reliable than two or three, all egging each other on for mischief.

Cris stood up and, now that he was alone, permitted himself the indulgence of a long, slow stretch. His muscles were still sore across his shoulders and deep in his thighs, but the walk uphill had done them good. By tomorrow he would be himself again, and now he needed to walk, stride out and work up a sweat and distract himself from the memory of a pair of amused brown eyes and the novelty of a woman who seemed to say exactly what she thought.

Why that was arousing he was uncertain, and he was not sure he wanted to explore why that should be. It was bad enough, every time he got close to her, to find himself imagining her naked under him as the surf pounded on the beach and the sun beat down hot on his back. The fantasy had kept him awake in the small hours of the night, too. It felt disloyal to Katerina, it disturbed his conscience and it was discourteous to his hostess.

Cris surveyed the rough track that led onwards towards the head of the valley. It looked challenging enough to drive any thoughts of sex out of his head for a while. How the blazes Collins had got the carriage over this road without breaking an axle was a minor miracle, he decided as he jumped a particularly evil pothole. He had thought the roads to Hartland Quay were bad enough, but this area appeared to have had nothing done in the way of road-making since before the Romans.

By the time he walked into the village he had taken off his coat, his body felt warm and limber and he had worked up a healthy thirst. There had to be an alehouse hereabouts. He surveyed the main street, which forked where he stood, the other arm presumably running to his right down to the quayside. The road was lined on both sides with single-storey cottages, some thatched, some with slate roofs. The whitewashed walls bulged and looked as though they were made with clay, but the quality improved slightly as the street rose from the fork, with a few two-storey dwellings, a public house with a faded sign showing a galleon in full sail swinging outside it, a shopfront and, rising behind the rooftops, the stumpy grey tower of the church.

Cris shrugged on his coat again and turned to walk up to the Ship Inn. The street was roughly cobbled, with narrow slate pavements raised on either side and, although he could see no signs of prosperity, neither did it look poor or neglected. A woman came out and emptied a pot of water into a trough of flowers that stood beside her door, stared openly at him, then went inside again, shooing a small child in front of her.

Two more women came down the street, baskets on hips, skirts kirtled up to show their buckled shoes and a glimpse of ankle. They smiled at him as they passed and broke into shy laughter when he doffed his hat. He kept it in his hand as he ducked under the low lintel of the inn door. 'Good day, gentlemen.'

The half-dozen men in the taproom fell silent, stared at him with the calm curiosity he was beginning to expect, then there was a murmur of greeting before they went back to their ale. He heard the click of dominoes from the table next to the window. The big man behind the bar counter waited, silent, as Cris made his way between stools and settles, then nodded. 'Good morning, sir. What can I do for you?'

'A pint of your best, if you please.' Cris leaned one elbow on the bar and half turned, letting the others take a good look at him. 'Is this cider country?'

'No, sir. Nor hops, neither, so we've no beer. We brew our own ale. Or there's brandy,' the landlord added.

'Your ale sounds just the thing at this hour.'

The brandy, no doubt, was French and smuggled. Cris picked up the tankard that was put in front of him and took a long swallow, then a more appreciative mouthful. 'A good brew.'

'Aye, it is that.' The man nodded, unsmiling, well aware of his own worth. He went back to polishing thick-bottomed glasses and Cris drank his ale and waited.

Finally one of the dominoes players slapped down the winning tile and shifted in his seat to look across to the bar. 'You be the gennelman down at Barbary?'

'I am.'

'Mizz Tamsyn fished you out the sea, is what we hear.'

'She found me staggering out and the ladies were kind enough to let me recover at their house.'

'Huh. Swimming. Don't hold with it, just makes drowning last longer.'

'It certainly seemed to go on a long time,' Cris agreed, straight-faced, provoking laughter from the other tables. 'I was most grateful to the ladies. Popular landowners hereabouts, I imagine.'

'Miss Isobel is that and all. A proper lady, for all that she's a bit scatty sometimes. Miss Rosie does a power of good for the school, too, poor lady, despite her afflictions. But Mizz Tamsyn makes certain it all runs right and tight.' There was a murmur of agreement round the room.

'They're having a difficult time just now, I understand. Rick fires, the sheep over the cliff.' Around him the dim room fell silent. Cris took another swallow of ale and waited.

'Nothing that won't get sorted. Mizz Tamsyn's one of ours now.' There was a warning in the voice from the shadows.

'What manner of man was her husband?' Now the silence was tangible, thick.

'Another one of ours,' the dominoes player said, putting down a tile and placing both formidable fists on the table. 'We look after our own. No need for strangers to get involved.'

It was said pleasantly enough, but the threat was quite plain. He was an outsider, this was not his business and if he continued to probe they would assume the worst and take action. He couldn't blame them for it, for all that it made life damnably difficult. Time to change the subject. 'Fishing good at the moment?'

As he spoke the latch on the door beside the bar snicked up and Dr Tregarth walked through, rolling down the cuffs of his shirt, bag under one arm. 'Your daughter will be fine now, Jim. It was a clean break. Just make sure she puts no weight on that leg until I say so or it will grow out of line. Now, where did I put my coat?'

'Here, Doctor.' The innkeeper produced it from behind the bar. 'I'm rightly glad to hear it ain't worse, given that she went down the stairs top to bottom. The little maid was crying fit to break her heart. What do I owe you?'

'A jug of ale and my noon meal will suit me just fine.'

He shrugged into the coat. 'I've got to go down to the Landing, but I'll be back directly.'

'Old Henry's rheumatics, that'll be,' the other dominoes player remarked.

'There's no privacy to be had around here,' the doctor said, turning with a grin, then saw Cris. 'Mr Defoe. How the blazes did you get up here?'

'Good day to you, Dr Tregarth. I walked.'

'Sore?'

'Some,' Cris returned, equally laconic. 'Exercise eases it, I find, once I get going.'

'First mile's the worst, eh?' Tregarth made for the door. 'I'll be back for that slice of pie, Jim. Make sure these rogues don't eat it all.'

'I'll walk with you, if you've no objection.' Cris laid a coin on the bar. 'Thank you, landlord. Good day, all.'

Outside, they walked in silence for a few yards. 'That will have provided more excitement than the last pedlar in the village a month ago,' the doctor remarked as he turned downhill. 'You'll be a major source of gossip and speculation for many a day.'

'More interesting than wondering how a strange dog got into Mrs Perowne's flock on top of a chapter of other incidents?'

'You've heard about that, then?' The other man's voice was carefully neutral.

'I have. Do you have any theories?' Cris ducked under a washing line slung across the street.

'As you say, a chapter of accidents.'

'I said incidents, not accidents.'

'At the risk of sounding rude, Mr Defoe, what concern is it of yours?' The doctor reached out the hand not encumbered with his medical bag, seized a runaway toddler by the collar and passed him back to his pursuing, breathless, mother. 'He's in fine form, Mrs Pentyre.'

Cris tipped his hat to the mother, sidestepped the struggling child. 'The ladies at Barbary Combe House may well have saved my life. It is clear something is wrong and, as a gentleman, I owe them my help.'

'And you know about agricultural matters?' Tregarth enquired. There was more than a hint of warning in his tone.

'Some. I know more about plots and sabotage, scheming and secrets.'

'And no doubt I wouldn't get a straight answer if I asked how you came by that knowledge. Mrs Perowne is an attractive lady.'

They had cleared the last cottage and the street bent into a rough track. Cris sidestepped sharply, forcing the doctor into the angle of the wall and a gate. 'Are you suggesting that I have dishonourable intentions towards the lady, Tregarth? Because if so, I am quite willing to take offence.'

Chapter Seven

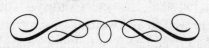

Cris watched the other man's eyes darken, narrow, and wondered if he was about to be asked to name his seconds. He knew he was being hypocritical because his thoughts, if not his intentions, were downright disgraceful as far as Tamsyn Perowne was concerned, but if he did not react he risked damaging her reputation with one of the pillars of the local community.

'Naturally, if you give me your word, sir.'

'That I do not wish Mrs Perowne harm? You certainly have my word on that, although as you do not know me from Adam, I am not sure how you judge the worth of the assurance.' What the devil was wrong with him? If he was observing this encounter, he would assume he was trying to force a fight on Tregarth, as though they were rivals for Tamsyn.

Oddly, the doctor relaxed. 'I trust you. Judging character is one of the tricks we medics must acquire, just as a horseman learns how to judge an unreliable animal. You, sir, have an odd kick to your gait, but I judge you are not vicious.'

'Thank you, for that,' Cris said drily, stepping back. He thought he had found an ally. Tregarth straightened his coat and they fell into step, as far as the surface of the track would allow. 'Miss Holt has a nephew.'

'The charming Lord Chelford. An acquaintance of yours?'

'I have encountered him in London. I would trust him as far as I could throw him. Possibly rather less if he had a deck of cards in his hand.'

Tregarth laughed. 'I suspect Tamsyn would say the same.' There was an awkward silence as the doctor realised he had used her first name. Cris did not comment, but noted it. 'He pressed her to marry him, quite persistently, and did not like getting *no* for an answer.'

'Before she married Perowne?'

'Then—and again after she was widowed. The first time she took refuge in marrying Jory, the second she had the iron in her soul and she sent him packing with no help from anyone.'

'Where did the iron come from?'

They rounded another bend and the land to the south fell away, giving a view of the sea and another towering headland. Tregarth nodded towards it. 'Black Edge Head. For a woman to see her husband hunted to his death it's either going to break her, or temper her steel.'

'He jumped from that?' Cris stared at the sheer face, the sea crashing at its foot, the snarling rocks. 'That is a long way down to regret an impulse.'

'Jory Perowne did not work on impulse. He was a realist and no coward. A man can dangle for half an hour on the gallows if the authorities are determined to make him suffer and Perowne had his pride. He would never have let them take him alive and jumping from there certainly made an impression.'

'And that old fool of a magistrate really thought he had to check that a strange man under Mrs Perowne's roof was not her husband? After he went over there in front of witnesses?'

'They never found the body and Jory was a legend. He had charisma, magic. No one would be surprised if he walked dripping out of the sea one dark night. Cornwall has King Arthur and, of late years, we had Jory Perowne. But if he does come back it will be as a ghost. Enough men saw him hit those rocks to know he died that day.'

Tamsyn had chosen marriage to a brigand who sounded like a swashbuckling rogue from the last century rather than submit to a man who would have given her status and title, if not happiness. She had survived seeing her husband's horrific death and lived with the consequences, and now she supported and protected two charming, and apparently unworldly, ladies. She ran an estate, kept a tart tongue in her head and she kissed like an angel. Cris was beginning to wonder who needed protection from whom.

'But where is he?' Aunt Izzy enquired plaintively for the fourth time. 'I cannot believe you simply abandoned the poor man like that and rode off, Tamsyn. Why, he might be collapsed in a ditch from exhaustion.'

'I did not abandon him, he is not a *poor man* and there are no ditches anywhere around there.' Exasperated, Tamsyn eyed the walking cane she had picked up when she rode home past the fallen tree. 'He was walking perfectly well and he can hardly get lost around here. He will turn up when he wants his luncheon, I have no doubt. He is a man, after all.' There was no doubt about that either. She braced her shoulders against the sensual little shiver that ran through her at the thought. She should tell them that Cris Defoe had exaggerated his weakness in order to have an excuse to stay there and protect them, but she suspected Aunt Rosie would be indignant and that Aunt Izzy would make a hero out of him.

'Here he comes now, from the beach,' Rosie said from her seat by the window.

'The beach?' And so he was, striding up over the lawn as though he had never experienced so much as a mild muscle twinge in his life. But how did he get there without being seen?

Cris raised his hat when he saw Rosie, then turned to take the path round to the kitchen door. Like all of them he had developed the habit of ignoring the front entrance. He obviously felt at home at Barbary Combe House and, strangely, the aunts, who were so protective of their privacy, seemed quite comfortable that he had become part of the household in only two days.

'Mr Defoe is back so I'll serve luncheon, shall I, Miss Holt?' Mrs Tape enquired. Through the open door his booted feet taking the stairs two at a time sounded quite clearly.

'By all means,' Tamsyn muttered as Aunt Izzy agreed with the housekeeper and they both went to help Aunt Rosie to her feet. 'Let us females wait upon the convenience of The Man.' She was thoroughly out of sorts and it was not helped by the fact that she felt guilty for being so scratchy. The aunts enjoyed having a man in the house again—Izzy to fuss over, Rosie to sharpen her wits on—and she was being a curmudgeon about it.

Booted feet clattered down the stairs again and she realised why she was feeling like this. The house had a man inhabiting it again for the first time since Jory's death. There were the male staff, but they were different; they did not fill the space in the same way. Nor did she desire them.

The sight of Cris as he came into the room affected her as though he had touched her, instead of immediately going to Aunt Rosie's side to offer his arm. Tamsyn tried to ignore the hollow feeling low down in her belly and the sensation that she was altogether too warm.

Whatever Cris Defoe had been doing had left him with colour on his cheeks and a sparkle in those blue eyes and he looked exactly what she had thought all along—a splendid male animal in his prime. *And a more cunning one than I have been giving him credit for.* But was he using his intelligence to help them or had he some other motives? Surely he could not be in league with Franklin? No one would risk drowning like that. Yes, he had been interested in Jory's legendary hoard…but the same objection held. All he'd have needed to do if he had wanted to be 'rescued' and taken in was to sink a boat in their bay or stage a fall from a horse outside the house.

'You came from the direction of the beach, Mr Defoe,' she observed when they were all seated. 'A remarkable feat, considering where we parted.' He looked at her with a faint smile. 'Do have a nice pilchard.'

'Thank you, but I feel sufficiently fishy for one day.' He sliced some ham and offered it to Aunt Rosie. 'I begged a ride back from one of the fishermen at Stib's Landing and his craft is liberally encrusted with fish scales. Dan Cardross, I think? He was going to lift his crab pots and said this was on his way.'

Dan had been Jory's right-hand man. Tamsyn tried not to read any significance into that. 'You had a long walk.'

'I went up to Stibworthy, had a pint of ale in the inn, encountered Dr Tregarth and walked with him down to the harbour. I will admit to being glad of the boat ride back,' he added to Aunt Izzy, who was making anxious noises about *overdoing it* and *recklessness*.

Tamsyn believed none of it. If he had needed to walk back, then Cris Defoe was quite capable of doing so. 'You must rest this afternoon,' she said, sweetly solicitous. 'Perhaps your manservant can give you one of his massages.'

'You are all consideration, Mrs Perowne, and I must admit, the thought of bed is a temptation.' His lids lowered over the sinful blue eyes, the only acknowledgement that he was teasing her with a *double entendre* that went right past the two older ladies. 'But I have correspondence to attend to, which will be restful enough. How does one get a letter to the post from here?'

'Jason will take it up to the Ship Inn, which is our receiving office. The post boy comes in every day except Sunday at about eleven, delivers the mail, picks up our letters and takes them to Barnstaple. Post going out of the county is taken to Bristol by one of the daily steam ships and from there by mail coach. A letter you send up tomorrow morning will be in London in three days.' Tamsyn delivered the information in a matter-of-fact tone, refusing to allow him to see the image that the conjunction of *Cris Defoe* and *bed* and *temptation* conjured up reflected in her expression.

'Steam ships?'

'They have been a boon for this coast because our roads are so bad. That is how the visitors to Ilfracombe and Instow arrive. We have quite a little sea-bathing industry in North Devon these days.'

'That is what gave us the idea for the bathing room,'

Aunt Izzy explained. 'I read how beneficial for rheumatic complaints the new hot-seawater baths are, but of course, Rosie could not tolerate the rough roads to reach Ilfracombe from here. So we decided to build our own.'

'Ingenious. Would you object if I made sketches of the plumbing? I am tempted by the thought of hot baths in my own houses.'

'Houses?' He had more than one? Aunt Izzy shook her head at Tamsyn's abrupt question but Cris showed no offence at her curiosity.

'The house in the country and a *pied-à-terre* in London,' he said vaguely. 'Would you pass the butter?'

Tamsyn handed him the dish. 'How lovely, to be able to go to London whenever you please.'

'Shops?' Cris enquired. He was teasing her, she could tell. The infuriating man did not so much as smile, but she was learning to watch for the slight dimple that appeared at the corner of his mouth when he was hiding amusement and the crinkle of laughter lines at his eyes.

'Of course.' She would not be drawn into a defence of shopping. 'And bookshops and theatres and the sights— St James's Palace and Carlton House and the parks.'

'You enjoyed your season, then?'

'I never had one. But as for the social round and the Marriage Mart, I am not sorry to have missed those.'

'Your absence was society's loss, Mrs Perowne. Think of all the bachelors deprived of the opportunity to court you, all the balls and assemblies ungraced by your presence.'

'I am sure those bachelors survived heart-whole. After all, they had no idea what they were missing.'

Aunt Izzy laughed and turned to Rosie. 'Do you remember at that assembly in Exeter, the evening before my eighteenth birthday?' In moments they were lost in reminiscence over some private joke.

'Yes, the poor souls have been languishing in ignorance,' Cris said slowly, answering Tamsyn, ignoring the laughter beside him. He raised his glass of ale to his lips and sipped, his eyes on hers as he did so. 'It is incredible that one can continue for years unaware of a gaping hole in one's life.'

Surely he did not mean that he recognised her as something missing from his life? No, he must mean that she was existing here, cut off from the world, not realising what *she* was missing. That was more likely. How very...*humiliating* to be pitied. 'And it is incredible how difficult it can be for some people to recognise when others are happy, just because they value different things,' she retorted.

There was a sudden flare of emotion in Cris's eyes. 'I think we may be at cross-purposes, Tamsyn.'

'Probably because we come from two very different worlds.' So, he had not meant to insult her, but the exchange had served to remind her how distant from polite society she was, here at the edge of England, cut off by sea on one side and rough tracks on the other. She was country gentry, teetering on the verge of slipping into something else since her marriage. The small resources that she felt gave her everything she needed were pitiful against the wealth that Cris Defoe was obviously used to with his beautiful boots and elegant coats, his valet and his London home. She must seem pathetically provincial and unsophisticated.

And in danger of slipping into self-pity and unjustified feelings of inferiority. I'd like to see him striking a bargain in a cattle auction or setting up a village school or teaching himself French from books ordered from an Exeter bookshop. I would like to see one of the elegant ladies of his acquaintance running a farm and a fishery.

They finished the meal in polite, prickly silence with each other, letting the two older women take the burden of conversation. *How complicated men are,* Tamsyn thought as she dropped her napkin on the table and nodded her thanks as Cris pulled back her chair for her when, finally, Aunt Izzy stopped chattering and noticed that they had all long since finished eating.

He went to offer his arm to Rosie and Tamsyn followed them out. 'That is a good walk with wonderful views that you took this morning,' Rosie was saying as he led her to the drawing room. 'It must be five or six years since I could manage it. I should not repine, this is a lovely house and I have an ever-changing view of the sea from the garden, but I confess that I miss being able to stride along the clifftops, see the expanse of the ocean and Lundy Island in the distance with the ships sailing by.'

If they could spare the money she would have the track up to the village made into a proper lane, with a surface levelled and graded by Mr McAdam's new method, but it would cost more than they could spare and Aunt Rosie would no doubt protest at the idea of spending so much on something intended for her pleasure alone.

'A penny for your thoughts?' Cris had stopped beside her at the foot of the stairs and was regarding her with a quizzical smile. Tamsyn realised she must have been standing there, staring blankly at the front door.

'I was speculating on road building,' she admitted. 'An expensive investment.'

'You, Mrs Perowne, are a constant source of surprise to me,' he murmured. 'You will allow me to stay for a few more days, despite my pretence of feebleness being exposed?'

'I suppose so.' Her dark mood lifted as rapidly as it had descended. 'I can hardly cut short your seaside holiday, now can I?'

'Holiday?' Cris's mouth twisted into a wry smile. 'It was hardly that.' He turned to climb the stairs.

'What was it, then?' She reached out and touched his hand as it gripped the carved ball on top of the newel post.

For a moment she thought he would not answer. Then he twisted his hand to catch hers within it and lifted them, joined, to his lips. 'A journey from reality, from the loss of a dream, from the acceptance of what is inevitable,' he murmured against her fingers. 'Perhaps that is the definition of a holiday.' His breath was warm, the touch of his lips no more than the brush of a feather. His fingertips were against the pulse of her wrist and he must have felt the thunder of the blood, the surging response, the desire.

It was madness, a dangerous madness if it could be so powerful when ignited by such a light touch, such a gentle caress. *I want him and he would not say* no *if I came to his bed.* But how did one carry on an *affaire*, however brief, under the same small roof as two doting and observant aunts? And how could she risk it—her reputation...*my heart*...for a few moments of pleasure with a man who would be gone within days?

Behind her, from the window embrasure out of sight of where they stood in the hallway, she could hear her aunts discussing their latest order to be sent to the circulating library in Barnstaple. Innocent, safe pleasures. This was not innocent and not safe and suddenly she had no desire for either. Tamsyn reached up and slid her fingers into Cris's hair, just above his nape, pulled down his head and lifted her face to his. One kiss, surely she could risk that?

Chapter Eight

His kiss was not tentative, nor respectful. Certainly it took no account of where they were. Cris turned from the stair, took her in his arms and swept her back against the front door, the length of his body pressed against hers, the thrust of his arousal blatant, thrilling. Tamsyn twisted and got her hands free so she could lock them around his head, the shape of his skull imprinted on her palms, the heavy silk of his hair caressing across her fingers.

Her mouth was open to him, his tongue forceful, demanding that she open more, let him taste her, explore her. She pulled back so she could nip at his lower lip, making him growl, low and thrilling, the sound reverberating from his chest to her breast, before she drove her own tongue into his mouth, refusing to allow him mastery. If this was to be nothing else, there would be equal desire, equal responsibility.

They broke apart, panting. Tamsyn wondered if she looked as stunned and wild as he did, with his hair tousled, his eyes dark. She reached behind her, turned the doorknob and staggered back on to the porch, pulling him with her. 'Summer house.'

Without waiting to see if he was following her she

ran across the lawn, round the corner of the dense shrubbery that sheltered one side of the garden, and into the little summer house that looked out over the beach. Cris followed her, the door banging closed behind him. Tamsyn collapsed on the bench, her knees failing her.

Cris stood with his back against the door as though glad of its support. 'What in Hades was that?' he demanded. 'I've been on the edge of an avalanche in the Alps and it was rather less violent. It was certainly less frightening.' She realised that he was smiling. It transformed the austerity of his face, changed him from beautiful to real.

'I thought a kiss would be…' *Nice? Do not be ridiculous.* 'I wanted to kiss you again.'

'You will get no argument from me on that score.' He still had not moved from the door.

'I noticed.' She could feel her lips twitching into an answering smile. It had not occurred to her that there might be anything amusing in giving in to this attack of desire. 'That is all it can be, you realise that? Just a kiss. This is quite inappropriate.'

Cris's smile deepened at the prudish word. 'With so many other people around, perhaps. But lovers have always found ways and means to be together.'

'We are not lovers.' Tamsyn found she had lost the desire to smile.

'Not yet.' Cris pushed away from the door and went to sit at the other end of the bench, out of touching distance unless they both stretched out a hand. 'There was something, there had to be, right from the start, in that moment of madness on the beach. I am not married, Tamsyn, and you are not an innocent. What is to stop us?'

Reputation, risk, prudence? 'And you are not committed to anyone?' she asked, wondering suddenly why such an attractive, eligible man should be unattached.

He did not answer her immediately and when she looked at his profile she found he had closed his eyes as though to veil his thoughts.

'Cris?' she prompted.

His eyes opened and when he turned his head to look at her the smile was on his lips alone. 'No, I am not committed to anyone.' He got up, a sudden release of energy like an uncoiling spring. She jumped. 'You are correct. This is quite inappropriate. You might have been married, but that does not give me the right to treat you like one of the sophisticated London society widows. They know the game and how to play it and they move in circles where these things are understood.' Cris opened the door and stepped out on to the daisy-spangled lawn. 'Forgive me.'

By the time she had realised what he was doing and had reached the door, he was striding away towards the house. The front door closed firmly behind him. A succession of Jory's riper curses ran through her mind.

Damn him! That was not about me, or at least, not entirely about me. There is someone and I made him think of her. Now you have got exactly what you told yourself you wanted, Tamsyn Perowne. You got your kiss and that was all. You are safe, respectable. And frustrated.

The tables had turned so fast she had been taken completely unaware. One moment she had been hesitant and he eager, the next she had pushed aside her qualms and he was backing away. She tried to make some sense of those past few hectic minutes. Cris had been a gentleman—once he had stopped kissing her like a ravening Viking pillager. She had said it would be inappropriate and he had agreed. And, just as she was telling herself that she should seize this opportunity and argue against herself, her question about other women had stopped him in his tracks. He had said there was no one else now, but she must have made him face a memory that hurt.

Tamsyn went down the slope of the lawn and took the steps to the foreshore. The sea had always helped her think, but now, as she watched the Atlantic waves come rolling in to end a thousand miles' journey in a frill of harmless lace on the sand, she knew there was nothing to think about. She wanted Cris Defoe, beyond prudence and reason and despite knowing quite well that he would leave this place very soon, whatever she felt or wanted. That meant that she had a decision to make. Was she capable of seducing a man—and would it be right to do so?

'Muscles paining you, sir? Would you like a massage?' Collins got up from the window seat looking out to the track up towards Stibworthy and put down what looked like a book of German grammar.

'No. Thank you.' Cris bit back the oath. His fault, his temper, and no need to take it out on Collins. He would think about what had just happened later when he had his breathing under control and some blood had returned to his brain from where it was currently making itself felt. 'I need paper and ink. Wax. And a seal.'

'Not your own, of course, sir.' Collins removed a key from his watch chain and opened the large writing box that sat on the dresser. 'The plain seal?' He laid a seal on the table in front of the window and set out paper and an ink stand with steel-nibbed pens, then struck a flint to light a candle. 'Which colour wax, sir?'

'Blue.' Cris picked up the seal and rolled it between his fingers. His own seal ring, securely locked away, showed the de Feaux crest, a phoenix rising from flames, a sword in one clawed foot. *From Ash I Rise, In Fire I Conquer.* The crest was an ancient pun on the similarity in pronunciation between *feu*—fire—and *Feaux*. This version showed only the flames, but it was known to his friends.

'Cipher, sir?'

He thought about it, then shook his head. 'No. Can you see anyone in this household opening a guest's correspondence?'

Gabriel Stone was in London, up to no good as usual, and perfectly placed to send Cris information about Franklin Holt, Viscount Chelford. Gabe might be Earl of Edenbridge, but he was also a gambler, a highly successful, ice-cold, card player, and he would know just what Chelford was about, whether he was in debt and any other scandal there was to be had.

Send whatever intelligence you can find—and especially anything about Chelford's relationship with his aunt, Miss Holt, of this address, and his inheritance of her estate after her death.

He put down the pen and stared out of the window as he ran through the things he wanted Gabe to find out.

He wished he could ask him to send down a couple of burly Bow Street Runners, or better still, a couple of doormen from one of the tougher gambling hells, but they would stick out like daffodils in a coal cellar down here. Then his eyes focused on the stony track and he smiled. Of course, that would kill two birds with one stone. He dipped the pen again.

You recall that little incident in Bath and our two Irish friends? If you can locate them and send them here with their equipment, I have use of both their old trade and their willingness to use their fists.

All correspondence should be directed to Mr C. Defoe.

He folded and sealed the letter, addressed it to *The Earl of Edenbridge*, then folded it within a second sheet and addressed that to his solicitor in the City, sealing it for the second time. However scrupulous his hostesses might be about other people's correspondence, there was no need to raise questions over letters to the aristocracy.

'Thank you, Collins. If you take that down I am told someone will take it to the receiving office in the village. That will be all for the moment.'

Alone, he got up and prowled around the room as he finally allowed himself to think about Tamsyn and that kiss. It was like unravelling tangled string, sorting out what he felt, what he ought to feel, what she wanted—what was right. She was not an innocent, but neither was she experienced with men other than her husband, he could tell that. Whatever she had been doing since Jory Perowne's death, Tamsyn had not been sharing the beds of any local gentlemen. This was a tiny, unsophisticated community where everyone knew everyone else's business and where a reputation lost would be common currency within hours. If this…attraction…flirtation… madness…whatever it was, went any further, then he would have to be very careful indeed.

And what was he thinking of anyway? Part of his anatomy was sending him very clear signals indeed, but it had been months since he had lain with a woman, not since he had set eyes on Katerina. He could simply be suffering from an attack of lust, which was something very different from what he had felt for Katerina. To have even thought of another woman while he was seeing her every day had been impossible. But she was far away and unobtainable and always would be, and he, as he kept reminding himself, was not cut out for celibacy.

Cris sat on the window seat and stared at a clump of gorse. It was sentimental tosh to feel that kissing another woman was disloyal to Katerina. She had never been his, he had never been hers, they had never spoken the words he read in her gaze, that he felt in his heart.

But the desire he felt for Tamsyn was shaking his certainty about his feelings for Katerina. Was it love? He felt uncomfortable with the doubt. It had certainly been more than pure lust. But was desiring Tamsyn just a selfish need to lose himself in a passionate encounter that he would walk away from in a few days?

Perhaps he should tell her who he was. Cris examined the idea and realised he was enjoying the freedom too much. For the first time as an adult he had none of the burdens of his title on his shoulders, none of the demands or the expectations. He was just Cris, a man who was attracted to a woman and who saw the need to protect her from the danger that threatened them. It would do them no good to know who he was, only make them feel awkward.

The whole thing was academic, anyway. He had kissed Tamsyn as though he was about to rip off her clothing, there and then in the hallway. He had almost had her standing up against the door, like some drab in a back alley, and he had topped off a thoroughly unpolished performance by informing her that she was not from the sophisticated world he inhabited. If Tamsyn would give him the time of day next time they met, then it was more than he deserved.

Something moved on the road. Cris focused and saw it was Jason, a satchel slung on his shoulder, riding up the track. The mail was on its way. Now he just had to remind himself who he was, what he was, and somehow recapture the man he had been before that wild impulse had sent him off the road at Newark, driving across country into oblivion.

There was absolutely nothing like a pile of account books for setting a woman's feet firmly on the ground. Or, in the case of the farm's accounts, in the mire. Nothing was adding up this afternoon, not the price of oats, not the farrier's bill, not even the egg money. Tamsyn gritted her teeth, turned over a sheet of paper covered in crossings-out and started again. All that was wrong with her, as she was very well aware, was that her brain was off with the fairies, her body was pulsing with desire and more than half her attention was focused on listening for footsteps on the stairs.

'Letters, Mizz Tamsyn.'

She jumped, sending her pen in one direction, the account book in another and a large ink blot on to her page of calculations. 'Jason, you startled me.'

'Sorry, Mizz Tamsyn.' He came into the room and emptied the contents of the satchel on to the table. 'You were daydreaming, it looked like.'

'Er…yes.'

Dreams of night, not of day. Of beds and rumpled sheets and mindless pleasure. And impossible dreams. There had been a moment as she daydreamed that she had heard wedding bells. And that would never be. Her stomach cramped with remembered pain and she bit her lip before she could turn back to the waiting groom.

'Thank you, Jason.' She dabbed at the spreading blot, made it worse, screwed up the whole sheet in sudden exasperation and began to sift through the pile of post. Several newspapers, two days out of date, a notification from the circulating library that three novels she had asked for were now available. Several bills, including another from the farrier, an invitation to dine at the vicarage in a week's time when the moon was full and the roads consequently less hazardous, and a letter with their solicitor's seal.

Something about leases, or perhaps an answer to her query about buying that small warehouse in Barnstaple she'd had her eye on. The heavy paper, expensive, like Mr Pentire's excellent services, crackled as she broke the seal and started to read.

'What?' The shriek hurt her throat, but that did not stop the next words being wrenched out. 'The *swine*. The utter, unmitigated *swine*.'

There was a thunder of boot heels down the stairs, Aunt Izzy's cry of, 'Tamsyn? What is wrong?', then the door flew open to reveal Cris with, of all things, a pistol in his hand.

'What is it?' He cast one searching look around the room, then strode in, jerked her out of the chair and into the curve of his arm. 'Who was it? Where did they go?'

Aunt Izzy hurtled into the room, gave a cry at the sight of her niece in the clutches of a man holding a gun, and collapsed into the nearest chair. 'What happened? Why do you have a gun?'

'What gun?' The question came from the doorway where Aunt Rosie, grim-faced and clutching the poker in one arthritic hand, clung to the doorpost.

'There is nobody, Aunt Izzy, please be calm. Cris, put that thing down and let me go. Aunt Rosie, let me help you.'

He beat her to the doorway, taking her aunt gently by the arm and thrusting the gun into the waistband of his breeches. 'It isn't loaded, which is more than I can say for this poker. Do let me take it, Miss Pritchard. Mrs Perowne, what provoked that scream?'

'Pure temper.' She picked up the letter and flapped it at them. 'This is from Mr Pentire, our man of business. Our bankers wrote to him because they had received information that we were about to withdraw all our funds to meet sudden and unexpected debts. In effect, that our credit was no longer good. And half today's post is bills—word must be spreading. Pentire has reassured the bank, but now we may expect a flood of demands for payment of all our accounts and it may take months for confidence in our credit to be restored.'

All energy gone, Tamsyn sank down in the chair and dropped the letter.

'Can you afford to meet all your creditors in full?' Cris asked.

'Yes, I never let accounts run on and we always settle up completely. Luckily we are almost at quarter-day when the rents will come in. But it is the principle of the thing and it will put doubts into the minds of people who do not know us well. This must be the work of Franklin, I cannot believe anyone else has a grudge against us and would do a thing like this.'

'But Franklin can have no grudge,' Aunt Izzy protested. 'I know you do not like him, dear, and I have to admit he is a sore disappointment as a nephew, but—'

'But nothing,' said Aunt Rosie. 'Tamsyn's right.

The man wants us out of here. I just wish I could work out why.'

'We are not moving and that is that,' Aunt Izzy said, with remarkable firmness.

'Forgive me, but does your right of possession here rely upon your residence?' Cris hitched one hip on the table edge and looked round at the three of them. 'If you move away, what becomes of Barbary Combe House and the estate?'

'I retain ownership and the revenues,' Izzy said promptly.

'And your nephew knows this?'

'Certainly.'

'So he would not gain control of it until, forgive me again for being so blunt, your death?'

Izzy gasped, Rosie went pale. Tamsyn got a firm hold on her panicking imagination. 'But Franklin offered you a house on his estate, Aunt Izzy. I agree he wants us out of here, but I do not think he is too worried about the estate as such. The farms brings in enough for our needs, but hardly the sort of income that will rescue him from some financial crisis, and land prices are very poor, so selling it would hardly help either.'

She looked at Cris and found his gaze fixed on her face. Of course, there was Jory's mythical treasure. If Franklin got them out of the house he could helpfully supervise getting it prepared for tenants—all to help his dear aunt Isobel—and search to his heart's content. 'There is no need for alarm about your personal safety, Aunt Izzy.' She directed a narrow-eyed look at Cris, daring him to say any more. 'I have organised some watchers for the livestock and we are quite secure down here. Any stranger would be spotted a mile away, we are so remote.'

'Of course. I am being over-cautious, and over-imaginative, too.' Cris stood up. 'I am sorry, Miss Holt, ladies, for alarming you.'

'No need for that.' Aunt Rosie was brisk. 'You talk a lot of sense, we should take more care. Help me back to the drawing room, Isobel. No, you stay here.' She waved a twisted hand at Cris as he came forward to help her. 'Soothe Tamsyn's ruffled feathers before she calls Franklin out for his idiocy.' She gave a wicked little cackle of laughter. 'I would lay several guineas on her being the better shot.'

Cris closed the door behind her and turned back. 'My apologies.'

'For what?'

'For alarming your aunts…and for what happened in the summer house.'

'They are made of sterner stuff than it might seem,' she said. 'And nothing happened in the summer house.'

'That, perhaps, is what I should be apologising for.'

Chapter Nine

Now, perhaps, was the moment to be bold, to reach out and admit, frankly, that she would welcome him as her lover, that she wanted him, that he had nothing to fear from her, that she would not cling or make demands. But that shadow—the one that had killed the heat of desire in his eyes—that haunted her. She would not be a substitute for another woman, nor would she demand he forget.

'There is nothing to apologise for in behaving like a gentleman.' She shrugged and smiled, making it light, slightly flirtatious. Unimportant. 'I was uncertain and you, very thoughtfully, did not press me. Now, if you will excuse me, I must finish these accounts or we really will be in a pickle if any more demands for payment come in.'

She thought he was going to offer his help with the books, but a smile, as meaningless and pleasant as her own, curved his mouth and he nodded. 'Of course. I will leave you in peace.'

Tamsyn stared at the account books for a long while after he had gone. The path of virtue was the right one to take, and the least embarrassing, as well as the decision that would carry no risks at all, for either of them. Safe.

'Safe is dull, safe kills you with rust and boredom,' Jory's voice seemed to whisper in her ear.

'Take care,' she had pleaded with him so often. *'Do not take risks.'*

'Risk makes your blood beat, fear tells you that you are alive,' he would respond with that charming flash of teeth, the smile that was as enchanting as Hamelin's Piper must have been. The smile he had given her before he had turned and sprinted for the cliff edge and oblivion.

And risk made you dead, Jory, Tamsyn argued back now, in her thoughts.

Yes, his voice seemed to echo back. *But I lived to the end.*

A week later Cris was still installed in the back bed-chamber, Collins had his feet firmly under the table in the kitchen and both of the older ladies protested strongly whenever Cris suggested that he really should be moving on. Not that he wanted to, not until he heard from Gabe and had a clearer idea of what Chelford might be up to, and not until his surprise for Aunt Rosie arrived.

The ladies insisted he call them Aunt Izzy and Aunt Rosie, exclaimed with pleasure over each small service he did for them, made a great fuss over him—even when he tangled Izzy's knitting wool into a rat's nest or beat Rosie at chess. He needed a holiday, they insisted, and his presence was as good as one for them, too. Again, as it did almost every day, the truth was on the tip of his tongue, and once again he closed his lips on it. Hiding his identity was becoming dangerously addictive, like losing himself in drink, and he justified it to himself again, as he did every time. He needed the rest, he was doing no harm to anyone.

The only blight on this amiable arrangement was Tamsyn. She protested that they should not detain him, that he must be bored or uncomfortable or, when he choked over one of her more blatant attempts to dislodge him one dinner time, in need of a London doctor.

None of this made him want her any less. He found himself in a state of arousal which long punishing walks along the cliffs, or up through the woods, did nothing to subdue. If he couldn't stop reacting like a sixteen-year-old youth soon he was going to have to resort to several cold swims a day. That particular form of exercise he had been avoiding, wary of encountering Tamsyn, who apparently saw no reason to curtail her own daily swims just because there was a man in the house.

He wanted her, he admired her spirit and her directness, her love of her aunts, her work ethic, her courage and her humour. Taking her as his lover would be healing, he sensed, provided he could manage a short-lived *affaire* without harming her in any way. On the other hand, finding a bride, plighting his lifelong fidelity and affection, that was another matter altogether. That would be a betrayal of Katerina. As soon as he thought it he felt uncomfortable, as though he was dramatising himself and his feelings. But if he was in love with Katerina...

He came in through the front door that morning after an unsatisfactory, brooding, walk on the beach, trying to conjure up the memory of Katerina and finding it damnably difficult, and found Tamsyn in the hallway arranging flowers in the big urn at the foot of the stairs. 'Can I be of any help? That looks heavy.'

'It will be staying here, thank you for offering.' A polite smile, a polite exchange, a not-very-polite urge to sweep the basket of foliage on to the floor and take her here and now, on the half-moon table amidst the flowers and the moss.

Cris pushed the fantasy back into the darker recesses of his imagination, from whence it should never have escaped in the first place, and took the stairs to his bed-chamber two at a time. Increasingly he found it difficult to be in Tamsyn's company and pretend there was nothing else he wanted beyond a polite social friendship.

Collins was sorting out laundry and managing to take up most of the space in the room in the process. 'I'll be out of your way in a moment, sir. I've just got to put these shirts away, the rest can wait.'

'No, carry on.' Cris took off his coat, tugged loose his neckcloth as he went to stand in the window embrasure and stare out over the roofs of the stable yard to the steep lane. Someone was coming, a rider, low-crowned beaver hat jammed on over windswept curling black hair, and behind him the roof of a carriage was just visible with, strapped on top, something that looked like a giant coffin with windows.

It was Gabriel. He had come himself without warning, riding into a situation he knew hardly anything about and quite apt to let all of Cris's secrets out of the bag if he wasn't stopped. Cris threw up the casement, climbed over the sill and dropped the ten feet to the rough grass path behind the house.

'Sir!' He looked up to see Collins leaning out. 'May I assist, sir?' He kept his voice to a discreet whisper. It was not the first time both he and Cris had left a building by way of the window and Cris suspected that the valet enjoyed missions where there was a strong element of cloak and dagger work as much as he did.

'Lord Edenbridge is riding down the lane, I need to head him off.' He was off, running, before Collins could reply, shouldered his way through the narrow gap in the shrubbery behind the house and sprinted up the lane past the entrance to the service yard.

Gabriel reined in, his hand on the hilt of his sword, the moment Cris emerged. The horse, battle-trained, went down on its haunches, ready to kick out, then Gabriel relaxed, clicked his tongue and the horse was still.

'My good fellow,' he drawled as Cris arrived at his stirrup. 'I am looking for my friend Cris de Feaux. Elegant, well-dressed gentleman, a certain dignity and refinement in his manner. Anyone answering to that description around here?'

Cris shoved the hair back out of his eyes. 'Buffoon.'

'*I* am a buffoon? By the sainted Brummell, what have you done to yourself? Your hair hasn't been cut, you're as brown as a farm labourer—and your clothes!' He surveyed Cris from head to foot. 'What the devil has happened to you?'

'I just climbed out of the window. What are you doing here? I wanted information, not the dubious pleasure of your company. And it is *Defoe,* not *de Feaux.*'

'It all sounded intriguing and I needed to remove myself from temptation in London.' He shrugged when Cris raised an interrogative brow. 'A sudden impulse of decency in regards to a woman.' His habitually cynical expression deepened. 'A lady. I thought it better to remove myself before I discovered that I was on the verge of becoming reformed. So here I am, complete with the cargo from Bath, armed to the teeth and looking for adventure. And, judging by the state of the roads hereabouts, this is probably the end of the known world, so adventure should be forthcoming.'

'You will fit right in. There are smugglers hereabouts and I would guess we're about two generations from pirates.' With his unruly black hair, his gypsy-dark eyes, his rakehell attitude and the sword at his side, Gabriel Stone, earl or not, looked as though he was up for any criminal activity. 'Listen, we must make this fast. I am plain Mr Defoe and you had better be simply Mr Stone. This is not a part of the world used to the aristocracy and I do not want to cause complications.'

'Or raise expectations. I assume there's a woman in the case?'

'A lady.' Gabriel grinned at the echo of his own phrase. *Lord, Tamsyn married one rogue, I just hope for her sake she doesn't take a fancy to this one...* 'There's some kind of trouble and I haven't got to the bottom of it yet, but until I do, there are two ladies of a certain age who would be better for some protection whether they want it or not.'

'Hence our Irish friends?' Gabe looked over his shoulder at the carriage with its incongruous load.

'Exactly. I'll just have a word with them, then we'll go on down to the house. The ladies will offer you a bed, I have no doubt. You'd best accept unless you want to make your way back to Barnstaple today—there isn't more than an alehouse for ten miles in any direction.'

He went up to the carriage, nodded to the coachman, and opened the door. The inside was filled with Gabe's luggage and two very large Irishmen. 'Good day to you, me lord!' the black-haired one exclaimed. 'And a pleasure it is to be seeing you again.'

'Seamus.' Cris nodded to his red-headed companion. 'Patrick. Now listen. I am Mr Defoe—forget I ever had a title. I've a couple of very nice ladies who need an eye keeping on them, but they aren't to know that. As far as they are concerned I've sent for a sedan chair for the one who can't walk far and the two of you are here to train up a couple of likely local lads. And you'll have trouble finding the right ones, if you catch my drift?'

Seamus cracked his knuckles and grinned, revealing a gap in his front teeth. 'Someone causing them grief, eh? Don't like bullies who upset nice old ladies, do we, Patrick? You can rely on us, Lord…Mr Defoe, sir. We're doing very nicely with the bodyguarding business you helped us with, it's a pleasure to take a job in the country for you, that it is.'

Patrick, a man of few words, grunted.

'Unload the chair now,' Cris decided. 'Get it set up, then follow us down in ten minutes. You'll be a surprise for the ladies.'

What they would make of two massive chairmen, Irish as most of the Bath chairmen were by long tradition, goodness knew. These two had waded into the action when Cris and Gabriel had found themselves cornered in a dark alleyway by a gang who did not take well to Gabe's legendary game-winning skills with cards. When the dust had settled and the four of them had been binding up their injuries and drowning the bruises in brandy at the nearest inn, Cris had suggested they might find acting as bodyguards a profitable sideline. After he had put some business their way the two were building quite a reputation and they made no bones about expressing their gratitude.

'Tamsyn, there is a carriage at the gate,' Aunt Rosie called. 'And a gentleman on a horse. Who on earth can it be?'

She jammed the rest of the flowers into the vase with more haste than care, whipped off her apron and threw open the front door. And there was Cris, who only ten minutes before had been upstairs while she had been filling vases at the foot of those stairs the entire time. She shot him a questioning glance as she approached, blinked at the sight of shirtsleeves and loose neckcloth, and blinked again when she saw the man dismounting from a raking bay horse. Presumably she was not dreaming and transported into some Minerva Press novel, so this was not a dashing gentleman highwayman. She took a deep, appreciative breath. Goodness, but he certainly looked like every fantasy of such a romantic character.

'Mrs Perowne, may I introduce my friend, Mr Gabriel Stone.' Cris gave her a very old-fashioned look as though he knew exactly what she thought of the newcomer. 'I wrote to him on a business matter and did not make myself clear that posting the information would be sufficient.'

Mr Stone doffed his hat. 'Mrs Perowne, my apologies for the intrusion. Just as soon as my coachman can work out how to turn the carriage on this track, we will be on our way.'

'Mr Stone.' She inclined her head in response to his half-bow. 'Are you in haste, sir?'

'No, ma'am, not at all.'

'Then you must stay. If your man takes the carriage further down he can turn where the lane opens out to the beach. Then the stable yard is just up behind the house. Oh, I see Mr Defoe is already organising him.'

And Mr Defoe wants you to stay, now you are here. I wonder just what that matter of business is.

She turned towards the house, inviting the intriguing Mr Stone to follow her as Cris strode across the lawn to rejoin them.

'If Miss Holt and Miss Pritchard are able to come to the door, I have a small gift for Miss Pritchard. I will go and fetch her a chair out to the porch.' He was gone before she could ask what possible present could necessitate Aunt Rosie coming outside.

It took a few minutes for Michael to carry out a chair and for Aunt Rosie to be settled on it and introduced to Mr Stone. There was the sound of feet on the stones of the lane and then, completely incongruous in the wilds of the Devon coast, two burly men appeared carrying a sedan chair between them. Cris opened the gate and they marched across the lawn, deposited the chair in front of Aunt Rosie, opened the door between the shafts and whipped off their hats.

They were certainly an imposing pair in their dark-blue coats, black tricorns and sturdy boots. The sedan chair gleamed and the seat was deeply padded. 'Would you care to try it, ma'am?' the black-haired man enquired in a broad Irish accent.

'Why…' For a moment Aunt Rosie seemed lost for words. 'Why, yes, I would. But we have no city pavements here, you will find it hard going.'

'We're from Bath, ma'am, and that has hills as steep as you'll find anywhere and cobbles like walking on ice. We're strong lads, that we are. We won't drop you, ma'am.'

'You brought them here?' Tamsyn asked Mr Stone as they watched Michael and Cris help Aunt Rosie into the chair. He nodded as the men picked up the poles and set off smoothly around the lawn, then through the gate and off up the hill.

'I'll be able to go with her on my mare.' Aunt Izzy ran across the grass and took Cris's arm as he stood watching the chair's progress up the lane. 'We can go for picnics and Rosie can visit our friends again and go up on the clifftops. Oh, thank you, Mr Defoe.'

'Mr Stone brought them,' he said with a smile.

'But you sent for them.' Tamsyn joined them at the gate. 'How long can they stay?'

'The chair is yours to keep. Seamus and Patrick will stay until they've found you a pair of local men to train in their stead.' He looked down at her, his face austere again. 'They are very reliable men, I can vouch for them. Very strong, honest. No harm will come to your aunts with them around.'

The chair was returning and Aunt Izzy ran out to join it. Tamsyn hardly noticed her going. 'You sent for bodyguards,' she said as the realisation struck.

'That is a side benefit. I thought of the sedan chair when your aunt was saying how difficult it was to get around, then I remembered these two. Will it be a problem feeding them? They probably eat like bullocks.'

'No, not at all, and there is space in the living quarters over the stables. But, Cris, you don't truly believe we are in danger, do you?'

Mr Stone, who had strolled over to the wall to watch the progress of the chair, remarked, 'Rider coming. Looks military.'

Cris joined him, leaving her question unanswered. The horseman reined in, his way blocked by the sedan chair, and even at that distance Tamsyn could see the colour in his face and the angry set of his mouth. He did not like being held up and neither did he seem to enjoy being stared at.

The chairmen came back into the garden, took the chair right up to the seat and began to help Aunt Rosie out. She and Izzy immediately broke into animated conversation, then fell silent as the stranger dismounted at the gate and strode in.

Around her Tamsyn was conscious of the men closing up. The two chairmen were standing in front of her aunts like a solid wall of muscle. Cris and Mr Stone flanked her. This was ridiculous. It was only one man, apparently on official business judging from his dark-blue tailcoat with insignia on the high collar and the naval sword at his side.

'Sir?'

He halted in front of her and made a sketchy bow, lifting his tall hat as he did so. 'Ma'am. I am looking for the householder.'

She was aware of his gaze shifting between the two large men beside her, Cris dishevelled in shirtsleeves, Mr Stone managing to look piratical despite his sober, conventional clothing. 'My aunt, Miss Holt, is the householder. And you are?'

'Lieutenant Ritchie, newly appointed Riding Officer for this beat of the coast. And I was told it is Mrs Perowne that I need to speak to.'

Was it her imagination or had Cris growled, low in his throat.

'I am Tamsyn Perowne.' She tried to sound calm and welcoming, but the man's hard, unfriendly gaze was setting her hackles up. 'And Mr Defoe and Mr Stone are our house guests.' She should invite him in, she knew. The Riding Officer had about the same status as the doctor or the curate and would expect to be received in gentry houses, but she did not want this man, who seemed to radiate hostility, over their threshold. 'What can I do for you, Lieutenant Ritchie?'

'The Revenue service has been informed of a new smuggling gang in these parts. What can you tell me of it, Mrs Perowne?'

'Nothing whatsoever. There is no gang here, not since—'

'Not since your late husband's death?' he enquired.

'Precisely.' She took a hold on her temper, sensing that her supporters would react violently at any sign of distress from her. A fight on the front lawn was the last thing they needed. 'I imagine smuggling still goes on, here and there, in a minor way, but I defy you to find any stretch of coastline in England where it does not.'

'And so it will remain while the local gentry take such a casual attitude to law-breaking. Ma'am.' The last word sounded like an afterthought. 'I came to give fair warning that we will be on the alert hereabouts now.'

'There is no *gang*, Lieutenant Ritchie. And I can only assume you mean you wish to advise us to take care and lock our doors. Any other *warning* would be nothing short of insulting.'

'Take it as you will, ma'am,' he snapped.

'Mrs Perowne is too much of a lady to respond to an insult in kind.' Cris took one step forward. He sounded perfectly calm and yet his tone held a threat that sent a shiver down her spine.

'And you are, sir?' The Riding Officer's square chin set even harder.

'As Mrs Perowne said just now, Crispin Defoe, a visitor.' Now he sounded as haughty as a duke.

'Gabriel Stone. *Another* visitor,' the mocking voice on her other side echoed, equally arrogant in its own way.

Ritchie's gaze rested on the faces in front of him, then shifted as though to study the chairmen. Tamsyn could almost feel them glowering behind her. 'Good day to you, gentlemen. Ma'am. You appear to have quite a private army here, Mrs Perowne.' He touched his whip to his hat, turned the horse and clattered back up the lane.

Chapter Ten

Tamsyn turned to find that the two Irishmen had taken Aunt Rosie inside by the simple method of picking up the armchair she was sitting in and carrying it into the house.

Aunt Izzy remained, her face creased with puzzlement. 'What an unpleasant man. I couldn't hear all of what he was saying, but he seemed almost aggressive.'

'Merely a jack-in-office,' Cris said. 'Newly appointed and officious. Nothing for you to worry about.' He turned and looked at Tamsyn. 'If he tries to cause any trouble, I will deal with him.'

It was necessary to take in a breath right down to her diaphragm. Somehow *she* was going to have to deal with this crisis and the aunts' willingness to live without men suddenly became very understandable. Her life was far too full of them—Riding Officers trying to scare her, the mysterious Mr Stone arriving without warning and securing an invitation to stay without the slightest effort, large Irish chairmen who were carrying Aunt Rosie about as though they had been in her service for years and now Cris calmly announcing that he would *deal with* a government official.

'And just how will you do that?' she demanded. 'Forgive me, Mr Defoe, but you are hardly the Duke of Devonshire, are you?' He stood there, competent hands on admirably slim hips, the breeze from the sea stirring the thin white linen of his shirtsleeves, a glimpse of skin at his throat, a long green stain that looked remarkably like lichen up the length of one buckskin-clad thigh. 'But of course, dukes do not go scrambling out of windows, do they?'

Behind him Mr Stone gave a snort of laughter. 'Cris, a duke? He certainly acts like one on occasion, I will give you that.' He appeared to find the idea inordinately amusing.

'Mr Stone, perhaps you would excuse us for a moment? No doubt you would like to freshen up after your journey. If you cannot see either of my aunts when you go inside, then our housekeeper, Mrs Tape, will take care of you.'

'Very crisp,' Cris remarked as his friend, still chuckling, strolled off towards the front door.

'I feel very crisp. In fact, I feel positively brittle. Just what, exactly, is going on, Mr Defoe? Why are you climbing out of windows and threatening Revenue officers and why does the idea that you are a duke convulse your exceedingly relaxed friend with amusement?'

'You are allowing yourself to become agitated, Tamsyn.' He touched her cheek with the back of his hand. 'You are quite flushed. Come and sit in the summer house and compose yourself.'

Grinding one's teeth was not ladylike, but then she did not feel so very ladylike, just at the moment. 'By all means, let us go to the summer house.' She waited until he had stepped into the shadowy interior behind her, then swung round and jabbed an angry finger into the middle of his chest. He caught her hand and held it, pressing the palm against the warm linen. Somehow she managed not to let her fingers curl, gathering the fabric up, pulling him closer.

'Being married to Jory Perowne was not all joy, but at least he never patronised me, never treated me as though I was incapable of looking after myself and never, ever, told me I was becoming *agitated* when I was rightfully annoyed!'

'But you aren't married to me, Tamsyn.' If she had not been flushed already, the suggestive growl in his voice would have turned her cheeks crimson. 'Was I being patronising? I apologise if I was.' He did not let her go and his fingers curled around hers as he took a step forward, trapping their joined hands between their bodies.

'No, you were not. Not until you told me I was becoming agitated,' she conceded. Stepping back would be admitting that his closeness, his touch, affected her. Confessing that she had found his presence at her side had given her strength was too much like accepting weakness. She lifted her chin instead and made herself meet the cool blue eyes. 'Up to then you were merely… lordly.'

Cris shrugged. 'London style, that is all. Take no notice of Gabriel, he finds the idea of his old friend being a duke amusing, the sarcastic devil. Do I seem like a duke to you? After all, I am the kind of man who almost drowns himself in foolish swimming incidents, climbs out of windows and is acquainted with Bath chairmen.' His face was austere, but she recognised the slight crease at the corner of his eyes, the start of a smile he was not allowing out.

She was not going to let him get away with charming her into smiling back at him. 'Explain the window.'

'The chair and the men were a surprise for your aunts. I wanted to stop Gabriel and make sure they arrived with it all set up for her.'

And you could not have run downstairs and out through the door? No, not without alerting me, she answered herself. Cris had wanted to talk to Gabriel Stone first. The pair of them made her uneasy. They had an aura of power and confidence about them, something that went beyond mere competence. They were used to being obeyed and to making things happen. Their way.

Tamsyn moved forward, closer, until she could feel the beat of his heart against her fingers, could see his pupils dilate with surprise, or perhaps, pleasure. 'Tell me,' she murmured sweetly, and he bent his head, to listen, or to kiss. 'Do I seem a helpless little female to you? Do I appear unable to take care of myself and my aunts? Do you think that I need a big, strong man to protect me?' She did smile then, showing her teeth in a clear warning that she could, and would, bite if provoked.

She expected Cris to respond with an attempt at mastery, a hard kiss to show her what she was missing. Or perhaps a display of affronted male pride and a declaration that she did not know what she was talking about and had quite misunderstood him. Instead he did the last thing she expected. He laughed.

It was infectious, open, genuine, and she laughed, too, not knowing why, only that this was completely disarming.

And *then* he kissed her. There were perhaps three seconds to make up her mind on how to react and she was aware of each of them in the thud of her pulse. Three seconds to decide whether to be charmed, or to be resentful, to be mastered or to fight. Or, perhaps, to meet him on equal terms.

One, two, three… Cris lifted his head, eyes watchful. He would not force her, she knew that. Whatever else this man was hiding from her, it was not a willingness to ill treat a woman. Tamsyn wrapped her arms around his neck, pulled his head to hers again and nipped at his lower lip, deliberately provoking. He laughed again against her lips, then probed with his tongue, risking her teeth, provoking in his turn.

This was the man from the sea, the man she had kissed in the surf without knowing why, only that it was right and she wanted him. Then they had been naked and that had been right, too, and they were wearing far too much now. Her hands ran down over the thin linen of his shirt, over the long, beautiful muscles of his back, down to the waistband of his breeches and she tugged, impatient, careless of rips.

He stepped back, breaking the kiss, to let her pull the shirt free and over his head, then his own hands were busy with buttons and pins and her gown was sliding from her shoulders, down to her feet and she was back in his arms, his skin hot and smooth under her palms, his mouth hot and urgent on the swell of her breasts above the neck of her chemise.

'Yes,' she said, closing her teeth on the tendon where his neck met his shoulder, biting gently, tasting his skin, tasting him. *'Yes.'*

'Cris!' The shout from outside froze them in place.

'Hell's teeth.' Cris stepped back, looked round wildly for his shirt. 'I must be out of my mind—the middle of the day in a confounded *shed* in the garden within a stone's throw of the house and a dozen people. Are you all right?' He dived into his shirt, dragged it on, stuffed it into his breeches while Tamsyn just stood and looked at him. 'Get dressed! What are you doing?'

'Looking at you.' She wanted to smile at the sight of him, uncharacteristically harassed and urgent, dishevelled and flatteringly aroused. This was not the cool, calm and mysterious Mr Defoe, this was another man altogether and she was charmed as well as attracted. The sound of Mr Stone's voice calling Cris came closer.

'Dress, Tamsyn!' He found the ends of his neckcloth, whipped it into some sort of knot, then moved to get between her and the door with its old glass panels fogged with salt spray. Through them, as she turned, she could see the blurred figure of the other man standing with his back to them. He seemed to be scanning the beach.

Suddenly seized with Cris's urgency, she pulled up her gown, fumbled the fastenings closed, twitched the skirts, patted at her hair. 'Am I decent?'

'More or less. You'll be the death of me, woman.' He pushed in a few of her hairpins and smiled at her, suddenly tender, his hand cupping her cheek. 'Do you want to be ruined?'

'Yes, please,' Tamsyn said demurely.

'But not here—'

The door swung open behind him. 'There you are. Cris, what the blazes are you doing?' Gabriel Stone took a step inside, took one look at her, turned on his heel and went out again. 'Or, rather, why the blazes are you doing it here and now?' he enquired without looking back.

'Insanity,' Cris said without turning, his smile still promising things that made her feel reckless and eager. He stroked his fingers down her cheek and murmured, 'We'll talk.' Over his shoulder he asked, 'Is the coast clear?'

'Completely.' Gabriel Stone stepped aside to let them

out on to the gravel in front of the summer house. 'Everyone is in the yard admiring the sedan chair and arguing about which of the locals might be employed to carry it.' He was still looking out to sea, presumably tactfully sparing Tamsyn's blushes. She was amazed to discover she did not have any. 'It will be a while before you can find two men suitable, I would suggest, Mrs Perowne. They need to be matched in size and strength, have good balance and endurance. Carrying a sedan chair is harder than it looks.'

'You suggest I do not search too hard?' She grappled to focus her mind on the issue and not on her pounding pulse, the excited flutter low in her belly, the ache in her breasts, the need to reach out and touch the man by her side. 'But how long can these two men stay?'

'As long as I am here, I will pay them,' Cris said. 'Call it a return for my board and lodging,' he said when she began to protest. 'When I leave they will stay for as long as you choose to employ them because this is their work these days.'

'Bodyguards? You cannot pay for them as well as give us the chair.'

'It is for my own peace of mind,' Cris said. He offered his arm to her and she slid her hand into the crook of his elbow. Mr Stone fell in on the other side and offered his arm as well.

'I feel very well protected between two gentlemen,' she remarked lightly as they strolled across the grass. The switch from reckless passion to a sensible discussion was disorientating, and the presence of Gabriel Stone with his rakish understanding at finding them in a compromising position in the summer house only added to the feeling.

Gabriel Stone chuckled.

'What is so amusing?' she asked.

He turned thick-lashed dark brown eyes to study her. 'In London you will find many who would say we are a disgraceful pair and that you are not safe with us at all. Certainly we would not add to your respectability.'

'You would not? Mr Defoe seems entirely respectable to me.' *Except when he kisses me. You, on the other hand...*

'We are two of four close friends, referred to bitterly by the dean of our university as the Four Disgraces. We worked hard at proving him right and did not lose the habit when we went out into the world. Two of us have married this year, so are probably removed from any further temptation to be disgraceful, but Cris and I have a reputation to uphold.'

'Speak for yourself,' Cris said. 'I am, as Mrs Perowne says, *entirely* respectable.'

'You cultivate the appearance of it, but underneath you are as much of a rakehell as the rest of us.' Mr Stone tucked Tamsyn's hand more firmly into his elbow. 'If you saw Cris at court, doing the pretty amongst the ambassadors and the courtiers and the politicians, to say nothing of their wives, you would not recognise this man in his shirtsleeves facing off with Riding Officers.'

Beside her Cris seemed to go still, although he continued to walk, his steady pace unchecked.

'You are often at Court? I thought you said you were a landowner.'

'I am. I just happen to be well connected enough to attend St James's, which is nothing very unusual. It is hardly as exclusive as its habitués would like to make out.' He shrugged. 'I find politics and diplomacy interesting. Unlike Gabriel who is as close-lipped as a clam most of the time and as indiscreet as a village gossip when he does open his mouth.' There was an undertone of threat in the teasing words.

There was something he was not telling her, although she could guess what it was. Crispin Defoe was not the country landowner he pretended to be, he was someone who mingled in society, someone used to London. Someone used to authority and privilege. So what was he hiding? And, more to the point, why was he hiding it?

Try as she might, she could not think of any reason that Cris might be a danger to her, or to those at Barbary Combe House. He had come into their world by accident and the fact that he was being less than open about his own life was probably simply reticence and not in any way sinister. *And I want him.* Was her desire for him blinding her to concerns she should be feeling? No, she decided. Franklin made her uneasy, unsettled, suspicious. Cris made her feel safe, even when she knew her feelings were definitely *un*safe.

Aunt Izzy came to the front door, saw them and waved. 'Dinner in thirty minutes,' she called. 'We have quite lost track of time with all this excitement and Cook is threatening a disaster with the fish if we are late.'

'I must go and tidy myself up,' Cris said. 'Return to my entirely respectable self.'

'And I will show you to your room, Mr Stone. Hot water will have been taken up for you.'

'I'm confused.' Gabe lounged into the dining room, where Cris, decently washed, dressed and combed, was waiting for the rest of the household.

'*You're* confused? I can't imagine what you are doing here—and don't give me that line about curiosity. You are never so curious as to put yourself out with a journey of over two hundred miles to one of the most inaccessible parts of England.'

'I told you, I'm removing myself from temptation and telling myself I am not quite such a rogue as to ruin a respectable young lady.' He shrugged when Cris lifted an eyebrow. 'And Kate is worried about you. She thinks you are in love and moping. But the timing is awry, unless you met Mrs Perowne earlier this year.'

'Kate said…' *Hell's teeth.* Had he been that obvious when he and Gabriel had visited their old friend Grant Rivers, Lord Allundale, and his new wife, Kate? He had thought he had concealed his heartache over Katerina very effectively behind his usual cynical exterior. Apparently not.

Thinking about Katerina did not bring the jab of pain he had become used to. The shock of that realisation almost took his breath away. Was he so shallow, so hard-hearted, that he could shrug off the heartbreak of true love, simply because he was distracted by a lovely woman and a mystery?

Unless, of course, he had not been in love in the first place. Cris moved down the length of the room, away from the door and into the deep window embrasure to absorb that thought.

'Kate was mistaken,' he said quietly. 'There was a woman I could not have. It preoccupied me for a while, that is all.' It occurred to him that there had never before been something that the Marquess of Avenmore wanted badly, yet could not have. Was that all that had been wrong with him? An attack of pique, added to sexual frustration and a heady dose of forbidden romance and he had thought himself in love? If that was the case, he was not at all sure how that made him feel.

The doubt made him almost dizzy. Ridiculous. He was never doubtful, certainly not to the extent of rocking on his heels as though he had drunk too much. Cris steadied himself with one hand on the window frame. He was always in command of his emotions, clear about his motivation. But now... Had he almost drowned himself out of sheer inattention because of the *delusion* he was in love?

Gabe, card-player *extraordinaire*, was watching his face, his own expressionless. He did not have to say anything. It was obvious he thought that Cris had ricocheted from one unsatisfactory *amour* to another.

'I was not in love.' *I think. Perhaps. Damn it, I should know, surely?* 'I am not in love,' he repeated more firmly. 'And I do not intend to find myself in love. I intend to leave here when I am confident that the ladies are no longer in any danger and I am then going to find myself a suitable, sensible wife. Kate hardly knows me. What she calls moping was merely the gloom brought on by contemplating matrimony.'

Gabriel's mouth twisted into a wry smile, but he did not respond to the attempt at levity. 'So what, pray, was going on in the summer house just now? And what is this I hear about you almost drowning yourself?'

'If I have to explain to you that Tamsyn and I are verging on the edge of an affair, then it is you we need to worry about, not me. As for the near drowning, I underestimated the power of the currents off this coast. I was not paying attention, that is all.'

'You always pay attention, Cris,' Gabriel murmured. 'And you are never transparent. Now I can read you like a book and you lose focus almost fatally. I think—'

Whatever he thought was, mercifully, interrupted by Aunt Rosie being helped into the dining room by the footman, Isobel and Tamsyn behind her. Cris let out the breath he had not been aware of holding and set his face into the blandest and most neutral of all his diplomatic expressions.

Chapter Eleven

Cris ate and smiled and kept up his share of the conversation, which was not difficult when the two older ladies could talk of little else but the wonder of the sedan chair and all the expeditions they could take with Isobel riding her hack and Rosie being carried, safe and comfortable at her side. He had taught himself to carry on a dinner-party conversation in three languages while puzzling over a coded letter, planning a meeting and thinking about a new pair of boots. This cheerful domestic meal, even with Gabriel's sardonic eye on him, was child's play.

It gave him the opportunity to think about the self-revelation Gabe had forced on him. He had, somehow, deluded himself that he had fallen in love with Katerina and that was inexplicable. Yes, she was an attractive, intelligent woman—what he knew of her, which was very little. Yes, she had been attracted to him. But that was all. He had never been in love before, he was not in love now. There was no point in trying to convince himself that he had not lost temporary control of his reason over a woman.

It could have been a disaster. If he had not been so

strong with himself about duty, honour and the need to protect both their reputations, the whole affair could have blown up into a diplomatic scandal, meant ruin for Katerina and probably someone dead on the duelling ground. And he would be a disgrace, tied to a woman who was quite intelligent enough to see through whatever protestations of devotion he made to her once their ruin had been accomplished.

What had come over him? He was not some green youth talking himself into love with an unobtainable beauty. He was, on the other hand, a mature man facing the prospect of making a suitable marriage and resenting it. He had always prided himself on his detachment and his independence and the only relationship that he had ever allowed to become personal, to matter, was his friendship with Gabe, Grant and Alex Tempest, Viscount Weybourn.

Was that what this was about? Had he armoured himself against the faceless, unknown, woman he was going to marry by telling himself that his heart was already taken, that marriage was a matter of form, of convention and of convenience, something that would not get close to him, could not hurt?

'Mr Defoe?'

It took him a moment to remember that was who he was, that someone was speaking to him. It seemed that he had been over-confident and his dinner-party skills had disintegrated along with everything else. 'I am sorry, I was distracted for a moment.'

'I was just remarking what a spectacular sunset there is this evening,' Aunt Rosie remarked.

The wall behind her was suffused with pink and those with their backs to the windows turned to admire the sight as the hot red disk of the sun dropped into the sea.

'You almost expect to hear it sizzle,' Tamsyn said as the colour faded. She rang the little hand bell by her side plate and when Michael came in, she gestured to him to light the candles. 'There will be a full moon tonight.'

'A smugglers' moon?' Gabriel asked.

'Certainly, if there is a big run, then moonlight helps, especially if they are going to load it straight on the ponies and head inland,' Tamsyn explained, surprising Cris with her lack of reticence in talking about the subject. 'But the men know the coast so well that they can land with only the aid of a few dark lanterns on shore.' She sent him a quizzical look. 'You don't want to take any notice of what that Riding Officer said. That's just some foolish rumour. There's no serious smuggling going on around here these days. I would know.'

She kept them entertained with tales of the last century when the gangs ruled the coast, then teased the two men with local ghost stories.

'I'll be safe riding back tomorrow, will I?' Gabriel demanded with mock alarm. 'No fear of finding Old Shuck loping at my heels, or headless horsemen or drowned sailors or any of those other horrors in broad daylight?'

'Surely you are not leaving us so soon, Mr Stone?' Isobel asked. 'Do stay a little longer. I am sure you cannot have had time to discuss your business with Mr Defoe yet.'

'This evening after dinner, ma'am...' Gabriel began.

'Not after the long day you have had,' Rosie said firmly. 'You relax this evening and see to your business tomorrow morning, then we can all take a picnic up on to the clifftops to celebrate my wonderful new sedan chair.' When he hesitated she reached out her twisted fingers and touched the back of his hand. 'Won't you indulge me with your company? We are so quiet here that a charming and intelligent guest is too precious to lose.'

'Ma'am, you overwhelm me with your hospitality. I would be delighted.' It brought Cris out of his uncomfortable thoughts to see Gabriel succumbing to the charms of a woman old enough to be his mother, if not his grandmother. He normally avoided respectable older women like the plague and confined his conversation, and his attention, to high-flyers and dashing society matrons.

Tamsyn rang the little bell again and got to her feet as Michael came in. 'We will leave you gentlemen to your port and nuts.'

Amidst the minor flurry of helping Rosie from the room Cris drew Tamsyn aside. 'Where can we talk?'

'Talk?' She looked up at him and blushed. 'The summer house at midnight.'

'That is too close to the house—and uncomfortable for…conversation,' he said, making her blush harder.

'Uncomfortable for talking? I think not. But I will take you on a walk, if you are not frightened of meeting Black Shuck. Wear good boots for rough ground. Coming, Aunt Izzy!'

When he turned back Gabriel had returned to his seat and was pouring ruby port into the pair of fine Waterford crystal glasses Michael had set out for them. He raised his glass and sniffed. 'Excellent port, duty paid or not.'

Edgy, Cris picked up the other glass and walked round the room to study a pair of sketches in the alcove by the fireplace. 'They've some nice pieces here.

I like the ladies' style—Miss Isobel in particular will take some earthenware jar from the local potter, fill it with wild flowers and stand it on an exquisite Sheraton side table and it will look perfect.'

'Stop fidgeting, it isn't like you.' Gabriel watched him, lids half-lowered over his gypsy-dark eyes. 'I like your fierce little widow.'

'She isn't mine.' Cris dropped into the nearest chair and reached for the wine. 'We may have a…thing. For a short while, that is all.' That was all it could be, of course. He knew exactly the sort of wife he needed, his father had explained that to him, young as he was. Marquesses married for dynastic reasons—connections, land, bloodlines. Tamsyn stirred his blood, but she was an obscure widow of a scandalous marriage without any of the attributes that would make a permanent connection acceptable in his world. But, as a widow, then a discreet *affaire* was perfectly acceptable.

'A *thing*.' Gabriel rolled his eyes. 'Are you quite certain that my friend Cris de Feaux has not been kidnapped by smugglers who put you in his place? I am missing the articulate, smooth, cynical man I know.' Cris lobbed a walnut at him. He caught it one-handed and cracked it between his long card-player's fingers. 'Joking aside, if there is something wrong, tell me, I'll help.'

'I know. And there's nothing wrong with me.'

Liar. My brain is scrambled eggs, all the blood in my body is heading straight for my groin and I have no idea what I've been thinking for the last few months.

'But there is plenty amiss here. I'll be interested to hear what you found out about Chelford tomorrow. Meanwhile, pour me some more of that excellent port and tell me the latest London news.'

* * *

'You are here already?' Cris followed the thread of lamplight across the grass to the dark lantern that was set on the step of the summer house.

'I am always prompt.' A hint of laughter, a suspicion of a nervous tremor, a suggestion of excitement. He could not see Tamsyn's face in the shadows, but he knew, quite certainly, that they would be making love that night.

'Where are we going?'

'Follow me.' She picked up the lantern and handed him another, its shutter closed so that only the heat of it and the smell of burning tallow told him it was alight. She crossed the lawn, heading away from the lane, opened the shutter of her lantern a little to show him the stones sticking out of the wall to make a stile and climbed nimbly over. 'We can open the lanterns more now,' she said as the ground began to rise. 'This sheep track winds around the side of the headland, we'll be out of sight of the house in a moment.'

She walked steadily up the steep path, moving with the confidence of someone who was both fit and familiar with where she was going. As they climbed the moon came out, full and brilliant, painting the short turf with abrupt black shadows. They gained the top and Tamsyn strode out, not waiting to see if Cris followed her, then turned abruptly, right on the edge.

'Take care!' He reached for her as she dropped out of sight, then relaxed as he saw she was on a lower path, cutting down below the lip of the cliff by about the height of a tall man. Once they were down it became flat and smooth, just wide enough for one person. Tamsyn ducked, moved sideways and, with an unexpected creak of hinges, vanished into the cliff face.

Cris opened the shutter of his lantern to show a squat hut, built back into the face of the cliff. From what he could see in the flickering lamplight it had been constructed from sea-weathered wood, perhaps hauled up from the beach below. The roof was turf and in the moonlight he could make out the needle-point leaves and round heads of sea thrift, sharp against the midnight sky.

He bent to get under the low lintel and found a square space, long enough for a tall man to lie down in. Across the back was a platform of crude planks. Tamsyn dragged a metal trunk out from under it and Cris crouched to help her, inhaling the scent of old lavender as she opened the lid and hauled out a thickly padded quilt.

They spread it on the planks, then added the pillows she took from the trunk along with a pile of blankets. Tamsyn patted the bed they had created. 'Close the half-door and come and sit here.'

It was divided like a stable door and he did as she asked. All that was visible as they sat there was the sea, filling half the view with the sky above and the reflection of the moon trailing silver across the waves. Tamsyn sighed and leaned into his side, so Cris put an arm around her shoulders and pulled her in snugly.

'An old haunt of yours?'

'It must have been a looker's hut once.' He made a questioning sound and she explained. 'A watcher for the Revenue service. But it was long abandoned when Jory and I found it as children. Later, when things were… difficult, I would sleep here sometimes because it is so peaceful.'

'Difficult? You mean when your husband died?'

She was silent for a moment as though thinking his

simple question through. 'Yes. It was my special place when I wanted to be alone and being alone helped sometimes.'

'Tamsyn.'

'Hmm?'

It had to be said. 'You know I am not staying, that I will be gone in a week or so.'

'Of course.' She wriggled upright and the air struck cool where she had been pressed, warm and soft, against his side. 'We are about to have the conversation about not getting attached and do I really want to do this and you respect me, but…'

There was a trace of amusement in her voice, so he let himself be frank. 'Yes, that was exactly it. You may rely on me to be very careful, but if there are consequences, I also rely on you to let me know.'

'Of course,' she said abruptly. 'I am not worried about that.' The shimmer of amusement had gone now, she sounded almost sad. This businesslike discussion was neither erotic nor romantic, he supposed.

'Tamsyn, if this does not feel right to you, we will go back now. And don't think I am going to sulk, or leave immediately or be less anxious to help you and your aunts.' He turned on the hard bed, reaching to caress her cheek. 'This matters to me, my mermaid. I'll not hurt you.'

'Mermaid?' She laughed, low and husky, the sound like an intimate caress. 'I thought you were a merman, coming out of the sea like that. If you wish to make a woman cautious, you should not appear looking quite so desirable.'

'I was ice-cold, half-drowned and probably covered in goosebumps.' He began to nuzzle her neck and she tilted her head to give him better access.

'I did not notice the goosebumps. I noticed the muscles and how blue your eyes were and your…proportions.' Her hand slid to the fall of his breeches in graphic demonstration. Her breath was coming in little gasps now as his flesh rose to meet her hand.

Cris lifted his head to look at her in the dim lantern light. 'My proportions? It was freezing, I doubt I had any proportions to speak of.'

'Oh, yes, you did. I was most…ah…impressed.'

'Hussy.' Ridiculously flattered, he stood and closed the half-door, then fully unshuttered both lanterns. 'If we are going to take any clothes off, I want to keep warm, regardless of how well I stand up to the cold.'

'You first.' She was sitting with her legs drawn up, her arms wrapped around them, her chin resting on her knees, those great dark eyes watching him. Cris stripped as fast as he could, given that he had to stoop under the low ceiling. It was not cold, but it was cool enough not to want to prolong undressing. And besides, he was beginning to desire nothing more than to be skin to skin with Tamsyn now, to discover whether her body was as tempting warm and dry as it had been wet and shivering.

He sat on the edge of the bed to pull off his boots and she reached out to run her hand down his spine, lingering over each bump of vertebrae. 'I love your back.'

It was difficult to pull off a pair of Hoby's boots when a desirable woman was beginning to twine herself around you. Cris persevered, resisting the temptation to tear off her clothes, rip open his breeches and take her with his boots on. It was an arousing prospect, but he did not know her well enough to judge whether she would find that exciting or insulting.

Barefoot, he stood up to pull off his breeches and she

came up on her knees, her hands sliding over his torso, her mouth trailing down his ribs. Cris stilled, breathing hard, his hands arrested on the fastenings of his falls as he tried for some self-control. Much more of this and she would have him spending like a green youth. He could not remember when a woman had made him quite this aroused so fast.

He kicked off his breeches and to his relief she sat back on her heels and just looked. 'If you touch me, I won't answer for the consequences,' he warned as she gave a low hum of approval.

'Very well.' She began to undress with a straightforwardness that matched his own, shrugging off a simple gown to reveal nothing beneath it but bare woman.

Cris almost swore, swallowed the oath and kept his eyes fixed on her fingers as she pulled the long braid of her hair over her shoulder and began to loosen it. 'Your hair is beautiful.'

'Thank you.' She bent her head and shook it so the mass of dark brown shifted and fell, wavy from the plait. When she looked up it covered her breasts, shadowed the junction of her thighs as she knelt on the bed. 'Cris…' Her voice trailed away, then she seemed to gather her courage. 'I have only slept with one man before. I will not have the skills of the lovers you are used to.'

'You have the skill to bring me to my knees,' he said, and went down on them beside her, pulling her beside him on to the mattress and dragging the blankets up over them. 'I desire you intensely. Can you doubt that?'

'No.' She buried her face in the angle of his neck and shoulder, suddenly shy, it seemed. But her hands were not shy, or clumsy.

'You are sure?' He had never doubted his self-control

before, now he knew that a few more moments of this and he was lost.

'Sure.' Tamsyn slid under him, like the sea creature he had imagined her as, and her damp, hot, softness met his desperate body and he drove into it and stopped, almost shuddering with the pleasure of it, his weight on his elbows, his forehead resting on hers. *'Ah...'* she murmured, and her hands fastened on his shoulders and her legs curled around him until her heels were in the small of his back.

'You are perfect,' he said on a breath that was almost a gasp. 'Perfect.' Then he ceased to know where her body ended and his began as they moved together. It was as though they had done this a thousand times together and yet never before. There was a rightness, a harmony, balanced by a freshness and the wonder of discovery. Somehow he hung on until her eyes opened wide and then closed in ecstasy and she convulsed around him. Somehow he found the strength to withdraw and find his release, straining against the strong, soft, wonderful body in his arms.

For a while he lay dazed, conscious only of their heartbeats, their breathing, the sound of the sea crashing far below. Then he rolled to one side and Tamsyn came with the movement, curling around him, her head on his chest, her body relaxed and trusting. Her lips moved against his skin with silent words, or, perhaps a kiss, then she was still. He sensed her slipping into sleep and closed his own eyes.

But oblivion would not come. He was utterly relaxed, utterly satisfied, warm, content and completely awake, and his mind was apparently determined that he would enjoy none of it. A few months ago, before Katerina, he would simply have been grateful to have experienced such mutually satisfying lovemaking. The fact that he hardly knew Tamsyn, that she was from another world completely, would not have mattered. They were mutually attracted, he could make love with her without compromising her and it would have been a perfect idyll, one that would be ended naturally with a departure that she expected and accepted.

But now he could not help examining his motives, his desires. He was not in love with Tamsyn, but he no longer knew what that meant, not after the shock of self-realisation over Katerina. Was he just using her? But she was not an innocent and she had her own needs, too. The urge to toss and turn, pummel the pillow, had to be suppressed because of the woman draped, limp and trustful, over him.

He should return to London, find a suitable bride, court her, wed her, he told himself. And then stay faithful to her. Gabe the ultimate cynic, was prepared to believe that their friends, Alex and Grant, had fallen in love, but to hear him talk about this was as rare an event as finding a unicorn in the back garden. According to him the remaining two disgraceful lords had no excuse for tying themselves to some woman's apron strings. If he explained his thinking to his friend, Gabriel would laugh at him, tell him that this attack of conscience, of sobriety, was the onset of old age.

Cris opened his eyes and stared up at the weathered old wood of the roof while Tamsyn's curls tickled the underside of his chin. If twenty-nine was old, then he might as well open that door, go back down the cliff and walk back into the sea to finish the swim that had brought him here.

Chapter Twelve

'What is wrong?' Tamsyn swam up out of the sleepy, satisfied haze and found Cris beside her, his arm heavy across her waist. She could feel the tension in him, despite the sprawl of his long body. 'I can hear you thinking.'

He laughed, an almost convincing sound, but she had come to know him very quickly over the past week and he was not amused.

'Are you regretting what we have done?' she demanded, wriggling round so she could sit up and look at him properly.

'No.' This time the smile was quite genuine, a small, sensual twist of his lips. 'I was brooding, that's all. Gabriel would say I am getting old.'

'Truly?' Feeling wicked, she slid one hand under the blanket and explored. 'I don't think so.'

Cris caught her hand, but did not move it from where it lay, her fingers lightly curled around the hardening length of him. 'Mentally old.'

'A sudden attack of responsibility? That is very ageing.' She tried to make a joke of it, but he only frowned.

'No. I've always been responsible, I think.' He

shrugged. 'I was brought up to be, to accept who I was, what I needed to do to fulfil that role.' There was an edge of bitterness there that puzzled her. What kind of burdens had his upbringing laid on him? 'Whatever hell I might have been raising, I always did what needed to be done, looked after the people who relied on me.'

'As you are doing here,' Tamsyn pointed out.

'I don't like men who try to get what they want by intimidating those who can't fight back.' He winced as she closed her fingers rather too tightly. 'I know you can stand up for yourself, but you shouldn't have to. I told you I wouldn't stay long. I must go home, settle down, stop doing things like this.'

She found her fingers had curled into claws. Cris closed his eyes as she let them rake gently over his hot flesh instead of digging them in. 'What exactly is *this*?'

'Making love without commitment.' His hand tightened over hers, moved.

'There is someone you should be settling down with? Someone to whom you should be committed?' She kept her voice light, surprised by the sharp lance of envy.

'No, there is no one.' His face was slightly averted, she wished she could read it. 'There should be. Duty. Responsibility again, I suppose.' His hips rose as she stroked down and up. '*Ah*. That is so good.'

'If there is no one, then you are not being unfaithful.' She thought his face tightened, but that might simply have been the effect of what she was doing to him. 'I believe you are simply experiencing the melancholy and introspection that sometimes comes after lovemaking.'

'*La tristesse*, the French call it. Well, I'm not suffering from melancholy now.' He kicked away the blanket, reached for her and held her so he could torment her right nipple with teeth and lips. Then he suddenly let go and she collapsed on to the bed with him in a tangle of limbs and kisses, and forgot jealousy, and worry, in bliss.

'Tamsyn, dear, have you been sleeping properly?' Aunt Izzy peered anxiously at her over the fruit bowl in the middle of the breakfast table. 'You look a trifle heavy-eyed.'

'I am sure Tamsyn is perfectly relaxed, dearest,' Rosie said before Tamsyn had a chance to collect herself from her improper recollections. Her aunt's smile was bland. *She knows.*

As for the expression on Mr Stone's face, the man was looking so innocent that it was bound to be false. Presumably he was quite well aware what had passed last night between his friend and herself.

'Too much time spent with the account books, that is all I am suffering from,' she said. 'I am looking forward to our picnic lunch. That will wake me up.'

They went their separate ways after breakfast. The two men strolled down to the waterside, deep in conversation, presumably to do with whatever business had brought Gabriel Stone there in the first place. Aunt Rosie went for her hot soak to get herself, as she said, 'In prime condition for my jaunt.' Aunt Izzy shut herself in the kitchen with Cook to create the perfect picnic luncheon and that left Tamsyn staring at the farm's feed bills and trying to focus.

She had to get the accounts straight in case they were sent any more invoices following the mischief with the bank and the damage to their reputation for creditworthiness. It was important and urgent and every time she smoothed her hand over a page in the book all she could feel was Cris's skin under her palm. When she nibbled the end of her pen, all she could think of was his mouth on hers, and once she let her mind wander along those paths, then the heaviness settled low in her belly and the little pulse started its wicked beat between her thighs, and her breasts ached.

I want him again. Now.

It frightened her, a little, the intensity of the need. She had been celibate for all the long months since Jory had died, that must be it. She was a young woman, used to lovemaking. Of course she missed it, even though she had submerged the need as deep as her grief for Jory. That was why last night had been so *magical*. She took the word, turned it in her mind, shivered. There was something charmed about the way Cris had come to her out of the sea, almost out of the jaws of death, something other-worldly about his blond beauty, those haunting blue eyes. If she was not an adult, modern woman she might start imagining things, supposing he had come from some mysterious world of Celtic legend to help her. She had read Scottish tales of Selkies, seal people who came out of the sea to seduce human beings. They would always return to the water, leaving their earthbound lovers desolate.

That was a depressing turn of thought, but of course Cris would leave, she accepted that. Whoever he was, whatever his life at home and in London, he was a man who moved in circles far removed from her rustic, un-sophisticated world. Even if he had wanted her in any other way than for this brief, amorous, encounter, then he would not when he knew the truth about her. All men wanted heirs. She realised her hand was resting over her stomach and snatched it away, angry with herself for still yearning, still grieving for what she had lost and could never have.

She had never had illusions about men. Jory had loved her in the only way he knew, as a familiar part of himself. They had married out of desire and because she had loved him in so many ways, although none of them was the romantic love she had always dreamed of. He had wanted to keep her safe because he was fond of her and she was one of his possession. And she had wanted to *feel* safe, a ridiculous illusion with Jory, who did not know the meaning of the word when it applied to himself.

She propped her chin on her cupped palm and stared out of the window overlooking the garden, trying to shake the mood, and saw the men were pacing back and forth along the long seawall at the end of the lawn. Then they broke apart, faced each other. Gabriel Stone drew the sword from the scabbard that seemed to be permanently at his side and she was half out of her seat before she realised that he was demonstrating something. He parried, Cris moved fluidly to one side, then in a blur of movement was behind him, reaching for his sword arm. Stone disengaged, moved out of trouble. They faced each other again, armed against unarmed. Then Cris shifted again, she saw Gabriel's head turn, he recovered, just too late and the sword went spinning out of his grasp and speared point-down, quivering in the grass.

He flourished an elaborate bow, retrieved the weapon, wiped the point carefully and sheathed it. Cris draped one arm around his shoulder and they began to walk up and down again.

Tamsyn sat down with a thump, closed her mouth, which was inelegantly open, and frowned at the two men. That had been disgracefully arousing and it had also been a demonstration of speed and skill and of complete trust. There would have been no fencing button on the point of that sword. One slip and Cris could have been badly hurt. Or if he had been less accurate, his friend might have been wounded in the disarm. They obviously knew each other very, very well.

She wondered why Gabriel Stone was armed with a sword. Gentlemen carried pistols with them in saddle holsters, or in their carriages when they travelled, but usually these days only military officers wore a sword at their hip. It suited him, she decided, went with the slightly sinister presence, the dark, mocking eyes. If Cris trusted him, then she must, but he unnerved her.

Whereas Cris confused and delighted and confounded her. She indulged herself by watching the tall figure sauntering along, silhouetted against the sea, then made herself look down and wrestle with the columns of figures once more.

The picnic expedition set off at eleven o'clock. Aunt Rosie was helped carefully into the chair, the men stepped between the carrying handles, ducked their heads under the leather straps, took a firm grip and lifted. Tamsyn mounted Foxy, Aunt Izzy was helped on to her placid hack, Bumble, and Jason loaded the pack pony with the rugs and hampers.

As Gabriel Stone mounted his own horse, Tamsyn looked down at Cris. 'You are going to have a long walk, I'm afraid.'

'Collins is saddling my horse. Didn't you realise he's been in your stables eating his head off ever since Collins brought the carriage over?'

'No one mentioned it and I've been too busy to visit the stable yard.' Which just went to show how distracted she had been by Cris's presence. Normally nothing stopped her from doing the complete rounds of the house and outbuildings daily.

A raking hunter emerged from the gate further up the lane. There was no one at its head, but when Cris whistled and walked out on to the track it trotted down and butted him in the chest with its big head. 'This is Jackdaw.'

'Because he is black?'

'And wicked and thieving,' Cris said, as he swung up into the saddle. 'Stop that.' The black tossed its head as though in denial that it had even thought about taking a chunk out of Gabriel Stone's bay. 'You are old enough to know better.'

'But not very old.' Tamsyn edged Foxy closer and Jackdaw snorted and rolled his eye.

'He's just four.'

'And not English, I think.' There was something about the powerful rump and the set of the animal's head that seemed different.

'Danish,' Cris said shortly and moved off after the sedan chair.

'Denmark?' Tamsyn said out loud. She had never encountered anything Danish before.

'He shipped him back.' Gabriel Stone brought his bay alongside Foxy. 'It's a nice beast and worth the effort and the cost.'

'You mean Cris…Mr Defoe, has been to Denmark?'

'Oh, yes, last mission he was on.' Gabriel said it vaguely, as though he was not creating even more mysteries. She had a very strong suspicion he knew exactly what he was doing. *Stirring the pot, Mr Stone?* Cris reined in and joined them again, presumably wary of what his friend was saying about him.

'Mission?' she asked, obediently playing Gabriel's game.

'Diplomatic.' Cris's expression did not change, but

Jackdaw sidled across the lane uneasily. 'I occasionally help out.' He managed to make it sound as though he handed the drinks round at embassy parties.

'Help who out? The government, you mean?' She dropped her hands without meaning to and Foxy broke into a trot, jolting her inelegantly for half-a-dozen strides until she got control.

'The Foreign Office. When they want someone who isn't, shall we say, a fixture in the diplomatic circles I drop in on…situations. Help out.'

Do you indeed? She was beginning to wonder just who this man was. The government used him as a part-time diplomat, and, she suspected, in tricky circumstances. He was tough, fit and capable of disarming the dangerous-looking Mr Stone, he could afford to import horses from the Continent and he had time to spend on a little local difficulty in a remote Devon hamlet.

Tamsyn tried to think of a question that did not sound like the bare-faced curiosity that it was. The trouble was, she found the mystery only added to the attraction, which was a dangerous state to be in.

Infatuated, she told herself severely. *That's what you are. You should settle for a nice, ordinary man, like Dr Tregarth. He is pleasant-looking, intelligent, hard-working, respectable, stands up for himself…*

He might even be willing to accept her the way she was. At least he would understand it was not her fault.

She lectured herself all the way up to Stibworthy and had just reached the conclusion that she did not fall for men like the doctor because they obviously did not find her attractive enough to show any interest, when the little procession met him striding down the street.

'Why are you blushing like a rose?' Cris enquired,

his voice carrying to Gabriel Stone, who twisted in the saddle, grinned at her and only made things worse.

'*Shh!* Good day, Dr Tregarth.' She waved, but he was by the sedan chair, smiling and nodding approval to Aunt Rosie while the chairmen set down their burden and stretched.

'Good chap, but too staid for you.' Cris moderated his voice, just a little, but he was still speaking loudly enough for Mr Stone to hear, judging by his expression. 'If he doesn't notice that you blush when you catch sight of him, well, one despairs of the fellow.'

'I am not blushing over Doc...over anyone. I am just a little windblown, that is all. I should have worn a veil.'

'Do you own one?' Cris enquired, all innocence.

Tamsyn brought Foxy tight up against Jackdaw and muttered, 'Do stop teasing me, you provoking man.'

'But I like it when you blush. It makes me wonder what I must do to provoke that pretty colour when we are alone.' His voice had dropped to an intimate murmur. 'Ah, so that's the trick of it,' he said, his eyes laughing at her as the heat flooded her cheeks.

She was saved from having to reply by the chairmen lifting their burden again and the party setting off once more.

'Where are we going?' Gabriel Stone reined back to ask.

'Up through the village and then we turn north on to the headland above Barbary Combe House. There's a wonderful view from up there.'

It was not her aunt's favourite, that had always been the prospect from Black Edge Head to the south, but Tamsyn knew she was far too tactful to take them to the scene of Jory's final confrontation with the militia.

'Mrs Perowne.' Dr Tregarth stepped out into the

street as they passed him. 'A word in your ear, if I may. I did not want to worry your aunts.' He cast a rapid glance at the retreating sedan chair party.

'We will ride on,' Cris said with a nod to Gabriel.

'No.' Tregarth held up a restraining hand. 'I think it would be a good thing if you heard this, too, Mr Defoe. There is word going around that Jory Perowne's gang is active again. They say the sign of the silver hand has been chalked up on walls, even on the door of the Revenue's building in Barnstaple.'

'That's impossible.' Tamsyn bit back the rest of the words that sprang to her lips and made herself think calmly. 'I suppose someone could be using the old name, the sign. This is what that objectionable Mr Ritchie was hinting at the other day, I suppose.'

'There is more.' Tregarth looked up at her, his face serious under the brim of his low-crowned hat. 'There are not only rumours, there is speculation as well. People are asking if the Silver Hand is operating again, and who is leading it?'

'I have no idea. Jory had no lieutenant. A second in command, yes, but no one who could take control of a gang like that.' Then Cris's intake of breath, the earnest expression on the doctor's face, made her realise what Tregarth was worried about. 'They think it is something to do with *me*? That is preposterous. Smugglers would not take orders from a woman.'

'They might from Jory Perowne's woman.'

'No.' She jerked Foxy's head round, used her heel and sent him cantering up the street towards the vanishing picnic party. The Silver Hand gang working again? It was impossible. Surely she would know if someone with Jory's skills and deviousness and leadership had set up the network again anywhere near here. But all she could be certain of was that it was not her leading even one rowing boat, let alone a gang. Yet if someone who knew her as well as Dr Tregarth could look at her with that question in his eyes, then others might think it, too. People who were far more dangerous than a friendly village doctor.

Pounding hooves caught up with Foxy before she reached the others. Cris and Gabriel fell in, one on either side of her, and she reined in to a walk. She did not want to talk about this within earshot of the aunts.

'Silver Hand gang?' Cris asked.

'Jory had inherited a silver charm. A hand, about two inches long, broken off a religious statue by the look of it. The story was that it was a relic from the Armada shipwrecks, found by an ancestor who had a ring fixed to it and who wore it round his neck on a chain. When Jory inherited it he wore it, too.' She remembered it hanging against his chest, the silver chain glinting through the curling dark hair. When he had been feeling defiant—which was often—he would wear it outside his shirt, answering questions about it with the bland assurance that it was simply an heirloom and it wasn't his fault if people used it as a symbol.

'It became part of the mythology around him,' she continued. Trust Jory to have to be dramatic. 'The men would chalk a hand on casks when they left them on doorsteps, so people knew who to thank for the gifts the gang left in return for silence. Not that anyone would have betrayed Jory and the others. When the Revenue put up posters advertising a reward, someone would always scrawl the hand over it.'

'And where is it now?' Gabriel's question jerked her out of her memories.

'He was wearing it when… It was round his neck

that day.' She had seen it in that moment when he had turned to face her, the moment she realised now was when he had made up his mind to jump and save them both the horror of a trial and an execution. If only she'd had his courage, could have stayed strong and defiant, not collapsed with shock and lost the only thing she had left of him.

'You wouldn't need the actual object,' Cris said thoughtfully, jerking her out of her memories. 'Not with something so well known. I suppose there isn't another, it would be unique.'

It was a question. 'There is another,' she admitted. 'Jory had a replica made for me as a wedding gift.' *Other women get earrings, a pretty gown, flowers from their lover. I get a smuggler's talisman.* 'But it isn't the same as his. He had our names engraved on mine, with a heart and an anchor.'

'Where is it?'

'Locked up in the strongbox with the legal papers and our bits of jewellery. I am not wearing it next to my heart, if that is what you want to know.'

'I know you are not.' Cris's whisper made the blush come back like the flooding tide. 'But it might be a good idea to get it hidden away somewhere a search party couldn't find it. The Riding Officer might see it as a sign of guilt, not as a love token.'

'Yes, I suppose you are right, but I cannot believe they would take it as far as searching the house.' But they had when Jory was alive. It had become almost a routine, tidying up after a party of Revenue men, or the militia, had rummaged in the cellars, the attics, under the beds, through the haystacks.

The ground beneath the horses' hooves began to level out. They were through the trees and at the edge of the clifftop pasture now and off to the left was the head of the path that she and Cris had climbed the night before.

'We are right above the house, surely?' Gabriel stood in his stirrups to look down.

'It is the only way up unless you are on foot. There are few rabbit holes up here—too many buzzards keeping them down—so we can gallop.' She turned Foxy off the track and gave him his head. Behind her she heard the sound of the other two horses in pursuit. Foxy, excited by the competition, stretched out his head and she laughed aloud with the thrill of it as they thundered across the clifftop.

They were neck and neck, the three of them, as she reined in. 'Take care now, it dips down to the next stream, we'd best turn back.'

They trotted behind Gabriel, who spurred his bay into a gallop again. 'Are we climbing our cliff path tonight?' Cris asked.

'Or...' She blushed saying it, it seemed so forward. 'I could come to you. I was thinking about it this morning.' More blushes when he sent her a swift, smiling look. 'Your room is so isolated, no one would know.'

'And the bed is softer,' Cris agreed, his face perfectly composed. Ahead across the clifftop they could see the picnic party flapping out rugs, setting up the folding chair that had been strapped on the pack pony. Cris leaned across, caught her round the waist one-handed, and dropped a rapid, searing kiss on her lips. 'And I am not. Softer, that is.'

'*Cris!*' She was still laughing, and still flushed, when they reached the others.

'Oh, it is so good to hear you laughing out loud again, my dear.' Aunt Rosie smiled up from her chair set amongst the scattered picnic things. 'And I could laugh like a girl, too. Thank you so much, Mr Defoe, Mr Stone, for this wonderful gift. And to my two stalwart bearers.' She beamed at the chairmen who were lifting tankards to their mouths. 'Just look at this view—you can see Lundy in the distance, see, gentlemen? And—' She broke off. 'Who is this coming?'

A procession was wending its way along the track they had just used. Three men on horseback, three militiamen on foot, the white cross-belts stark against their scarlet coats, muskets at the slope on their shoulders.

Cris nudged Jackdaw closer to Foxy's side. Gabriel moved his big bay until it stood between the advancing party and Aunt Rosie's chair.

'Squire Penwith,' Tamsyn said as the party approached closer. She found her voice was not quite steady. She sat up straighter in the saddle and got it under control. 'And the coroner, Sir James Trelawney. And someone from the Revenue by the look of his uniform.'

The group halted at the edge of the spread rugs.

'Sir James, Squire Penwith. Good day to you.'

'Mrs Perowne. Ladies.' Sir James lifted his hat. 'I apologise for interrupting your picnic.'

'I have no doubt it is a matter of urgency, Sir James.' She managed to sound just a trifle haughty, she was glad to hear.

'It is, Mrs Perowne. I very much regret to say that the Riding Officer, Lieutenant Ritchie, has been murdered.'

Chapter Thirteen

'Murdered?' Foxy backed as Tamsyn's hands clenched on the reins. 'How? When?'

'Last night, in Cat's Nose Bay. He was shot in the back,' the rider in uniform said harshly. 'I am Captain Sutherland of His Majesty's Revenue Service.'

'That is appalling news indeed,' Cris said before she could do more than gasp. 'But might I ask why you accost these ladies here with such a tale, told so brutally?'

'I will be holding the inquest on the body of Lieutenant Ritchie. I require the attendance of Mrs Perowne to give evidence and to answer questions.' Sir James narrowed his eyes at the two men so protectively close to the women. 'I do not believe I have had the pleasure of your acquaintance, gentlemen. Sir James Trelawney, Coroner for this district, at your service.'

'Crispin Defoe, of London and Kent. My friend, Gabriel Stone, of London. Your servants, sir.' Cris, his voice perfectly civil, managed to make the polite introduction sound like a declaration of war, without one word out of place.

From horseback Gabriel bowed. As he straightened his hand lay lightly on the pommel of his sword. The two chairmen lumbered to their feet, pewter tankards tight in their massive fists.

'The inquest will be held in two days' time. I require Mrs Perowne to reside at my house, chaperoned, naturally, by my wife, until then.'

'You are *arresting* me?'

'You have a warrant?' Cris no longer sounded civil.

'I have not. Nor am I arresting Mrs Perowne. This is for her own protection.' The coroner was icy. Beside him the Revenue Officer was glaring at Cris, and Squire Penwith was flushed with anger, or excitement, Tamsyn thought, wondering why she did not feel more frightened. Sick, yes, but not as terrified as she ought to be. But Cris was there, of course. It was time she stood up for herself.

'Against what am I being *protected*?' she enquired.

'Against the members of the gang responsible for this outrage,' Trelawney snapped. 'They will not want you giving evidence, I'll warrant.'

'The implications of that statement are insulting, Sir James.' Cris cut across her furious reply. 'To say nothing of prejudicial to a fair hearing. I see you are escorted by the militia. If you are fearful for Mrs Perowne's safety, then I suggest that stationing them outside her house on guard will be more than adequate. It might also persuade the lady not to take a civil action for wrongful arrest, unlawful detention, kidnapping and defamation of character.'

'Defamation?' Penwith spluttered. 'A smuggler's moll has no character to be defamed, sir!'

Cris jerked his head at Gabriel, who circled his horse and brought it in on Foxy's other side. As soon as he was in position Cris walked Jackdaw forward until the big black was nose to nose with Penwith's horse.

'On the last occasion we met, sir, I suggested a meeting in a field. At dawn. That still seems to me to be an admirable idea.'

'Duelling is illegal,' Penwith said. His horse began to back up; Jackdaw pressed in closer.

'So it is,' Cris said silkily. 'A minor disadvantage. A greater one in this case is that it requires two *gentlemen* who both possess a little courage.'

'Enough of this.' The coroner directed a scornful glance at Penwith. 'Your suggestion is sound, Mr Defoe. Sergeant Willis, you will deploy your men at Barbary Combe House and deliver…*escort* Mrs Perowne to my court the day after tomorrow for a ten o'clock hearing. Good day to you all. Enjoy your picnic, ladies.'

'Insolent wretch,' Aunt Rosie said, her voice cutting through the clear air. 'I knew him when he was a boy, and he was a pompous little no-account then.' Sir James's ears turned scarlet, but he did not turn. 'And as for that jackass Penwith, you are wasting your time attempting to arrange an affair of honour, Mr Defoe. He has none.'

'Cris—'

He rode back, dismounted and held up his hands to her. 'Courage, Tamsyn. They are blustering. It can only be a bluff. Now come down, eat this wonderful picnic, admire the view.'

'Of course.' She managed a smile. 'I cannot let those idiots spoil Aunt Rosie's special day.'

'That's my girl,' he murmured as she slid into his hands, down the length of the hard steady body. 'I'm here, they won't hurt you.'

She stood for a moment, just leaning into him, feeling the strength and the reassurance flowing from him to her, wishing she could put her head on his shoulder.

Instead she pushed away and walked towards the militiamen. *Do not weaken. He won't be here forever.*
'Sergeant Willis, isn't it? Do make yourselves comfortable. None of us are going anywhere for a while and I am certain our picnic will stretch to give you your luncheon also.'

'Ma'am.' The sergeant looked hideously uncomfortable. He cleared his throat and looked round as though for inspiration.

'Might I suggest your men stand guard, one at a time on rotation, while the rest of you sit over there with our staff and refresh yourselves?' Cris scanned the surrounding area. 'I feel certain that the country hereabouts is open enough to give good warning of the approach of dangerous gangs of smugglers intent on subverting Mrs Perowne's evidence.'

'Er…yes, sir. Just as you say, thank you, sir. Perkins! You heard the gentleman. On patrol for half an hour, then you, Downton.' They marched off stiffly.

Tamsyn fought a rather hysterical giggle. 'This would be funny. If it—'

'Wasn't,' Cris finished. 'Quite. A very bad farce. Come and sit down.'

She managed a rueful smile for the aunts, both of whom, she was relieved to see, were fuming rather than fearful. 'I simply cannot believe that there really is a large-scale smuggling operation going on,' she said, once they were settled with slices of raised pie and cheese and apples. 'Things were becoming more difficult even before Jory died. With the end of the war and the changes in taxes, there just isn't the range of things to smuggle to make it worthwhile. Not on this coast, at any rate.'

'I suppose they cannot overlook a murder,' Aunt

Rosie said, obviously struggling to be fair. 'But they must be demented to think Tamsyn has anything to do with it.'

'After the inquest it will be quite apparent there is no evidence.' Gabriel sprawled with careless elegance across one corner of the rug, a chicken leg in one hand. 'I assume you have been nowhere near this Cat's Nose Bay, Mrs Perowne?'

'Not for several weeks,' she said. 'But I know it. It was one of Jory's favourite landing beaches and it is probably still used for some small runs. But violence has never been the way down here, not since Jory was running things. He always found a way to slip past the militia and the Revenue. Someone must have been desperate, or cornered.'

'You don't shoot a man in the back if he's cornered you,' Cris pointed out drily.

Aunt Izzy was beginning to look anxious. Tamsyn took a deep breath and found a smile from somewhere. 'The inquest will be held in Kilkhampton, so I will be able to get some shopping done at that excellent milliners Mrs Holworthy recommended. We must make a list of what we need.'

Always assuming I am not being hauled off to the lock-up right after the inquest.

Her tone and smile must have been suitably optimistic, for Aunt Izzy brightened up and reminded her that there was also a very good stationers and they needed sealing wax and black ink.

Somehow they managed to ignore the militiamen marching up and down, a discordant flash of scarlet in the corner of the eye, however hard everyone looked the other way and pretended they were not there.

Eventually Rosie announced that she was becoming

a little tired and perhaps they should return. The picnic was loaded on the pack pony, the sedan chair set off down the hill and the two men flanked Tamsyn with the militiamen bringing up the rear.

'Right, now we are out of earshot of your aunts, let's have a serious discussion about this,' Cris said briskly. Tamsyn felt an irrational wave of relief that he was not going to pretend everything would be all right. It was not and she needed help, not soothing. 'First thing, we get that silver hand of yours out of the house.'

'How? They will stop any of us leaving, I am certain. And if they search, they will search everyone's possessions.'

'I've a secret compartment in my carriage. It has defeated virtually every border guard on the Continent. If you go and get the hand out of the strong box immediately when we get back, then I'll find an excuse to be in the stables, getting Jackdaw settled.'

That was a relief. She pushed to the back of her mind the question of why Cris needed a secret compartment in his carriage.

'I am assuming this is another of Chelford's little games,' he continued.

'Franklin? But this is murder…' She thought about it while Cris rode on in silence, waiting for her to catch up with his reasoning. 'He spreads rumours about a new smuggling gang, he shoots that poor man and somehow implicates me? That would explain Sir James's confidence. But there cannot be any evidence.'

'That is what is worrying me,' Gabriel said. 'It means that something has been fabricated and it is likely to be something so obvious that even that blockheaded coroner will swallow it.'

Perhaps, after all, it would be nice to be treated like

a damsel in distress and not be subjected to this bracing dose of reality. As if he sensed her wavering courage Cris reached out and closed his hand over hers on the reins. 'Don't worry, we're here. If you can just get it clear in your mind that you are not going to be hauled off to gaol and hanged, you can relax and enjoy this.'

'Relax!' It came out as a shriek before she could help herself. 'How do you expect me to enjoy this?'

'We are going to tie Chelford in knots,' Gabriel said with relish. 'Hang him up by the ba—that is, by the toes and leave him swinging in the wind.'

'There is no need to mince your words for me, Mr Stone,' Tamsyn said crisply. 'I like the idea of suspending Franklin by the balls. It appeals very much indeed.'

'To which end, I'd be glad if you'd go back to London, Gabe, and carry on with the investigations we discussed this morning.' Cris released her hand with a small squeeze.

'After the inquest. I might pick up some more information there.'

'Mr Stone is here for more than the delivery of the sedan chair, is he not?' she demanded.

Cris shrugged. 'He has been investigating Chelford in London for me.' He leaned forward so he could look at his friend across her. 'There was no reason, other than incorrigible curiosity, for him to have come down here himself instead of writing.'

'I told you,' Gabriel said laconically. 'I am running away from a woman.'

It was not until they reached Barbary Combe House that Tamsyn realised that the two of them had managed to keep her distracted and laughing with their inconsequential teasing, all the way back. She let Cris help her down from Foxy, allowing herself the indulgence, this time, of sliding down his body, and then stayed close, enjoying the heat and the feeling of strength and the evidence that her body next to his aroused him.

She was conscious of the sergeant watching them and deliberately raised her voice as she broke free from Cris's supporting hands. 'If you wait just a moment, I will bring you what is left of the herbs that the farrier gave me for Foxy's sore hoof. If Jackdaw is favouring his off hind, it might help.'

The militiamen made no move to stop her as she ran into the house, through to her study, and took the key to the strongbox from its hiding place behind the desk. The old lock creaked and protested as she turned the big key, but it opened easily enough and she rummaged quickly, burrowing beneath the documents for the box with the silver hand. It was not there.

She searched again, then once more, tossing the papers out on to the floor, heedless of deeds and indentures mixing with a roll of banknotes. There was no box except the aunts' jewellery and those boxes were all too small, or too flat, to hold the pendant. There was no silver hand, not even the chain. She scooped it all back, just as it was, slammed the lid on the chaos and locked the strongbox, then ran to hide the key and on to the stillroom to find a mixture of harmless herbs.

'There was no need to hurry so,' Cris said when she reached his side again. He was talking to one of the militiamen and gave him the sort of look that always made her want to slap a man. *Silly female, still, we have to tolerate them, don't we?* it said. The sergeant smirked.

He is getting him on his side, Tamsyn realised. 'What I was looking for was not there any more,' she said brightly. 'But I thought this might help with any swelling.'

Cris took the bowl from her hands, sniffed it. 'To be applied as a poultice? Can you show Collins?' He glanced at the militiaman. 'We are just going up to the stables. Are you coming?'

'Don't see how I needs to, sir.' The man shifted his feet uncomfortably. 'Load of foolishness, if you asks me. The sergeant said I was to watch the lane, not follow anyone about. Dan's round the back, Sarge is looking at the beach. You're not going nowhere, are you, ma'am?'

'No, I am not. You're Willie Downton's brother, aren't you?'

'Yes, ma'am. Jed. I liked Mr Jory, I did. I'd known him since I was a boy. They've no cause to be hounding his widow, not no how.'

'Well, thank you, Jed. But you must obey your orders, I don't want to get you into any trouble. If you stand there, then you are keeping an eye on the stable yard and the lane.'

In the yard Collins was unsaddling Jackdaw. 'Is he favouring the off hind?' Cris asked. The man grunted, his gaze sweeping the yard and surroundings while Cris ran his hand down Jackdaw's leg and lifted the hoof.

Tamsyn came and studied it, close by his side. 'The hand has gone,' she whispered. 'And the chain. Nothing else is missing, not even a roll of banknotes or the jewellery.'

'When did you last see it?' Cris made no attempt to moderate his voice and Tamsyn copied him. Being seen whispering would only look suspicious.

'Months ago. It was in a black bag. I wouldn't notice it unless I was looking especially for it.' She bit her lip in thought. 'I haven't seen it since before Franklin was last here. He could have taken it easily.'

Cris made a remark to Collins about Jackdaw's hoof,

handed him the herbs and took Tamsyn's arm to walk back down to the house.

'He must have been planning this ever since Aunt Izzy refused to move to the dower house,' she said, as they went in through the kitchen door.

'He has taken an object that not only ties you in closely to your late husband, but is a potent symbol of his smuggling activities.' Cris sounded grim.

She swung round to face him. 'You are worrying me now.'

'And you are not already concerned?' His wry smile sent a jolt of panic through her. 'There is no point in me treating you like some feather-headed chit and pretending everything will be all right without us putting some effort into it. What would Chelford think would happen to your aunts if you were hauled off to prison to await trial?'

'He would never believe they could manage on their own.'

'He would expect them to retreat, trembling, to your aunt Isobel's nearest male relative for shelter.'

'But they would not. They would hire a steward, take on more men.'

'He underestimates them, in effect. But he is only going to discover that too late.' Cris kept going, through the bathing room and into the drawing room, which was deserted.

'I confess I would rather he did not have to find out that way.' Somehow she kept her voice from trembling. Murder was a capital offence.

Cris turned, frowned. 'You think I would let it get that far? You do not have much faith in me, do you?'

'What can you do? They must have some evidence, even if it is false.' She wanted to wring her hands, pace about. Instead she made herself stand still, look the thing firmly in the eye and face facts, deal with it.

'The day after tomorrow is the inquest, not a trial. It is to establish the cause of death and to record the circumstances. Come here.' He pulled her to him a little roughly, held her, and for a second she thought his hands shook. Then he was stroking one firmly down her back as though soothing a spooked horse and his voice, which had roughened, was steady and reassuring. 'Tamsyn, I swear to you that I will keep you safe.'

'Why?' She jerked away before the safety of his body, the reassurance of his arms, left her so weak she would not be able to stand on her own two feet. 'You don't belong here, you hardly know me. Why should you get involved in this mess?'

Cris answered without stopping to analyse it. 'Because I probably owe you my life. Because I like you, and your aunts. Because you are my lover. And, when you come right down to it, I'll be damned if that little weasel Chelford gets away with this. Whatever it is.'

And because dealing with this keeps my mind from thinking about all those things I don't want to deal with. The mess I got my head into over Katerina. Thinking about the wife I must acquire. My respectable future and how to fill it. Leaving you.

'Oh. That is certainly a comprehensive list.' There was a hint of a smile now and her colour was coming back. He had not liked her calm, her control. It had looked too much like shock to him. Either that or an inability to see just how serious this might be if it was not dealt with hard and ruthlessly. He wanted her aware of the dangers, but confident and ready to fight. It shook him, how much he worried about her. For a moment there he had almost let his feelings overwhelm him. He had wanted to kiss her senseless, overwhelm her with assurances, treat her like some fragile little miss who had to be tucked away in cotton wool.

And that was foolish because he would be gone soon, back to London, back to his own, real life, and Tamsyn would be here, carrying on with hers, needing to stand on her own two feet. Just as soon as she was out of danger.

'Tell me your plans,' he said, pushing her to think, watchful that he did not push too far.

'Cheer up the aunts, get the accounts straight, choose the best outfit for appearing at an inquest—and carry on racking my brains for some hint as to what Franklin is up to.' Her chin was up, her voice was steady. Yes, she was all right to leave now. Fussing over her would only make her more unsettled.

'That sounds comprehensive to me. I'll go and find out what Gabriel's plans are. He should be heading back to London as soon as possible.'

'Cris.' Tamsyn was half turned from him, the colour up charmingly on the curve of cheek that was visible to him. 'Tonight…'

'Will you come to my bedchamber? It is quite isolated, as you said.' Now that sweet curve was rosy with embarrassment. 'I do not keep Collins hanging around after dinner. If you were to drop by for, shall we say, a nightcap at about eleven I think you might find me unable to sleep.' It was unexpected, the way he felt his heartrate kick up, how his body was already hardening at the thought.

This is a pleasant diversion. A temporary thing. A reaction. I will forget her and this world of fishermen and smugglers and sheep soon enough when this is all over and I am back in London.

Even so, for all that cold water dash of realism, he found he was looking forward to the night with the eagerness of a young man with his first lover.

Chapter Fourteen

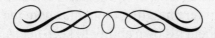

'Cris!'

'What?' he demanded with more aggression than good manners.

'I have addressed two full sentences to you and you sit there gazing out of the window like some lovelorn youth. What is the matter with you?' Gabe sauntered into the drawing room and hitched one hip on to the table edge.

'Thinking. You have to concede, there is plenty to mull over.'

'And none of it the sort of thing that might put a foolish smile on your lips,' Gabriel jibed. 'I shall have to send a letter to Alex and Grant with the news that Cris de Feaux has been seen to smile.'

In a moment he would be blushing and that *would* be worthy of a newspaper headline. What the devil was wrong with him? Denmark had apparently confused him far more than he was letting himself believe. 'I've been known to, usually when you aren't around to aggravate me.' Cris waved a hand vaguely at the window. 'It is a pleasant view.'

Gabe made a complicated sound of derision. 'Views, my left buttock. This is developing into something decidedly murky.'

'The view?'

'The persecution of Mrs Perowne.' He grinned. 'Which sounds like the title of some Minerva Press novel.'

'Knowing Chelford that is probably where he got the idea.' The feeling of relief that Gabe would be there, at his back, for one more day, was worrying. He had always operated alone, been confident and self-sufficient. Now there were niggling thoughts about the danger to Tamsyn, about his own ability to keep her safe when he had no idea where the next threat was coming from. 'I was telling myself that Chelford did not have the brains to set up something like this merely as a distraction for another attack, and Patrick and Seamus are a regiment in themselves, but even so, I'm glad of someone here in case things do awry at the inquest.'

'I've got your back,' Gabe said. He gave Cris's shoulder a buffet, then left his hand there for a moment. It was as close a demonstration of emotion as Cris had ever experienced from him. Gabe stood up, pulled out a chair and sat square to the table, producing the inevitable pack of cards from somewhere about his person. He dealt two hands, flipped them both over and began to play against himself.

'Something else strange happened today,' Cris told him about the missing silver hand.

'And what does that mean?' Gabriel threw down the cards he was holding and frowned. 'I don't like the way that it was taken without any apparent damage to the lock.'

It had been at the back of Cris's mind, too. 'Chelford used to run tame here when he was younger. He would have been the kind of sneaky brat who would steal copies of keys so he could pry.'

'That and the fact that I don't think any of the servants here are disloyal makes it almost certain it is him, or some agent of his. Provided you don't need me here after the inquest, I'll go back to London, see what I can do to trace his recent movements.'

'Thank you.' There was no need to say anything more effusive than that.

Gabriel gathered the scattered pack with one sweep of his long-fingered hand and stood up. 'I like her, Cris.' He paused at the door and looked back. 'But don't get in too deep. You are who you are and she is…'

'Intelligent, interesting, strangely beautiful?' Cris enquired coldly, wondering why he did not get up and land Gabe a facer. Wondering at his own depth of anger, the way the need to hit the other man had just surged up from nowhere.

'A smuggler's widow and exceedingly ineligible for—'

He did get to his feet then. 'I know. Don't say it.'

'—someone in your position,' Gabe said and left with the ease of a man who had a great deal of practice in extricating himself from dangerous gaming hells.

To hell with him. Gabriel liked to tease and he particularly enjoyed poking at Cris, simply because he knew his friend valued self-possession and self-control. 'I like to see ice cracking,' he had admitted once with his wicked smile. 'It is more exciting to skate on.'

Cris glanced up at the mirror over the fireplace, kept his face completely emotionless as the cold blue eyes stared back at him. Could Gabe see something he could not? Was the ice cracking?

The wind was getting up, fretting at the old house, worrying at a loose slate here, a shutter there, sending the rags of cloud scudding across the full moon so that the clear white light that reflected on the polished boards of the passageway kept vanishing, plunging Tamsyn into darkness for seconds at a time.

But she knew every inch of the house and the creaks and groans were not frightening, merely a useful cover for any noise she might make. It seemed strange to be creeping around Barbary like this, as though she had left behind the impulsive, passionate girl years ago and had grown sensible and staid. Not that she and Jory had ever misbehaved here. Before he had shaken her by offering marriage they had been friends and she would have no more flirted with him than she would a brother.

After they were married there had been many places for lovemaking, places that Jory found stimulating in direct proportion to how outrageous and dangerous they were. She wondered now, as she had begun to increasingly in the months before his death, whether it was that edge of danger that aroused him and not her at all.

On that thought she arrived at Cris's bedchamber door. What did *he* see in her? She halted before the threshold and stood, fingers closed around the handle, and felt her confidence draining away to her chilly, bare feet. Convenience, perhaps. Or novelty. She was presumably unlike the ladies with whom he normally mixed. Or he felt pity for the poor widow, who must be pining for the attentions of a man.

The door opened and, as she was clutching the handle in a death grip, she was towed into the room and fetched up sharply against the solid wall of silk-covered muscle that, she realised after a moment's ineffectual flailing, was Cris in a heavy brocade robe.

'Wait a moment.' He reached around her, closed the door quietly and then put something down on the dresser by the door. The light of the one chamber stick that stood there sparked fire off the chased silver mounts of a small, sinister pistol.

Tamsyn suppressed an exclamation and managed a coherent question. 'What are you doing with that?'

'When someone stands outside my bedchamber door at almost midnight, shifting uneasily from one foot to the other so that the boards creak, in my experience they are either there to cut my throat or to join me in bed.'

His arms were around her now, holding her against him so her senses were full of the feel of silk and skin and the scent of man and the thrill of his hands stroking lazily down her spine to cup her behind and pull her up against his erection.

'Does it happen very often?' she asked, the words muffled as she explored the tantalising vee of bare skin exposed by the neck of his robe.

'Which? The assassins or the offers?'

'Either.' The crispness of hair tickled her lips. She used the point of her tongue to probe into the dip at the base of his throat and his breath caught. 'Both.' The offers seemed more likely than assassination attempts, but she was beginning to realise that most of the truth about Cris Defoe was hidden from her. She wondered why. Either he was a very private man, or he had a sinister secret or he was deliberately keeping his distance from her.

'One more frequently than the other,' he murmured, as his lips moved down from her temple.' You have such a beautiful curve to your cheek.' His tongue swept over it. 'And you taste like salt on peaches.'

Somehow she found enough space to wriggle her hands between their bodies and catch hold of the knot that secured the sash of his robe. She wanted to see him naked again, not, as he had been last night, obscured by the half-darkness, tumbled in the coarse blankets. In response he pulled her in tighter, moved so that her hands slipped, found the thrust of his erection under the lush fabric.

She began to caress him through it, not attempting to push the sides of the robe apart. The silk slid over his hard, heated flesh and he made a sound between a growl and a groan as his teeth closed gently on the vulnerable angle between her neck and shoulder. The gesture was powerfully possessive and the image of a stallion she had once seen mounting a mare, his teeth bared as they closed on the arch of her neck, holding her for his domination, filled her mind with shocking clarity.

But she was no mare to be dominated. One-handed she pulled at the sash and the robe opened. She raked her nails lightly down the flat belly, into the dense tangle of coarse hair, down to touch him with a demand as fierce as his.

The response was instant. His right hand took her nightgown by the neck, twisted, tore it so that it gaped open, and he lifted her, stepped forward so she was trapped between his body and the door. Instinctively Tamsyn curled her legs around his hips, her arms around his neck as he held her there, open to him. She knew she was wet, was ready for him. She had been from the moment her tongue had touched the skin of his throat. With a growl as demanding as his she shifted and lunged, taking him into her in one glorious movement.

Cris made a sound of astonished pleasure and was still, his brow resting against hers, his forearms bracing him against the door on either side of her head. 'Vixen.' His voice was rough, naked, powerful and yet vulnerable. She had shaken him. Which was only fair. He had shaken her to her foundations and beyond.

The position was exquisitely, erotically, uncomfortable. The door was unyielding behind her shoulder blades, she had to lock her ankles together, harden her thigh muscles to keep from sliding on the silk that still draped across his hips, and she could scarcely move. It was bliss, but it couldn't last. Cris was so aroused that he would take them both over the edge in a few powerful thrusts.

He began to move and she realised that she was wrong. He had the strength to move slowly, agonisingly slowly. Tamsyn could feel his muscles lock rigid as she hung on to his shoulders, she could hear the effort of control in his breathing, but he did not break. He was relentless and she could do nothing but let him fill her, pleasure her, drive her insane.

'Cris…please.' She had no pride left, all she could do was beg and gasp and strive to break free from the ropes of desire that he was tying tighter and tighter around her.

'Not…yet.'

'I can't.'

'You will.' She felt his effort to breathe, to find more words. 'Look…up.'

'Why?' Somehow she lifted her head.

'I don't…want…you screaming.' His lips sealed over hers as he gave one more thrust and the ropes tightened and broke her into a thousand pieces and she screamed into the heat of his mouth and then she was flying, moving through the air, and the aurora burst behind her eyelids.

'Tamsyn.'

She had been flying, so now she was lying on clouds. When she looked down, what would she see? The whole ocean spread out beneath her? She dragged open heavy lids and found her nose was buried in the thick fluffy coverlet, her body sprawled diagonally across the bed. It was an effort to turn her head towards Cris's voice, but she managed it. He was lying parallel with her, on his back, his hands behind his head.

'That,' he said seriously as she blinked at him, 'was infinitely preferable to having my throat cut.'

It made her choke with laughter, gave her enough energy to roll over and curl up against him. 'I would hope so.'

'Are you all right?' He sat up, giving her an admirable view of his muscles at work, and ran his hand down her back. 'Have I bruised you?'

'Don't know,' she mumbled, kissing the only part of him that she could without sitting up, which happened to be his right hip bone. 'Don't care.'

'I do not think anyone has ever kissed me there before.' He sounded lazily content as he flopped back. 'Do you think you can find anywhere else like that?'

'I've got to do all the work of exploration, have I?'

'I did all the work just now,' he said reasonably, as though he was negotiating a deal. The almost-dimple was back at the corner of his mouth.

'Very well. Lie on your stomach.'

He rolled over obediently. Tamsyn thought for a moment, then got up on her knees, straddled his legs and bent to kiss the tendon that ran up from his heel.

'That's one,' he conceded.

She switched position, leant down and nipped one firm buttock, then soothed the sting with a kiss.

'No, those have had kisses lavished on them.'

'Don't be smug. Just because you have a very superior rump—'

He moved so fast that she was pinned beneath him before she had a chance to retaliate. 'Is it? Superior?'

'I think so.' Yes, he was definitely smug. 'Almost as superior as Mr Stone's.'

'Hussy.' He slid into her and she bowed up to meet him, loving the way her breasts were crushed against his chest, loving the darkness in his eyes, just before he closed them to hide the depths of his pleasure from her, loving the way their bodies moved together without shyness or hesitation.

Loving him.

The shock of finding herself in love distracted Tamsyn all through the next day. It was hard to focus on keeping the aunts calm, let alone on listening to the advice Cris was giving her, when all she wanted to do was to sit looking at him, trying to come to terms with what her unruly heart had done.

'I would suggest wearing something respectable and practical. You don't want to give the impression that you are attempting to act the fluttering female to sway the jury and they know you, I imagine, so pretending to be some helpless little thing won't work either.' He leaned back against the front of the summer house, rocking the bench a little on its spindly metal legs.

He is beautiful, but I haven't fallen in love with those blue eyes or that superior rump...

'Tamsyn?'

Or that decided voice or those well-formed lips... 'I thought my newest riding habit. I will have to ride over in any case and it is a severe cut and deep-blue colour.'

'Excellent. I imagine it will make you exceedingly angry, but—'

Although those all help. It is his courage and his kindness and...

'—it is essential that you keep calm. You are willing, of course, to help the authorities, but you are baffled—'

...as to why I love you when you keep secrets from me and I am not of your world, whatever it is, and you will be gone soon and I will never see you again.

'Are you listening to a word I'm saying, Tamsyn?'

'I am baffled,' she repeated obediently. *Although you make love like an angel. Or perhaps a devil and that helps, too.* 'I will try my best to keep my temper, be helpful but confused. And, if he persists in this nonsense, indignant. I'm a lady and respectable, whatever my late husband might have done. After all, a wife is a mere chattel of her husband's, is she not? I cannot be held responsible for what Jory did.'

'If you were ever any man's *mere chattel*, I will eat my hat.'

Oh, and I adore that rare, rare smile of his.

'I will have the advantage that, being men, they will assume I am incapable of organised thought or sophisticated planning,' she said and looked out across the garden to the sea. It was impossible to think when she was looking at Cris, all she could do was count the things about him that mysteriously merged together and made a miracle.

'I am trying to think of it as a duel, me against Franklin. I must keep a cool head and fight strongly but prudently.'

'Sensible,' Cris admitted. 'And when we do find out what he is about it will be my pleasure to make that duel a reality.'

'You cannot!' She spun round so fast that the bench rocked and almost tipped her off on to the grass.

'Why ever not?' Cris was suddenly the austerely aloof, distant man who sent a shiver of awe down her spine. 'He has behaved in the most appalling way towards a lady, therefore it is the duty of any gentleman to call him to account.'

'If he murdered poor Mr Ritchie, then he will hang. Would you cheat justice and spare him the ordeal of the courtroom and what follows?' she asked fiercely, knowing as she spoke that what she felt so passionate about was Cris's safety, not the abstract idea of justice.

'I doubt he pulled the trigger himself. Why should he when there are so many villains to hire in the rookeries of London who would cut their own grandmothers' throats if you made it worth their while?'

'You mean he could get away with this?'

'I think it very likely. After all, what proof do we have?'

'There may be some after the inquest,' Tamsyn told herself that rushing to meet trouble was not going to help, she had enough to cope with as it was, not least was the prospect of a broken heart in the very near future.

Chapter Fifteen

'This court will rise for Sir James Trelawney.'

Awkward in their best clothes and solemn with responsibility, the jury shuffled to their feet from their double row of benches. The audience, jam-packed into the main part of the Ram's Head Inn's little assembly room, stood, too, nudging and whispering and staring at the front row, where all those to be called as witnesses were seated.

Sir James took his seat behind the table set on the rather shaky dais that the local joiner and coffin-maker had knocked up hastily, fussed with his cushion, his pen and his papers, donned a pair of spectacles and cleared his throat.

'Silence in court!' The parish constable was enjoying himself. 'Be seated!' He turned to Sir James, who nodded. 'Call the first witness! Thomas Gedge!'

'I be 'ere, Fred Dare, you old fule. Sitting right in front of you. No call for yelling.' An elderly man in a smock and sea boots got to his feet.

'You stand there.' Red about the ears, the constable pointed to the witness stand, another of the carpenter's constructions. 'And here's the Bible.' He handed it over, read the oath, still at full volume, and sat down.

'…so help me God,' the old man concluded.

'You are Thomas Gedge, fisherman?'

'Aye, sir.'

'And you frequent Cat's Nose Bay?'

'Don't know about frequent it. I keeps me fishing boat there and me shed with me nets and all.'

Sir James glowered. 'And were you there on the night of Wednesday last and for what purpose?'

'Aye, I was there, having a bit of a smoke in me shed. The wife's mother had come to visit and a man can't get any peace in his own home with two women clacking. It was a good, warm night, so down I go to the cove. I was there from when the church clock struck eight to past one.'

'Aye, and with a brandy bottle, too, I'll be bound!' someone called from the back.

'Silence in court! And you could see the beach?'

'The door to the shed was open, but I can't see the beach on account of the shed's with the others, up aways. I could see the track down to the beach.'

'And did you see anyone go down it that night?'

'Aye, I did that.' A whisper of interest ran round the room. 'It was that new Riding Officer, Ritchie. Recognised his hat and the cocky way he has…had…of walking. And the moonlight caught his face as he went past. I thought to myself, you'll find no one down there to bother, you interfering devil, you.'

'Did you see anyone else?'

'I did. About ten minutes after, it was. Figure in a cloak, all muffled up and walking quietly, like they didn't want to be seen.'

'And is that person in this court?'

'How would I know, your worship? He was all muffled up, like I said.'

'Was it a man?'

'Could be. Might have been a tallish woman, I suppose.' He shrugged. 'I had a bit of a doze. Then I woke up and was just thinking the mother-in-law would have gone to bed and it'd be safe to go home when I heard a shot. I thought about it a bit, then I closed the door of the shed and waited until I heard footsteps going up the track. Then I waits some more and then I went to have a look and there was Ritchie on the beach in the moonlight with a bullet in his back and blood all over the stones.'

'Why did you wait before going out to look, man?' Sir James asked irritably.

'Because I didn't want a bullet in me head, of course. Then I went and got Fred Dare out of bed, much good he was.'

'That will be all. You may go back to your seat. Frederick Dare, take the stand.'

Gabriel Stone leant forward as the constable took the oath and murmured across Tamsyn to Cris, 'And that is it? One cloaked figure of indeterminate sex?'

'There will be more,' Cris said.

The constable recounted being woken, getting dressed, fetching some of the local men in support and finding the body on the beach.

'And were there any traces of the murderer to be seen?'

'Aye, there was, your worship. There was an object lying under the body. It's that there object in the black bag before you, your worship. We carried the body up to the church, and woke up the vicar, then I went to tell you and you told me to search the neighbourhood for any strangers or news of anyone behaving suspiciously, and that I did. That night I didn't find anyone, but the next day I came across this traveller in the inn and he said he'd been out for a walk and had seen something odd. So I brought him to see you, Sir James.'

'Thank you, Dare. You may stand down and call the next witness.'

The local doctor came to the stand and explained in lengthy and gruesome detail that the deceased had been killed by one bullet to the heart and showed no other signs of injury.

Tamsyn found she was watching the proceedings, slow and rustic and ponderous, as though they were a rather bad play. She ought to feel something, fear, or curiosity at least, but all she felt was numb.

Beside her Cris whispered, 'Now we come to the interesting witness.'

A thin man with a very ordinary, instantly forgettable face, took the oath and stood clutching his hat and staring stolidly at the coroner. He had brown hair pulled back in an old-fashioned queue, brown eyes, a brown suit of decent, but plain clothes.

'State your name and occupation and business in this parish.'

'Paul Goode, solicitor's clerk of Gray's Inn Road, London.' Tamsyn felt a sudden prickle of interest. The accent was southern, the man a total stranger. 'I was sent by my employer, Mr Ebenezer Howard, on a business enquiry, which took me further down the coast from here. I was making my way back and stayed overnight at this inn, your worship. I'd been hoping to get to Barnstaple, but the roads defeated my old horse, so I rested us both up.'

'Tell us what you might that will throw light on this business, Mr Goode.'

'I went for a walk after my supper, sir. I wasn't

sleepy. It was a nice moonlit night and the seaside is a novelty for a city man like myself. I wasn't sure where to go, but I saw a man walking down the track that I discovered later led to the beach and I followed, assuming if he was going down it, it must head somewhere. I got a stone in my shoe, so I sat down on the bank and took it off and someone else passed me. I followed along, rather cautiously, sir, because I thought maybe I would be interrupting a tryst and that would be a bit embarrassing.'

'A tryst?' Sir James looked at him over his spectacles and Tamsyn thought he was tense now, like a weasel about to leap on its prey. 'An odd word to choose, Mr Goode, for a possible meeting between two men. You may stand down, but do not leave the room.'

'Why doesn't he hear all the man's evidence?' Tamsyn whispered to Cris.

'No idea. He's stage-managing the whole performance.'

'Call Mrs Tamsyn Perowne to the stand.'

Cris rose with her, his hand under her arm until she turned with a smile and shook her head. 'I'll be fine.'

Once she was no longer waiting it was easier. She took the stand, repeated the oath, folded her hands on the rail in front of her and turned the calmest face she could manage on Sir James.

'You are Mrs Tamsyn Perowne, widow of Jory Perowne, leader of the Silver Hand gang of smugglers.'

'I am Jory Perowne's widow,' she agreed. 'But I have never heard his relationship with that gang confirmed in a court of law.'

'You knew the victim of this murderous attack?'

'I had met Lieutenant Ritchie on one occasion. He came to Barbary Combe House and introduced himself. A brief conversation on the front lawn was the extent of our encounter. I have not seen him before or after that.'

'And did he issue a warning to you?'

'He told us that a gang of smugglers was operating. I took that to be a caution in case they proved violent.'

'Did you, indeed? A curious construction to put on it, considering your late husband's business.' When she merely stood impassive and waited for the next question he snapped, 'And who is this *us* you speak of?'

'Myself, my relative Miss Holt, with whom I live, her companion, Miss Pritchard, our staff and two gentlemen who are our guests. You met them the day before yesterday. Mr Defoe and Mr Stone are sitting in the front row now.'

'Did your husband wear a charm around his neck?'

'Yes,' she agreed. 'A silver hand on a silver chain.'

'And is it unique?'

She had expected a question about the whereabouts of Jory's charm, but she answered immediately, knowing that hesitation would only create a bad impression. 'I owned one also. A replica with an engraved message that was a gift from my husband.'

'And where is it now?'

'I have no idea. It appears to have been stolen from the locked chest it was kept in.'

There was a whispering of excitement and speculation in the court. 'Stolen, you say? It must be a valuable piece, why has no reward been offered for it?'

'Because its loss has only just been discovered.' As soon as she spoke she felt a twinge of fear.

Sir James smiled. 'Indeed? Constable, show the witness the contents of the black bag, then pass it to the jury.'

Tamsyn did not need to see the river of silver links that spilled into Dare's calloused hand to know what this was, but she waited until he handed it to her and made a point of examining it carefully. 'This is the hand and chain given to me by my late husband. It is engraved J and T with a heart.' She let it run back into the constable's outstretched hand and wondered if she should remove her handkerchief and permit herself a brave sniff and a dab at her eyes, but the thought of play-acting sickened her. Let them believe her or not, she would give them the truth and nothing else.

The coroner waited until the hand had been passed along the rows of jurors and returned to him. 'This chain and the attached charm were found clasped in the dead hand of Lieutenant Ritchie as he lay on the beach at Cat's Nose Bay. As you have heard, gentlemen of the jury, the witness has identified them as her property.'

Put there to incriminate me. The words were almost out of her mouth before she caught them. The jury did not need her to underline the conclusion they were being led to.

'You know the cove in question, Mrs Perowne?'

'Certainly. I visit it occasionally. I believe the last time this year was in March when a fishing boat belonging to me was washed up there.' It felt like standing on a frozen pond, hearing the ice cracking, feeling it shift under her feet, wanting to run. But she had to stand there, stay calm, not defensive.

'Mr Goode, return to the front of the court. Remember you are still on oath.'

The whispering increased as the thin man made his way forward and stood, perfectly composed in his respectable drabness, looking at the coroner.

'You told the court that you saw a cloaked figure following Lieutenant Ritchie down to the beach. Can you describe that man?'

'I can, sir. But it was no man, it was a woman. She was wearing a cloak, but the hood was down and I could see her plain in the moonlight. Quite tall she was.'

The whispering broke out into exclamations. Tamsyn's hands hurt and she looked down to see them locked on the rough bar at the front of the stand. A split ran all along the seam of the right index finger of her glove.

'Silence in court! And can you see that woman in this courtroom?'

Goode hesitated, bit his lip. 'It bleaches the colour out, does the moonlight.'

A nice touch, she thought, wondering at her own detachment.

'Try, Mr Goode,' the coroner said with an encouraging smile.

The man turned to the stand and made a show of studying her. She made herself stare back, expressionless, while her stomach seemed to drop into a pit and her heart rate kicked up to a gallop.

'Er…if the lady could turn sideways to me?'

'Mrs Perowne, please do as the witness asks.'

She made her feet move although her legs were trembling, turned to face Sir James, lifted her chin and met the coroner's gaze steadily.

'That's her! That's the lady I saw. I couldn't mistake that profile, the moonlight lit her up, clear as day.'

Tamsyn turned back slowly to face him. 'Liar,' she said without emphasis, wondering if she was about to faint. The coroner's words to the witness were a blur of sound as she focused on breathing, on keeping the blackness at the edge of her vision from moving in.

'Mrs Perowne, you heard the witness. What have you to say?'

'He is either lying or he is mistaken. I was not at the cove, I was at home at Barbary Combe House.' As she spoke the reality hit her. She had been at home, but not in the house. She had been in the lookout with Cris, making love, lying in his arms, tiptoeing back into the house at three in the morning.

Something must have shown in her face, for Sir James leaned forward. 'Are you certain of that, Mrs Perowne?' When she nodded he smiled, thinly. 'And can you prove it?'

'No,' she said bleakly.

'Yes,' said Cris Defoe, coming to his feet.

Sir James narrowed his eyes at him. 'You wish to present evidence, sir?'

'I wish to take the stand and swear to an alibi for Mrs Perowne.'

'Very well. Mrs Perowne, return to your seat. Mr... Defoe, is it not? Take the stand.'

'No,' she whispered as Cris passed her. *'It will ruin me.'*

Cris took the oath. She stared, uncomprehending, as Gabriel Stone sat beside her muttering, 'Bloody fool, he must know where this will end up.'

'Give the court your name, if you please, sir.'

'Anthony Maxim Charles St Crispin de Feaux of Avenmore Park and St James's Square.'

'The—'

'Yes,' Cris said abruptly and with emphasis. 'I believe that is sufficient to identify me.'

'I understand. Well, m...sir, what have you to add to the proceedings?'

'I do not know who Mr Goode saw, but Mrs Perowne was with me that night.'

'We are aware that you are a guest in the house and that you would expect your hostess to be there in her own chamber after the party had broken up and gone to bed. However, the shooting occurred at past one in the morning.'

'When I say that Mrs Perowne was me that night, I mean that I was with her,' Cris said, his face an austere mask. 'We were together. All night. Do you require me to draw you a diagram, Sir James?'

The courtroom exploded into a hubbub. Tamsyn knew she had gone white, she felt as though there was no blood left in her head at all. What was he thinking? He had ruined her.

After much banging of the coroner's gavel and shouting by the constable, order was restored.

'Do I understand you to mean that Mrs Perowne is your mistress, my...sir?'

'Certainly not,' Cris snapped. 'The lady is my affianced bride.'

Beside her Gabriel Stone was swearing under his breath, a litany of obscenities that, mercifully, she could hardly make out through her fog of relief, dismay and confusion.

'Ah. In that case, naturally, it becomes apparent that Mr Goode must be mistaken. Mr Goode?'

The constable looked round wildly as people began to crane their necks. 'He's gone, sir.'

'Then you must see that he was lying, that he had been put up to this by the real criminal—or that he himself was the murderer?' Cris demanded.

Sir James hesitated, then snapped, 'Constable, find that man Goode and arrest him! Gentlemen of the jury, you must disregard everything you heard from that witness. Thank you, sir, you may stand down.'

'But I will not.' Tamsyn found she could think, speak, and that she was on her feet. 'Sir James, Mr Defoe has most gallantly spoken out to save me from this accusation, but the inference you have drawn from his words is incorrect, as he intended it to be. Yes, I spent that night in his company, late into the night, in fact. But we were up on the cliffs walking because I was distressed over a family matter and could not sleep, and Mr Defoe was protecting me with his escort when I insisted on going out so late.'

'But he has said you are betrothed to him.'

'What else could a gentleman say when he has, for the best of reasons, ruined a lady's reputation? He was not lying—after all, having led you to believe the worst he obviously felt himself honour-bound to make me his wife, even though he has said nothing to me.'

'I see. This is all most unfortunate. The witness may stand down and the court accepts that there is no stain on Mrs Perowne's virtue and therefore no need for... er... Mr Defoe's gallant action.' For a moment Sir James appeared flustered, then he cleared his throat. 'Gentlemen of the jury, you have heard the evidence, you must now decide your verdict.'

Tamsyn sat numb as Cris came back to the seat beside her. He had put himself in a position where, in order to safeguard her reputation, he had offered to marry her. Did that mean, could it mean, that he loved her? She hardly dared think beyond the burgeoning warmth that was defeating the numbness now.

Nothing was said as the jurymen trooped out to debate their verdict. It took them all of ten minutes.

'Your worship, we do find that Lieutenant Ritchie was foully and deliberately murdered by a gunshot fired by a person or persons unknown. And we are all agreed it ain't likely to be a woman, neither, and specially not Mrs Perowne, who's a lady we all know of and respect. And we agrees with you and Mr Defoe that that man Goode was lying. And that's the opinion of us all.' The foreman sat down with a thump and was patted on the back by his fellow jurors.

Cris stood, took Tamsyn by the arm and walked her out, Gabriel on their heels. He led them to the stables, stood in silence while their horses were brought, then boosted her up into the saddle, mounted himself and headed out of the stable yard at a trot that turned into a canter the moment they were clear of the street.

When they reached the open space at the crossroads, he reined in and waited for Tamsyn and Gabriel to catch up.

'Cris, why on earth did you do that?'

Please tell me you realised you love me…

'I have saved you a trial,' Cris said, getting Jackdaw under control as the stallion plunged and backed as Gabriel thundered up. 'They would have put you in prison and I could not allow them to do that to you. And it exposed Goode as a liar and probably as the man who pulled the trigger.'

'Of all the damn-fool things to have done!' Gabriel exploded into speech the moment he was within earshot. 'Couldn't you have done something that didn't almost involve you marrying a totally unsuitable woman?'

'Mind your tongue, Stone.' Jackdaw plunged again as Cris wheeled him to face Gabriel. 'You will not speak disrespectfully of Mrs Perowne in my hearing.'

'Disrespectful? She is a charming lady, an intelligent, beautiful lady, a wonderful hostess and great company.' Gabriel, his face grim, sketched a bow from the saddle to Tamsyn. 'She is also a smuggler's window and, forgive me, ma'am, of simple gentry stock. She is not a suitable wife for a man in your position and you know it.'

'Will you both please stop discussing me as though I am not here?' Foxy had caught Jackdaw's restlessness and was sidling away from the other horses, tossing his head. 'What *is* Cris's position?' An awful thought struck her. 'No, you aren't going to tell me he is a duke and that you were not joking the other day.'

'No, he is not a duke,' Gabriel said furiously. 'Allow me to introduce the Marquess of Avenmore.'

Chapter Sixteen

'A marquess?' It was a joke, of course. They would both laugh in a moment.

They did not.

And then it all began to make sense. Cris's fine clothes, his superior manservant, his air of utter confidence, his foreign travels. His whole attitude of assurance.

'My name is de Feaux.' He gave it a slight French intonation. 'Not Defoe. I was not trying to lie to you, but my voice was hoarse.'

She waved away the explanation with an irritable flick of her hand. 'You could have told the coroner anything—that we had both been up looking after a sick horse, that Mr Stone played cards with us all night—anything than let everyone think we were lovers.'

'But that would not be true,' Cris said with maddening reasonableness. 'I do not lie under oath. If I could have seen a way to prevaricate, I would have done. If what I said was going to ruin you, then I would have had to keep silent for now. But once I said I intended to marry you there was no danger of that, Tamsyn.'

'And thanks to my own willingness to tell half-truths you are not leg-shackled to a wife your close friend regards as a disaster! Why did you do it?'

'Because it was an explanation that convinced both the coroner and the jury and, as for your reputation, almost anything will be forgiven to the betrothed of a marquess.'

'And anything at all will be forgiven of a marquess, I suppose?'

'It is the way of the world.'

'Maddening, but true,' Gabriel observed.

'Thank you, Mr Stone, I do not need you to point that out to me,' she snapped.

'I am the Earl of Edenbridge, actually,' he said with a rueful grimace. 'I suppose I had better tell you while we are laying our cards on the table.'

'And the ruse served its purpose. Goode ran, exposing his own guilt.' Cris shrugged. 'No one has to marry anyone.'

'I suppose I got in with my explanation just as you were about to explain your cunning deception to the coroner.'

'Yes, of course.' Cris had both his voice and his horse under perfect control now.

She was so angry that she was unsure whether it was with him, or with herself for being so shamefully weak in wanting him to love her, to tell her it had been no ruse at all, but a ploy to make a humble country girl the wife of a marquess. Tamsyn gathered up the reins, dug her heel into Foxy's side and gave the gelding his head, thundering along the road that led back towards Stibworthy. Anything but think, anything but risk him reading the feelings in her face.

'We must keep her in sight.' Cris spurred Jackdaw in pursuit.

'But I would advise you not to actually catch her.'

Gabriel jammed his hat on his head and drew level with Cris. 'That is not a happy woman.'

'She is an unhappy woman who is not sitting in a cell awaiting the next assizes,' Cris said grimly.

'She might not be in a cell, but you as near as damn it landed yourself in a parson's mousetrap. And don't tell me you were about to tell the coroner it was all a ploy—you didn't think of that until she was on her feet digging you out of the hole you'd made for yourself.'

What in Hades was I thinking? I do not need Gabe to tell me that I was risking creating a storm in London, in the diplomatic corps, at Court.

But he had simply been incapable of watching Tamsyn stand there, brave and honest and truthful, while the snare tightened around her. 'So I should have let her be accused by the coroner's jury, allowed her to be carted off like a felon to prison and let her languish there with prostitutes and Lord knows what scum while I worked out how to disprove that so-called solicitor's clerk?'

'Yes.'

'I can always rely on you for the ruthless answer, can't I?'

'You can. Tamsyn would have survived a few weeks in gaol. She's not some sheltered society miss.' They reined in as a flock of sheep swept across their path, spooked by a circling buzzard. Gabriel pushed his mount in front of Jackdaw. 'Cris, listen to me, I am worried about you. You are half-tempted to tell her you won't withdraw your offer, aren't you? You've slept with her and I know you when you've a fit of gallantry on you.

'But think what you owe to your name, your reputation. You might not want to help out the Foreign Office again and you certainly don't need the money, but you enjoy the work. You'd lose that—which ambassador's wife is going to want to receive a smuggler's widow? The Queen most certainly wouldn't have her at Court. Let Tamsyn go now, let her calm down. Ride back slowly, take her at her word that she doesn't want you.'

'I know all that. Don't think I haven't had what is expected of me dinned into me since I was old enough to understand.'

But she didn't say she did not want me. What if she loves me? What have I done?

The frustration and anger came down like a red mist in front of his vision. Cris urged Jackdaw forward alongside his friend's mount, bunched his right fist and hit Gabe square on the jaw. He held his panicked horse in check for long enough to see Gabriel sit up on the heather, rubbing his chin and swearing, then kicked into a gallop after Tamsyn.

He had no time for thinking as he raced after her. She knew this country like the back of her hand, and so did Foxy, but he did not and the track was treacherous. He caught sight of her only as Jackdaw plunged skidding and sweating down Stibworthy's cobbled street past the inn, and by then she was already vanishing down the track to Barbary Cove.

He reined in, reassured that she was going home and that nothing much could happen between there and the house. Jackdaw was tired, but game, and proved a handful to keep to a trot. On impulse, when they reached the fork that led to the clifftop where they had picnicked, he dismounted, tied the reins up and slapped Jackdaw's rump. When the big black trotted on down to the stable Cris walked up to the summit, then made for the almost hidden path to the lookout hut.

Inside, he shut the lower half of the door, sat down

on the bench and stared out at the square of blue sea, blue sky, until his anger with Gabriel subsided and his brain started working clearly again. He had done the only possible thing, he told himself. The only honourable thing. He had slept with Tamsyn and that had put him even more under an obligation to defend her. But he had no obligation to marry her now. Unless she expected it. But she had rejected him in court when she thought he was plain Mr Defoe and had been horrified to discover he was a marquess.

The crunch of feet on stone was the only warning he had before the hut door opened and someone ducked inside. For a moment there was simply a figure in silhouette against the brightness, then he recognised her at the same moment that she saw him. 'Tamsyn.'

'You.' She recoiled in shock and he leapt for her, his stomach clenching in fear at the thought of the closeness of the cliff edge, the narrowness of the path. He caught her by both wrists as she teetered on the brink, yanked her back into the hut and fell with her in a tangle of limbs on the hard wooden bench.

She was quivering in his arms and he realised he was shaking with the sheer horror of that moment when he thought she was going over the edge. Then his mouth was on hers and her hands were clenched in his hair and they were kissing with a ferocity that swept everything away but the urgency to mate, there, then, on the hard wooden bench.

Tamsyn's hands were on his falls and he twisted to give her access even as he dragged up her skirts and found the hot, wet core of her. She pressed into his hand as she freed him from the tangle of shirt tails, the constriction of breeches that had become too tight on his aroused flesh.

'Cris.' It was a demand, a plea, an order, and he came down over her, into her with a single thrust. She came apart on the instant and her cry, the hot, tight grasp of her, almost sent him over the edge before he could withdraw.

There was a moment's perfect bliss as they lay in a hot, tangled, sticky heap, the aftershocks of his release sending spikes of pleasure through him. Then Tamsyn shoved at his shoulders, hit out, writhed beneath him.

'Stop fighting me, damn it.' He sprawled on top of her as she bucked against his weight and in sheer self-defence he caught her wrists above her head.

'Let me go.'

'The moment you promise not to scratch my eyes out or go rushing out on to that cliff edge again. You took ten years off my life, woman.'

She subsided, panting, and Cris sat up, keeping his distance as much as possible in the cramped space as he stuffed his shirt back into his breeches and fastened his falls.

Tamsyn wrenched down her skirts as she struggled up. 'You lied to me.'

'A moment ago you were crying out in ecstasy in my arms.'

She buried her face in her hands, then pushed back her hair impatiently. 'I don't know what that was.'

'Fright, relief, sheer irrational lust. And I did not lie to you. I withheld information.'

'Why?'

Cris had asked himself the same question often enough over the past few days. Now, as the mists of sexual release began to clear, he forced himself to focus. 'Because I found I enjoyed being Mr No One in Particular. I can hardly recall what it was like not being the Marquess of Avenmore. This is the first time, as an adult, that I have ever experienced that freedom. I found I liked Barbary Combe House and its inhabitants. I found I valued the peace and the informality and the lack of fuss. If I had said who I was, what I was, you would all have treated me differently. I did you no harm by not telling you my title.'

'I would never have slept with you if I had known.'

'Why not? A naked marquess is no different from any other man in a bed.'

'Don't be disingenuous.' Tamsyn sounded more weary than angry now. She was flushed and he could see a red mark where the collar of his riding coat must have chafed her neck. 'You know perfectly well why not. You might like to take a holiday from who you are now and again, but the rest of us cannot. You had the arrogance to think that it did not matter, deceiving me. You enjoyed playing the knight in shining armour and setting out to protect me, and now your pride has almost landed you with a scandal that you have escaped by the skin of your teeth.' She drew up her legs and wrapped her arms around them, rested her head on her knees so he could only see part of her face.

'Tamsyn, you should take no notice of Gabriel. He is my friend and he is simply trying to protect me. Dukes have married actresses before now and the heavens have not fallen.'

'But presumably they both wished to be married to each other.'

The sarcasm in her voice was like a slap on the face. Cris realised that he had believed, deep down, that Tamsyn *would* want to marry him, and her rejection, whilst it had to be a relief, was an assault on his pride. He was eligible beyond her wildest dreams, they were good in bed together, they seemed to get on well—yes, she was angry and upset about him implying that they were lovers in open court, but once she had got past that…

'You wouldn't want to be married to me?' He should take her rejection thankfully, and leave it, leave her. He was free to marry the right wife for the Marquess of Avenmore. And yet some demon had control of his tongue. 'Leaving aside my title for a moment—' He ignored her muttered response to that, ignored his own common sense telling him not to pursue this argument. 'What else makes you react like this?'

'I cannot marry you.' There was something desolate in her tone before her chin came up and her voice hardened. 'One of the benefits of being an ordinary peasant, dust beneath your lordship's boots, is that one can marry whom one loves, someone who loves you back. And ours would have been no love match, would it, my lord?'

'I am not sure what being in love means.' That was certainly true. He had almost died because he had got his head into such a mess over Katerina. 'I like you, I desire you, I would have tried to make you happy.'

Leave it, drop the matter, you have done all that honour demands.

The memory came of his father's voice as they had walked down the long gallery at Avenmore Park together. He had pointed out each ancestral portrait and enumerated the reasons why each wife had been chosen, her bloodlines, her connections, her dowry.

'Each marriage strengthens our house, our line. There is nothing more important than the choice of your marchioness, the mother of your children.'

'You cannot.' Tamsyn gave a deep, shuddering sigh. 'And I know it, even if you cannot accept that you would not be every woman's dream husband.'

Well, that answers that. She is not in love with me, she doesn't want to marry me. I am, quite definitely, free. Perversely it did not make him feel any happier, but presumably that was his wounded pride.

'What do you want to do now?' Cris asked. He knew what he wanted, which was to take her into his arms and let her weep, something he suspected she was fighting against with every ounce of her willpower. He wanted to tell her to look after herself, cosset herself against the stress of the day, but she would only fling that back in his face as patronising.

'I will go back down to Barbary, tell the aunts that everything is all right, tell them…tell them what happened in court so they do not hear rumours and gossip and be taken unawares.'

'Will you tell them who I am?'

'No. Not until you have gone and perhaps not even then. They would not understand why you could not tell us.' She stood up, hunched under the low roof. 'And you are going, aren't you, Cris? Soon.'

He followed her out along the narrow ledge, up on to the cliff, acutely conscious of the drop to his right, of the sea crashing on the rocks beneath as she stood looking out to sea, the wind whipping her uncovered hair back into a ragged banner behind her, her skirts tight around the long horsewoman's legs.

'You want me to leave?'

'Yes. I want you gone.' She said it without apparent anger, with a weariness that hurt more than harsh words would have done.

'And I want you safe.'

'I will pay the two chairmen to stay here as bodyguards, I will puzzle out what it is that Franklin wants so badly he will kill for it. I will employ more of the villagers to guard the farm and the flocks. I will do all those things I would have done before you ever came into my life, my lord.'

My lord. She uses the title like an insult. Yes, he would go and he would pursue Chelford with every resource he could muster and, if he could not find out what the man wanted with Barbary Combe House and its occupants, if he could find no proof that would stand up in law, then Franklin Holt was going to find himself in the hold of a ship bound for Australia.

He watched Tamsyn walk away from him, back straight, head up. This was the woman who had seen her husband leap to his death like a hunted stag, who had faced down a courtroom, who had dragged him from the sea. And she was walking out of his life, and he must be glad because that was what she wanted.

She could not face the aunts, not yet. Tamsyn closed the door of the summer house and struggled to find some composure. What was she becoming? What was this nightmare doing to her? One moment all she wanted was to be part of Cris in the most carnal way possible, the next she was seized with disgust at herself for throwing herself at a man who wanted her only for the moment.

This mystery had brought her Cris, and love, but she could not be glad, not even for the memories of those two perfect nights in his arms. He would be gone soon, back to London and the world that he belonged to and to the search for a wife who was a well-bred, well-dowered, well-connected virgin who would bear his children. *All the things I am not and cannot be.*

Eventually, when she had her hair and her clothing and her face under as much control as she could manage, she ran across the lawn and slipped in through the front door. There was no sound of anyone talking, the aunts must be in their room. She reached the foot of the stairs when a heavy tread made her turn. 'You.'

'Yes, me, the nasty Lord Edenbridge.' He leaned against the table on which she had left her flower arrangement, his gypsy-dark, dangerously masculine looks a startling contrast to the wispy grasses and the lush femininity of roses. 'Where is Cris?'

She shrugged. 'Up on the cliff.'

'Where you made love and had a thundering row, I suppose. Tamsyn—'

'Mrs Perowne to you, my lord.'

How does he know what we have been doing? I suppose I still look as though I've been tumbled like some country trollop. Which is what he thinks I am anyway.

'Mrs Perowne. I mean you no ill, but Cris is my friend and I'll not see him brought down by an entanglement.'

She held up a hand to stop him. 'I have *un*tangled him from my lures, such as they are. He will go back to London very soon, rest assured, my lord. You will have him safely back in his rightful environment, far from scandal and unsuitable women.'

Something changed in his expression, some slight shift towards sympathy. 'Are you in love with him, Tamsyn?' He did not wait for an answer. 'It is better this way, believe me. Cris is a prisoner of his responsibilities to Avenmore and he would not thank you for freeing him from those chains.' He turned abruptly and walked away, his elbow catching a spray of roses, sending the soft crimson petals shaking and tumbling on to the polished oak.

Tamsyn picked up the trailing skirts of her riding

habit and climbed slowly up the stairs to her aunts' door, tapped and went in.

Izzy, always demonstrative, jumped up from her embroidery and ran across to hug her. 'Oh, my dear, that nice Mr Stone looked in to tell us it was all right and that you were on your way home, safe and sound. He said you'd found it rather upsetting, so not to expect you back immediately.' She went back to her chair beside the sofa where Rosie was lying and the pair of them gazed at her expectantly.

Tamsyn found a chair, took a deep breath and began to recount the story of the day, accompanied by gasps and exclamations from Izzy, solemn nods and shakes of the head from Rosie.

When she finished with the jury's verdict they looked at each other in one of the silent exchanges that Tamsyn had never been able to interpret. Behind them on the wall above the bed, the two small oil paintings that were Aunt Rosie's favourites glowed with the vibrancy of rich red fabrics against the lustrous naked flesh of gods and goddesses feasting and loving, and she thought of the fallen rose petals on the table below, of the texture of Cris's skin against hers.

'So,' she said briskly, 'with that out of the way Mr Defoe will be going back to London very soon.' She even managed a smile.

Chapter Seventeen

'But he asked you to marry him.' Aunt Izzy shook her head in puzzlement. 'That is wonderful. Yet you refused him?'

'It was a ruse and I would prefer not to be seen as the woman who entrapped a man who had to marry her to save her reputation,' Tamsyn said firmly.

'Yes, dear. But surely he wouldn't have thought of it if he hadn't already been considering asking you. Don't you want to marry him?'

'No, certainly not.'

Aunt Rosie's eyebrows rose in disbelief, but Tamsyn stared her out until she shook her head and turned to look out the window. 'There he is now, walking across the front lawn.' She pushed the window a little wider. 'Mr Defoe! Do come up. We are both so anxious to speak to you.'

'You won't say anything…?' Tamsyn began, panicking at the thought of the two of them assuring Cris that she really did want to marry him and that they thought it would be an excellent idea.

'Naturally we will thank him,' Aunt Rosie said, then called, 'Come in,' in answer to a tap on the door. 'Mr

Defoe, thank you so much for taking care of Tamsyn today,' she said, beaming as he entered.

To Tamsyn's eye he looked less than his usual elegant, unruffled self, but neither of the aunts appeared to see anything amiss, let alone the mild dishevelment of a man who had been making love in a hut half an hour before.

'Things became a trifle fraught,' he said with a smile for Rosie and without a glance at Tamsyn sitting at the foot of the sofa. 'But we brushed through all right in the end. Mrs Perowne is held in esteem by many people around here, even if the authorities are still determined to visit her late husband's sins on her head.'

'You consider not being required by your stratagem to marry Tamsyn is *brushing through*?' Rosie enquired, with no attempt to hide the tartness in her voice.

Cris turned a level blue gaze on her and his expression assumed a polite aloofness that sent a shiver down Tamsyn's spine and made Aunt Izzy's eyes widen in surprise. 'Mrs Perowne's wishes in the matter are paramount. It will, no doubt, help reduce any further speculation if I remove myself back to London tomorrow. I have presumed on your hospitality more than enough.' Izzy opened her mouth, and he added, 'I will, of course, continue to investigate Lord Chelford's involvement in the problems you have been experiencing. I may well be better placed to do so in London in any case.'

'We will miss you,' Izzy declared with a reproving glance at Rosie for her acid tone.

'And I, you.' Cris's smile returned, the chill vanished. 'You have made me very welcome here—as well as saved my life. I will miss your company and this charming house.' Tamsyn saw him look up at the paintings on the wall over the bed. 'Its endless small treasures are a constant pleasure.'

The three of them began to talk about art and the handsome set of Hogarth engravings on the walls of the landing and Tamsyn indulged herself by watching Cris's face. He was enjoying talking to the aunts, she realised, recognising the deepening of the laughter lines at the corner of his eyes, the softening of the severe line of his mouth with its betrayingly sensual lower lip.

She pulled her attention back as he shifted his position to gesture to the pictures over the bed. 'Those two oils, for example. Magnificent, like gems.'

'I know,' Izzy said with satisfaction. 'They are perhaps a trifle *warm* for display in the public rooms, but the colours and the energy in them have always pleased me.' She shook her head. 'One cannot wonder at the classical gods having so much energy for, er…'

'Life?' Cris supplied, the crease at the corner of his mouth deepening.

'Exactly. They used to hang in Papa's study, but he knew I liked them, so in his will he said I must have them to give me colour through our windswept winters here on the coast. I have no idea who the artist was, but dear Papa always said they had been in the family for a long time.'

'May I?' Cris stood and reached for the left-hand painting, lifting it down when Izzy nodded. He carried it to the window, looked at it closely, then propped it up on the sill and went back for the other. 'You know, these are not just good, they are exceptional. and I have seen this artist's work before, I think.' He looked at Izzy whose smile faded at his seriousness. 'I think they may be by Rubens.'

'*Rubens?* But that would mean they are worth thousands,' Rosie gasped. Then her expression hardened. 'That is what Franklin wants, those paintings.'

'They will be listed in the inventory of Holt Hall, won't they?' Tamsyn moved to sit by Izzy, taking her hand in hers.

'I am sure they will be,' Aunt Rosie said. 'And that is in Franklin's hands now.'

'They belong to him?' Cris asked.

'They do, as virtually everything in this house does, but he cannot touch them, let alone sell them, during my aunt's lifetime,' Tamsyn said thoughtfully. 'You must be right, Aunt Rosie. We always knew he had debts. What if they have become pressing? What if he has read the inventory, noted that we have something very valuable here and decided to get his hands on it? Moving us out of here into a small house on the estate would mean Izzy would have to reduce the furnishings and pictures. Or two little paintings might get lost in the move...if you did not know what they were.'

'And then we refused to move so he tried to scare us away and when that failed he attacked you. If something dreadful had happened to you, then I do not know if we would have been able to carry on alone here. We might well have agreed to move to the dower house. It all makes perfect sense now.' Aunt Izzy clasped her hands to her chest. 'But to murder a man to incriminate you, Tamsyn! I cannot conceive of such wickedness.'

'He must be desperate,' Tamsyn said. 'I hate to think of him getting away with it, but unless anyone can lay hands on that so-called solicitor's clerk who gave evidence at the inquest there is nothing but our suspicions to go on.'

'Let me take the paintings to London and get them appraised by experts,' Cris offered. 'Then at least you will know where you stand. If I am wrong, you can let Franklin know they are not valuable, make a story out of your excitement and then disappointment.'

'But what if they *are* genuine?' Izzy asked. 'What will we do then?'

'Cross that bridge when you come to it,' Cris advised and Izzy smiled, soothed, as she always seemed to be, by Cris. 'At least you will know why the attacks have been happening. You will have the facts and that puts you in a position of strength.'

Tamsyn slipped out of the room. She needed to think and she needed to calm the churning anger that her cousin could act that way, kill a man, threaten her, because of his own weakness and cupidity.

Cris would charm the aunts and smooth their ruffled feathers and when he was gone they would talk often of 'dear Mr Defoe', she thought as she went to her room, fighting the desire to simply get into bed, pull the covers over her head and pretend the whole exhausting, bitter day had not happened. She would not tell them they had taken a marquess and an earl under their humble roof, she decided. They would worry that they had not entertained them in style and that would spoil their innocent pleasure in the little adventure of Cris's arrival.

He would write with news of the pictures and of Franklin's activities. That would hurt, she accepted as she changed out of her riding habit and into something suitable for the evening. She didn't want to see his handwriting, to imagine his voice as she read his words. She wanted to forget him and she knew she never would, however angry she was with his secrecy and his wretched, wretched title.

A marquess, for goodness' sake! One step below a duke and I have to go and fall in love with him.

He must not guess for a moment how she had felt when he had declared that they were betrothed, how the treacherous little flame of hope that this was a declaration from his heart and not his honour had burned clear through the fog of fear, only to be quenched when she remembered that her daydreams could never be, however he felt about her.

She finished dressing, put up her hair with more care than usual and donned her few pieces of jewellery along with a smile that she was almost confident looked genuine. Cris would see that she was perfectly happy to see him leave and the hostile Lord Edenbridge would see that, despite his opinion, she had the manners and the poise to match the Marquess of Avenmore.

'You will take care?' Cris stood by the gate, Jackdaw fidgeting beside him. Gabriel himself sat on his horse by the stable-yard entrance, all too obviously not watching them. His carriage was already on its slow way up the rough track with Cris's vehicle following it.

'Of course. I told you, I will hire the two chairmen to guard the house.'

'It is already taken care of.'

'I do not need or want your charity, my lord.' They were safely out of earshot of the aunts who were watching from the drawing-room window.

'Do not call me that.'

'Why not? Your dear friend Lord Edenbridge would tell me I should curtsy respectfully as well.' She did so, with grace and a straight back.

'Gabriel will learn to watch his tongue one of these days. But if we are to be formal, Mrs Perowne, it is not you who has the say in the matter of hiring. I consulted your aunt Isobel, who is, after all, the mistress here, and convinced her that this was a good way to protect you and that I would be deeply hurt if she did not allow me to make the gesture.'

'You always get your own way, do you not?' She said it politely, with a smile on her lips, both for her own pride and for the watchers in the house.

'Not always.' He was smiling, too, a charming expression that did not reach his eyes. 'And sometimes it is right that I do not.'

She would never see him again, that must be the explanation for her reckless question. 'There is someone, isn't there? Someone you are in love with and cannot have.'

'I thought so.' He spoke readily, but his eyes were bleak. 'I was wrong, but it clouded my judgement badly enough to almost get me drowned through sheer inattention.' He turned and mounted, collected the restless horse with a light hand on the reins. 'I would have done my best to make you happy, if marriage was what you wanted.'

'What I want, my lord, is my old life back. I wish you a safe journey and a happy return to your old life. Thank you for your help and for taking the pictures to be appraised.' She could still hardly think of them without feeling ill.

He inclined his head, turned Jackdaw and spurred off up the lane, not slowing as he drew alongside his friend, but cantering on. She waited, but Cris did not look back.

Thank you for your help. Thank you for two nights of bliss in your arms. I wish I had never seen you, because I do not know how my heart will heal.

It was more difficult than she could have imagined to walk back briskly into the house and join the aunts in the drawing room, but it was good discipline, Tamsyn told herself. Soon, if she kept on smiling and pretending everything was all right, she would begin to get used to this hollow ache.

'Such nice young men,' Izzy said, patting the sofa beside her. 'I will miss them.'

'We will hear from Mr Defoe soon enough, I expect,' Rosie said. 'He did not think it would take the expert long to assess the paintings.'

'Dear Mr Defoe will know what to do,' Izzy said, apparently comforted by the thought.

'*Dear* Mr Defoe is having the pictures valued for you, not investigating the crime,' Tamsyn pointed out.

'If Franklin had come to me in the first place, told me he needed the money and wanted to sell the pictures, then I would have given them back,' Izzy lamented. 'I still would if it were not for that poor man's death.'

'With no proof, there is not a lot we can do, although I hate to admit it,' Tamsyn mused. 'We must be on the alert here and hope some way to deal with Franklin occurs to us.'

As she spoke the bulky figure of Seamus the chairman passed the window. He was apparently strolling casually, but Tamsyn noticed the truncheon hanging at his side when his coat was blown back by the breeze. At least their bodyguards were in place, but unless she could come up with some plan then they were never going to be free of Franklin's shadow.

The London papers arrived, courtesy of the vicar, four days after publication. A week after Cris and Gabriel had left, Tamsyn sat and attempted to read an account of the antiquities of Devon—also thanks to the vicar, who was generous with his library—and told herself that she was managing very well without Cris de

Feaux. She'd hardly thought of him at all—not more than every hour or so—although it was unaccountably difficult to concentrate on manorial history for some reason. It was hard to sleep as well, but that must be because of her worries over the pictures and what Franklin might do next, and the faint crunch of footsteps as one or other of the Irishmen made their nightly patrols.

'Franklin's name is in the paper,' Izzy announced suddenly, making Tamsyn jump.

'It is?'

Her aunt folded the *Morning Post,* pushed her spectacles further down her nose and peered at the small print. 'Here, I glimpsed his name somewhere under "Fashionable Arrivals and Departures". In "Arrivals" it says, "The Duchess of Devonshire to Ashbourne's Hotel; the Marquess of Avenmore to St James's Square; the Earl of Edenbridge to Half Moon Street; Dowager Countess of…" Here it is. "The Viscount Chelford from Holt Hall."'

So Cris and Gabriel were in London. She wondered what Cris's house was like. It must be very grand, she supposed. Even if she had never been to London she knew that the St James's area was fashionable and that the legendary Almack's was just off St James's Square, which was convenient for Cris in his pursuit of an eligible wife. With Franklin out of town, at least there was no risk of the two meeting.

'Here comes the post,' Rosie observed before Izzy could launch into futile speculation on Franklin's movements and motives.

A few minutes later Jason brought in the letters. Tamsyn's correspondence was all exceedingly dull until she reached the letter from Mr Pentire, their man of business, who was delighted to report that since their banker had received a letter of guarantee from no less a person than the Marquess of Avenmore, he had been energetically quashing all rumours about the state of finances at Barbary Combe House.

It should have been a huge relief, of course. *Damn him*, Tamsyn fumed. *In he strolls, setting my life straight with the bank as well.* Dear Mr Defoe, *says Izzy.* Interfering, patronising marquess, *I say.*

It was unworthy and ungrateful and she should think of the aunts' security and happiness, not her own wounded heart and dented pride. She was still talking herself out of the sullens when Rosie gave a shriek.

'They *are* by Rubens! The oil paintings, Mr Defoe says they are by Rubens and worth—oh, my goodness, I must be misreading his handwriting. Isobel, dear, you see what it says.'

Izzy took one look, added her own shriek. 'I don't believe it! That much, for two little pictures? Whatever am I going to do? I am very fond of the paintings, but hardly to the extent that I would see anyone hurt to keep them.' She looked as though she might weep at the thought.

'Nothing,' said Rosie fiercely. 'If your nephew had been a decent young man and you had discovered this, then of course you would tell him. But he is responsible for that poor man's death, whether he intended it or not. Your father wanted you to have the pictures. That should be enough—it is not as though you could or would sell them and they will go back to the estate eventually.'

'If he takes them, he will only be stealing his own property,' Tamsyn said thoughtfully. She got up and went to sit beside Izzy, put an arm around her and gave her a hug. 'I am trying to think of what we could accuse him of if there is no evidence about the murder. He would be breaking the terms of your father's will and he would be breaking and entering, I suppose.'

'We must think on it when we have got over the shock,' Rosie said. 'Ring for some tea, Tamsyn dear, and let us open the rest of our post.'

Even tea did not entirely stop Izzy's agitated mur-murings, but eventually she opened the remainder of her letters. 'This is from Cousin Harriet—do you recall her, Rosie? Sylvia's daughter, such a nice girl, and she made a good marriage, to Lord Pirton, and had three sons and a daughter, Julia. I haven't heard from her in an age, but she says she has been in a whirl with her daughter's come-out and marriage! Goodness…to Lord Dewington. And she—Harriet, that is—says she was quite cast down with anti-climax and Pirton is insist-ing on staying in London during the summer because of some government business and she's been meaning for an age to invite us all to stay, but couldn't because of Julia—' Izzy paused for breath '—and would we like to come now?'

'But—' Tamsyn began.

'But neither Rosie nor I enjoy cities,' Izzy contin-ued. 'You could go, though, dear. You have never been to London, after all.'

'I couldn't leave, not now, with all this going on. And surely Lady Pirton knows about my marriage and Jory. She wouldn't want me visiting, surely?'

'Yes, she knows and she was very sympathetic and understanding at the time. And it is not as though the season is under way,' Rosie said. 'You could see the sights and keep her company for a week or so, do a little shopping. We will be quite safe here with our two sturdy bodyguards. And Mr Defoe says in his letter something about the dealer he took the pictures to.' She searched painfully through the scattered sheets in her lap until her arthritic fingers found the page she was looking for.

'Yes, here it is. He says that the dealer has put the pictures into his own strong room until we decide what to do about them. I really think it would be best to go and talk to this Mr Masterson and get all the details, don't you? He may have advice about looking after them.'

But... No, she couldn't just sit there mouthing the same word over and over. Tamsyn made herself look at the issue objectively. The aunts had their large and capable bodyguards and she was certain that if she asked him, Dr Tregarth would call in daily. She had strengthened the security on the farm and the livestock. It would be sensible to talk to the dealer about the paintings now that they knew what a responsibility they were. She might even find out more about Franklin and whatever mess he had got himself into. Which left the real reason she did not want to go to London—Cris was there.

Coward. 'Yes, I will go,' she found herself saying before she could think about it any more. 'I will go to London.'

Chapter Eighteen

'Excellent,' Aunt Rosie said. 'You deserve a holiday, my dear, and you will enjoy London.'

Will I? Tamsyn had her doubts, starting with the risk of encountering Cris, through qualms about her lack of familiarity with society beyond the local gentry and assemblies at the nearby towns, to the prospect of making the longest journey she had ever attempted.

She mentally stiffened her spine and told herself not to be feeble. She could do this. 'Will you write at once, Aunt Izzy, and say I would be delighted to come for a week? And I will send a note to the Golden Lion in Barnstaple and book a seat on the stage for the day after tomorrow.'

'I will say a month,' Aunt Izzy said from her seat at the writing desk. 'It is too far to make a week's stay worthwhile. The roads are better than the last time I went to London, but they are still poor as far as Tiverton, so you will be a good two days on the road, besides having to set out from here the day before to stay at the Golden Lion. You had best take Harris with you, you can't go staying at inns by yourself and we can manage with Molly. I can always get in more help from the village if necessary.' Purposeful now the decision had been made, she was writing rapidly as she talked.

Tamsyn went to her own desk and wrote a note for the doctor, then another to the inn to reserve a room and two inside seats on the stage, and finally a list of things to do that took up three sheets of notepaper. It was not until she fell into bed that night with a grateful sigh that she realised that she had not thought about Crispin de Feaux for at least eight hours. That seemed like a small, but significant, victory.

Tamsyn swam up through clouds of sleep into a pale blue light and, for a moment, had no idea where she was. She fought her way upright against a heap of pillows, looked around and remembered. She was in London. Had arrived yesterday afternoon and had been swept into the warmth of Lady Pirton's welcome.

'My dear Tamsyn! May I call you Tamsyn? Such a pretty name. Welcome to London!'

Her hostess, in a flurry of silken skirts, had come across the drawing room, hands outstretched as Tamsyn collected her scattered and travel-tossed wits and executed a respectable curtsy, trying not to stare like a yokel at the elegance of Lady Pirton and her drawing room. 'Lady Pirton, thank you for your invitation.'

'Harriet, dear. Why, we are almost cousins, are we not? Now then, are you exhausted? What would you like best? A nice bath and your bed? A little something to eat? A walk in the fresh air? You must tell me just what would suit you.'

'A bath, something to eat and my bed, Cousin Harriet,' Tamsyn had admitted honestly. 'I do apologise, but I have to confess that the room is jolting up and down and I forget when I last had more than a few hours' sleep together.' And when she had closed her eyes it had been to fall into a restless doze, full of anxious dreams about the aunts and disturbingly erotic fantasies of Cris.

As she had travelled, grown more weary of the jolting, crowded coach, the hectic, grubby inns, the constant need to look out for their possessions and to find their way in unfamiliar places, she had felt both her uncertainty about what to do deepening but her determination to do *something* about Franklin strengthening.

'You are a heroine for even attempting a stagecoach journey of that length,' Cousin Harriet said with a shudder. 'Now, up to your suite and I will send my woman to look after you. I have no doubt yours is in as much need of a rest as you are.'

And now it was full morning, judging by the light. A bell pull hung by the bed and she tugged it, wary of just who might appear and hoping it would not be Cousin Harriet's very superior lady's maid, Fielding, who had helped her into her bath, unpacked her battered valises and had refrained with crashing tact from showing any reaction to her workaday, unfashionable wardrobe.

But, thank goodness, it was Harris who came in, neat as a pin as usual and looking as rested as Tamsyn felt. 'How are you feeling, Harris?'

'Much better, Mizz Tamsyn. Sorry—madam, I should say.' Harris wrinkled her nose. 'Lord, but they're a starched-up lot below stairs, for all they've made me very comfortable. All precedence and Miss Fielding this and Miss Harris that. And a butler called Pearson with a poker up his—yes, well, you know what I mean.'

Tamsyn snorted with laughter and felt better. 'It is all very grand, is it not? What is the time?'

'Eight o'clock, madam. Her ladyship says, would you

care for breakfast in your chamber or will you join her in the breakfast parlour in half an hour?'

'I'll go down, I can't lie about in my room any longer.' Tamsyn slid out of bed. 'It will have to be the green morning dress, I think, Harris. It is the better of the two.'

Cousin Harriet was just entering the breakfast parlour as Pearson, the stately butler, showed Tamsyn to the door. She managed to say, 'Thank you, Pearson', without giggling over Harris's pungent description of him and took her seat.

'Now then, what would you like to do, my dear? I have all kinds of suggestions, but this is your visit.' Lady Pirton heaped her plate from the buffet with an enthusiasm that belied her slender figure and gestured to Tamsyn to help herself.

'I have a few errands, and some shopping for myself and my aunts, but you must tell me how I might be of use to you, Cousin Harriet.'

'By keeping me company and letting me come shopping with you. I miss my darling Julia and you must stop me moping and keep me young. Now, what are your errands?'

'There is a picture dealer I must visit on behalf of Aunt Isobel and a shopping list of alarming proportions for both her and Aunt Rosie—I suspect I will be visiting every bookshop in London.'

'And dress shops for yourself?' Lady Pirton buttered another slice of toast and reached for the strawberry conserve.

'Yes, I fear my wardrobe is hopelessly out of date and provincial,' Tamsyn confessed. 'Not that we have an extravagant social life in Devon, but I would like something pretty for the occasional assembly and certainly for local dinner parties. And perhaps a new riding habit and a walking dress or two.' She looked down at her sprigged green skirts. 'And a morning dress.'

'And shoes and shawls and all the trimmings. Excellent.' Lady Pirton beamed. 'And I have invitations to some select little parties you will enjoy, so I suggest we visit my *modiste* first so she can make a start and then we can go to your art dealer and the bookshops. You won't need to dress up for either of those.'

Which implies that I'm not yet fit to be seen in any of the fashionable lounges like Bond Street or Hyde Park, Tamsyn thought with an inward smile.

The visit to the *modiste*, who proved to be the famous Mrs Bell, much to Tamsyn's alarm, was thoroughly embarrassing. She was stripped down to her plain and functional underwear, which was *tutted* over, then she was measured, peered at, discussed and turned around like a doll in the hands of a group of little girls.

'I think I might... Do I really need...? But how much...?' All was ignored until she pulled herself together, put up both hands and said, 'Stop, please! I need to know how much each garment will be before I commit myself. And I most certainly do not require a ball gown.' It was not as though she could not afford a new wardrobe, but her practical soul revolted at the idea of wasting her money on things she did not need and would never use.

Finally she escaped with an order that satisfied both practicality and a purely feminine desire for a few frills and furbelows that were, perhaps, not entirely necessary.

'That is a reasonable start,' Cousin Harriet commented as they took their places in her smart town carriage with its hood down.

Tamsyn tried hard not to stare about her like a yokel. Bond Street, Albemarle Street, fashionable squares and elegant town houses. And the traffic…and the people and the noise. By the time they reached the pleasant side street close to Grosvenor Square she was both dizzy and exhilarated and had to calm herself down in case she let slip too much slip in front of Cousin Harriet when they entered the dealer's shop.

Fortunately the older woman appeared to think that Aunt Izzy was thinking of selling the paintings and therefore took herself off discreetly to one side to study a Fragonard while Tamsyn spoke to the dealer.

'Yes, Mrs Perowne, they are undoubtedly by Rubens. I took the precaution of seeking a second opinion from an expert who considers them excellent, although small. If your aunt wishes to place them on the marketplace, I would be happy to act as her agent.' His eyes gleamed, presumably, Tamsyn thought, with the prospect of the commission.

'The disposal is not entirely in my aunt's hands,' she said carefully. 'Will you be able to keep them securely for a few more weeks? Would there be a charge for that?'

'As I am acting on behalf of the Marquess of Avenmore in this matter, and he is an excellent customer of mine, it would be entirely *gratis*, ma'am, I assure you.'

It niggled at her pride to be beholden, yet again, to Cris, but common sense told her this was the safest place. All she had to do now was to try to think of a way of dealing with Franklin, which was proving as hard here in London as it had in Devon. With a mental shrug, Tamsyn allowed herself to be swept off by Cousin Harriet for more shopping. The important thing, she assured herself, with half an ear on Harriet's discourse on the best place to buy ribbons, shawls and lace, was to keep calm, and then a solution would present itself.

Three days later the only things that presented themselves were a pile of dress boxes from Mrs Bell, Lady Pirton's *coiffeuse* to give her a fashionable crop and an alarming pile of invitations.

'Now that your hair has a modish touch and you are outfitted in style, what is to stop you from going to parties? Lady Ancaster's informal supper dance tomorrow will be just the thing. It will not be a crush, the food and music will be excellent and Hermione's little gatherings are always delightfully unstuffy.'

'*Hermione's little gathering*' appeared to consist of about two hundred beautifully dressed people all talking at the top of their voices. Tamsyn told herself that she, too, was beautifully dressed, in sea-foam-green net over matching silk with cream lace at neck, sleeves and hem. She had borrowed pearls at her neck and in her earlobes and a simple ribbon threaded through her smart new crop. She found her smile and her poise and lunged into the throng.

Half an hour later her hair ribbon slipped. 'Just through the arch on the left,' Harriet advised. 'Then down the passageway and you'll find the ladies' retiring room. I won't have moved far when you come back.'

Tamsyn found the arch and then discovered three possible passages. She took the left one at random, rounded a corner and walked into the back of someone large, solid and male.

'I do beg your pardon, sir.' He turned. 'Oh. Lord Edenbridge.'

Behind Gabriel a tall blonde girl with lovely blue eyes put her hand to her mouth, turned and hurried away.

'Come back!'

The young woman stopped, looked back with something close to despair in her eyes.

'Don't be a fool. You don't have to marry him and you don't have to…damn it, I've burned the thing.'

'A promise is a promise,' the blonde said, chin up. Tamsyn recognised someone holding back tears by sheer pride and willpower. 'But if you do not want me—' She shrugged, turned and walked away.

What on earth was that all about? Tamsyn eyed Gabriel's furious expression and began to back warily away.

'What in Hades are you doing here?' he demanded as the brown gaze focused into recognition. 'Does Cris know?'

'Certainly not. I do not need Lord Avenmore's permission to visit a relative.'

'Come with me.' He took her arm and swept her back into the main reception room and up to a handsome couple who were in the middle of what looked like a heated, but amiable, discussion.

'Alex, Tess, stop bickering.'

'But Alex says I must not cut my hair.' The woman Gabriel had addressed as Tess turned deep-blue eyes on him. 'And I want to be in the mode.' She smiled at Tamsyn. 'I want a crop like yours, with the curls at the front and long at the back. Who did it for you?'

Tamsyn made a dab at her slipping hair ribbon as the man called Alex smiled at her apologetically. 'Darling, we haven't been introduced. You cannot interrogate people about their hairdressers without an introduction.'

'Don't be stuffy—'

'Alex, Teresa, allow me to present Mrs Perowne,' Gabriel cut in, earning a rap over the knuckles with Teresa's fan. 'Mrs Perowne, the Viscount Weybourn, Lady Weybourn. This,' he said, turning to his friends and ignoring Tamsyn attempting to curtsy, 'is the person I told you about. Cris's problem.'

'Gabriel,' Lady Weybourn gasped.

'I am no one's problem,' Tamsyn said hotly at the same time.

'In here, I think.' The viscount, smiling amiably, took Tamsyn's arm with his right hand and a firm grip on Gabriel's elbow with his left and walked with apparent casualness towards one of the small retiring rooms. Lady Weybourn came, too, muttering under her breath about *overbearing men.*

The room was, thankfully, empty. Lord Weybourn, showing rather more decision than Tamsyn had assumed from his amiable appearance, promptly locked the door. 'Now, what's going on?'

His wife took Tamsyn's hand and urged her to sit next to her on the sofa. 'Yes, what *is* going on? That was rude, even by your standards, Gabriel.'

'Mrs Perowne is the widow of a smuggler who cheated the gallows only by a lethal leap from a cliff. She is embroiled in a feud with Lord Chelford and she has seduced Cris into a declaration of marriage in front of a courtroom full of yokels.'

'They were not yokels and I have not seduced anyone,' Tamsyn said, furious.

Lord Weybourn studied her face, which she could feel was pink with anger. 'No? I must say, I had not thought anyone was capable of seducing de Feaux against his will. I was about to congratulate you, ma'am.'

'Cris is to marry you?' Lady Weybourn caught Tamsyn totally off guard by planting a kiss on her cheek. 'Kate and I told you he was in love,' she added triumphantly to the two men.

Who on earth is Kate? 'No, he is not! At least, not with me. It was a ploy, because otherwise I was going to be accused of murder and he was establishing an alibi for me.'

'Murder?' Lord Weybourn sat down. 'You told us that Cris had formed an unsuitable attachment—and I must say, coming from you, Gabe, that is rather rich— but you said nothing about the lady in question being a murderous seductress.' His smile to Tamsyn was teasing and she realised he thought her neither of those things.

'Cris might show the world a façade of ice, he might be a marquess and none of us have ever seen him put a foot wrong, but that does not mean he isn't vulnerable and that when he is, that we don't guard his back, just as he guards ours.' For once Lord Edenbridge's air of care-for-nothing cynicism had slipped and Tamsyn found herself liking him for his fierce loyalty, if nothing else.

She stood up. 'If you are Cris's friends, then ask him to tell you all about his time in Devon, but believe me, I want nothing to do with him, ever again. Will you kindly unlock that door, my lord?' Stepping out into the crowded reception was like plunging into roaring surf. Tamsyn took a deep breath, fixed a smile on her face and went in search of the retiring room once again.

Chapter Nineteen

Cris regarded the stolid figure of the Bow Street Runner seated across the desk from him as he finished his description of the lying witness.

'Thin, forgettable face and brown hair? Shabby, respectable and with an Essex accent? Aye, I know that one. What's he calling himself, my lord?'

'Paul Goode, solicitor's clerk.'

'That's what he was before he went to the bad.' Jem Clarke, the Runner, nodded, his satisfied smile holding a wealth of promises for Mr Goode. 'I'll be glad to lay my hands on Paul Gooding, which is what his real name is. What's he done this time?'

'Murder and perjury, for a start,' Cris said.

'Hanging crimes.' The Runner was beaming now. 'How strong is the evidence?'

'The perjury, good enough. For the murder, I think we'll need to trick a confession out of him and do that by confronting him with the man who paid him. And he, I fear, is a viscount.'

'Tricky. The corners of the Runner's mouth turned down, then he brightened. 'But you're a marquess.'

'I am. Let me tell you the background to this.'

228 The Many Sins of Cris de Feaux

* * *

He was almost finished with the explanation when Dyson, his butler, scratched on the door and opened it just enough to slide inside. 'I know you did not want to be disturbed, my lord, but Lord Edenbridge—'

'Insists.' Gabriel followed the indignant butler into the room. 'Sorry to interrupt. You entertaining, de Feaux?' His intelligent gaze skimmed over the Runner in his blue coat and red waistcoat. 'Or investigating?'

Tempting though it was to try to eject Gabe, he would be as persistent as a dog with a stolen bone. Cris waved him to a seat and introduced him to the Runner. 'My thought was to get hold of Chelford, let him think we have evidence of what are actually only suspicions and confront him with Goode, after telling him the man's turned King's Evidence. With any luck they'll both say too much.'

'I'm with you on that. How do we get hold of them both?'

'I'm relying on Clarke here to find Goode, or Gooding or whatever he's calling himself this week. When he has, then I'll invite Chelford to a nice intimate dinner.'

'I can't condone kidnapping, my lord.' The Runner did not look too worried at the thought.

'Heaven forfend,' Cris said piously, making Gabriel snort. 'The doors in this house have locks that are prone to stick, but that's a minor inconvenience. I'm sure they would prove easy to open if you, for example, were to try one.'

'I'll get right on to Gooding's tail now, my lord.' The Runner got to his feet. 'I know who'll know where to find him, if you follow my meaning.'

'Let me know if you need to grease any tongues,' Cris said as the man took his leave.

'Right, now we're alone, you can help me think through how to handle Chelford.'

'Later.' Gabriel strolled over to the decanters and splashed out two brandies. 'Your Mrs Perowne is in town.'

'She is not my—*what* did you say?'

'Bumped into her at Hermione Ancaster's little affair last night. Dressed to the nines with a fashionable hairdo that Tess admires. Spitting tacks in my direction.'

'Why should she be doing that?' he asked as he grappled with the news. Tamsyn in London. Tamsyn within reach of Chelford. He stared at the glass in his hand and found it was empty.

'I warned her off you again.' Gabriel sat down at a safe distance, which was sensible.

Cris put down the glass. 'Why? You are acting like an hysterical society mother whose little lamb is straying into the jaws of some rake like…you. I, in case you haven't noticed, am male, almost thirty and no one's little lamb.'

'But you are an honourable man and she is a not-unattractive lady in distress who has turned up virtually on your doorstep for no good reason that I can see. If you are not exceedingly careful you are going to find yourself leg-shackled to her. And, if my memory is not failing me, you were only saying a few months ago that you'll be looking for a bride this coming season.' Gabriel, on the receiving end of Cris's most icy stare, smiled innocently. 'And I'm your friend, so I must look out for your interests.'

'What is she doing here?'

Gabriel shrugged. 'Said something about visiting a relative, but not who. Or where. Just as long as she is not chasing a husband.'

Landing his infuriating friend another facer was tempting, but not constructive. Cris got to his feet. 'I'm going out. Do help yourself.' He gestured ironically towards the decanters.

An hour later, after a visit to Masterson in the Albemarle Street shop, Cris used the knocker on the door of an elegant town house in Grosvenor Street.

'Lord Avenmore to see Mrs Perowne,' he said as the butler opened the door.

'I am not sure Mrs Perowne is at home, my lord.' Cris stepped forward, the man gave way before him and he found himself in the hallway.

'No? Perhaps you would check. If she is not, then I will wait.'

The man looked as though he would protest. Cris dropped his card on to the silver salver on the side table, raised one eyebrow and waited.

'Perhaps if your lordship would care to take a seat in here, I will make enquiries.'

Cris settled himself in the small salon and summoned up some patience. He had hardly crossed one booted leg over the other when the door burst open.

'What are you doing here?'

He stood up, taking his time about it, admiring the vision of fashionable womanhood who had swirled to a halt in front of him. 'I could ask the same of you.'

'I am visiting a relative of Aunt Isobel's, doing some shopping and consulting the picture dealer. Why have you called?'

'Gabriel told me you were in London. I was concerned about you.'

'Concerned that I might be pursuing you?'

'No. Concerned for your safety. You are looking very fine.'

She did not sit, but swept over to take a stand in front of the fireplace, giving him an admirable view of pale primrose skirts and upswept hair that exposed the temptingly soft skin at the nape of her neck. 'Thank you. I can look respectable if I wish, you see.'

'I was going to say, I preferred you as I remember you.'

'Why?'

He was only a stride away, too close to give himself the opportunity for second thoughts. She was in his arms before he was aware of moving, straining back against his hold, but not struggling, her eyes wide, dark, as she searched his face. 'I remember you naked in the sea, in my arms. I remember you windblown and laughing on the cliffs, I remember your long legs, strong and lovely as the old riding habit blew back against them.'

'Oh.' It was a gasp and she wrenched out of his hold and retreated across the room to take refuge behind a low armchair. 'Do you have to remind me?'

'I don't need reminding and I don't believe you do either.'

'You arrogant man!'

'Why is it arrogant to praise your passion and your beauty?' He stayed where he was, not wanting to provoke her into fleeing the room or ringing for a chaperone.

'Stop it, you are flustering me.'

'Good.' She turned her head away, but not before he saw the colour flooding her cheeks. The movement gave him an excellent view of the vulnerable soft nape of her neck, the elegance of her figure in the well-made gown. *Damn, but I want her...*

'Your friends have made it very clear to me that I should not be associating with you.'

'No doubt Gabriel has, but I'm not so sure about Tess and Alex. I am not going to be barred from Court simply for knowing you, Tamsyn.'

'No?' She sounded wistful, but her back was still ramrod straight, her head still averted.

'I missed you. Did you miss me?' As he spoke he moved closer, skirted the chair.

'Of course I did.' Still she would not look at him. 'But it will pass.'

He should go. She was right. It would pass, this feeling, whatever it was. And he could not, must not, court another woman with his mind distracted by Tamsyn Perowne. 'I wish it would not, Tamsyn.' And he touched her arm, curled his fingers over the smooth, warm flesh and saw her eyes widen as she started and turned at the touch.

Then she flung her arms around his neck and brought his head down so she could reach his lips and they were lost. He could have sworn he smelled the sea salt on her skin, in her hair, that he could hear the surf pounding on the beach and the gulls crying overhead. The taste of her, the feel of her in his arms, was familiar, yet different, right and yet unsettling. As he swept his tongue into her mouth, finding her again, claiming her, the salt scent yielded to rose water. As his hands spanned the familiar curve of her waist and hip, his fingers encountered fine lawn and the structure of stays.

Tamsyn broke the kiss, laid her head against his chest, held him. 'You overwhelm me.' But she did not let him go. 'I did not want this.'

'I did,' he admitted, his mouth buried in her hair.

'I will not be your mistress.' It was a fierce declaration and he wished he could see her face.

'No. I would not ask it.' Lovers, yes, but he could not bear to see her brought to a position of a dependent, living on his whim, obligated to please him, to pleasure him. Tamsyn was wild and free and her own woman.

'And I am not negotiating, that was not a demand for something more.' She broke away, seemingly angry with herself, not with him. 'I should never have come.'

'Why *did* you come? And do not tell me, shopping.'

'I wanted to deal with Franklin, to make him stop, to find a solution to this.'

She sat down and he pulled up a stool so he could sit close, catch her expression. 'It is dangerous for you. I am dealing with it.'

'Cris, it is not your problem to deal with.'

'No?' He reached out and cupped her cheek. 'It has become so.' When she shook her head he added, 'Let me tell you what I have been doing.'

'Lord Edenbridge—' Tamsyn said when he had finished telling her about the Runner and his discussion with Gabriel.

'Ignore Gabriel. He is going to find my right fist in his teeth if he does not stop this nonsense. It is insulting to you and it is driving me to distraction. You need have nothing to do with him and he'll pull himself together soon enough and be of some use.'

'There is a woman, I think. I don't know her name, but she is…upsetting him. I saw them at Lady Ancaster's reception. I do not know what exactly is going on, but I do not think he knows how to deal with her.'

'Excellent. That will be the first time a woman has tied Gabriel in a knot. It might stop him attempting to nursemaid me.' What was it that Gabriel had said when he arrived at Barbary Combe House?

A sudden impulse of decency in regard to a woman. A lady. I thought it better to remove myself before I discovered that I was on the verge of becoming reformed.

'I can help,' Tamsyn said.

'No.' It made his blood run cold to think what might happen if she sailed in to attack Chelford, all indignation, banners flying. 'It is bad enough that you've been flitting about London unguarded as it is. You could have bumped into him at any time.' He wanted to keep her in the house, wrapped in cotton wool, protected.

Tamsyn snapped, 'He is not going to make me a prisoner, or afraid, any more than he is going to make me a pawn in his selfish, greedy plans.' Her eyes were narrowed, her mouth set and her chin was up.

A warrior queen, Cris thought with a sudden jolt under his sternum. To treat her like a victim was to deny who she was, a fighter. 'We need to get our hands on Gooding first, otherwise all we have is pure speculation. Even when we do, it will be his word against Chelford's unless we can trick him into some kind of confession before witnesses, preferably our Runner.'

'If he discovers I am in London then that will unnerve him, surely?' Tamsyn turned to him, caught his hands in hers in her eagerness. Cris quietly closed his fingers and enjoyed the flutter of her pulse, the warmth of her palm against his. 'He'll wonder what on earth I am doing here and it might provoke him into rash action.'

'If he tries rash action in your direction, I'll break his neck.' He discovered he meant it. 'But it might be a good tactic. What we need is for both of you to be at the same party, one we can control and where I can keep you safe. I'll see what I can persuade Tess and Alex to put on, I doubt Chelford knows we are friends.'

'Thank you.' She looked down at their clasped hands and made no move to free herself. 'And thank you for agreeing to involve me. I know your instincts are all to shut up the women and children and man the barricades.'

'I only want to shut *you* up safely.' He lifted his hands until he could kiss her knuckles. 'But it would be like caging a wild hawk, and besides, you wouldn't let me do it.'

Tamsyn made a tiny, inarticulate sound and sought his mouth, fiercely urgent, pushing away the knot of their hands so she could find his lips. The heat surged through him as he caught her by the shoulders and pulled her on to his knee.

Mine. The word beat in his brain, drowning out common sense and caution.

'Tamsyn!'

She recoiled from his grip back into her chair, sending the stool he was sitting on rocking. Cris got to his feet with a twist and regained his balance to find a trim matron in her forties regarding the pair of them with something between horror and amusement.

'Lord Avenmore.'

'Lady Pirton.' How in Hades a grown man was supposed to maintain his dignity when he was caught in an amorous tangle by the chaperone of the lady concerned he had no idea. 'I can explain.'

'There is absolutely no need. Mrs Perowne may naturally count on my protection if she feels in need of it, but as she appears to be an entirely willing participant in your, er, conversation I will retire to the Green Salon and ring for tea. Perhaps you can both join me shortly?'

Cris found himself without words as the door clicked shut behind Lady Pirton. Then, as Tamsyn collapsed into a fit of helpless giggles, he caught sight of his own rigid expression in the over-mantel mirror and gave way to laughter, too.

He folded up on the floor by Tamsyn's chair and groped for a handkerchief. 'Will she send you home, do you think?' he managed when they had both sobered up enough to speak.

'I'm sure not and if she should ask me to leave, why, I will hire myself a lady companion and take us both off to a respectable hotel.' Tamsyn got up, mopped her eyes and held out a hand to him. 'Stop sprawling on the floor. It is conduct unbefitting a marquess, as I am certain the very respectable Earl of Edenbridge would remind you.'

That was a glimpse of a different man altogether, Tamsyn thought as she sat sipping tea with perfect decorum, and a suspiciously pink nose, ten minutes later. She would never have believed the cool and collected man she thought she knew could have given way to amusement in quite such an uninhibited manner. It was, she decided ruefully as she watched him accept a cucumber sandwich with perfect composure, exceedingly attractive.

'I was not aware that you were acquainted with Mrs Perowne, Lord Avenmore.' Cousin Harriet poured tea with a steady hand, but Tamsyn could almost see the calculation going on behind her bland expression.

'We met in Devon. Mrs Perowne came to my aid when I almost drowned. I was delighted, but surprised, to discover she was visiting London.'

'Oh, then you were not expecting to meet?' Harriet

was apparently having trouble controlling her curiosity as her gaze flickered back and forth between the pair of them.

'No,' Tamsyn said, softening the flat negative with a smile. 'It quite took us by surprise.'

'So I see.' Cousin Harriet blushed and put down the tea pot with a clatter. 'Will you be leaving London for the summer, Lord Avenmore? Your country estates, perhaps? Or the seaside?'

'Later, no doubt. I have some business to complete first.'

Tamsyn felt his gaze resting on her and slid him a sideways glance. His mouth was just twitching into a hint of a smile. Then he ran the tip of his tongue over his lips in pursuit of an errant crumb and a wave of desire hit her like a rogue wave. She was mad to have kissed him just now, to have incited that outburst of passion. It seemed he felt as ardently as she did— about making love, at least. Parting again was going to be hellish.

To her relief Cousin Harriet appeared to expect her to see Cris to the door and stayed behind in the salon after shaking hands. But with the butler waiting with Cris's hat in his hands there was no opportunity for conversation, let alone any more stolen kisses.

Cris stopped her with a hand on her arm, just out of earshot. 'I will let you know how things progress, but do not go out alone, or with only a maid. Take a hefty footman, at the very least.'

She didn't point out that Cousin Harriet appeared to employ footmen for smart good looks and not for bulk. 'I will take care. I just wish I knew the best thing to do about those pictures.'

'We'll think of something.' Cris caught her hand in

his, raised it to his lips, the courtly, almost old-fashioned gesture at odds with the heat of his mouth as he lingered a moment longer than decency allowed. 'Do not worry.'

Chapter Twenty

Tamsyn got through the next few days by a mixture of intensive shopping, sightseeing and sheer willpower. She added a flirty little veil to her bonnet, intriguing Cousin Harriet, who teased her about trying to set a new vogue, but soothing to her nerves when she was outside. Surely Franklin would not recognise her dressed to the nines, veiled and hundreds of miles from where he thought her to be?

Lady Weybourn came to call, fortunately while Cousin Harriet was out, because she proved to be charmingly frank. 'Let's use first names, shall we? You mustn't mind Gabriel, he's in a muddle with some woman, which is doing nothing for his mood, and he is worried about Cris.'

'But why? I am not trying to entrap him, and besides, Lord Avenmore is a grown man of experience. He can look after himself.'

'He has changed since he went to Devon. No...' Tess shook her head, contradicting herself. 'No, he had changed before that, when we were up in Northumberland visiting Kate and Grant—Lord and Lady Allundale. Kate thought he was in love. He seemed on the surface his usual self, all cool detachment and lofty self-confidence, but there was something in his eyes, some…bleakness. I wondered if she had died, now I suspect he had to give her up, leave her.'

'I think so, too,' Tamsyn said. The other woman looked a question. 'We became close.' Tess smiled and Tamsyn shrugged. 'Oh, very well, we became lovers. But he does not love me, I knew that from the beginning and I never expected it, or marriage. I knew it was an affair of the moment and he would leave, we both did. And I do not need Gabriel Stone to tell me I am not the wife a marquess should be looking for. He needs someone with a pedigree of note, a young woman who will give him an heir.'

'You are not some rural bumpkin,' Tess said. 'You may live in the depths of the country and you may have married a smuggler, but you are perfectly well connected. Don't pretend otherwise,' she added sternly when Tamsyn began to protest. 'Country gentry, I presume? There's nothing wrong with that. I'm illegitimate and I'm married to a viscount who'll be an earl one day.' She settled back more comfortably into the corner of the sofa and Tamsyn saw the way she rested one hand protectively over her stomach for a moment.

'Does he know he's going to be a papa next year?' Tamsyn asked.

'Oh! How did you know?' She followed the direction of Tamsyn's gaze to where her hands had settled again and laughed. 'No, he doesn't. I wanted to be certain, and now I am and I will tell him tonight.'

Tamsyn was happy for her, she truly was, and she thought her smile showed nothing but delight for the other woman, but Tess was both observant and sensitive. 'Tamsyn? Have you—have you a child from your marriage?'

'No.' Now her smile was too bright, she could feel it. 'No, I was not so fortunate. Jory and I were not married long. Just nine months before he died.'

'I heard what happened, Gabriel told me. You were there?'

Tamsyn nodded.

'It must have been appalling.'

'It was…quick. Better than prison and a trial and a noose. But it was a terrible shock.'

She kept her tone as neutral as she could, but Tess was intuitive. 'It was more than a shock, wasn't it? Were you pregnant?'

'Yes.' She looked down at her hands, willed them to stillness.

There was a little silence, then Tess turned the subject and began to talk about the reception Cris had asked them to hold in order to entrap Franklin. 'He said to make it for a week today. He seems very confident he can amass the evidence he needs for then.'

'I have the suspicion that if he hasn't he will bluff and I'm sure he will be excellent at that. But if his Bow Street Runner can lay hands on the so-called Mr Goode, then I think it will be all right.'

They chatted about decorations and the menu for supper and whether a string quartet or Pandean pipes would be best and by the time Tess took her leave, off to give her husband her glad news, Tamsyn found that the need to retreat to her room and weep that she had been fighting for an hour had left her.

You see, she told herself. *You can manage this. You can leave him without your heart breaking.*

* * *

Five days passed. Tamsyn fretted about the pictures, wrote long, chatty letters home, spent too much on clothes and helped Tess with the planning for the reception.

Despite it being July there were still enough people in London to garner a respectable number of acceptances, including, to everyone's relief, Lord Chelford's.

'I made sure he heard there would be plenty of card tables and some heavy play.' Alex sat on the arm of his wife's chair, his hand possessive on her shoulder. He was having to fight not to fuss over her as though she was spun glass, Tess had confided.

They were at the Weybourns' town house, expecting Cris and Gabriel for a council of war, as Alex termed it. 'And about time,' he added as the two were announced. 'There's only four days to go.'

'Jem Clarke, the Runner, has got Goode safely locked up at Bow Street,' Cris said, dropping into the chair next to Tamsyn's and sending her a rapid assessing glance followed by a hint of a smile. 'He is singing like a canary because the magistrate has hinted that if he only meant to wound Ritchie, and if he gives us the full story, then he will be transported, not hanged. It means that we'll not be able to get Chelford for conspiracy to murder, because I doubt any jury is going to believe that Goode would be hired to kill and not carry it out, not with his record.'

'If this is the only way he is going to be brought to justice—' Tamsyn broke off, shivered. 'I hate the thought of anyone hanging. One thing worries me, though.'

'Only one?' Cris reached across and took her hand, ignoring the interested stares of the other three.

'Aunt Izzy is going to be devastated by the scandal. Franklin is her nephew, after all, and if he comes to trial I do not know how she will cope with it.'

'So we had best make certain he finds a pressing necessity to leave the country and not come back,' Gabriel said dryly.

'It is hardly justice,' Alex commented. 'What of Ritchie's family?'

'I have made enquiries,' Cris said. 'Fortunately he was not married, had no parents living and I can't locate any dependents. He seems to have been something of a loner, which is one small mercy.'

'Who is Chelford's heir?' Tess asked.

'His younger brother, Michael. A nice young man as I seem to remember,' Tamsyn said. 'I haven't seen him for years, but Aunt Izzy said he is a lawyer somewhere in Somerset and is married with a family.'

'Couldn't Chelford discover he has weak lungs and must go and live in Italy, or the South of France or Greece or somewhere hot?' Tess said. 'I am only thinking aloud, but if he hands over the estate to his brother in return for a pension—'

'A modest one,' Alex said.

'Yes, although the world at large need not know that. Then the brother could take over and have the benefit of the estate and Chelford would be exiled for the rest of his days.'

'We could see to that, certainly,' Cris said with a thin smile that made Tamsyn shiver. 'There would be no scandal for the family.'

'What about his debts? They must be serious if he is prepared to do what he has and if he needs to sell a pair of Rubens's paintings to cover it.'

'Yes, those must be paid.' Cris pinched the bridge

of his nose in thought. 'I'll cover them, then talk to the brother about making it a long-term loan on the estate. He's a lawyer, he can sort something out.'

'Now we just need to make sure Goode doesn't name Chelford in court,' Gabriel said. 'And hope his brother will see this the same way as we do. He has a young family and the opportunity to save the estate and family name for them. That should do it.'

'We are conspiring to help a criminal to escape justice,' Tamsyn said worriedly. 'Just because the family is going to hate the scandal… Is this really the right thing to do?'

'We are conspiring to subvert the law,' Cris said. He was still holding her hand. 'But I think *this* is justice. We cannot be certain Chelford would be convicted in court—it would be the word of a habitual criminal against a peer of the realm.'

'But we have got to convince him that it will go to trial, that he *will* be convicted,' Gabriel said. 'Then we can *reluctantly* offer him a way out and he should snatch at it.'

'It's a plan,' Cris agreed. 'And this is what we will do on the night—'

'But not Tess,' Alex said.

'Alex, I am not ill,' his wife protested. 'It is a perfectly normal state of affairs.'

'You've news for us?' Gabriel asked with a grin.

Tess blushed, but nodded. Gabriel got up and shook Alex's hand, but Cris, to Tamsyn's surprise, went to Tess and bent and kissed her cheek. 'Can I hope to be a godfather?'

'Of course!' Tess laughed.

Gabriel took Cris's seat and leant towards Tamsyn. 'Cris is as soft as butter over children. You wouldn't think it, would you? He's going to make an excellent father.'

'Yes,' Tamsyn said, a growing hollowness below her diaphragm. 'I am sure he will.' Why was she upset? She had known all along he was not for her. Why should this revelation hurt so much? Perhaps she had been harbouring ridiculous dreams after all, she thought drearily. And all the time she had told herself she was being realistic and keeping control of her emotions.

Cris reclaimed his seat and she pulled herself together. 'I know what to do about the paintings, if we can't get Franklin out of the country. When we meet at the reception he will want to know why I am in London. I will tell him and while he is reeling from that, you men can spring your trap.'

'Tell us,' Cris said. 'Then we can weave our noose.'

Tess had planned a glittering reception with an orchestra in the gallery of their town house, masses of flowers and greenery in every corner, card tables set out in one room and little sitting areas scattered throughout to allow for intimate conversations.

The staff were hurrying back and forth, setting out the buffet tables, when Tamsyn arrived early to find Cris waiting for her.

'You look like a mermaid,' he said as he drew her into an alcove screened by a vast display of ferns and orchids. He studied her gown of sea-green silk with a mass of white net foaming over it and an edging of tiny pearls and little shells made of mother of pearl. His eyes darkened, his lids lowered with what she was all too aware was arousal and she found herself short of breath in the confined space.

'That was rather the idea,' she confessed. 'I simply

could not resist it when I saw the fabric and the trimming.'

Cris reached out and trailed one ungloved fingertip along the edge of the scooped neckline, over the curve of her breasts. He made no attempt to delve beneath it, or to pull her closer, but the gesture was both possessive and provocative.

'You will spoil my concentration,' she murmured. 'I need all my wits about me tonight.' It was difficult not to sway towards him, to beg with her body for his hands, his mouth.

'Come, then, see what we have arranged.' He led her to a little grouping of chairs. 'That is the door to the card room just there. We are certain Chelford will make directly for it when he arrives—it is his normal pattern of behaviour. You will be seated here, talking to Gabriel, who will inevitably gather a small group around him. He appears to have a magnetic attraction for a certain kind of young lady and for rakish young men who wish they were just like him.'

'He is very attractive,' Tamsyn said, with deliberate intent to provoke.

'I know,' Cris said grimly. 'There should be a law against it, at least according to most anxious mothers.'

'You are very attractive, too,' she conceded, still in a teasing tone, meaning every word.

'I am exceedingly respectable, boringly eligible, debt-free and apparently sober, most of the time. I could have the looks of a horse as far as the ambitious mothers are concerned.'

He probably has to beat the fluttering debutantes off with sticks, Tamsyn thought, suddenly plunged into gloom.

'Anyway, you are seated here, facing the way he will

come. Even if he doesn't recognise you and react, you will see him. Call him over with no sign that you've the slightest suspicion of him, drop your bombshell about the pictures and one of two things will happen. Either he'll make a scene, in which case Gabriel and I will get hold of him and steer him out of the room, which will make an unfortunate, but hopefully small, disturbance. It will be better if he is thrown into confusion by your revelation and so distracted that we can quietly cut him out as he goes into the card room and get him away without a fuss.'

'And the Bow Street Runner and Goode are here?'

'Yes, with Sir Peter Hughes, a magistrate, behind a screen with another Runner on guard.'

She nodded, as much to quiet the butterflies in her stomach as to reassure Cris that she had it all clear.

'Nervous?' They were in full sight of the bustling servants now and the sounds from the entrance were signalling the first arrivals. He did not touch her, but the concern in his expression was enough to bring her chin up.

'Certainly not. Just excited and keyed up.' Cris's left eyebrow rose and she had to laugh. 'Oh, all right! I admit it. I am quivering like a jelly inside.'

'No one would ever guess.' He stepped in close as the servants began to leave the room, or take up position around the walls. 'You've got courage, Mrs Perowne. Your Jory would be proud of you.' Cris's kiss was swift, hard, scandalous, a moment of affirmation and desire, then he was striding away across the room towards the card room. He paused in the doorway, turned and looked back. 'I won't let anything happen to you, I swear.'

Then he was gone. Tamsyn sat down, tried another

chair, told herself to relax and instead fidgeted with her gloves. They were new, made of pearl-grey kid as soft as satin, and they fastened above the elbow with ribbons. Cousin Harriet had assured her that the slightly loose fit was perfectly fashionable, but, unused to evening gloves, she found the sensation that they might slide off at any moment unsettling.

Worrying the ribbons until they were even looser occupied her for a frustrating five minutes, then Gabriel wandered over, two young bucks on his heels. 'Mrs Perowne.'

'Lord Edenbridge. On your way to play cards?' The young men, who had not been introduced, looked enthusiastic at the thought.

'Later, perhaps. There does not appear to be anyone to make up a serious game, as yet.' The young men wilted. 'May I?' He indicated the seat beside him and, at Tamsyn's smiling gesture, folded his length into it. He should have looked out of place in a formal setting, Tamsyn thought. His evening dress had been beautifully cut, but was worn with a carelessness that included slightly wilted collar points, a loosely tied neckcloth, an off-centre stick pin in its folds and a crimson silk handkerchief escaping from the pocket in his coat-tails.

Against the two young men, starched and groomed to a point of utter perfection, he looked feral, dangerous and, she acknowledged, worryingly attractive. No wonder anxious mamas kept their daughters away and wise fathers forbade their sons to follow him into gaming hells or even less reputable places.

She smiled at the two lads and Gabriel obligingly said, 'Mrs Perowne, may I make known to you Lord Brendon and Mr Elliott. Gentlemen, Mrs Perowne, a visitor from Devon.'

She shook hands, encouraged them to sit and no sooner had they embarked on a careful conversation about the beauties of Devon and the possibilities for stag hunting than three young ladies fluttered past, giggling, just as Cris had predicted.

'Oh, Lord Brendon, good evening.' The boldest, a plump and pretty blonde, came to a halt, smiled at the young man and managed, at the same time, to bat her eyelashes at Gabriel.

Hiding her own smile, Tamsyn obligingly invited Lord Brendon's friends to join them and, camouflage complete, settled down to make conversation and watch the entrance door without appearing to do so.

Guests began to arrive, the room filled up and Tamsyn stayed in place, resisting all invitations to take a turn around the room, admire the paintings in the gallery or accompany any of the young ladies on an expedition to find the retiring room.

How long was it since she had seen Franklin? Only months, she realised, calculating while she tried to keep at least part of her mind on social chitchat. 'Yes, indeed, Miss Wilberforce, a very striking colour for a gown.' It had been when he came to invite the Barbary household to take up residence in his dower house so he could 'watch over them'. 'Thank you, Lord Brendon, I think I will sit a little longer. No, some ratafia a little later, perhaps.' So she couldn't have failed to recognise him. But where was he?

The crowd shifted and he was walking directly towards her. Tamsyn suppressed a gasp. He looked changed and not for the better. His blond hair was still carefully groomed, yet somehow seemed lank. He had put on weight and at only medium height could ill afford it. There were dark circles under his eyes and his gaze shifted restlessly around the room as though he expected an attack at any moment. It passed over her without recognition so she fluttered her fan in a clear gesture of greeting.

He stopped, looked and took a step backwards. Then he seemed to recover himself and came forward to make a jerky half-bow. '*Tamsyn*. Mrs Perowne! What a surprise to see you here.'

Beside her she felt Gabriel gathering himself, although he still sat elegantly at his ease. 'So formal, Cousin Franklin. Or must I call you Lord Chelford?' she chided him. 'It was Cousin Tamsyn last time we met. But doubtless you will tell me I am showing my country manners.' This was the man behind the 'accidents' on the farm, the man who had tried to implicate her in murder. She had no doubts now she was face-to-face with him, his eyes failing to meet hers, his mouth hardly capable of maintaining a social smile.

'Not at all, not at all. But I must confess my surprise at seeing you here.' The smile was more successful now.

'Shopping, you know.' She smiled vaguely. 'Oh, and tasks for my aunts. I must go down to Dulwich soon.'

'Dulwich?'

'The picture gallery, surely you know of it? Aunt Isobel has a pair of paintings at Barbary Combe House that she thinks deserve to be shown to a wider public, and I believe the gallery could accept them on a long loan. So much safer as well, don't you think?' She appealed to the men in the group. 'Do you agree, gentlemen? Works of art deserve an audience, and, besides, I am not certain a remote country house is the best place for treasures.'

There was a chorus of agreement and some flattering remarks about the generosity and vision of Tamsyn's aunt.

Franklin was sweating. He pushed his hair back from his forehead, seemed to realise what he was doing and patted it flat again. 'But dear Aunt Isobel is not—'

'She is the custodian for her lifetime,' Tamsyn said, turning to the others in the group with a proud, affectionate smile. 'She takes her responsibilities very seriously. Oh, you are leaving us, Lord Chelford?'

'I am meeting someone in the card room, excuse me.' He gave a jerky bow and strode off.

'Excuse me, Mrs Perowne, ladies.' Gabriel got to his feet. 'I am reminded that I, too, have a rendezvous.' He followed Franklin into the card room and Tamsyn wished her imagination was not conjuring up images of silent black panthers padding in pursuit of their prey.

There was no point in worrying. She had done her part, she told herself. Franklin was unsettled and off balance. It was all in Cris's hands now. Cris's hands and Justice's scales.

'Do you know, Lord Brendon, I think I will accept that drink you offered me. But a glass of champagne, if you would.' Ratafia was nowhere near sustaining enough.

Chapter Twenty-One

Cris watched the exchange between Tamsyn and Chelford, then crossed the card room to intercept the man just as Gabriel reached his side. As he passed he took a glass from the tray a footman was holding, stumbled and spilled the contents down Chelford's waistcoat.

'My dear fellow! So clumsy of me, here, let me help.' He dabbed heavily at the stain, took the furious viscount by the arm and marched him towards a door leading to the corridor. 'Retiring room through here, we'll have that sponged off in no time.'

Cris was conscious of Gabriel on the other side, exclaiming about his carelessness, taking Chelford's arm, despite the man's attempts to bat him away. Then they were out and into the corridor without anyone noticing anything amiss beyond a tipsy encounter and an accident.

Gabriel took Chelford's wrist, wrenched his arm up his back at a painful angle and, as Cris held the door, pushed him into the room where Jem Clarke sat stolidly at a table, Goode next to him. A screen stood across one corner. There was silence, broken only by the click of the key in the lock and Chelford's heavy breathing.

'What is this?' he demanded.

The Runner introduced himself. 'And I believe you know this man, Goode, or Gooding, my lord.'

'Never seen him before. This is an outrage. I'll have the lot of you for kidnapping.'

'Do you recognise him?' Clarke asked Gooding.

'Aye, I do that. Paid me fifty guineas to injure that Revenue man down in Devon, then swear in court I saw some female do it.'

'That's a lie,' Chelford spat.

'And that's on top of the money he gave me to fire a rick and some other things like that.'

'That'll be the Revenue man you killed. Conspiracy to murder, that is, my lord.'

'This is outrageous. I never—'

'Him dying was an accident,' Gooding said hastily.

'You can't take any notice of the things a criminal like that says. With his record, he's…' His voice trailed off as he realised what he had just betrayed.

'So you admit you know him?' The Runner made a note in his Occurrences book. 'So what was it? A set-up that went wrong, or murder?'

'Neither, I have nothing to do with this.'

'Met me at the Waterman's Tavern, down near Tower Steps,' Gooding said. 'I gave you the dates and times. The landlord will remember him.'

'Nonsense,' Chelford blustered. 'How could he, in a crowded place like that and weeks ago?'

'You really aren't very good at this lying business, are you, Chelford?' Cris moved away from the wall and came to stand beside the man. 'Or is it just because your nerves are shot to pieces with wondering what Dapper Geordie's enforcers are going to do with you when they track you down? Oh, yes, we found out about your debts. The last man I know of who welshed on Dapper Geordie had both thumbs cut off. Devilishly difficult to hold a hand of cards when you've no thumbs.'

Chelford moaned and sagged at the knees. Gabriel caught him and pushed him unceremoniously into a chair. 'Gooding has turned King's Evidence. We've got witnesses, we've got hard evidence and circumstantial evidence. We know about the Rubens oils. You might as well make a clean breast of it.'

At the mention of the paintings Chelford's head came up and his sagging features hardened into fury. 'It's Tamsyn behind this, isn't it? She's influenced Aunt Isobel to stay down there, squatting on all those things that ought to be mine to do what I want to with. I offered them a home, the unnatural coven that they are. Those two old women—disgusting, living together like that— and she's as bad. I offered her marriage, honoured her with my attention and what does she do? Turned me down and married that criminal Jory Perowne!'

'So you tried to get your hands on what's yours by rights,' the Runner said, sympathetically. 'I mean, seems unfair they turned their noses up at a perfectly good home you'd offered them. No wonder you tried to shake them up a bit, show them some real life.'

'That's it exactly.' Chelford leaned forward, apparently thankful to find someone who understood. 'Tamsyn trying to run an estate, a farm, as if she was a man. Turning me down. Like I said, it's unnatural.'

'Still, getting her blamed for smuggling, that attack on the Revenue man—that's going a bit far.'

The Runner was playing him like a master, Cris thought, gesturing to Gabriel to keep back, out of Chelford's line of sight.

'Of course she's mixed up in the smuggling. Where

do you think Perowne's ill-gotten gains have gone? There's some hidey-hole she knows about. If the Revenue man had got any closer, she'd have dealt with him, mind my words.'

'That's what you said to me when you paid me to have a go at him,' Gooding said suddenly. '"Make it look like that fool woman's done it," you said.'

'Almost worked, too,' Chelford said. 'Still don't understand how she got out of it.'

'By being innocent, no doubt.' The dry voice came from behind the screen. Chelford jumped to his feet as it was moved back to reveal an elderly gentleman in an old-fashioned bagwig. 'I've no doubt of your implication in this matter, Lord Chelford. I am Sir Peter Hughes of the Bow Street magistrates' court. The question remains of the exact charges to be brought, which cannot be settled here.'

Got him, Cris thought on a wave of relief. *We've got him scared of the court on one hand and Dapper Geordie on the other. He'll agree to whatever escape route we offer him.*

The elderly magistrate moved forward. The Runner stood up, sending the table rocking, made a grab for it, knocked the screen with his elbow and suddenly Chelford moved, pushing the old man into the screen, shoving the table back into the Runner, who fell against Gooding. Cris reached for him and found his arms full of furious, flailing magistrate. The unlocked door behind the screen banged back and Chelford was gone.

'Servants' stair,' Cris snapped as he and Gabe forced their way through the bodies and furniture and out into the passageway. 'You follow it down, I'll take the main staircase, then we'll catch him in the middle when he comes out into the hall.'

As he ran, bursting out into the corner of the reception room, heads turned. 'Cris?' It was Tamsyn, pushing her way to the front of the crowd, who were craning and jostling to see what was happening.

'Stay there.' He turned his back on her and ran out on to the wide landing at the head of the sweeping curve of the main staircase, deserted now except for a few footmen.

He took the stairs two at a time, landed skidding on the marble floor of the hall and came face-to-face with Gabriel, who erupted from the green baize-covered door to the servants' area. 'Where the hell is he?'

'Don't know.' Gabriel swivelled, searching the hall. 'The staff say no one went through there, there wasn't time for him to have got through the front door—'

He broke off as someone screamed on the landing above. Then there was silence. They turned as one to the foot of the stairs.

'Stay where you are.' Chelford had Tamsyn by the arm, one-handed, the other holding a long knife. The blade glittered in the candlelight, lethally sharp against the pale skin of her neck.

'Carving knife from the refreshment buffet.' Gabriel moved to one side to let Cris come up beside him, three steps from the hall. It felt like a hundred miles from Tamsyn.

'You can't escape. Put the knife down before someone is hurt,' Cris said, pitching his voice to reach the shocked crowd who filled the doorway into the reception room. He could only pray none of them made a rash move.

'I don't give a damn who is hurt,' Chelford snarled. He looked almost hysterical with fear and anger.

'He bolted before we could tell him there's a way out,

that he could leave the country,' Gabriel said to Cris, his voice low. 'He thinks he's going to hang.'

'He will if he hurts Tamsyn,' Cris snapped back. 'If there's anything left of him to hang.' He raised his voice again. 'Chelford, let her go. Something can be arranged. You can leave the country.'

'Liar!' It was almost a scream.

'He's beyond reason,' Gabriel said, taking a step back. 'I'll get round the back, see if I can find a pistol, take him out from up there.'

'Don't move!' Chelford yelled and Gabriel froze as he moved towards the head of the stairs, dragging Tamsyn with him by the arm, the knife waving at the cringing onlookers.

Cris strained to see Tamsyn, who was twisting and turning, trying to free herself. It must be agony; Chelford had large hands that looked strong, for all his dissipation. Then he saw what she was doing. Her long evening glove was loose, twisting on her arm as she distracted Chelford by screeching in his ear. In a moment, unless he realised what she was about, she could slide her arm out of his grip, leaving him holding the glove.

Gabriel realised, too. 'There's nowhere for her to go when she frees herself. That part of the landing is effectively a balcony and he's between her and the door. He'll cut her throat or stab her. If she jumps…'

Cris eyed the distance between balustrade and floor. The height was too great, the floor, without so much as a carpet, was mercilessly hard marble. If she jumped without anything to break her fall, she would die.

He stepped backwards to the floor, making Chelford shout and brandish the knife.

'Tamsyn!' Her head turned. 'Remember Jory. Do what he did,' he shouted.

For a moment her eyes widened in shock, then she gave a frantic twist and pulled her arm from the glove, wrenched away from Chelford and swung herself over the rail. *She's strong,* he told himself as he ran to stand beneath her.

Tamsyn balanced on the far side of the balustrade, her toes on the narrow ledge, then she crouched, seized two of the wrought-iron uprights and swung down to hang over him.

He couldn't touch her even if he stretched. A shoe fell off, hit him a glancing blow as Chelford leaned over the rail and swung at her with the knife.

'Let go! I'll catch you.'

The jolt to her shoulder joints as she swung free with all her weight hanging from her hands made her cry out. Tamsyn risked a glance down and almost passed out, the floor beneath her a shifting pattern of black and white moving dizzily as she swung. *Too far, I'll break my neck, my back.* The memory of Jory's broken body in the seconds before the wave took it came back with sickening force.

Franklin leaned over, white with fear and anger, swiped at her with the long blade, slicing her knuckles. Tamsyn clenched her fingers in agony as the blood welled and he shifted to try again.

'Let go! I'll catch you.' Below her, out of sight. *Cris.* He had told her to jump and she had trusted him. He must have got something for her to land on, a sofa, some cushions. As the knife whistled down she forced her fingers to open and fell.

She crashed into something, something solid that collapsed down with her. Hands held her, she was pulled hard against cloth and she was still falling and then, seconds after she had let go, she was down, jolting and gasping on to a solid, yet yielding object. Something lashed around her ribs, holding her tight, then fell away.

The fall knocked the breath out of her for a moment, sheer shock kept her eyes closed, then the rising volume of shouts and screams forced her to open them. She was lying face down, her nose pressed into white fabric. She lifted her head and discovered it was a neckcloth and above it was Cris's face, eyes closed. He was quite still. He had caught her with nothing to break his own fall.

'Cris!' Gabriel was on his knees beside them. 'Are you all right, Tamsyn? Is anything broken?' He was not looking at her, his fingers busy loosening Cris's neckcloth, then sliding underneath to search for the pulse in his neck.

'No.' She rolled off Cris's body, landing in a sprawling heap on the floor, the hard, unyielding floor that he had crashed down on to without his hands free to save himself. Down on to his head, his spine, with her whole dead weight on him. She ignored the pain to her overstretched arms, the blood from the knife cut on her hand, as she scrambled to her knees. All she was conscious of was terror. 'Is he dead?'

'No.' Gabriel sat back and shouted, 'Get a doctor!' Then he bent to look closely at the side of Cris's head. 'No blood from this ear. Your side?'

'No.' She knew that was a bad sign if blood came from the ears, but there was so much else to worry about.

Someone came rushing up with a rug, pillows. 'Don't raise him or touch his head. Keep him flat.' Dr Tregarth had told her that when she had helped him with three boys who had fallen from a barn roof. She spread the rug over him and looked across at Gabriel, whose expression was grim. 'His head, his spine... Gabriel, do you know what to do?'

'I know not to move him and I know not to let some damned leech of a doctor bleed him.' His fingers were still against Cris's jugular.

Tamsyn hardly dare touch the unconscious body. Carefully she threaded her bloodstained fingers through his still left hand and tried to send every ounce of her strength, of her love, to him. Someone brought more rugs, spoke to her. Alex.

'Our doctor's coming. He used to be an army surgeon, he'll know what to do.' He, too, reached out and laid his fingers on the column of Cris's neck. 'The pulse is strong. Chelford's dead. He tried to struggle with the Runner and the knife—' Alex broke off as Cris's lips moved.

'Curses,' he whispered. 'I wanted to break his neck myself.'

'Cris.' Her voice wavered and she bit down on her lip until she could master it. 'Don't move.'

'I don't intend to.' Incredibly there was the thread of a laugh in his voice. 'Who is fondling my neck with those cold hands?' His eyes were still closed.

'Gabriel and Alex.' She managed a smile for them both and they lifted their hands away. 'Can you move your fingers?' There was a pause, as though he was recalling where they were, then the hand in hers contracted, squeezing her fingers.

'Tamsyn, are you hurt?' He opened his eyes, dark with pain or shock.

'No, I am perfectly all right, thanks to you. And your feet?'

That time the pause was longer, but after an eternity that was probably only five seconds, the rugs over his legs shifted. 'Wish I hadn't done that,' Cris remarked as his eyes rolled up and he lost consciousness.

'The doctor, my lord.' Both the men got to their feet, helped Tamsyn to hers. Gabriel swept her up in his arms, carried her across to the bench against the wall and set her down on it, keeping one hand on her arm as she tried to get up again.

'Let the dog see the rabbit,' he said mildly.

Someone had moved screens around Cris's sprawled body. Beyond them she could hear the guests making their way down the stairs, Tess's voice as she reassured them, thanked them for their understanding, wished them a good night. The doctor, lean and white-haired, knelt beside Cris, his hands running lightly over his body while Alex told him what had happened, how Cris had moved his hands and feet. She found she was praying under her breath, 'Let him live, let him live, don't let him be crippled.'

'Ah, you're with us,' the doctor remarked and she realised Cris was conscious again. 'We'll have you off this floor soon, just tell me if this hurts…and can you move that? Good, and now, I'll just try bending this.'

Cris's muttered comments sounded profane, but Tamsyn was just happy he was conscious and able to swear. Tess came in, wrapped a shawl around her shoulders. 'Come along, we'll get you undressed and check you over.'

'I can't leave him.'

'Yes, you can. Look, Dr Langridge is organising the footmen to put him on a tabletop and carry him to a bedchamber. He wouldn't do that if there was any danger. And you can't follow him in, they'll be stripping him.'

'I've—'

'Yes, I know you have, but we don't want the doctor

being shocked, do we? Come on.' Tess coaxed her to her feet, away from Cris, slowly up the stairs. 'There's a nice bedchamber just here.'

Tamsyn managed to get through the door and then, for only the second time in her life, she fainted.

Chapter Twenty-Two

'Cris?' Tamsyn demanded as Tess slipped back into the bedchamber. Her ferocious lady's maid, White, carried on easing her into a borrowed nightgown, positioning herself firmly so that Tamsyn could not get out of bed.

'Battered, but there is nothing seriously wrong, I promise,' Tess said before she even had the door closed. As Tamsyn sagged back against the pillows she added, 'Twisted ankle and knee on the right, several broken ribs, a lump the size of a plum on the back of his head and apparently bruises in just about every place possible.'

'I feel dreadful,' Tamsyn confessed. 'What the marble floor didn't do, I must have, landing on him like a sack of potatoes.' She tried to smile and hide the fact that she wanted to burst into tears of sheer relief after twenty minutes of imagining Cris with a broken spine or a fractured skull.

'You aren't *that* heavy,' Tess said, laughing.

'I'm not some dainty little debutante either.' White moved away and she promptly threw back the covers. 'I want to see him.'

'You stay right there, ma'am.' White tucked in the covers like a straitjacket. 'The doctor said you were to rest and the marquess is not to be disturbed until at least tomorrow.'

'Franklin.' The memory of why all this had happened came back with an unpleasant lurch in her stomach. 'They said he was dead or did I imagine it?'

'He is. Perhaps it is for the best,' Tess said, although she sounded dubious.

'The scandal…and your lovely party ruined.'

'We're putting it around that he suffered a brainstorm and was experiencing delusions.' Tess perched on the edge of the bed, ignoring White's's disapproving expression at such bad deportment. 'It is early yet, but so far, from what I can hear, people are accepting that. Apparently he has been acting oddly recently—Alex said he was in the grip of a really frightening money lender and most of the gentlemen are quite prepared to believe that was enough to drive anyone insane.'

'I must write to my aunts before they hear this in the newspapers.'

'Just a note then. In fact, I will do it for you now and send it to catch the next post. I'll reassure them everyone else is safe and make sure they know about the brainstorm story.' She slid off the bed and took Tamsyn's hand. 'You rest and I'll just go and tell Cris he can stop worrying about you. Try to sleep,' she added as White blew out all the candles, leaving only the little oil lamp by the bed. 'All is well.'

All is well. Tamsyn lay, eyes wide open. When she closed them she could see Franklin's face, contorted by fear and rage, see the marble floor far below her dangling feet, see Cris's face, white and still.

The trial for the murder of poor Lieutenant Ritchie

would go ahead with, she suspected, no mention of Franklin's involvement. The aunts were safe and so was the estate and everyone on it. The worthy lawyer cousin and his family would move into Holt Hall, which could only be a good thing for that estate, and soon Franklin would be a fading memory, an unsatisfactory nobleman who had gone to the bad and suffered for it.

And she would go home, back to Barbary Combe House, back to her life at the edge of the sea, to remember two men. One who had married her as he might have adopted a stray kitten and whom she had loved as a friend, the other who had shown her gallantry and the glories of physical love and whom she loved with what she feared was everything she had in her heart and her soul.

Tamsyn drifted off to sleep at last and woke, stiff and sore and confused in a strange bed with the light seeping through the curtains on the wrong side of the room. Then she recalled where she was and the events of the night before came back to her like a hammer blow. Next door to her chamber she could hear doors opening and closing carefully, a murmur of voices, footsteps on the landing and then silence. Perhaps that was where Cris was.

She needed him, she needed to see him just one more time, touch him, reassure herself that he truly was not seriously injured, store a few more precious memories away. She got out of bed, clumsy and sore from the fall, and pulled on the wrapper Prescott had left for her. There were no slippers, but then, she was not supposed to be wandering around. The clock on the mantelshelf struck five with thin, silvery notes as she eased open the door and found the corridor outside deserted.

The door to the next room opened with well-oiled silence, but even so, the man on the bed turned his head towards her as she slipped inside. 'Tamsyn.'

'Don't move.' His hand when she took it was warm and his grip reassuringly strong. Tamsyn sat down on the chair beside the bed without letting go.

'I didn't know whether they were telling me the truth when they said you were unhurt,' Cris said. He was lying completely flat with no pillows and there was a hump in the bed where some sort of framework had been put over his injured leg. 'Tell me the truth. Were you injured?'

'No, of course not.' She managed to smile and adopt a rallying tone rather than throw herself on his battered body and just hug him as she wanted to. 'How could I be injured when I had a large man between me and the floor? I could wish you were rather better padded with fat and not solid muscle, though. It was like hitting a horsehair sofa.'

Cris snorted with amusement and winced. 'Do not, I beg you, make me laugh. Tamsyn, tell me truthfully, how do you feel about yesterday?'

She thought for a moment, then answered him honestly. 'I am sorry for Franklin, that his own weakness and folly led him to such an end. Part of me is relieved, because he cannot threaten Aunt Izzy any longer, but I cannot be glad, not at the loss of a life, however wasted. Tess says the scandal can be contained, explained, but I hate bringing violence and death into her home, especially now.'

'Now?' Cris raised an interrogative eyebrow.

'Now she is expecting a baby.'

He grinned. 'Alex is almost tying himself in knots trying not to fuss over her, the lucky devil.'

'You want children.' Of course he did, she knew that. He needed an heir, but beyond that, she could tell he wanted to be a father, with all that entailed.

'Naturally.' Cris shrugged, a thoughtless, nonchalant gesture that made him gasp. 'Have you any idea how much everything itches the moment you can't reach to scratch it?'

She forced a smile for him. 'When will the doctor let you get up?'

'He's calling again this afternoon to make certain my skull's all right, then I can sit up, he says. The man's seen too many head injuries during the war, it makes him over-cautious.'

'I would rather he was. I thought…I thought for a moment that you…were dead, or had broken your back.'

'Would you care very much?' The austere, cool expression was back on his face and he was looking up at the underside of the bed canopy, not at her.

'Of course I care! You saved my life, Cris. That was an incredibly brave thing to do, to risk. And I couldn't have jumped for anyone else, there is no one else I would have trusted. How did you think of telling me to do what Jory did? It confused Franklin, stopped him guessing for a few vital seconds.'

'I thought that would penetrate the noise, and the confusion, and reach you in a way that just shouting *Jump!* would not. If I thought at all. But I do not want your gratitude, Tamsyn.'

'Why not?' she asked softly. He seemed somehow angry and all she got for a reply was a shake of the head. 'You are in pain and I am making you irritable. I'll go, I just wanted to see for myself that you are alive and are going to get better.' She released his hand and got to her feet.

'I am not irritable,' Cris snapped.

'No?'

'No. I am working out how to propose to you from this ludicrous position.' He sounded completely exasperated.

'*Propose?* But, Cris, why?' Of all the unromantic offers of marriage she could imagine, being snapped at by a man flat on his back and in a foul temper must be top of the list. 'We have discussed this.'

'I love you.'

'Just because—' Her brain caught up with her ears. 'No, you do not.' How much more did this have to hurt?

'I think I may know better than you how I feel.' His eyes, blue and dark and unfathomable, watched her as he lay, unmoving.

'You are being gallant again. The scandal does not matter, I am leaving today.'

'*Today?*' Cris came up off the bed, cursing with pain, and twisted to take her by the shoulders with both hands.

'Lie down, *please*.' She tried to push him back, but he yanked her against him, kissed her until she stopped struggling and began to kiss him back. It was the last time, she justified to herself with what was left of her powers of reasoning. When they finally broke apart she reached for the pillows and piled them behind him in the hope he would at least lie back.

She moved the chair safely out of range. 'That is not love—that is desire. We know we feel it. What about the woman you were in love with before? Is this just the rebound from her?'

'How did you know about Katerina?' Cris was controlling his breathing with a visible effort.

'I did not, you have just told me her name. I guessed there was someone. Your friends thought so, too.'

'I believed I was in love with her. She was married and it was impossible. We exchanged one kiss—that was all. I think the very impossibility of it made me believe it was love. That first time I kissed you, in the sea, there was something that made me doubt my feelings for her and the more I thought about it, the more I realised it was not love I had felt.'

She should not ask him any more, because even if this was the truth, he was not for her. She was not for him. *But I am only human.* 'What makes you think what you feel for me is love?' she asked, her voice steady, her body shaking with the effort of will that took.

'The ache when I came to London and you were not here. The sense that something was missing, as if I had lost a limb, or a sense. And then last night, when I saw you fighting to be free from Franklin, when I saw you blazing with courage and determination and a refusal to give in and I thought I was going to lose you. Then I knew.'

'I am not the wife for you, for a marquess. You know that.'

He loves me. I love him and I cannot, must not, marry him.

'All my life I have thought I knew not whom I must marry, but what kind of woman. It was a certainty, like knowing that the land was entailed, or that I had a seat in the House of Lords. But I lay here last night, unable to sleep, and made myself listen to reason, to reality, to what I felt. I realised I could marry a yeoman's daughter tomorrow and a few eyebrows might be raised. And they would be lowered again if she proved to be elegant and cultured and knew how to behave in society.

And before you mention last night's uproar, the scandal is Chelford's. Only a small inner circle know how you are involved.'

'Jory—'

'Was a youthful love. A romance that happened a long way away from any of those raised eyebrows. Tamsyn, I do not have to marry for money, I do not have to marry for political alliances. I have only myself to please if I fall in love with a lady who can only enhance the family name, be a life's partner to me, a wonderful mother to my children.'

Her control did break then, as though he had hit ice, sending cracks and fissures spreading out, taking pain with them. Of course he did not know what had happened on that clifftop that day, not all of it.

'But I do not love you,' she lied as she stood up, sending the chair to the floor behind her. He was white to the lips as he stared at her, his hands already clenching on the bedclothes as though he would throw them off, try to follow her as she backed across the room to the door.

'I'll always remember you, but I cannot…'

Cannot lie to you any more.

'Goodbye, Cris.'

My love.

She was halfway across the room and he was half out of bed, the frame over his injured leg knocked away, one foot on the floor. Behind her the door banged open and Alex strode in.

'What the devil is going on in here? There was an almighty crash, I thought you'd fallen out of bed.'

'Tamsyn is trying to leave. Stop her.'

'I must go home, Lord Weybourn. Please could you ask someone to secure me a post chaise to leave at ten?

I must call at the dealer's shop and retrieve the paintings and I can hardly take them on the stage.'

'I'll send you in one of my carriages,' Alex said over his shoulder as he advanced on Cris. 'Get back into bed, man, for heaven's sake, or Tess will have my guts for harp strings.'

Tamsyn closed the door on them and ran. Tess and Gabriel would help her get away before she did something unforgivable and agreed to marry the man she loved.

It was good to be home. There was a peace to be found in the endlessly changing weather, the finality of land meeting ocean, the timeless rhythms of the farms and the fisheries.

A week after she'd returned home Tamsyn made herself walk to the clifftop where Jory had gone to his death. It was the first time since that afternoon and she knew now it was finally time to lay that ghost to rest. She sat down on a rock that pushed out of the rabbit-nibbled turf, its base fringed with purple thrift, and gazed out to sea. One day people would walk on these cliffs and look out at this view and they would know nothing of her, or her love or of tragedies long ago. That was strangely comforting.

The grass muffled footsteps and the man was almost on her before she heard him and turned. The tall figure was silhouetted against the bright sky and for a second her pulse stuttered and a wild hope ran through her, only to be crushed a moment later when Dr Tregarth stopped at her side.

'Tamsyn. They told me you were home again.' He sat down on the rock, took off his hat and let the wind ruffle through his hair. 'It is good to see you again.'

'And you. Is everything well in the village? The aunts knew of no problems to recount to me.' He was such a comfortable presence at her side that she was almost tempted to lean against his shoulder.

'Little Willie Stephens broke his arm falling out of Mr Pendleton's apple tree, the Penwiths' pigs got out and rooted up old Mrs Fallon's vegetable patch, and Lucy Williams was brought to bed of a fine pair of boy twins, which would be a cause for rejoicing if only she could work out who the father is.'

'The field of candidates being somewhat large, I expect.'

'Somewhat,' he agreed drily. 'Are you back to stay?'

'I am.' If anywhere could heal her, this place could. Or, rather, she could learn to live with the loss of Cris de Feaux here better than anywhere else.

'So…' He heaved a sigh as though exasperated with his own hesitation. 'Defoe. I thought you might marry him.'

'Mr Defoe is, in fact, Crispin de Feaux, Marquess of Avenmore.'

'Is he indeed! And so he did not ask you?'

'Yes. He did and I refused him.'

'Why on earth would you do that?'

Probably Michael Tregarth was the only man she could talk to about this. She was so healthy that she had never had to consult him, but if she needed a doctor, then he was the one she would go to.

'I cannot have children. I was pregnant when Jory died. I was there and the shock brought on a miscarriage and the doctor told me that I could never…' She swallowed the lump in her throat and pressed on, determinedly matter of fact and sensible. 'So there is no way that I could, in all conscience, marry a nobleman who

needs heirs. Besides all the other things, like the dispar-
ity in our ranks and his friends disapproving.' Although
it occurred to her that Tess and Alex did not seem to be
against her and Gabriel had definitely softened.

'Who told you that you could not carry another
child?' Tregarth demanded.

'Dr Philpott, who was here before you came. You
never met him, of course, he had a stroke and there was
several months before you arrived. I was quite ill after
Jory died, with the shock and the miscarriage. I was in
a fever for almost a week. When I was recovering he
said I would be...'

'Sterile. Hmm. How did Defoe—sorry, the marquess—
take that?'

'I didn't tell him.'

'Why not?'

'He is a very stubborn man and he is used to getting
what he wants. He would have brushed it aside and then,
later, regretted it bitterly.'

'So what reason did you give him for refusing?'

'I told him I do not love him.' A kittiwake soared
up from the cliff face, stiff-winged, white and free, its
gentle dark eye warily watching the human intruders
in its world.

'You lied. Hmm.'

'I wish you would stop going *hmm*! What do you
mean?'

'That perhaps you should have told him. It might
have made it easier for him to accept your rejection if
he knew there was a reason behind it, not simply that
you could not return his affection.' He shifted and she
knew he was studying her profile. Tamsyn kept her gaze
fixed out to sea. 'Which, of course, you do.'

'Yes.'

'I thought you did. Think on it.' Tregarth got to his feet and clapped his hat back on his wind-tangled hair. 'I'll bid you good day. I'm off to see how young Stephens is getting on, the little devil.'

Tamsyn watched him go, striding easily over the clifftop towards the precipitous path down to the bay. A good man, and a good doctor, so his advice was worth pondering on, however difficult it might be to take.

Chapter Twenty-Three

...and so, you see, even were things different, it would not be right for me to accept your proposal.

I hope your injuries are improving rapidly and that you are out of pain. Please give my warmest regards to Lord and Lady Weybourn and to Mr Stone—I cannot think of him as Lord Edenbridge, I fear.
Yours for ever

Tamsyn scrubbed at the words with her nib.

Your friend,
Tamsyn Perowne

There, it was done, and as near the truth as she could get without admitting to Cris that she loved him. Tamsyn sealed and addressed the letter and put it on the hall table to be taken up with the rest of the post.

She stood for a moment, her fingertips resting on the letter, then with a shake of her head, turned back to the drawing room. A line had been drawn, as it had when Jory had died and she had lost the baby. She would start again and she would get through this, just as she had before.

The tide was just on the turn, the sun was beating down and a more beautiful mid-August day for a swim would be hard to imagine, Tamsyn thought as she carried her rug and her armful of towels down the lane to the beach. The aunts had gone off on a picnic with Izzy riding and Rosie in the sedan chair, that was now carried by two of the village lads who had proved apt pupils for the brawny Irishmen who had returned to Bath two weeks before, much to the regret of several of the village girls.

There was no one at the house. Mrs Tape had gone to Barnstaple, shopping with Molly and Michael, and Jason was with Izzy and Rosie. Which meant she could yield to temptation and swim naked.

It would strike cold, even this far into the summer. Tamsyn ran, the breeze cool on her sun-warmed skin. There was no one but the gulls to hear her shriek as the water hit her stomach and no one to watch as she struck out for the Flatiron Rock that was above water now and would be until the tide was halfway in.

When Jory was twelve he had cut rough steps in the side of the rock after a summer of hard labour with a hammer and chisel and as children they used to clamber out and sun themselves on the smooth, wave-polished top. But it was years since Tamsyn had done so and certainly not since Jory died. She clambered up at the cost of a scraped knee on the barnacles that covered the sides and sat down, legs stretched out, and wriggled her toes in a big clump of bladderwrack seaweed clinging to the far edge.

Her toe caught painfully on a rough surface. 'Ouch!' She jerked back her foot. Behind her something splashed, but when she turned there was only a swirl of water close to the beach, lost immediately as a wave came in, its crest creaming as it built up to break. Then a head broke the surface, an arm came out, powered forward in a long, cutting stroke, and she came up on her knees, heedless of the scrape of barnacles and sand, as the swimmer reached the Flatiron. He trod water, looking up at her, and she could not help the shock of pleasure, of excitement.

'Cris.' He should not be here, it would all be unimaginably painful, but now, in this moment, all she could feel was joy.

'How do I get up?' He was smiling at her, her own happiness reflected in his face.

'There are footholds, just there.' She watched him climb easily, with none of her fumbling and scraped knees. Muscles taut, skin streaming water, hair slicked back to expose the austere planes of his face, he was like some sea god rising from the deep.

'Tamsyn.' She stumbled into his arms, heedless of sense or of anything but the moment. His body, under the chill of the water, was hot and so was his mouth on hers. *Oh, the taste of him. Cris.* Under her palms his back was smooth, broad, infinitely masculine, and she clung to him, taking and giving in a kiss that was trying to make up for over a month's separation.

When the necessity to breathe finally broke the kiss, they stayed locked together, not speaking, reading each other through their eyes. Finally Tamsyn could pretend no longer. 'Why are you here?'

'Because I love you.' Cris sat down, pulled her with him, knee to knee, his hand still on her arm.

'I told you that this is not possible.'

'You told me that you did not love me. And at first, I believed you.' He held her gaze, not hiding the pain in his eyes, not shielding his feelings as he always had before. 'Then you wrote to me.'

'But I explained why I cannot marry you. And it makes no difference to my feelings.' Now she was the one veiling her gaze, trying to keep him from seeing the futile hope.

'I know.' He lifted his other hand and cupped the fingers around her averted face, turning her back to face him. 'I asked myself why you would have written and told me something so painful to you, when, if you did not love me, it could make no difference. And the only answer I could find was that you *did* love me and that this tragedy in your past was why you were refusing to marry me.'

'But it is not in my past. It will be my future, too. It cannot be yours.'

'Tamsyn. Do not lie to me, because here, now, I will know, believe me. Do you love me?'

'Yes,' she burst out. 'Yes, I love you. And what difference does knowing it make, except to worsen the pain for both of us of what we cannot have?'

The tender expression in his eyes became something else, something hot and intense and possessive. 'I knew it, I could sense it. I knew you were lying to me before. Tamsyn, my love.'

She pushed back against his naked chest, even though it was like pushing against the Flatiron itself. 'It makes no difference.'

'You cannot have a child whether or not you marry me. I do not want one unless it is yours. It will be a grief for both of us, one we will share,' he said fiercely. 'I do not want children with any other woman because I *want* no other woman. Only you, Tamsyn. Only you.'

'But your heir—'

'He is a perfectly pleasant, intelligent young cousin who would have inherited if the woman I married bore only daughters, or if I had a son who died, or if I married someone else and we had no children anyway. I love you, you love me. We can be happy for the rest of our lives. We can build a good marriage and you will make a wonderful marchioness.' When she stared at him, wordless, he pulled her to him, breast to breast, mouth to mouth.

'I love you,' he said against her lips. 'I was washed up on this beach because I thought I had lost love and all the time I was on the verge of finding it. Don't deny us this happiness, my darling.'

Something broke inside her as if a dam had been breached, a stone wall that had been holding back her love for him. 'No,' she said. 'No, I won't. I love you too much.'

A bare rock, covered in limpets and seaweed and water, in the middle of a rising sea, was not the most comfortable place to make love, Tamsyn thought hazily. Cris lifted her on to his thighs, entered her with a gasp that held relief and joy and intensity, and then she forgot to think, or to feel the sun on her back or the friction against her knees or the slap of wet seaweed tossed up by the wind. All that was real was the power of Cris's body and the need to use hers to show him how much she loved him.

They broke together, clinging as they had done when they had first found each other in the sea, locked together now by love and the promise of a future.

Finally Cris moved and they untangled their limbs,

laughing a little at themselves, touching again and again, as though unable to believe this was real. He flopped back, full length on the rock. 'Lord, but I do love you. What the blazes?' He sat up again, rubbing his head and twisted to glare at the lump of bladderwrack that Tamsyn had been exploring with her foot earlier.

'Is it a crab?' She shifted to sit beside him, legs dangling, as he poked at the mass.

'No, it's hard.' He pushed the weed aside. 'Look— it's a ring bolt and a chain.'

'Pull it up.' A certainty that she knew what this was began to creep over her.

Cris hauled, his muscles bunching as he took the weight of whatever was at the end of the chain. He stood, braced his feet apart and hauled and suddenly a small, square, metal box broke the surface. He dumped it on the rock and stared at it. 'If I didn't know better, I'd think we'd found a pirate's treasure.'

'No. A smuggler's. This rock was Jory's place, ours when we were young.' Tamsyn ran her hands over the rusting iron bands that bound the box. 'There is no padlock, only a staple through the hasp.'

'You open it, you are his heir,' Cris said. In the end it took both of them to force it open, lift the lid, creaking, to reveal a canvas bag no bigger than a lady's reticule. 'Hardly pieces of eight and golden doubloons.'

'If it was full of money I suppose we'd have to give it to the Revenue,' Tamsyn said, trying to cover her disappointment with a show of reasonableness.

Cris put the bag in her hands and helped her open it. Inside was a gold chain and a handful of crystals. 'Cris, these aren't—?'

'Diamonds? Yes, I think they are. I think your first husband has left you jewels where no one else but you would ever find them.' They sparkled in his palm like the foam on the sand in the moment the sunlight caught it. 'You can have these made into a necklace you'll always remember him by.'

'You wouldn't mind?' she asked as he tipped them back into the bag, knotted it securely and hung it around his neck.

'That he made you happy? That he kept you safe? Of course I don't mind.' He stood up and reached down to help her to her feet. 'Come, we had best get ashore and decent before your aunts discover us disporting.'

'That's a good word, *disporting*.' But he had already dived into the sea and was treading water, waiting for her. She dived in, too, and swam slowly back to the point where their feet could touch bottom. 'We disported here before,' she said and slipped her arms around his neck and curled her legs around his waist. 'Shall we try it again?'

Later that evening, as they sat, hand in hand on the sofa, trying to make conversation with a deliriously happy Isobel and Rosie and not simply sit staring into each other's eyes, Molly came in.

'Letter for Mizz Tamsyn, just been delivered by the doctor's man.'

'Will you excuse me, I had better read it now. I can't imagine what it might be.'

The others talked while she took the letter to the table where the oil lamp stood and cracked open the seal.

Dear Mrs Perowne,
I have been meaning to read my predecessor's di-
aries, which I found stored in a trunk in the attic
of the house when I took over the practice, but

*have never found the time. After our discussion on
the clifftop I looked at the one relating to the date
of your husband's death and the following weeks.*

*I find that the late Dr Philpott was a believer
in the old theories of health and medicine, now
thankfully becoming a thing of the past. He wrote
that your bodily humours were unbalanced by
shock and grief and that your womb had no doubt
'wandered' as a result.*

*You may be familiar with the idiotic but widely
held theory that a 'wandering' womb is the cause
of feminine hysteria. No doubt at the time you
were understandably distraught at the tragic loss
of your husband and might be thought, by an old-
fashioned doctor, to be hysterical.*

*He wrote that it was very regrettable, but he
expected you to be rendered infertile as a result.
I can assure you that nothing in his notes leads
me to the same conclusion.*

*I would recommend you to attend a specialist
in these matters, possibly a London doctor—I can
suggest some names. Or you may simply wish to
let nature take its course.*

*I am, dear Mrs Perowne, your obedient servant,
Michael Tregarth, MD*

'Is anything wrong?' Izzy asked.

'No. Nothing is wrong at all. Dr Tregarth was simply
recommending a certain course of action to deal with
a problem I had discussed with him.'

Cris stood up and held out his hand to her. 'Shall we
take a stroll in the moonlight before bedtime?'

She let him lead her out on to the lawn and, out of
sight of the windows, curled into his embrace.

'Should I be concerned?' Cris asked her, holding her a little away so he could look down into her face as she smiled up at him.

'No, not at all.' She told him what the letter had said. 'I don't want to be prodded about by London doctors. I shall follow his advice and let nature take its course.'

Five minutes later, emerging breathless from his embrace, she murmured, 'My bedchamber is still the same one as before, my love.'

'Excellent,' Cris growled. 'Because after that kiss, my darling Tamsyn, I, too, fully intend to let nature take its course.'

* * * * *

THE UNEXPECTED MARRIAGE OF GABRIEL STONE

For the Quayistas – and the lovely staff at
Hartland Quay Hotel.

Chapter One

London—June 1st, 1820

'There is a young lady to see you, my lord.'

Gabriel Stone, Earl of Edenbridge, swung his feet down from the fender and sat up in his saggingly comfortable armchair to fix his butler with a quizzical look.

'Losing your touch, Hampshire? Young *ladies* do not come calling on me, not even with a bodyguard of chaperons.'

'Quite so, my lord. However, this is indubitably an unaccompanied lady and a young one at that.'

'Does this mythical creature have a name?'

'Lady Caroline Holm, my lord.'

'Holm?' That rang a bell. A very faint and slightly muzzy chime, given that Gabriel had been playing cards and drinking brandy into the small hours at a cosy hell in St Christopher's Place. He glanced at the clock and found it was now eleven o'clock in the morning. He really must summon up the energy to go to bed.

It had been a profitable night and the crackle of promissory notes in his pocket told him so as he lounged to his feet and stretched all six foot two inches of weary body.

Profitable to the tune of several hundred pounds, a very nice signet ring and the deeds to a small estate in Hertfordshire.

The estate... 'Ah, I have it, Hampshire. I presume Lady Caroline is the daughter of Lord Knighton.'

'The eccentric earl, my lord?'

'A euphemistic description, Hampshire, but it will serve. The man appears to suffer from occasional bouts of gambling fever and is notoriously obsessional about improving his estate in the intervals between his binges. Of his other peculiarities I have no personal experience, I am thankful to say.'

Gabriel turned to look in the over-mantel mirror and was confronted by a vision of unshaven, rumpled dissipation, guaranteed to send any gently born lady fleeing screaming from the house into Mount Street. That would be an excellent outcome, although possibly without the screaming. He had some consideration for his neighbours. 'Where have you put her?'

'The drawing room, my lord. Should I bring refreshments?'

'I doubt she'll stay long enough. Have my bathwater sent up, will you?'

Gabriel sauntered out of his study towards the drawing room, the details of the night before gradually becoming clearer. Knighton was the man who had lost the Hertfordshire deeds to him as a result of one ill-judged hand after another. He hadn't appeared particularly concerned at the time, certainly not to the extent of sending his innocent and respectable daughter to the home of one of London's most notorious rakes and gamesters to buy back the stake.

The innocent lady in question was standing before the unlit grate and turned at the sound of the door opening. Gabriel had time to admire a slim, unfashionably tall figure in a blue walking dress before she threw back her veil. The move revealed a chip-straw bonnet over neatly dressed blonde hair, a pair of admirable blue eyes a shade darker than her gown, a severely straight nose and, to balance it, a mouth erring on the side of lush.

Not a beauty, not with that determined set to the chin, but striking. *Tempting.* 'Lady Caroline? I am Edenbridge. To what do I owe the pleasure of this visit?'

She dropped a hint of a curtsy, nicely judged to reflect both his rank and his dishevelled state. 'You played cards with my father last night.' Her voice was normally warm and mellow, Gabriel suspected. She sounded anything but, just at the moment.

'I did. To save time, yes, I won the deeds to an estate in Hertfordshire from him in the process.'

'I know. I overheard Papa telling my elder brother about it this morning.'

'You have not come to tell me that it is your dowry, I hope?'

'It is not.' She took a few steps away from him, turned and marched back, chin up, apparently using the few seconds to marshal her words. 'It belongs to my younger brother, Anthony.'

'I regret to disagree, it now belongs to me. It is an unentailed estate, I gather, one that may be legally disposed of.'

'Legally, yes, morally, no.'

'Lady Caroline, I have very little time for morals.'

'So I understand, my lord.' A sensitive man would have flinched at her tone. 'My father is…'

'Eccentric.'

She seemed to weigh the word for a moment. 'Yes. And obsessed with both his title and Knighton Park, our home. That *is* entailed of course and my brother Lucas, Viscount Whiston, will inherit it. Anthony is only sixteen. Papa has decided that he will become a clergyman, installed in one of the livings at his disposal, and therefore he has no need of lands of his own. He doesn't understand Anthony like I do. I virtually brought him up and—' She must have realised she was losing his attention and her tone became brisk again. 'Springbourne is ten miles from Knighton Park, too far for it ever to be integrated into the main estate, so Papa thinks little of it.'

'The church is a common career for a younger son,' Gabriel observed. His own brothers seemed happy enough with their respective roles, but they hadn't been born first and saddled with the responsibility of title, tenants and lands. Let alone brothers. *Promise me, Gabriel...*

With the ruthlessness of long practice he pushed away memories of childhood and thought of his brothers now. Ben, the elder, a blood-and-thunder cavalry major, George, newly ordained as a vicar, a mild soul who tended to flinch when he encountered Gabriel, and Louis, painfully studious and conscientious and both sensitive and pugnacious, a difficult combination to handle. He was a student in his final year at Cambridge where he was reading law before taking over the family's business affairs, an outcome Gabriel was looking forward to immensely.

Now they were adults Gabriel gave them money when they asked for it, had introduced each to a good clean brothel when he judged them mature enough, warned them about predatory young ladies and their even more predatory mothers and beyond that managed to avoid them for months at a time. It was better for all of them that way.

'It may be usual,' Lady Caroline said in a voice that made him think of lemons inadequately sprinkled with sugar, 'but it is quite unsuitable for Anthony.' She glanced at him, then looked away hastily. It might have been the morning light shining directly into her eyes, it might have been the sight of him. The blue gaze flickered back, she bit that full lower lip and the hunting cat in him stirred, twitched its tail and began to purr. 'Anthony loves Spring-bourne. He isn't studious or intellectual. He is a natural farmer and countryman and it will break his heart to discover it has gone.'

'And you expect me to hand it back to you, just like that? Sit down, Lady Caroline. I have had a long, hard night and I cannot sit until you do.' Besides anything else, he wanted to watch her move.

With a small sound he assumed was exasperation, she sat on the nearest chair and studied her clasped hands as he subsided into the seat opposite. 'No, I do not expect you to do anything so altruistic as to save my little brother's dreams and future for no return.'

'Perceptive of you,' he drawled and was rewarded by a hiss of anger before she was back to being the perfect lady again. 'Do you intend to buy it back then?' He pulled the mass of vowels out of his pocket and sorted through the IOUs until he found the one scrawled in Knighton's hand. He held it up for her to see. 'That is the value your father put on it.'

Lady Caroline winced. 'No, of course I cannot buy it back. You must know that as an unmarried woman I have no control over my own money.'

'Then what do you propose?'

'You have a certain reputation, Lord Edenbridge.' Those gloves must be fascinating to require such close scrutiny.

'As a gambler?'

She closed her eyes, took a deep breath, then opened them and sent him a defiant stare before her gaze skidded away to settle on the fire irons. 'As a man of amorous inclinations.'

Gabriel tried not to laugh, but it escaped in a snort of amusement. 'That is one way of putting it.'

'I am a virgin.'

And one who blushed delightfully. 'So I should hope,' he said piously. The lush mouth compressed into a hard line and he had a sudden urge to capture it beneath his, tease it into softness and acceptance. Into pleasure.

'I propose an exchange, my lord.' She addressed the fire irons. 'My virginity for those deeds.'

Gabriel had always thought himself sophisticated in his dealings with women. After perhaps half a minute, during which time Lady Caroline's cheeks turned from light rose to peony and he revised his opinion of his own unshock-ability, he said, 'I am not in the habit of deflowering virgins, respectable or not.' *But in your case...*

'Perhaps you would consider making an exception? I understand men are almost obsessed with virginity, which seems strange, but then I know very few men.' And, by the sound of it, wished to keep it that way.

He flicked the IOU with one finger, making her start at the sharp sound and glance at him again. 'This debt is not your problem, Lady Caroline.'

She bit her lip and Gabriel drew in a steadying breath. Even talking about making love to her was having an uncomfortable effect on him. He could understand that men wanted a virgin bride because they needed to be certain their heirs were from their own seed. But maidens held no attraction for him. Forcing women was revolting and a willing virgin was doubtless a great deal more trouble than she was worth—tiresomely inexperienced with a price to pay in the form of a maddened father with a shotgun. Besides, he expected expertise and sophistication from his lovers.

And yet, this one... It has nothing at all to do with her

virginity. Those blue eyes and that mouth and the stubborn, innocent courage of her... Damn, she is not safe out when she has no idea the effect she has on a man.

'Oh, but it is my problem.' Lady Caroline was becoming animated now, her blush disappearing as she leaned forward earnestly, trying to convince him, or, perhaps his disordered neckcloth, which is what she was now fixed upon. 'Mama died ten years ago. Anthony is my little brother and I promised her I would look after him. I love Papa, of course, but he is…difficult. He would regard paying you to buy back the deeds as a waste of money that should go into Lucas's inheritance, or towards improving Knighton Park.' When Gabriel did not respond she said fiercely, 'Anthony is the only one of my family who truly loves me and I love him as though he was my own child, not just my brother.

'You have brothers, I know you have because I looked you up in the *Peerage.*' For some reason that brought the colour up again in her cheeks. 'This morning, I mean. I know, as a man, you can't feel about them as I feel about Anthony, but you would do anything you could to help them, wouldn't you?' It was more a statement than a question.

Yes. 'No.' He was not going to encourage her in this, allow her to see that her promise to her mother meant something to him. What his duty was as a man, as the eldest son, was quite different from hers as a daughter, a woman. 'Listen to me, Anthony is a boy. He'll find his own way in the world eventually. He isn't a child, your responsibility, any more. Your older brother will look after him.'

She was finally staring at him, although her expression suggested that it was because he had grown two heads. 'I do not understand you. I love him for himself, but Anthony is also all I have left of Mama. I know from the *Peerage* that your mother is dead too. Have you no affection for your own family? Don't you see your parents when you look at your brothers? Surely they are the most important thing in the world to you, even if sometimes you fall out with one of them?'

All I have left of Mama, she had said. He understood that too well. The blackness swirled down, the memories clamouring. *Promise me...the still white hand, limp beside the bottle...*

Gabriel shrugged the images away, unable to acknowledge what lay at the heart of them. He would kill…he would protect his brothers, of course he would. He had. They were his responsibility, his trust. He shrugged again. 'It is my duty. But I am a man and head of the family.'

'I am so sorry you feel like that, you must miss so much,' Lady Caroline murmured.

For an appalled moment Gabriel thought she was going to cry, she looked so upset. 'You are *not* going to sell yourself to me in exchange for those deeds. What will your husband say?' The heavens only knew where this impulse to decency was coming from.

'I do not have one. Yet.' Lady Caroline's expression changed from sad to rigid.

'You will, soon enough.' She must be in her early twenties, he guessed. Twenty-three, perhaps. 'And a husband means a wedding night.'

'Papa has a number of men in mind for me, but he hasn't made up his mind yet which would be the most advantageous match. Frankly I would be delighted to give any one of them a shock on the night.' She seemed to have recovered her spirit, but her gaze had slid away to the fire irons again.

'You do not have to obey him.'

'He is my father, of course I have to obey him. I have no choice.'

'Your duty, I suppose.'

She nodded, one sharp jerk of her averted head. 'Duty and lack of other options. My father tends to discourage suitors who do not match his wishes for me.'

'You don't really want to have sex with me, do you?' Gabriel smiled as she looked back, startled at the deliberate crudity of his words. He made the expression more wolfish than reassuring and ran one hand over his morning beard, drawing her eyes to his mouth. She stared and then swallowed and his arousal kicked up another notch. *Damn it.*

'To be frank, rather you, my lord, than Sir William Claypole or Mr Walberton. Or Lord Woodruffe.'

'Hell's teeth! Has your father made a list of every middle-aged bachelor in society?' If he had sisters he would not have been willing to match one of them to any of those men, least of all Woodruffe.

'Only of those with lands close to ours who would be willing to exchange them for me.' When he did not respond she said urgently, 'Please, Lord Edenbridge. I know you are supposed to be hard and cynical and to care for nothing and nobody, but deep down you must have family feeling. You must, surely, understand how desperate I am.'

The first part of that description was more or less accurate. 'You have managed to do a remarkable amount of research on me, considering that it is not yet noon.'

Lady Caroline blushed again. 'I have seen you about at balls and so forth. People talk.'

And you have been interested enough to ask about me? Gabriel laughed inwardly at himself. *Coxcomb. Flattered because some attractive girl has noticed you?* Women tended to look at him, just as he looked at them. But not well-bred virgins. He had a highly developed sense of self-preservation.

'I will take you up on your offer,' he said. She gasped

as though she had not expected it and the colour fled from her cheeks. 'I will send the deeds to you when I receive them from your father and you will give me an IOU for your maidenhead, to be surrendered when your marriage is definitely arranged.'

'But…'

'I may be a gamester and a rake with a shocking reputation, Lady Caroline. But I am a gentleman. Of sorts.' *Just enough of one not to barter your innocence.* On the other hand, if she thought they had an agreement it would prevent her doing anything else reckless in order to raise money to pay him. He could simply hand her the deeds and he *should* do just that without any conditions. But the hunter in him enjoyed having her between his paws. Not to hurt, just to play with a little. He was so damnably bored these days. 'On my honour I will speak of this to no one. What is your decision?'

She had expected to be sent packing with Lord Edenbridge's derisive laughter ringing in her ears, or to find herself flat on her back in his bedchamber, and had not been able to work out which of those was the worst of two evils. What she had not expected was this reprieve. Which was not a reprieve after all, merely a postponement, she realised as his words sank in.

'I accept.' Caroline wondered if she was about to faint. She was not given to swooning, but the room seemed unexpectedly smaller and there was a strange roaring in her ears that must be the sound of her blood.

'Please send the deeds to this address.' She found her piano teacher's card in her reticule and handed it to him without meeting his gaze. She had tried not to look at him, partly because the whole situation was so mortifying, but also because she knew she blushed every time she saw that rangy, carelessly elegant figure. Looking at his face, so close, would be too disconcerting. 'Miss Fanshawe understands the situation at home.'

'She is used to acting as a go-between for your illicit correspondence, is she?' The earl moved away towards a writing desk and Caroline realised that she had been holding her breath. A hasty glance at his back made her shiver. He was far too large and male and *animal* to be so close to. Whenever she had seen him before it had been across a ballroom floor at a safe distance and there his dark hair and the slight carelessness of his formal evening attire had been attractive.

This near, in the same room with him, his casual disregard for the niceties of fashionable male dress and grooming was shocking and more than a little unsettling. His hair was thick, slightly waving, rumpled as though he had run those long fingers through it. His face was shadowed by dark stubble, his neckcloth was pulled askew and his collar had been opened, exposing the base of his throat. He smelled of brandy and smoke and something faint and musky and his eyelids drooped with a weariness at odds with his drily intelligent voice. She wondered what colour his eyes were. Dark blue, brown?

At a safe distance he had attracted and intrigued her. The gossip about him was both titillating and arousing to a well brought-up young lady and she had fed her fantasies with it. Of course, she'd had no expectation of finding herself within ten feet of the object of her lurid imaginings. Aunt Gertrude, her chaperon, would have hysterics at the thought that Caroline might actually *speak* to Gabriel Stone.

His reputation was shocking and yet no one accused him of being vicious. He was amorous, said the whisperers, dangerous to a lady foolish enough to risk her heart with him and he was far too good at cards for the health of anyone reckless enough to cut a deck in his company, but

Caroline was not hazarding her allowance. Nor her heart, she told herself. In the shock and anger of discovering just what Papa had done last night, Lord Edenbridge had seemed like the answer to her dreams—amoral, unconventional, sophisticated and possessed of his own particular brand of honour. The man had disturbed those dreams often enough, so surely the bargain she was proposing would not be so very unpleasant to go through with, given that one had to lose one's virginity some time, to someone? Lord Woodruffe's stomach wobbled over the top of his breeches. She shuddered. *I will not think about Woodruffe. Think about this man.* Nothing about Lord Edenbridge wobbled physically, nor, apparently, mentally.

Caroline gave herself a mental shake. 'I do not have any illicit correspondence,' she said. 'But Miss Fanshawe is a friend.'

'Not much of one if she is encouraging you to come here.' He pulled back the desk chair for her.

'She has no idea what I am doing.' Caroline eyed the pen stand warily. She was not at all certain she knew what she was doing herself. It had seemed such a good idea at nine o'clock that morning. 'What should I write?'

'Whatever you feel covers our agreement.' The wretched man had a perfectly straight face and his eyes beneath those indecently long lashes were veiled, but she suspected that he was amused.

'Very well.' She dipped the nib and began, choosing her words with care. She was not, whatever he thought of her, completely reckless.

> *I agree to pay Lord Edenbridge the price agreed upon the arrangement of my betrothal.*
> *Caroline Amelie Holm*
> *June 1st, 1820*

She sanded the paper with a hand that shook only a little and pushed the note towards him. 'Will that do?'

'Admirably discreet.' He folded the paper and slid it into his breast pocket. 'This will reside in my safe, most securely.'

'Of course.' Strange that she had total confidence in his discretion and his honour—in keeping this a secret, at least. He would not be bragging in his clubs that he had made a conquest of the retiring and virtuous Lady Caroline Holm. *Would he?*

'Why do you trust me?' he asked abruptly, the question so near to her thoughts that she stared at him, wide-eyed, convinced for a moment that he could read her mind.

'I have no idea,' she confessed. 'Only my own impressions and the fact that everyone says how shocking and ruthless you are, yet you are never accused of dishonourable behaviour.'

'It is easy enough to be honourable if one is never tempted.' His voice was dry and his smile held little amusement. 'I confess that it is a novelty to be trusted quite so implicitly, Lady Caroline.'

The heat that had been ebbing and waning throughout this entire outrageous interview swept up her cheeks at the thought of what tempting this man might involve. She was innocent, certainly, but not ignorant. 'Obviously I have not tempted you beyond reason, my lord, given the very businesslike way we have concluded our bargain.'

'I did not say that I am not tempted, Lady Caroline.' He took her hand, raised it to within a hair's breadth of his mouth and held in there for a moment. His breath was warm, his fingers firm. She braced herself for the brush of his lips.

'How did you come here?' Lord Edenbridge asked,

releasing her without the slightest attempt at a kiss. He walked to the fireside and tugged the bell pull.

'In a—in a hackney.' *Damn him for making me all of a flutter, for making me stammer. For disappointing me.* Behind her the door opened and she bit back any more stumbling words.

'Hampshire, find the lady a hackney with a reliable-looking driver. Good day, Lady Caroline. I look forward greatly to the announcement of your nuptials.'

Her last glimpse of the earl was of him pulling his neck-cloth free and beginning to unbutton his shirt. Caroline did not deceive herself, her brisk walk down the hallway was as much a flight as if she had run.

Chapter Two

It had seemed such a good idea at the time. It had seemed the *only* idea at the time. Caroline took her place at the dinner table and wondered if the sinking feeling inside was guilt and shame or…anticipation. More likely, she thought as she made herself sip her soup, it was all three plus very sensible fear at what would happen if her father found out what she had been doing that morning.

'Something wrong, Caro?' Lucas, her elder brother, glanced across at her.

Her father, who was unlikely to notice anything amiss with anyone else, short of one of the party spontaneously combusting, ignored them. He had always been self-centred and selfish and she had given up years ago expecting any parental warmth and attention. She just prayed that Lucas would find a wife soon, someone who would stop him becoming just like his father.

'This soup is a trifle salty. I must speak to Cook about it.' Apparently her face did not convey the depth of her feelings, for Lucas merely nodded and went back to discussing with their father a planned visit to Coade's Artificial Stone Manufactory in Lambeth in pursuit of statuary for their latest landscape project.

She had noticed before that once her father had sustained a major loss he would stop gambling abruptly. It was as if the bubble of gaming fever that had built up in him had been pricked and he was back to normal, until the next time. At least he did not continue throwing good money after bad for very long, but the irrationality of his behaviour, the wild swings of mood, were an increasing worry.

'What new feature are you planning, Papa?' she asked as the soup plates were cleared.

'A hermitage. I will adapt the Gothic chapel that is already almost complete. The position where the path through the plantation has the view of the small lake is more suitable for a hermit's cell than for a church.'

'A hermitage there would be very dramatic and atmospheric,' Caroline observed dutifully, not adding *and damp*. That location faced north and the trees dripped moisture on to the mossy bank. But years of experience had taught her what to say to keep her father happy.

'Finding the hermit may take some time,' he commented, gesturing impatiently for Lucas to add more of the capon he was carving to his plate.

For a moment, despite all her years of experience with him, Caroline thought her father was joking, but he sounded perfectly serious. 'That might be challenging, I can see.' Somehow she kept her voice steady. 'I doubt the usual domestic agencies would be of any use. Perhaps an advertisement in the newspapers?'

'What kind of hermit had you in mind, Father?' Lucas was apparently fully behind the scheme. 'As it is a Gothic chapel then a Druid would be unsuitable.'

'I envisage a reclusive scholar,' their father declared. 'Once a monk, then expelled from the monastery by King Henry, now living alone in the ruins with the books and manuscripts he has saved from the Dissolution.'

'You intend him to actually live there, Papa? That way of life might be too rigorous for a modern applicant to accept,' Caroline ventured.

'Of course I have considered that. The chapel exterior will disguise a one-roomed cottage, just as I built accommodation for the gamekeepers into the folly tower.'

'And his duties?' What did a hermit do anyway? Herm, perhaps. Somehow she managed not to give way to her feelings. It would be all too easy to collapse into hysterical laughter this evening.

'I will want him simply to be there when anyone passes by. He must keep the hermitage in good order and maintain the area around it. I have no objection to him carrying on his own work—studying, writing and so forth—if he is a genuine scholar.'

'Will we be returning to Knighton Park soon, Papa?' Headlong flight down the hallway to the Earl of Edenbridge's front door was not enough, it seemed. Headlong flight out of London was beginning to feel much safer. 'The Season is drawing to its end in a few weeks.'

It had been the familiar round of socialising, of eligible young men who flirted and danced and then sheered off as soon as they encountered her father. Her looks were passable, her breeding acceptable, her dowry reasonable but her parent was the kind of father-in-law that bachelors were warned about. If she had ever met anyone who had wanted her for herself, loved her, then that would not have mattered, she supposed. But that had never happened and she was well aware of the whispers that Lady Caroline Holm was perilously close to being on the shelf. *Such a pity,* the old cats gossiped, *such a charming girl. But...* And then she had seen Gabriel Stone.

'We will stay in London for June,' her father said, jolting her out of her reverie. 'That will give the builders time to finish the hermitage while Lucas and I select the ornamental details and find the hermit.'

No escape then. Unfortunately it was not Lord Edenbridge from whom she felt she needed to escape, it was her own absolutely irrational desire to see more of him. *Playing with fire*, Caroline thought. *He is dangerously attractive and he is not for me. The man is downright wicked. As well as beautiful in that wild gypsy manner.*

Her food was becoming cold. Caroline applied herself to it and told herself she was suffering from an attraction that was as ridiculous as any schoolgirl's *tendre* for the music master. Only that was usually a hopeless passion, quickly forgotten. This was something that was going to lead her into the man's bed and might, if she was not very careful, end in scandal.

'The post, my lord.' Hampshire proffered the salver with so much silent emphasis that Gabriel picked up the pile of letters immediately, intrigued to see what had interested the butler.

The letter on top, of course. Sealed with a plain wafer, posted in London and addressed in an elegant feminine hand. He lifted it to his nose. Unscented and good quality paper.

The note inside was to the point. *The package has been received. I am most obliged for your prompt attention to the matter.* There was not even an initial.

'My *prompt attention*, indeed.' Gabriel tapped the note on the table. Lady Caroline would have done better to have written begging him to reconsider their agreement. He was in half a mind to stop playing with her, tear up her IOU and send it back to her via her obliging pianoforte teacher. He would never act on it.

Would I?

As a gentleman he most certainly should not, but part of him admired her outrageous logic. It was certainly one sure way to hit back at her father's schemes to marry her off advantageously whatever her own inclinations. Not that losing her virginity was going to save her from marriage, not unless she was prepared to inform her hopeful suitors in advance of the ceremony.

Yes, he should tear up the note and forget her and she would spend her entire married life giving thanks for a narrow escape. On the other hand he was bored, the situation was novel and a little internal devil prompted him to see just how this game played out a little longer.

He opened the next letter in the pile, noticing that it was from his old friend Crispin de Feaux and that the wax was impressed, not with the Marquess of Avenmore's usual seal, but with the discreet abbreviated version. Cris was up to something.

Not only that, he discovered, but requiring Gabriel to get himself involved as well. 'Collect information about Lord Chelford's debts…obtain a sedan chair and bearers… send to Stibworthy, North Devon… *North Devon?'* What the blazes was Cris up to now?

The study bookshelves returned no answer to his questions. This was too intriguing to deal with by post. Gabriel tugged the bell pull. 'Hampshire, I am going into Devon by way of Bath. I will want my travelling coach.' He glanced at Cris's letter again and smiled. 'Tell Corbridge to pack for action rather than amusement, I think.'

By the time he got back from whatever was brewing on the wilder western shores of England he would have located his better nature. He would do the right thing by the innocent Lady Caroline immediately and he would not yield to the temptation to discover just what the delicate skin at the base of her throat tasted like. Strawberries, perhaps…

June was drawing towards July, complete with sunshine, roses in bloom, a flurry of fashionable parasols—and no indication from her father that he would be leaving for the country for at least another week. Caroline could only be grateful because she had just realised the great flaw in her scheme, the gaping black hole in the centre.

She had the deeds, so Anthony's future was assured, she had told herself. Then, when she was locking them away in the base of her jewellery box, she realised that in solving one problem she had created another—or two, if she counted the looming shadow of Lord Edenbridge and her promise to him.

Anthony's estate was safe, but estates had to be managed. Plans must be made, orders must be given, wages paid, staff supervised, income banked and invested. Somehow Springbourne had to function for five years until her brother reached his majority and could take control. Meanwhile, she had no resources, no experience and no legal standing in the matter. Anthony was a minor, so neither did he. And if either of them tried to employ a solicitor or a land agent to act on their own behalf the first thing the man would do was consult their father.

Lord Edenbridge. Papa thought the earl was about to take over Springbourne and doubtless he had already notified all concerned. If Lord Edenbridge took nominal control it would solve everything. Would it be a huge imposition? Perhaps she could offer him a percentage of the income, or might he be offended by that? She needed to ask his advice.

It was the day she realised that she must speak to him

that Lord Edenbridge disappeared from London. She looked for him in vain at balls and parties, she heard no gossip about him and, when she contrived to have the barouche drive along Mount Street, she saw the knocker was off his front door.

There was nothing for it, she would have to write to him. Caroline sat in the little room optimistically referred to as her boudoir, chewed the end of her pen and racked her brains for a tactful way of phrasing a request that a virtual stranger take on the supervision of an estate she had extracted from him in return for the dubious value of her own virtue.

The knock on the door was almost a relief.

'Yes, Thomas?'

'His lordship requests that you join him in his study, my lady.' The footman had doubtless translated a grunted command to *fetch my daughter* into a courteous message, so she smiled at him, even though he had thrown what little she had managed to compose into disorder.

As she went downstairs she wondered what Papa wanted. Perhaps he had decided to go back to Knighton Park, in which case life would become immeasurably more complicated, for not only would all her correspondence with Lord Edenbridge have to go via Miss Fanshawe, but then be posted on to her in the country.

'You sent for me, Papa?'

For once he was not buried in a pile of plans and estimates, sparing her only a glance. To be the focus of his attention was unnerving. 'Sit down, Caroline. I have good news for you.'

That was *definitely* unnerving. 'Yes, Papa?'

'I have received an offer for your hand in marriage from Edgar Parfit, Lord Woodruffe. What do you say to that?'

'Lord Woodruffe? But he's…he's…'

'Wealthy, a good neighbour, in excellent health.'

'Forty. Fat. He thinks of nothing but hunting. His first wife died only a year after they were married.'

'It is hardly his fault the foolish chit fell off her horse.'

'Miranda was frightened of horses and she hated hunting. He forced her to ride, to follow the hounds. He is a bully.' *And he frightens me.* She managed not to say the words, for she had no justification for them, simply instinct.

'He is a well set-up, mature man who expects loyalty from his wife.'

'He can expect it of someone else, then.' Caroline found she was on her feet. 'I will not marry him.'

'You do not tell me what you will and will not do, my girl! Your duty is to accept this most advantageous offer that has been made to you.' Her father's face was already darkening with building rage at her defiance.

The match was far worse than she had been dreading and advantageous only in what Lord Woodruffe would be offering in the way of land to increase the Knighton estate. But she could do nothing until she had spoken to Lord Edenbridge, secured Springbourne for Anthony.

If Mama was still alive she would not let you do this. The words were almost out before she could control them. Mention of his late wife always triggered her father's worst rages. 'Yes, Papa.' She forced herself to meekness. 'But I hardly know Lord Woodruffe.'

'That didn't stop you spouting nonsensical opinions a minute ago,' he grunted. 'There's plenty of time to get to know him, no need to rush things. I'm too busy at the moment to worry about details like weddings and settlements.'

Reprieve…

'Next month or so is soon enough. We'll go down to

Knighton in a week or two, Woodruffe can do his courting, wedding in September.'

September? She had been hoping for six months, not
two. The thought of the baron's *courtship* made her feel
queasy. 'Yes, Papa.' It sounded weak, defeatist, but it
calmed him. He was unused to defiance from her, she realised. Perhaps there had never been anything to make a
stand about. Rebelling over being ignored and underval-
ued or complaining about her marriage prospects would
have been pointless. But this was different and she had
just won a little time to think.

First she had to locate Lord Edenbridge and settle Anthony's estate safely, then, somehow, she had to find a way
to escape from this marriage. Her brave words about losing her virginity and giving her husband a shock on their
wedding night were wishful thinking, she realised now.
Edgar Parfit's response to finding that his bride was not
what he expected was likely to be extreme: she had no illusions about the man, only fears that seemed worse because of their very vagueness.

'Will Lord Woodruffe be at Lady Ancaster's supper
dance this evening, Papa?' She infused as much interest
into her voice as possible.

'Doubt it.' He did not glance up from his papers. 'He's
still in the country as far as I know.'

A small mercy, she thought as she let herself out of the
study. If only Lord Edenbridge was at the dance, too, then
she had some hope of settling Anthony's future and with
that done, and her promise to Mama fulfilled, then perhaps she could find some way out of the mire for herself.

'You look very well, Caroline.' Aunt Gertrude, the
Dowager Countess of Whitely, was normally sparing in
her praise, but tonight, perhaps prompted by the news that

Caroline was to receive an eligible offer, she was positively gracious.

'Thank you, I was rather pleased with this gown, I must
confess.' It was an amber silk with an overskirt of a paler
yellow and she was wearing it with brown kid slippers and
her mother's set of amber jewellery.

'The neckline, however, is verging on the unacceptable.'
Her chaperon leaned forward in the carriage, the better to
glare at Caroline's bosom.

'I believe it is well within the current mode, Aunt.'

'Humph. And you are somewhat pale.'

It was a miracle that she was not white as a sheet with
tension, Caroline thought as she set her lips in a social
smile and prepared to follow her aunt out of the carriage
and into the Ancasters' Berkeley Square house. At least
the necessity to act in a certain way prevented her from
simply sitting down and having a fit of the vapours. She'd
had to dress, have her hair styled, talk to her maid, choose
her jewels, pay attention to Aunt Gertrude and now enter
the Ancasters' ballroom looking as though she had nothing on her mind except pleasure.

'Good evening, Lady Farnsworth... Yes, Lord Hitch-
combe, the floral decorations are charming... No, Aunt,
I will be certain not to accept more than one dance from
Mr Pitkin... Thank you, Mr Walsh, a glass of champagne
would be delightful.' She smiled and prattled on, just like
every other young lady in the crowded, hot room, while all
the time she expected to open her mouth and find herself
announcing, 'I have offered my virginity to Lord Edenbridge. I am deceiving my father. I am plotting to...' *To
what? Ruin myself, most likely.*

And there, strolling along on the other side of the room
as the company began to take their places for the first
dance of the evening, was a tall, black-haired figure. *Eden-*

bridge. He turned and went through a set of double doors that Caroline knew led to several sitting-out rooms and the ladies' retiring room.

She murmured in her aunt's ear.

'Oh, for goodness sake, Caroline! Why on earth didn't you visit the closet before we came out?' Lady Whitely demanded in a penetrating whisper. 'The first set is forming and you do not have a partner yet.'

'I really must,' Caroline whispered back. 'The rhubarb posset…' She escaped before her aunt could reply. With any luck she would attribute her niece's haste to natural urgency, not the desire to go chasing after wicked bachelors.

She was moving so fast that she almost cannoned into Lord Edenbridge around the first corner of the corridor. He was standing with one evening shoe in his hand, prodding at the inside with a long finger and frowning.

'Lord Edenbridge, I must speak with you. Where have you been? I have been looking for you for days…'

'And good evening to you, Lady Caroline.' He inclined his head in an ironical half-bow, shook the shoe and held up a small tack between finger and thumb. 'I will have words with Hoby about this.'

'Never mind your bootmaker, my lord, this is urgent.' At any moment someone could come along the passageway and find them compromisingly tête-à-tête.

He winced. 'You utter blasphemy.' But he replaced his shoe and opened the door opposite them. 'As I recall… Yes, excellent, and a key in the door. How accommodating of dear Hermione.'

He meant, she supposed, that this might be a refuge for lovers. There was certainly a *chaise longue*. Caroline pushed away speculation about how Lord Edenbridge knew this room was here and waited while he turned the key.

'Now, Lady Caroline, how may I help you? I have been

down in Devon,' he added. For all his light tone and the smile, she detected a wariness about him. From her urgency he must think she was pursuing him, which was embarrassing, to put it mildly.

She sat down squarely in the middle of the *chaise longue*, spread her skirts out on either side in a way that made it quite clear she was not expecting him to join her and almost smiled at the rueful twist of his lips. 'Perhaps you have misjudged the situation, my lord?'

'Perhaps I have.' He lounged across and propped a shoulder against the mantel-shelf looking for all the world like a Romany who had, for reasons of his own, donned an evening suit and strolled into a *ton* ball. She half-expected to see a glint of gold in his earlobes. His eyes, she realised, were brown. 'I do wish you would stop addressing me so formally. Call me Gabriel, Caroline.'

'And risk letting it slip out should we meet in company?' *Gabriel.* She liked the sound of the name and she liked her own name on his lips even better. Perhaps not such a gypsy after all, she thought, watching him from beneath her lashes. His hair had recently been cut, although it was still on the long side, he had shaved to perfection and it was only the carelessness with which he wore his expensive clothes and the feline ease with which he lounged that spoiled the picture of the fashionable aristocrat.

'Your chaperon would run me through with a hatpin before I got within conversational range of you, Caroline, so I think we are safe. Now, having established that you do not desire me to deflower you in a retiring room at HermioneAncaster's dance, which I agree would be unwise, however informal she insists the occasion is—'

'Oh, do not make me laugh! Not that there is anything to laugh about. I must be hysterical.'

'Just very anxious, I think. Ask me what it is you want

to know.' He sounded not bored, precisely, but certainly reassuringly unexcited by being dragged off for an intimate chat. The coolness was bracing. Then she met his gaze and saw heat and a raw masculine awareness of her as a woman. No, he wasn't cool at all, simply controlled and that very control was almost as arousing as the heat.

She could be controlled, too. She must be or he would read the utterly immodest carnal desire that was making it so hard to breathe. *Inhale.* 'How burdened are you with the management of your own estates, Lord Edenbridge?'

He straightened up, hooked an upright chair away from the wall and sat down. 'I am not easily surprised, Caroline, but I must admit that our meetings are presenting me with one novel situation after another. Would you care to explain why you wish to discuss estate management?'

'I have realised that securing the deeds to Springbourne for Anthony is useless unless there is some way we can run the estate. I cannot do it. As an unmarried woman I will never be able to open a bank account without my father's permission and Anthony is under age.'

'That is so. I have to admit, this had not occurred to me when I gave you the deeds back.'

'If I hand them back to you, will you manage the estate for Anthony until he is twenty-one?'

The silence seemed to go on for a very long time. Then Lord Edenbridge said, 'No.'

Chapter Three

'Naturally we could not allow you to be out of pocket, Lord Edenbridge. Perhaps your man of business could find a suitable manager and the estate would meet all the costs. It is perfectly solvent, I believe.' Caroline kept her tone as brisk and efficient as she could in the face of his frowning refusal.

'Money is not the point, Caroline. It is irrelevant.'

It is? How nice that would be, for money to be irrelevant.

'I employ perfectly competent people to run my own estates and my business matters. My own involvement will become even less as soon as my brother Louis leaves university. I can certainly add your brother's property to the portfolio and extricate it again when he reaches his majority, but you are asking me to assume a position of trust, to be responsible for another man's estate and income. That is a considerable responsibility. Who is going to audit the revenues and financial transactions?'

'Why, no one. I trust you. You are a gentleman.'

He ran both hands through his hair, turning it into something disordered and wild, then leaned forward to emphasise the words that emerged through what sounded like clenched teeth. 'Then you are an idiot, Caroline, and I had thought you innocent and trusting, but not empty-headed. You do not know me. I gamble and that in itself should raise warning flags. What if I suffer a big loss and see an easy way to *borrow* some funds?'

'I am not completely air-headed, Gabriel,' she retorted. The name was out before she realised what she was saying. He lifted his head, looked at her and the tight jaw relaxed as he smiled. Nettled by that little sign of male smugness, she pressed on firmly. 'I am a good judge of character. I told you I have heard the talk about you and no one accuses you of deceit or dishonourable behaviour, even the people who have no cause to love you. I was reckless going to your house the other day, proposing what I did. You could have taken advantage of me then and you did not.'

'You should not confuse financial probity with an unwillingness to pounce on young ladies when I am half-asleep and three-parts drunk.' His smile deepened, suggested that now he was not tired or drunk he might reconsider pouncing.

'Were you really? Goodness, I would never have guessed.'

'You thought I look like that stone-cold sober and after a good night's sleep, a bath and a shave? I am wounded, Caroline.'

'No, you are not, you are teasing me. And, yes, I do understand that I am asking you to shoulder a significant responsibility, even if it makes little actual work for you personally and involves no financial loss. How can I recompense you?'

The amusement faded out of the deep-brown eyes and they became harder than she could ever have imagined. 'I already hold one too many of your IOUs, Caroline. I will undertake this for you because you asked and because you are doing it for your brother, not because you have got yourself into this ridiculous mess.'

The smile edged back, curving the corners of his mouth, but not warming his eyes as he moved to stand beside the *chaise.* 'I have spent my youth and my adult life being disgraceful. A gambler, a hedonist. Being responsible is a bore. And yet now I find myself having to be the sensible one. This summer I have been attempting to talk a close friend out of a totally unsuitable marriage and now I am resisting the urge to take you up on your reckless offer. I do not know what is coming over me. Old age, possibly.'

Old age? Nonsense. Surely he cannot be above twenty-eight or nine? 'You still have my promise.' Somehow their fingers met, brushed, then hers curled into his. Not quite a hand-clasp, not quite a caress. She looked up and met Gabriel's unreadable gaze as his fingers tightened. 'And Papa tells me he has given Lord Woodruffe permission to court me.'

'Edgar Parfit?' Her hand was her own again and Gabriel was three angry strides away. 'That per— Is your father insane?'

She had often wondered what would be the verdict on her father's behaviour if he had been simply plain Mr Henry Holm, a shoemaker, perhaps. What in an earl was eccentricity would, surely, be treated rather differently in other circumstances. The obsessions, the mood swings, the recklessness and the utter disregard for other people were not normal, she knew. But to say the words was a step too far.

'No one has ever suggested my father is not legally competent,' she said carefully. 'Many in society would say Lord Woodruffe is an eligible match...'

'Well, quite obviously you cannot marry him. Besides his unpleasant preferences, he is probably diseased—'

What does he mean, diseased? Horrible suspicions presented themselves and she pushed them away, knowing they would come back to haunt her dreams. The atmosphere of closeness, of something trembling on the edge of desire, vanished in the cold chill of reality.

'What do you mean, *preferences*?'

He shook his head.

'Tell me! Preserving my innocence until I am actually married to the man is not going to help.'

'Some men enjoy pain as part of sex. Some want to receive it, be beaten.' His face tightened as though at some unpleasant memory. 'Others enjoy inflicting it. Woodruffe has a reputation for the latter.'

'Oh.' She felt sick as she recalled Miranda, Woodruffe's first wife. The bruises because she was *so careless*. The days when she did not leave her room because her health was *fragile*. Bullying her into riding despite her fear of horses had been the least of it.

But what could she do? 'Lord Edenbridge, listen to me. Your friend who is contemplating an unsuitable marriage is, I assume, male. He can choose. He is independent, free. I cannot choose and I am not free. Not legally, not financially and not emotionally. I have a family and I promised Mama I would somehow look after them.' *My brothers at least. Heavens knows if anything can be done for Papa.* She found she was on her feet. 'I will send back the deeds and I am truly grateful for your help. Please will you open the door now?'

'Caroline, this is the year 1820. Your father cannot force you to the altar.' Gabriel stood, unlocked the door, but kept his hand on the handle.

'Not physically, no,' she agreed, even as she wondered what bullying and bread and water might reduce her to if she defied Papa. Somehow she was going to have to per-

suade him because the alternatives, marriage to Woodruffe or fleeing her home and leaving Anthony, were too
horrible to contemplate.

She reached the door handle and he caught her fingers
in his, pulled her close until her skirts brushed his legs and
she could smell him—clean, warm man, starched linen,
brandy, a careless splash of some citrus scent, that hint of
musk again.

'Infuriating, stubborn woman. I do not know whether
to shake you or kiss you,' he said, his tone suggesting that
neither was very desirable.

'Kiss me then, for courage,' she said, seized with recklessness and something that must be desire: a hot, shaky
feeling, a low, intimate ache, a light-headed urge to toss
common sense out of the window. No other attractive man
was ever going to kiss her, it seemed. She must seize the
opportunity while she had it.

Gabriel lifted one hand, cupped her jaw, stroked his
thumb across her lips and the breath was sucked out of her
lungs. 'Have you ever been kissed before?'

She shook her head and he bent to touch his lips to hers,
caught her around the waist with his free hand and pulled
her, unresisting, against him. His mouth was warm, mo-
bile, firm. He pressed a little, shifted position, his hand
came up from her cheek to cradle her head and he made
a sound of satisfaction when he had her as he wanted.
Then she felt his tongue and the heat of his open mouth
and opened her own in response as he slid in, exploring
and stroking.

It was incredible and strange. It should be disgusting
and wet, but she found the taste of him exciting, the heat
inflammatory. She sensed his restraint, that he was holding back, toying gently with her, and she stepped forward

until their bodies were tight together, wanting more of this strange new intimacy.

His body was hard against her curves and there was the urge to rub against him, as a cat might burrow into a caress. But he was still and perhaps he would not like it if she did that…

Far too soon Gabriel ended the kiss, took his hands from her body, stepped back. 'Enough. Enough for your safety and more than enough for my comfort,' he added mysteriously, as he pulled open the door and looked out. 'Quickly, while there is no one about. Turn down Wood-ruffe, Caroline. Send me those deeds, then stay away from me.' He almost pushed her out into the corridor. 'Now go while I can still listen to what passes as my conscience.'

Gabriel had kissed her and now he did not want her. *Of course not, no doubt I was clumsy in my inexperience.* So what was that caress for if he did not desire her? There was something that had driven him to kiss her, something that had made that relaxed body tense. *I want him, perhaps he could come to want me? Madness.*

'Well, if you do not want me I shall not burden you any longer, Lord Edenbridge.' She made to sweep past him, annoyed that he could make her feel so much and yet obviously feel nothing himself.

There was a flurry of skirts, the muffled sound of a collision and a feminine voice said, 'I do beg your pardon, sir.'

Gabriel half-turned to confront the speaker and Caroline caught a glimpse of a tall young lady dressed in an exquisite sea-foam-green gown.

'Oh. Lord Edenbridge.' The stranger did not seem over-joyed to see him and he did not even respond to her.

Caroline stepped away, her hand to her mouth, not certain whether she was stifling a sob or trying to hide her face.

'Come back!'

She stopped, looked back.

'Don't be a fool,' Gabriel said. 'You do not have to marry him and you do not have to... Damn it, I've burned the thing.'

He had only been teasing her then, demanding that IOU that day at his home. She had gone through a maelstrom of emotions, through shame and fear and excitement and triumph that she had somehow rescued Springbourne for Anthony in return for that pledge, and all the time Eden-bridge had never intended to take her up on it.

'A promise is a promise,' she said, chin up. 'But if you do not want me—' She shrugged, turned and walked away, gathering the rags of her dignity around her.

Gabriel swore silently, then turned to confront the other female bedevilling his life, the widowed Mrs Tamsyn Perowne, who was tying his friend Cris de Feaux, Marquess of Avenmore, in knots.

'What in Hades are you doing here?' he demanded 'Does Cris know?'

'Certainly not. I do not need Lord Avenmore's permission to visit a relative.' The wretched female looked down her sun-browned nose at him.

'Come with me.' He took her arm and swept her back into the main reception room. There, thank goodness, were Alex, Viscount Weybourn, and his wife, Tess. They could help him deal with Mrs Perowne.

Goodness knew who or what was going to help him with Lady Caroline because that clumsy kiss had made him realise that he could not cynically despoil an innocent, nor was it fair to tease her. And yet she had somehow got under his skin. *Damn it, she is not my responsibility.* Knighton could never force her to marry Woodruffe if she refused. *Could he?*

* * *

The deeds came back to him three days later with a brief, rather hurried-looking note.

I am about to leave for the country. I doubt very much if I will be able to receive or send any correspondence from there as I have grievously annoyed my father, but I know I can rely on you to look after my brother's interests in the estate.

Thank you, you cannot know how much it means to me to have Anthony's future safeguarded.

So Caroline had refused Lord Woodruffe. That could be the only explanation for her *'grievously'* annoying Knighton. *Good for you, my girl,* Gabriel thought. He pulled paper and pen towards him and began to draft instructions for his man of business and solicitor to set in motion all the things that must be done to manage the estate and preserve the income for the young man.

None of it was very taxing, it merely required logical thought and meticulous attention to detail. His solicitor might well advise setting up a trust to safeguard both parties, but that was straightforward enough. Yet there was something niggling at the back of his mind, some sense that everything was not as it should be. Whatever it was, it was more than the memory of that innocent first kiss he had claimed, which was now wreaking havoc with his sleep. He reached for the brandy.

He had still been brooding when he fell asleep that night and he woke with a crashing headache and a feeling of unease. Corbridge, his much-tried valet, came in on silent feet and left a glass with something sinister and brown beside the bed, then wisely left without speaking.

Gabriel hauled himself up in bed, swigged back the potion without letting himself smell it, fought with his stomach for a moment, then lay back with a groan. His life was changing. Two of his closest friends were married now, Cris soon would be. Where there had been four, now there would be seven. He liked Tess and Kate. He would probably like Tamsyn when he got to know her. But the change to that close foursome only made his dissatisfaction with life worse.

He had been aware of being unsettled for months. He was bored with his life, no longer content with an existence in which winning was all that counted. Jaded, that was the word. He had a title, lands, money far beyond his needs or wants. What was he doing it for? Damn it, he had toyed with the idea of ruining a respectable young lady just for the novelty. He didn't much like the man who could do that. Perhaps it was time to change. But if he didn't spend his time gambling, socialising, drinking, what was the point to his life?

His three friends had been closer than his family, closer than he had ever dared allow his brothers to be. Cris, Alex and Grant had come into his life when he had been at his most desperate and vulnerable, at a time when they all needed the help that only others who had been wounded could understand. They knew his secrets, all but one of them—he could not burden them with the lies he had told the day his father died. That burden was his to carry, ever since he had made a promise to his mother, a woman so desperately unhappy she had taken her own life.

If he loved anyone, it was his friends and he knew they returned the sentiment, even if they would have died rather than admit it. From the hell that had been his childhood he had met them and learned that friendship gave what family never could, an equal give and take.

'Good morning, my lord.' Corbridge came in with hot water. Obviously he judged Gabriel to be back amongst the living,

'Is it?' Gabriel got out of bed and strode, naked, into the dressing room. 'What's the point of it all, Corbridge? Life, I mean, because I'm beginning to wonder.'

'My lord...is anything amiss?'

Gabriel was aware of the valet laying one hand protectively over the razors and, despite himself, grinned. 'It is all right, I'm not about to cut my throat, blow my brains out or otherwise put a period to my existence. I am simply wondering what I am doing with my life.'

'My lord, you are an *earl*,' Corbridge said repressively.

'That is a title, not a job description.' Although perhaps it was.

Manage the estates, look after the dependents, take my seat in the House, marry well, have heirs, teach the next generation to do it all over again... Focus on the title and not myself. Give up taking lovers? Step back and pray I can manage not to make a disaster of heading a family? But who would listen to my *prayers?*

He grimaced at his reflection and reached for the soap and sponge. He did everything he needed to do to keep the wheels of the earldom turning, but he did it at a mental distance that felt as though he had preserved it in ice. When the frost melted would he find something fresh and new to engage with or find only the rotted carcase of the past?

A disgusting image. He shook off the ghoulish thought with an effort. 'I'm getting old, Corbridge.' Is that why it was so hard to accept how his life was changing?

'My lord, you are not even in your prime yet, if I may be so bold.' The valet began to work up a lather with the shaving soap.

Gabriel grunted and scrubbed his toothbrush into the

powder. What he needed was a purpose and he supposed the obvious one was his earldom and, heaven help him, his brothers, although they would probably think he'd got a brain fever if he suddenly turned up showing a keen interest in their lives and welfare. It would certainly unnerve them thoroughly.

'I'm at home until this afternoon, then I'll be riding. I may as well put on buckskins and boots now.' There was business to finish, then he'd blow away the cobwebs with a good gallop and try to work out how to finally come to grips with his inheritance, all of it, on his own terms. His identity had been that of the care-for-nothing rakehell for so long that he wasn't certain he knew who the man underneath that mask was.

It was not until the evening that he sat down and began to sort through the jottings he had made on young Mr Holm's inheritance. He picked up Caroline's message again, feeling the same prickle of unease as he had experienced the day before. Something was not right with it. He rummaged in the papers until he found her first note and laid them side by side. Same paper, same ink, but while the first was neat and elegantly written, the writing in the second was uneven, straggling, untidy. It looked as though it had been produced in haste and by someone who was either not themselves or who found it difficult to hold the pen. One corner of the page was distorted and he picked it up to study it more closely. A water splash. Or one fallen tear…

I have grievously annoyed my father. Father, not Papa as she had always referred to him before. Something was wrong, very wrong. He had encouraged her to defy Knighton over the marriage and now she was exiled to the country, perhaps mistreated in some way, until she gave in. In his mind he heard the crack of the riding whip, felt the shock of the pain. He had withstood it, pride and sheer bloody-mindedness had seen to that. But a woman...

Surely Knighton wouldn't beat his daughter? Yet he wanted her to marry Woodruffe. Surely he realised what the man was? Or perhaps he really was so obsessional that he could ignore the man's reputation?

Just because his own father had been utterly ruthless in imposing his will did not mean that Caroline's father was. Gabriel pushed away the old nightmares, studied the slip of paper for a long moment, then folded it and put it in his breast pocket. He was imagining things were worse than they were, surely. Even so, he could not rest easy. The paperwork for her brother's estate was soon completed and he bundled it up to go to his lawyer, then got to his feet. He had a commitment to help Cris and that might take a day or so, but then he was going to find Lady Caroline Holm and undo whatever damage he had caused.

He imagined his friends' expressions if they knew he was contemplating involving himself in some chit's family dramas. But Caroline was not *some chit*, she was intelligent, courageous and determined, and he felt guilty about the way he had teased her, he realised. That was novel enough to provoke him into action. What that action might be he had no idea, but at least he was not feeling jaded any longer.

Chapter Four

Hertfordshire—August 1st

August was usually a month Caroline enjoyed, especially if she was in the country. Now Knighton Park was a hot, stuffy prison and the sunlit gardens and park outside were a bright, tantalising reminder of just how trapped she was.

It was not my fault, she told herself for perhaps the hundredth time. It was not her lack of duty, not her wilfulness, not her foolish whims—all the faults her father had thrown at her. *It is his. His tyranny, his temper. His lack of love.*

It had started mildly enough. Her father announced that they were moving to Knighton Park and, recklessly, she had chosen to make a stand, to announce that she would not marry Woodruffe, or any of the middle-aged suitors he had considered for her.

The bruises on her right cheek had finally vanished. She studied her reflection in the mirror and clenched her teeth. There was some soreness and a molar was still rather loose, but she thought if she was careful it would grow firm again. The marks on her arms had almost faded, too. She could write long letters to Anthony without discomfort. His future, at least, was safe now.

The image of her face faded and the scene she kept trying to forget swam up in its place.

'You will do as you are told, you stupid girl!'

'I am not stupid. I am not a girl. I am of age and I will not be bartered to some man for whom I have nothing but contempt for the sake of your obsessions.' Caroline had no idea what kept her voice so steady, what kept her standing there as his face darkened with rage.

Her father was a believer in corporal punishment for his children, although Lucas, the favoured elder son, always seemed to escape with only the lightest of canings. As a girl, her governess had been instructed to strike her once or twice on the palm with a ruler for laziness or inattention, or whenever her father deemed her deserving of punishment, which was often. But she had never been hit by him.

Her father had grabbed her arm, held her as she'd pulled back against his grip, her righteous defiance turned in a second to stomach-churning nausea.

'You will obey me.' He'd jerked again as she fought against the pain in her arm. It felt as though the bones were grinding together.

'No,' she'd managed. 'Woodruffe is—' But she didn't have the words for what Gabriel had told her. And then her father had hit her across the face, backhanded, knocking her to the ground to land in a painful sprawl against a wooden chair. She had no clear memory of being taken upstairs, only of coming to herself to find her maid bathing her face. There was a bandage on her arm.

Now, with the bruises gone, she had permission to leave her rooms, go downstairs, allow herself to be seen, provided she maintained the fiction of a virulent sore throat that had laid her up for almost two weeks. She sat down in the window seat and searched for some courage. There were tales of how prisoners were afraid to leave their cells and the security of a familiar confined space and now she could understand how they felt. But she was desperate to get out, away from the tedium and anxiety, away from the circling thoughts and desires for Gabriel Stone.

She should be ashamed of herself for having carnal thoughts about a man, because that was what they were. She couldn't deceive herself that these were romantic daydreams about love and marriage and family. This man was never going to be domesticated and when she imagined herself with him what she saw was a tangle of naked limbs, what she felt was the heat of his body and the pressure of his lips. Beyond that she was too inexperienced to imagine detail. All she knew was that this was shocking, sinful and impossible, because when she had offered herself to him on a plate even this hardened rake had not wanted her.

She had to stop thinking about him. *I am the only person I can rely on, no one is going to help me if I do not help myself.* And she could achieve nothing shut up inside, Caroline knew that. Her old world of certainties and duty and acceptance of the limitations of a lady's powers lay in ruins. She would not submit to marrying Woodruffe and that meant she must act.

She had even thought through a strategy over the past few days: go downstairs and assess Pa… *Father's* temper and intentions. If he had no intention of yielding, then gather money, jewels, information and escape. Somehow. There would be no help from Lucas, for although he had been shocked by their father's violent outburst, he still shared his opinion that Caroline should marry as he directed.

But Anthony was a constant worry. What if he did something to arouse such violence in his father? And if she left home it was going to be horribly difficult to meet with him. *One thing at a time*, she told herself. *If I am mar-*

ried to that man I would be equally helpless to look after Anthony. This way I can write, I could see him when he is at school perhaps.

She dressed with care and went downstairs. Her father and Lucas were at breakfast, the table littered with news sheets and the scattered pages of opened letters. Lucas stood up as she came in, her father merely grunted and went back to his reading.

Caroline found a soft roll and some scrambled eggs and took her place at the table and began to eat, favouring the left side of her jaw. Her father shot her a penetrating look, nodded, presumably with approval at her unbruised appearance, and turned to Lucas.

'The hermit has had his first night in the folly now. I'll not disturb him for a few days, let him settle in.'

She had not intended joining in the conversation, but this was startling enough to make her forget that. 'You have found a hermit, Father?'

He did not appear to notice that she had stopped calling him *Papa*. Somehow the affectionate diminutive was impossible to use for a man who had raised his hand to her.

'I put it about at my clubs that I was looking for one and he turned up, don't know how he heard about it, although the fellow is a gentleman of sorts. He seems ideal. Educated fellow, for all that he looks as though he hasn't had a haircut or a shave for six months. Says he's a poet or some such nonsense. Wants to write in peace and quiet. Told him he can do what he pleases as long as he wears the costume and looks the part. I'll not send warning that we'll be about when we do go, so I'll catch him unawares, see how he performs.'

'Are you going to the Home Farm this morning, Father?' Lucas looked up from his correspondence.

'Yes.' The earl lifted a bundle of papers. 'These are the

plans for the new Model Farm that Hardwick sent over from Wimpole Hall in Cambridgeshire. Their new buildings are excellent, we'll see how they'd do for our site.'

They left together soon afterwards. Caroline looked out across the sweep of the South Lawn, over the invisible line of the ha-ha to the shoulder of Trinity Hill. Just visible above it was the tower of an apparently ancient chapel which had, in reality, only just been completed.

She finished her cup of tea and pushed back her chair without waiting for the footman to help her. She needed exercise and fresh air and the *faux* hermitage was one place where her father was not this morning. An unkempt poetry-writing hermit might not tempt her to linger long, but at least he would give her walk a destination.

The slope of Trinity Hill was gentle, but for someone who had been shut up inside with no exercise for days it was enough to bring a glow of perspiration to her face and an ache to her legs. Caroline reached the point where she could look down on the lake and on the hermitage, apparently deserted in its shady grove of trees.

She was not at all certain she wanted to converse with a professional hermit, for he must be a strange creature, but curiosity drew her down the slope to the clearing. The door to the chapel stood open and in front, on the other side of the path, a rough trestle table had been created by balancing a slab of wood on two tree stumps. A log was set in front of it as a seat and the table was laid with a pitcher, a pewter plate and a horn beaker, the remains of the hermit's breakfast, she supposed. As she watched, a robin flew down and pecked hopefully around in pursuit of crumbs.

Treading with care, Caroline approached the chapel and glanced at the open door. No movement within, but she did not feel she had the right to pry by entering.

Then the sound of a twig snapping brought her round to face the path up from the little lake, the robin flew away in whir of wings and a tall robed figure walked into the clearing.

The man stopped when he saw her and stared, just as she was doing, she supposed. What did one say to a recluse, even an ornamental one? He was certainly not her idea of a hermit, which was a white-bearded, stooped figure supported by a staff. This man was big, with a mass of thick black curling hair that fell across his brow and shadowed his eyes and a beard that, although not long, covered his lower face completely. It made him look older than he probably was, for he moved like a young, fit man and there was no grey showing in the black hair that brushed the folded-back hood of his brown robe.

His hair was wet, catching the sunlight that filtered through the tree canopy, and droplets of water hung in his beard like improbable diamonds. He must have been bathing in the lake, she realised. In one hand he held a battered leather satchel, perhaps containing soap and a towel.

'Good morning,' Caroline ventured, wondering if a clean hermit was a contradiction in terms.

He inclined his head, but said nothing. Nor did he move any closer.

'Has my father forbidden you to speak? I am Lady Caroline Holm. I hope the kitchen sent you food or do you go down to collect it yourself? You must let us know if there is anything you need.'

His silence was unnerving, but not as unsettling as the feeling of familiarity that was growing as they stood there separated by ten feet of leaf litter and sparse turf. Then, maddeningly, he inclined his head again.

'Which of my questions is that an answer to?' she demanded.

The thicket of beard moved as though he was smiling, but with his eyes in shadow she could not be certain. Of course, if he had been forbidden to speak then it had been quite illogical of her to follow on with more questions.

'Are you required to keep silent?'

The man cleared his throat. 'No, my lady.' He spoke quietly, but the deep voice was quite clear in the still, warm air. It had an attractive lilt to it. 'I have food, I thank you.'

'You are not English, are you? Your accent is unfamiliar.'

'It is a Welsh accent, my lady.'

'Oh.' Then that sense of knowing him was completely illusory. How strange. It must be her need for someone to talk to, to confide in. To plan with, if she could trust them. But all her friends were in London, or away at country houses or at the seaside and she had hardly had a conversation for weeks, except with her maid. 'You are comfortable here?'

In response the hermit gestured to the open door of the chapel. He did not move and when she took a step towards the building he sat down at his makeshift table as though to reassure her that it was safe to enter, that he would not follow.

Inside all pretence of a religious building disappeared. There was a single whitewashed room with a bed made up with coarse sheets, blankets and a worn patchwork quilt. A table and chair stood in the middle of the space and a chipped stone sink was propped up on empty crates that served as makeshift shelves. A wide fireplace with logs stacked beside it was set into what must be the base of the tower, which would disguise the chimney, and a rag rug on the stone floor provided the only touch of decoration or comfort.

Bleak, but weather-tight and warm enough during the

summer. She only hoped her father did not expect the man to stay here in all seasons. There was a small pile of books on the table, some paper and an inkwell and pen. Tools for a poet, she supposed, resisting the temptation to see what he was reading—or writing.

When she left the folly he stood up again and she sensed he was smiling. 'It seems rather comfortless,' she observed. 'Are you certain there is nothing that you need?'

'I am a hermit, my lady. I am supposed to live the simple life.'

'You are *acting* the hermit,' she corrected. 'There is no need for you to endure such a Spartan existence in reality.'

'His lordship requires authenticity and he employs me.' He shrugged. 'When he brings visitors to view the scene nothing must jar.'

He was certainly conscientious. Caroline knew she would have been tempted to smuggle in some comforts if she was in his place. 'What is your name?'

There was a long pause and she wondered if she had disconcerted him. Then he said, 'Petrus.'

'That means Peter, doesn't it? Peter the Hermit. Why does that sound familiar?' Caroline wrestled with the elusive memory. 'Of course—Peter the Hermit, the First Crusade.'

Now she was certain he was taken aback. *Bother that impenetrable beard.* 'You are well read, my lady. It is simply coincidence, not a deliberate choice.'

'I will leave you in peace, Petrus, you will want to get dry...' Caroline could feel herself blushing. She most certainly could not discuss a strange man's washing arrangements. To add to her discomfort her imagination conjured up the vision of that tall, broad-shouldered figure naked in the lake, the water streaming off his chest as he stood up, the thick black hair tossed back from his face.

'Oh!' Before she was aware of moving, of turning to leave before her treacherous mind conjured up any more shocking images, her foot caught in something. She had a split second to realise it was a tree root as she went flying to land in a sprawling, inelegant heap. 'Ouch!'

'What hurts?' Petrus knelt beside her, then caught her by the shoulders as she tried to lever herself up.

'My left wrist.' Caroline managed to sit. 'The leaf mould is soft, but I put out my hand and I… I hurt it a while ago. No, it is all right—'

His fingers were circling her wrist, gentle and firm and all-enveloping. With the other hand he pushed back her sleeve to expose her forearm. There was silence as she went still in his grasp, watching the bent head as he studied the pattern of fading bruises that still encircled her arm. The sprain where her father had jerked her towards him, held her as she fell, was still a little sore.

'Who did that?' Petrus still did not look up and the lilting voice was steady, but she could feel the shock and the anger coursing through him even though she could not see his face.

'It was an accident. I fell and my…someone caught my arm to steady me.'

'No, they did not.' He rebutted her lie quite calmly. 'These are not the marks of someone catching you, but of someone holding you forcibly, as though they intended to hurt you. Who was it? Your brother or your father?'

'Lucas would never—I mean no one wants to hurt me.'

'So it was your father.' He stood and held out his hand so she could take it with her uninjured right.

There did not seem to be any point in arguing with him. Caroline allowed him to pull her to her feet. 'It is none of your business,' she said as she found herself standing with her nose virtually pressed against the rough cloth of his robe.

'And I am merely an employee,' the hermit observed. 'Of course, a husband is permitted by law to beat his wife with a rod no thicker than his thumb and a father may chastise his children. But you are not a child.' His voice became harder, angry.

'No. I am not.' *We are both adults.*

The fingers wrapped around hers were strong and still slightly cool from the lake water. Standing so close, she could smell damp wool from his robe and the sharp tannin scent of crushed bracken and leaf mould and something indefinable that must be the scent of his skin. A little shiver of recognition, as elusive as a breath of wind, stirred her and he let go of her hand and stepped back.

'I am sorry, my lady. It is not my business, as you say. But is there no one to take your side, for you to confide in? Who looks after you?'

'Why, no one! I am twenty-three, Petrus the Hermit, and I have people to look after, not the other way around. Or do you think all women are feeble little things who need keeping in cotton wool?'

'No, I do not. Nor do I think they are fair game for any man who feels he has a right to bully and abuse those who cannot fight back, for whatever reason.' He walked away from her towards the chapel, then stopped and half-turned in the doorway. 'You should go, my lady. You should not be here alone with me.'

The sense of recognition was almost *déjà vu* now. Something about the way he stood there, one hand on the door, the way the broad shoulders filled the frame, the utterly relaxed pose that hinted at an ability to move instantly if the need arose… Caroline gave herself a brisk mental shake. She had never met a bearded Welshman before, her mind was playing tricks on her. The only tall, black-haired, broad-shouldered man she knew was miles away in London, probably nursing a hangover or totting up his gambling winnings. Or just getting up from the bed of some sophisticated and beautiful woman.

Petrus lifted his head, no longer relaxed. 'Someone is coming. Two horses.'

Without a word Caroline turned and plunged down the narrow path that led through the bushes to the lake. It must be her father and Lucas, but she would be safe down here, the path was too steep and narrow for riders to follow.

She reached the shelter of an ancient oak tree and moved behind the massive trunk, round to where honeysuckle had created a tangled screen. Looking up, she could see the area in front of the chapel door where Petrus stood waiting.

The horses moved into the space, large hunters, ridden with no thought that they might be intimidating to a man on foot. Petrus stood his ground, then bowed, his hands inside the wide sleeves of his habit, the gesture somehow utterly lacking in servility and with a hint of the exotic about it.

'You have made yourself at home, I see.' Her father's voice carried clearly. 'What are you up to?'

'Eating my breakfast, bathing in the lake, contemplating a rhyme for *bruise*, my lord.' Petrus's voice was respectful and yet lilting through it was a thread of laughter, of mockery that had a dangerous edge to it.

Bruise. He had been angry when he saw her arm, angry when he realised who had inflicted the fading brownish-purple fingermarks that circled it like a malevolent bracelet. She should have been wary, on her guard approaching a complete stranger like that, and yet she had felt safe, even when he had touched her, even when the savage note had marred the liquid music of his accent.

Her father appeared to have noticed nothing amiss with the hermit's tone, but then he would never believe that an employee would dare to mock him, let alone threaten him. What was the status of a professional hermit anyway? Was he a servant or did he have a professional standing akin to an artist or architect called in to provide a service? she wondered, smiling a little at her own whimsy.

'Very good, carry on as you are.' No, her father had heard nothing amiss and his self-centred imagination had not picked up on the oddity of Petrus's remark about bruises. 'I have house guests arriving in three days' time. I will send word of when I want you to be here, but the first evening I think you should be seen at a distance, wandering across the hillside. It will intrigue the company before dinner, make a topic for conversation. You will receive detailed instructions.'

House guests? Who? And why hasn't Father told me? Now she had to get back to the house without being seen and wait until he deigned to inform her. She could hardly ask straight out or she would betray where she had been. When she looked back her father and Lucas had ridden on and the little clearing was empty.

It would be quickest to return to the chapel, cut down through the slope above the kitchen gardens and enter the house from there. She would then appear to have been inspecting the vegetable and flower crops if anyone noticed her slightly muddied boots.

Caroline crossed the clearing silently. The chapel door was still open and she could hear the hermit moving about inside. As she tiptoed past he spoke, one loud, angry swear word that made her gasp. Then something hit the door and fell to the ground. For an appalled moment she thought the brown huddle was an animal, then a fold flopped over and she saw it was his robe.

Which meant the chapel contained one angry, damp, naked hermit. She picked up her skirts and fled.

Chapter Five

'Woodruffe will be visiting in three days,' her father announced at dinner. 'Thought I would make a house party of it so Calderbeck's coming and Turnbull—they are sound on landscape design—and Lucas has invited some friends.'

'Yes, Father.' Caroline's heart sank. She had always thought it an exaggerated phrase, but it perfectly described the unpleasant lurch in her chest at the thought of her unwelcome suitor's presence in the house. 'Who have you invited, Lucas?'

'Frampton, the Willings brothers and Perry Ratcliff.' Lucas hardly looked up from his attempts to carve a tough chicken.

'Seven, then. An all-male party?' She tried to sound interested and positive.

'Yes.' Her father helped himself from the dish of buttered peas.

'I had best ask Aunt Gertrude to stay.' Caroline chased a sliver of beef around her plate. For once the idea of her aunt's fierce chaperonage was welcome.

'I don't want my sister's Friday face around the place for a week. What do you need a chaperon for when you're in your own home with your father and brother? I've no time for this missish nonsense.'

I need it for protection with Edgar Parfit prowling the corridors at night and a houseful of men I hardly know, she thought, but held her tongue.

'You complain that you don't know Woodruffe well enough to wed him, so this will give you plenty of opportunity. I'll have old Humbersleigh over to draw up the settlements while he's here and tell that useless parson to sort out the licence.'

'But, Father, what about my bride clothes?' Best to pretend that she had given in.

That brought his head up and his attention full on her. Caroline put up her chin and fought the instinct to cringe back in her chair.

'You've spent weeks in London doing nothing but shop. If you don't have enough gowns now you can buy them when you're wed and Woodruffe can pay for them. Hah!' Obviously pleased with the thought of fobbing off expense on his prospective son-in-law, her father returned to his roast.

Protesting to him was not going to work, not with two hundred acres of Woodruffe's land almost within his grasp. Caroline reached for the potatoes and bit into one with sudden determination. She would have to give Woodruffe a distaste for her, make him realise she would not stand to be dominated by him. Being missish and meek had not helped his first wife, he had simply bullied and beaten poor Miranda into submission. No, she would have to be bold and brassy, stand up to him, then he would think her too much trouble to wed. And if that failed, then her desperate plan to flee was the only alternative.

She bit down on her sore tooth without thinking and winced, reminded of what her father's temper could do if he discovered her scheming. But first she had to worry about preparing for a house party of seven with only two days to do it in.

'That's a fine prospect, Knighton, I must say.' Lord Calderbeck shaded his eyes as he looked out from the terrace across the garden to the slopes of Trinity Hill. 'I like what you've done with that tower—it has an air of age and mystery about it, makes a man want to take a walk across the park and explore.'

'That's my latest project.' The earl pulled his pocket watch out of his waistcoat and peered at the time. The shadows were lengthening as the summer evening drew in, but the sun still illuminated the far hillside. Caroline scanned the treeline, realising what her father was waiting for. She had been so busy over the past two days that she had hardly spared the hermit a thought. Certainly, all that afternoon, preoccupied as she had been with greeting the guests and avoiding Lord Woodruffe, she had quite forgotten him.

'Who the devil is that?' young Marcus Frampton demanded, pointing.

'It looks like a monk!' Mr Turnbull, an author of lurid Gothic tales, clapped his hands in delight. 'That's wonderful, Knighton, you have found yourself a monk.'

'A hermit, actually. The building you can glimpse is a chapel and there he lives in solitude.' Her father was beaming now, more than satisfied with the effect of his creation on his friends.

Caroline picked up the telescope that was lying on the bench and trained it on the distant figure. Petrus was walking slowly, using a long staff to good effect, for it showed the fall of his full sleeves. As she sharpened the focus he turned to face the house and flung his arms wide in a gesture that might have been a blessing. Or perhaps a curse.

'Do let me help you, Lady Caroline. That is too heavy for dainty female hands.' A large body pressed against her and one hand came around her waist as the other clasped her fingers on to the telescope, pressing hard so the metal ridges bit into her skin.

'Oh!' Caroline gave an exaggerated start of alarm and stepped back. It had the unfortunate effect of pressing her closer into Lord Woodruffe's belly, but it also brought the narrow heel of her evening slipper down hard on his toes. He staggered, pulling her with him, and she lifted her other foot clear off the ground so her entire weight was on the one heel. When he let go of her hand she allowed her arm to fall so that the end of the telescope swung back in an arc to hit him squarely in the falls of his breeches.

The sound Woodruffe made was gratifyingly like a pig seeing the approach of the butcher. He bent double, his hands clutching his groin as the other men turned to see what all the noise was about.

'Oh, Lord Woodruffe, I am so sorry, but you pulled me quite off balance. Are you badly hurt? Perhaps our housekeeper has a salve you could rub in.'

Seeing where Woodruffe was clutching himself the two Willings brothers snorted with laughter. Even Lucas was struggling to suppress a grin. Caroline fluttered about, full of innocent concern, and her father glowered at the interruption to his discussion about stone quarries with Lord Calderbeck. 'What the devil?'

'I trod on Lord Woodruffe's toes, Father. I am so sorry.'

'Then why in blazes is he clutching his…er…?' The fact that he was addressing his daughter appeared to dawn on the earl and he stopped mid-sentence. 'Brace up, man, and stop whimpering!'

Woodruffe straightened, shot Caroline a malevolent look that made her shudder and limped back into the house.

It was a good start. Now she had to balance her behaviour on the knife edge between giving Woodruffe a disgust of her and betraying what she was doing.

The telescope had rolled across the terrace and she went to pick it up. It was a good instrument and there was a dent in its brass casing now. Caroline raised it to her eye to check that the lenses were not damaged, scanning round as she fiddled with the focus screw. Yes, it was working perfectly, thank goodness.

The trees on the far hill came into sharp definition and there, strolling back to his chapel, was the hermit. *He probably thinks no one is looking at him now he's finished his performance,* she thought with a smile as the tall figure turned and walked up towards the path into the trees. Again that sense of recognition swept over her and this time, without the beard and the accent to distract her, she placed him.

Lord Edenbridge. The image swooped and blurred as her hands shook. *Gabriel Stone. Petrus, the Latin for stone or rock. How could I not have realised?*

'I say, do take care, Lady Caroline, you almost dropped the telescope again.' Mr Turnbull took it from her lax grip.

'Thank you, Mr Turnbull. So foolish of me, but staring through it made me suddenly light-headed.'

Somehow she chattered on, made conversation as the party drifted back into the drawing room. *Gabriel Stone. Here. Why?* It had to be something to do with her. He had no reason to be taking employment of any kind, let alone something as peculiar and uncomfortable as fulfilling an eccentric man's expensive fantasies about landscape features. But what did he want?

'Dinner is served, my lord,' their butler announced, making her jump.

Caroline got a grip on herself. Dangerous peers of the realm might be lurking in the shrubbery—literally and mysteriously—but she had a dinner party to deal with. 'We are a most unbalanced group, are we not?' she said with an attempt at a gay laugh. 'Lord Calderbeck, may I claim your arm? The rest of you gentlemen must escort yourselves in, I fear.'

She had set out the place cards with strict attention to precedence. Marcus Fawcett, Viscount Frampton, sat on her left hand as she occupied the hostess's chair at the foot of the table with Lord Calderbeck on her other side. Woodruffe, a baron, was left watching her from his position midway down the table. She turned and began to flirt lightly with the viscount. The stare turned to a glare and young Lord Frampton sat up straighter, his expression faintly smug.

Just as long as I do not have to deal with him as well! Caroline accepted a slice of beef with a smile and asked the viscount about his horses. From experience, he could be relied upon to bore on for hours once started on that theme, which had the dual benefits of distracting his mind from flirtation and also allowing her time to think about a certain earl.

Why on earth hadn't she recognised Gabriel immediately? That beard and the curling mane of hair, she supposed. And the fact that when they had met before she had been too embarrassed to study his face closely. It was that rangy body with its easy movement that had always attracted her and that was what she had recognised through the telescope.

'Spavined? How distressing,' she responded automatically to Frampton's ramblings about one of his matched bays, then closed her ears to an account of just what the farrier had advised doing about it and what his head groom had thought.

But what was Gabriel Stone doing here with his Welsh accent and his poetry? She would wager her entire allowance for a year that the man had never so much as rhymed a couplet in his life. Surely he hadn't come with a view to collecting on her shocking IOU after all? No marriage had been announced, no betrothal announced, so the terms of the bargain were not met in any case.

They had parted with angry words, on her part at least, but if Gabriel had wanted to make his peace with her he was going to preposterous extremes to do so. Besides, he had not revealed his identity when they met at the hermitage and he had made no attempt to contact her since.

'And what do you think of your father's hermit, eh, Lady Caroline?' Lord Calderbeck's voice was loud enough to draw the attention of all the diners.

'I...I haven't...I mean I don't...' She was blushing, she knew she was. And stammering and generally behaving in a most suspicious manner. 'I have not had the opportunity to view the man at close quarters,' she managed. 'I have been rather occupied. But I consider the impression he creates from a distance to be most picturesque. My father has such a good eye for a landscape effect.'

That at least earned her an approving look from the far end of the table. Perhaps her father's violent anger with her had been forgotten for now, although she could not delude herself that the truce would hold once she defied him again over Lord Woodruffe. And she would defy him, she was even more certain of that now as she watched her suitor eating his way through the mound of food on his plate without the slightest sign of appreciation or discrimination. His eyes, when they met hers, held promises of retribu-

tion that banished the image of a portly, middle-aged buffoon, replacing them with threats of domination and pain.

Gabriel dumped the bucket he had carried down to the
stream to deal with his after-dinner washing up and closed
the door of his cell. It was cool now that the sun was down
and the mossy grove seemed to stay damp however high
the daytime temperature. He had performed his first cha-
rade for his employer, seen the glint as the sinking sun
had caught the lens of at least one telescope, and there was
small risk the house party guests would leave after dinner
to inspect him. It was safe to relax.

The fire was still alight after his culinary efforts earlier and he tossed on some wood, more for the cheerful
flicker of light than for the warmth. For a man who had
never had to so much as make himself a cup of tea before he was quite pleased with his cookery, even if all he
was doing was converting the food sent over from the big
house kitchens. He had heated soup without scalding it, he
had chopped up what he assumed were the leftovers from
yesterday's roast along with onions and a carrot, fried the
result with beef dripping and consumed the savoury mess
along with a hunk of bread that was only slightly stale,
washed down with a mug of the thin ale that had been
provided in a firkin.

Not what he was used to, he thought as he stretched out
his legs in front of the fire, but he was getting accustomed
to it and the constant fresh air was sharpening his appetite,
even for his own cooking. It was certainly easier to adapt
to the food than it was to the long skirts of his robe. How
the devil did women cope with the encumbrance? To say
nothing of the fact that it was decidedly draughty around
the nether regions.

The chilling effect of cold air had probably been an advantage to monks fighting the temptations of the flesh in their quest for celibacy. Not that cold draughts had been necessary the other day when he had found himself with Lady Caroline in his arms. It had been anger that had heated his blood then, fury that anyone could manhandle a woman, let alone her own father.

He had expected to discover that she had been bullied, but not that she was suffering actual physical harm. Bullying he had expected to be able to deal with by giving her moral support and by finding something on Woodruffe that would persuade the man to drop his pretensions to Caroline's hand. His dubious sexual proclivities were well enough known for that to be ineffectual as a pressure point—Gabriel must find something else. It might amount to blackmail, but he had no qualms about that in this case. And probably Woodruffe would prefer it to facing him down the barrel of one of Manton's duelling pistols, which was Gabriel's fall-back plan. It wouldn't be difficult to work up some kind of quarrel with a man as objectionable as Edgar Parfit.

But if Caroline was being mistreated then the whole business became more serious, for if her father blamed her for Woodruffe's withdrawal then she could suffer more than bruised wrists.

Gabriel lifted the bottle of brandy from behind the log pile, poured himself two fingers into a horn beaker and sipped while the heat of the spirits settled the faint nausea that came with some ruthless self-examination. He had shaken his head over Caroline's lack of foresight beyond her aim of retrieving her brother's estate, now he wondered if he had been equally thoughtless.

He had landed himself in this situation on a sudden impulse when Alex Tempest had reported overhearing Knighton at White's talking about his advertisement in

The Times. He had been brooding on what to do about his unease over Caroline's welfare and Alex's gossip seemed like the answer on a plate, so he'd snatched at it.

Pretend to be a hermit—there would hardly be competition for the post—combine an amusing small adventure with the opportunity to soothe his nagging conscience over Caroline, get himself out of his London rut for a while. It had all seemed like the perfect answer.

Perhaps if things had not fallen into place so easily he might have reconsidered the masquerade and found some other way of discovering how Caroline was faring. But the necessary delay while his 'agent', otherwise known as Corbridge his valet, had negotiated on his behalf, and he ostensibly travelled from Wales, had given him time to grow an impressive beard and for his untrimmed hair to develop an unfashionable shagginess. He had to shave twice a day to maintain an acceptable appearance for a gentleman and the resulting thicket of neglected growth was enough, he was confident, to hide his identity from a self-obsessed man who had only seen him closely in a poorly lit gaming hell.

The Welsh accent that he had learned to mimic when he had stayed with his Great-Aunt Gwendoline near Caernarvon as a boy had come back easily. Alex had been so amused and impressed by his disguise that they had even tried the imposture out on Alex's wife, Tess, although with Gabriel in ordinary clothes and not his monkish robe. Lady Weybourn had carried on almost five minutes of polite social chit-chat in Green Park with Mr Petrus Owen, the gentleman from Wales, before her husband's poorly suppressed laughter had made her suspicious.

It was a shock to find Caroline at the chapel when he'd returned from his morning dip in the lake and he'd been surprised, too, that she had failed to recognise him. With the painful discipline of self-examination that he had imposed on himself recently Gabriel pondered whether his reaction to that lack of recognition was hurt pride. They had, after all, discussed becoming lovers—one would expect a woman under the circumstances to have looked closely at the man she was proposing such a bargain with.

'Coxcomb,' he muttered to himself. Caroline had been in turn embarrassed, mortified, shy, angry and afraid during both of their encounters. It would have been a miracle if she had recognised him in the street, let alone hiding behind all those whiskers. *Which cover all my best features*, Gabriel thought with a grimace as he tugged at the offending growth.

He needed to talk to her again, reveal his true identity and discover the truth about her situation. That might be easier said than done, because catching her alone so that any startled reaction was not observed was not going to be easy. He found that it was not just the fire and the brandy that was warming him. The thought of Caroline Holm was…stimulating. *In much the same way as a hair shirt, no doubt,* Gabriel told himself as he reached for a book and moved the candles closer. She was likely to cause him nothing but trouble, anxiety and hard work, all things that he normally avoided like the plague.

He had become unused to worrying about anyone else's welfare. His employees were easy enough—you paid them properly, made your expectations clear and dealt fairly—and mistresses were much the same. His brothers more or less looked after themselves now they were adults and, except for the occasional request for money, seemed quite happy with the state of affairs.

But Caroline was alone and courageous. She had been hurt, was probably still at risk, and he could no more stand by and see a woman injured than he could fly. And she had blue eyes like speedwell in sunlight and soft, soft skin under his fingers. That thought was almost worse for his peace of mind than fighting old nightmares, but he could not walk away and leave her, not if he wanted to live with his conscience afterwards. Gabriel removed a bookmark and applied himself to an analysis of the post-war European political situation.

Chapter Six

Gabriel, staying firmly in the role of Petrus Owen, poet and hermit, had bathed, broken his fast and tidied his humble residence. He was contemplating a visit to the kitchen door of Knighton Park in the hope of discovering if the mistress of the house came down to give her orders to Cook or sent for her, when the sound of approaching riders brought him to the threshold of the chapel.

He picked up the large book that he had selected, thinking it looked like an appropriate text for a hermit to be studying, shut the door on the domestic interior and took up a position looking out over the wooded dell down to the lake.

The horses filled the clearing behind him, hooves tramping on the leaf mould, bits jingling, breathing heavy after what must have been a gallop up the long slope on the other side of the crest. There were at least half a dozen of them, perhaps more, but the riders fell silent as they saw him and he could not be certain.

Gabriel waited, counting up to twenty in his head in Welsh to make certain his accent was firmly in place. The sound of movement subsided, leaving only the occasional snort and stamped hoof.

When he turned he made the movement slow, scanned the clearing until he saw Lord Knighton, then bowed, straightened and waited, his gaze on his employer's face. The man was pleased, he could see that. Pleased to find his hermit in the right place, pleased with his bit of theatre and pleased, too, by the admiring murmurs from his guests.

There were nine mounted men facing him. Seven guests in addition to Knighton and his son and, on the edge of the group, Caroline on a neat bay hack, her habit a deeper shade of the blue of her eyes, a pert low-crowned hat on her head. He let his gaze pass over her, frustrated by the veil that hid her expression from him.

'So this is your hermit, eh, Knighton!' Woodruffe, of course, was always ready to state the obvious, probably because it saved thinking. 'What are you doing, fellow?'

Gabriel turned by a few degrees, met Woodruffe's stare and bowed again. 'Meditating.' He let the silence hang heavy and saw the two youngest men, the Willings brothers, if he was not mistaken, shift uneasily in their saddles. He had spoken as though to an equal and they were uncertain, he guessed, how to react to that. 'I was pondering upon the transience of glory and the fall of pride.'

Woodruffe nodded, as though he understood some great truth. 'Good show.'

Gabriel managed not to roll his eyes and waited.

'You are a poet?' That was Calderbeck. No fool, the old man, and someone who had known him distantly since Gabriel's childhood. This was no time to be complacent.

'A bard.' He deliberately thickened his accent.

'So you sing?' That was Frampton, who had lost two hundred guineas to him only a month ago. Gabriel bowed assent. To deny an ability to sing would undermine his Welsh credentials if they held to that stereotype.

'You will come down to the house and perform your work for my guests, in that case,' Knighton ordered.

'When it is ready, my lord, with pleasure.'

'You have nothing but what you are working on now?' Calderbeck demanded, bridling at Gabriel's indifferent tone.

'Nothing that is of the spirit of this place.'

'Well, perform something else,' Knighton said impatiently. 'Tonight, nine o'clock.'

'And bring your harp to the party,' Frampton added, making the younger men guffaw with laughter.

'I sing unaccompanied,' Gabriel said. *Hell and damnation.* Could he recall any of the Welsh tunes his great-aunt and her housekeeper had taught him as a child? He could sing well enough, but he had not been prepared for this.

'No doubt your hermit is wary of performing to an audience after so much time alone, Father. Or perhaps he fears his voice is not all he boasts of.' The words, spoken indifferently, brought the men round to stare at the speaker as though they had forgotten there was a woman with them.

'We do not want a poor performance. Not with such distinguished guests,' said Lady Caroline as she rode forward into the clearing. She put back her veil as though to study him more closely and her expression, as she stared down at Gabriel, was suited to a lady who has found the chimneysweep's boy on her new Oriental hearth rug. He risked a quick assessing glance. Her face was unmarked and she seemed to be managing her horse without any difficulty. He let out a breath he had not realised he'd been holding.

'Why not have him come up to the house later this afternoon, Father? Blackstone can show him the salon and let him practise his voice a little.' She shrugged. 'Or not, as you choose. I merely thought it might save us an evening of strange discords if I were to hear what he can do.'

Gabriel kept his eyes lowered, respectfully not staring, it must have seemed, when in fact he was having difficulty keeping the surprise off his face. Where had the Lady Caroline he knew vanished to? This bored, haughty creature was surely not the blushing, passionate, brave woman who had made him that outrageous offer, who had come to visit her father's hermit to assure herself of his welfare?

'A good idea, Caroline.' Gabriel looked up and saw that Knighton was nodding approval. He had no qualms, it seemed, about exposing his daughter to the close proximity of his hermit. Presumably he had every faith in her chaperon. The earl gestured abruptly at him. 'Come to the kitchen door at three. We'll all be outside, no one for you to disturb.'

Except your daughter, but apparently she does not count. 'My lord.' He was finding it mildly amusing to discover the amount of meaning—and insolence—one could convey with an apparently subservient bow. He must see if his own and other servants possessed the same skill.

Gabriel stood at the edge of the clearing and watched the riders make their way along the twisting track that skirted the contour of the hill before descending to the far side of the lake.

'Grottos…'

The word floated back on the still air. Another of Lord Knighton's landscape follies in planning. Gabriel wondered what he would want to ornament his grottos. Water nymphs, perhaps, or tritons.

He watched until the last of the horses, the bay hack with its blue-clad rider, vanished into the trees, ignored and unpartnered. Woodruffe took a complacent approach to his courting, Gabriel thought as he sat down on the log seat. Or perhaps the matter had been agreed and he was behaving as neglectfully as a fiancé as he would as a husband. From what he knew of the man, neglect would be infinitely better for Caroline than his attentions.

The summons to the house solved the problem of gaining an interview with her. If he had not known better he would have thought she had arranged matters in order to speak with him in private, but apparently this confounded beard was enough to hide from even the most perceptive young lady. He tugged at it and thought longingly of his razors before he began to dredge through his memory for Welsh songs, poems or even sermons.

'You are very clean for a hermit.' Mrs Gleason, the cook, eyed Gabriel up and down as he stood in the doorway of her immaculate kitchen looking as meek as he knew how. Subtly mocking Lord Knighton was one thing, but cooks were the empresses of their domains and even their employers treated them with respect if they knew what was good for them.

'I wash in the lake every day, Mrs Gleason.'

'And what's your name then?' That was Molly, the kitchen maid, all freckles and crooked teeth and a big grin that showed them both off.

'Petrus Owen, Miss Molly.'

That triggered the giggles again. 'Ooh, *Mis*s Molly!'

'You'll be Miss Out On Your Ear, my girl, if you don't finish those potatoes,' Cook snapped. 'And you, you big Welsh lummox, stop lurking about like something out of those novels Lady Caroline's maid is always reading, go on through to the end of the passage and knock on Mr Blackstone's door. You give me the cold grues, standing there in that Popish outfit.'

'Yes, Mrs Gleason.' He winked at Molly as he passed and was out of the door before her giggles erupted again.

The butler answered the knock on his door after a good

minute. From the waft of violet pastilles on his breath Gabriel deduced he had been having an after-luncheon snooze to recover from the onerous duty of finishing off the leftover wine.

'Oh, it's you. His lordship said to take you up to the Blue Salon.' He glowered at Gabriel, apparently found nothing obvious that he could object to, considering his employer was misguided enough to employ such a man, and stalked off along the passageway to the foot of the servants' stairs.

'Bring that with you.' He gestured in passing to one of the hard wooden hall chairs. 'I'll not have you sitting on the good upholstery. That robe or whatever it is looks as though it would shed.'

Where Mrs Gleason's distrust merely amused him, the butler's attitude filled him with a strong desire to apply one booted foot to his chubby buttocks. Gabriel picked up the chair by the back rail and hefted it into the salon without replying.

Blackstone waved a hand towards the piano. 'Lady Caroline said you might need to play it.' His expression showed strong doubt that the silent hermit was capable of such a feat.

Gabriel, without acknowledging he had heard, shifted the piano stool, dumped down the chair, sat and ran his hands up and down the keyboard in a series of perfectly accurate scales. He rarely played the piano, but he could recall enough of his lessons to manage that, at least.

'Ha! Don't touch anything else. I will tell her ladyship you are here.'

It was almost silent when Blackstone's footsteps died away. There was the draught from the open door on his cheek, the sound of birdsong through the window and, distantly, the lowing of cattle in the meadow beyond the ha-ha. It was curiously soothing, this bucolic peace. If he was not careful he would find himself seduced—

'What on earth are you *doing*?'

Gabriel brought his hands down on the keys in a jangling discord and swung round and to his feet. 'Lady Caroline.'

'Lord Edenbridge.'

She knows me. 'Not so loud.' He reached her side in three long strides and pushed the door half-closed. 'Where the blazes is your chaperon?'

'Unnecessary, according to my father.' She was tight-lipped and pale and he felt his temper rising.

'Your maid, then?'

'Upstairs immersed in a pile of fine mending and a lurid novel I deliberately left just by the mending basket. Never mind that, we are alone for a few minutes at least, so tell me, what are you doing here? And like this?' Her sweeping gesture encompassed his beard, hair, robe and the scuffed toes of his oldest pair of boots showing beneath the frayed hem. 'I do not know whether to laugh or run and hide in a cupboard.'

'From me?'

'No, of course not from you,' Caroline said with a laugh that wavered dangerously before she closed her lips tightly upon it. 'From my father when he discovers this imposture.'

'What imposture? He cannot seriously delude himself that I am a genuine Welsh hermit. He assumes I am a gentleman or scholar fallen on hard times, but if I am an earl eccentric enough to wish to seclude myself in a chapel and write poetry for a few weeks then that makes me no more peculiar than the earl prepared to employ me.'

'But that is not why you are here, is it?' She had retreated to the far side of the piano and from there was studying his face with an expression somewhere between bemusement and alarm. 'I wish I knew what you were thinking. That beard is extraordinarily effective in concealing both your features and your expression.'

'I am glad to hear it. But how did you realise, if you did not recognise me close up that first day?'

'I was watching from the terrace with the guests that evening. There was something about you that was nagging at the back of my mind and then, when I saw you moving, without the distraction of the beard and Welsh accent, I realised.' She blushed for some reason.

'I came because I was worried about you. Your note saying you were leaving London was written in a hand that shook and you mentioned your father's displeasure. I know what kind of man Woodruffe is and I feared you were under intolerable pressure to marry him. If you are, then I could…discourage him.'

'You were worried? Why should you be? I am no responsibility of yours.'

Gabriel gave a half-shrug. Honour? He supposed it must be that. And he liked Caroline, which in itself was a puzzle. He was unused to liking women for themselves, not as sexual partners, or flirts. Perhaps associating with the wives of his close friends, three brave, intelligent women, was changing his perspective. It was unsettling the way he felt so protective of Caroline. *As though she was a sister*, he thought, then discarded the idea. It felt strangely wrong.

'I am not used to associating with well-bred virgins, but it seems that an encounter with you was enough to lay bare the few gentlemanly instincts I do possess,' he said, unwilling to express his half-understood feelings. 'I was concerned, as I say, but what I did not expect was to find that you had been physically mistreated. I cannot walk away from that.'

'I told you, it was an accident.'

'That is not true, we both know it, Caroline. Women tell those lies to shield the men who mistreat them.' *Mama's voice as she explained away another bruise. So careless, she had been, so clumsy.* His father had hit his own wife and he found the sight of a bruise on a woman intolerable. And now he was an adult he could do something about it. He felt his voice begin to rise and regained control with an effort. 'Your loyalty is misplaced.'

She made a little gesture of rejection, whether of his persistence or of the violence, he could not tell. Nor did he realise he had moved until he found himself beside her, her hand in his. He lifted it and pushed back the sleeve, feeling her skin under his fingertips, satin-smooth, rather cool. 'The bruises are almost gone. Do you have new ones?'

She should make him let go of her hand. Caroline did not stir, letting the warmth from the long, sure, fingers soak into her skin. *Calloused horseman's hands, perhaps swordsman's hands*, she thought. *Strong.* 'No, there are no new ones. My father is content that I am allowing Lord Woodruffe to court me.'

'Is he? Courting you, that is.'

'No, not really. He is behaving as though he already owns me and has no need to exert himself to win my approval. He expects my father to deliver me at the altar steps as a neatly wrapped parcel complete with dowry, in return for his acres that adjoin our land. One daughter disposed of, Lucas's inheritance expanded—all with minimal fuss and bother.' Her aunt would warn her sharply about the bitter tone. So unladylike, so undutiful.

Gabriel was tracing the veins in her wrist with his fingertip. She should free herself, she was not *that* careless of proper behaviour. *But why should I? I want his hands*

*on me, I like the strength and the gentleness and the anger
on my behalf that is in this man.*

'What is the solution, then?' he asked. 'I could shave
off this confounded beard, reappear as myself and chal-
lenge Woodruffe to a duel.'

Was he being whimsical? 'You will do no such thing!
On what pretext? What if you kill him? And think of the
scandal in any case.'

His fingers still circled her wrist, they were close
enough to kiss, close enough for her to breathe in the now
familiar scent of him. Gabriel's lips parted, she caught her
breath. 'You do not worry that he might kill me?'

She gave an unladylike snort of disbelief, shattering the
fragile moment, and saw the laughter lines crease at the
corners of his dark eyes.

'I am flattered by your confidence, Caroline. But to be
serious, I agree that duels are a last resort because of your
reputation. Is there no one you would wish to marry? No
suitor ready to carry you off across the border?'

He had released her wrist and she concentrated on not
closing the fingers of the other hand around it to trap the
sensations that still teased the skin. 'No. There are suitors,
yes. But anyone I would wish to marry? No. Certainly no
one ready to carry me off at the risk of scandal and my
father disowning me.'

'Then we will have to think of another solution.' Without leaving her side Gabriel let his fingers stray over the
keyboard, a ripple of notes, the beginning of a tune she
did not know. 'I have only just arrived and begun to think
around the problem. There is time yet, do not despair.'

'I am not despairing,' she said stoutly. 'If the worst
comes to the worst I will simply run away—once I have
thought of a way to support myself respectably until Anthony comes of age and I can live with him.'

Gabriel raised an eyebrow, his expression dubious. 'He is what? Sixteen? Five years to hide and support yourself is a long time.'

'I know. But I will think of something.' She shrugged. 'I must. Other women support themselves.'

His quizzical look was plain to read. *Most of them do it on their backs.* 'I was considering blackmail.' Gabriel completed his one-handed tune with a flourish. 'Something that would suggest powerfully to Woodruffe that he would do better to leave you alone. Catching the man cheating at cards would be useful.'

'It would. I cannot believe we are discussing blackmail, elopements and duels.' She watched him as he stood so close, head bent, studying the black-and-white keys as though they were all that was important here.

Gabriel glanced up towards the door. 'Someone is coming.' He crossed the room to the rug in the centre. 'I think it would be better if I recite rather than sing, my lady,' he said clearly, the Welsh lilt back to colour his voice.

Blackstone looked round the door, then came in, nose almost twitching with curiosity. 'May I bring your ladyship refreshments?'

'Yes, please, Blackstone. Some lemonade and macaroons. Bring two glasses and plates.'

When he had gone, his face stiff with disapproval, Caroline stayed where she was. 'Why not sing?'

'Because I cannot remember sufficient songs,' he confessed. 'But I can recite Welsh poetry long enough to send an entire house party to sleep. It is a hot day and this evening will be warm. A stage set of sorts on the terrace will give maximum drama and keep your father happy.'

'But why are you doing this? You hardly know me,' she began. 'Why are you helping me?' *It isn't as though you desire me.*

'Hush, my lady. *Mawredd gyminedd, a weli di hyn? Yd lysg fy nghalon fel etewyn—*' He broke off as a footman came in with a tray, placed it on a side table and left on well-trained, silent feet.

The man must have incredible hearing. 'How did you—?'

Gabriel shook his head at her in silent warning. 'That is from a warrior's lament, my lady, many hundreds of years old.'

Blackstone entered, glanced at the lemonade jug as though checking on the footman and went out again.

'"My heart is burning like a brand of flame",' Gabriel translated incongruously as she poured lemonade. 'What time should I make my appearance this evening? "I praised their wealth..."'

'Ten o'clock.' Caroline made herself think of practicalities, not the rich, dark voice weaving ancient magic. 'Have a biscuit.' There were few things more prosaic than biscuits. 'Tell me why.'

'You know perfectly well I cannot just abandon you now I know you are being ill-treated and that your father is forcing Woodruffe on you,' Gabriel said, waving away the macaroons. 'And, if I am to help, this performance consolidates my position here and it gives me the opportunity to get something on Woodruffe that I can use to apply pressure.'

'Blackmail?' Gabriel spoke of it as though *putting pressure* on someone was a normal business practice.

'You don't handle men like him with kid gloves. Or at all, if you can help it,' Gabriel added with a smile that made her think of sharp teeth and dangerous shadows. 'You must set the scene. Flambeaux, a brazier, a pile of furs if you have them, a horseshoe of chairs with the open end to the steps to the terrace.' Gabriel finally took a biscuit and bit into it. 'We want drama and every possible cliché.

You don't have any mead on the premises, have you? Pity, it fits the whole Welsh mystical mood so well,' he added softly as she shook her head, bemused. 'Honeyed wine would do and some soporific if you have anything like that. I'd like to send Woodruffe to bed for a very sound sleep and be able to search his room. If we can solve this by simple pressure on his weak spots, then so much the better. A love letter from the wife of a senior cabinet minister, a handbook on cheating at whist with annotations in his hand or a diary entry on a wartime career as a French agent would be handy.'

'There is laudanum,' Caroline suggested, trying not to think of Lord Woodruffe in an illicit and amorous encounter. Or any amorous encounter, come to that. Of *course* it was normal to be discussing drugging guests with a Welsh bard over lemonade on a summer's afternoon, contemplating blackmail. She was not going to give way to hysterics and the strong desire to run to her room and put her head under the pillow for the rest of the day.

'I recall the exact dose Dr Latimor prescribed when my father had a broken ankle. He and Woodruffe are of a similar build, so it ought to knock him out safely, provided I can manage to serve it to him.'

'Excellent.' Gabriel put down his glass and took her hand in both of his, lifted it and this time just touched the back of her fingers with his lips. 'Courage, my lady. We will get you out of this one way or another.' Then he turned to the terrace door and was gone in a swirl of brown robes.

Chapter Seven

The servants, used to their master's whims, responded well to Caroline's requirements for the after-dinner entertainment. The gardeners produced braziers and flambeaux, set around a semicircle of the most throne-like chairs she had been able to glean from remote corners of the house. A large stool had been heaped with sheepskins with an ancient wolf pelt at the foot and set in the centre, where the steps from the terrace led down to the lawn. Footmen collected armfuls of cloaks against any evening chill and Blackstone was concocting the nearest mixture he could invent that resembled mead.

'I regret we do not have sufficient drinking horns for all the guests,' he apologised to Caroline, who assured him that goblets would do. Slipping laudanum into a drinking horn would be decidedly tricky, she thought, touching the carefully measured dose in the little phial in her pocket. Much as she disliked the man she wanted to do Woodruffe no harm and she had rechecked the doctor's notes and her own measurements.

The guests, well fed and glowing with plentiful wine, came out as she was casting a final look over the stage set. They had forgone their port and she set Blackstone circulating with the honeyed wine as soon as they were all settled. The candles were extinguished in the house behind them, leaving them in the summer night beneath a clear sky with the afterglow of sunset to keep the stars at bay.

The men continued to talk, but gradually the atmosphere seemed to reach them and the volume dropped, conversation became sporadic. In the house the clocks chimed ten and Caroline, eyes straining, made out a flicker of movement approaching across the lawn. She nudged William, the footman with the most impressive bass voice.

'The bard approaches!'

She thought she knew what to expect. This was all smoke and mirrors, a performance, and yet as the tall figure came up the steps and into the firelight she caught her breath, seized with an almost superstitious awe. Robed and hooded in black and holding a long staff, Gabriel had become a figure from the remote past, a mystical creature of magic and power, both spiritual and physical. This was not a grey-bearded Merlin, stooped and ancient, this was a virile man in his prime, as likely to draw a sword as a magic wand.

Around her there were sharp intakes of breath, the sounds of men straightening themselves in their chairs— or leaning away as though faced with a threat. Gabriel stood, head bowed for a moment, then threw back his hood and sat down on the heaped animal skins with the air of a tribal chieftain taking his place on a throne. He held up his hand as if for silence, although save for the crackle of the fires and the hooting of an owl in the Home Wood, there had been no sound.

'*Marwnad Cynddylan Dyhedd deon diechyr...*'

The words dropped into the night air, soft as the owl's wingbeat. Only one person there understood their meaning and yet, shivering, Caroline thought they all knew this was a lament, an ancient warrior's song of glory, loss, death.

The rich, dark voice strengthened, deepened and Caroline lost herself in the sound, lost herself in the enchantment the enthroned figure was weaving. She had no idea how long Gabriel spoke for. When the liquid Welsh stopped it took them all a moment to realise it. Caroline released an unsteady breath and heard around her the others doing the same. One or two of the guests shook their heads as though rousing from a dream. No one applauded, but the very silence was filled with appreciation.

She rose, took the wine jug from the nearest footman and began to circulate, topping up the goblets in the men's hands. They hardly seemed to notice her. Woodruffe certainly did not as she tipped the laudanum from the phial in the palm of her hand into his wine.

She resumed her seat and the spell was spun again.

'Mawredd gyminedd, mawr ysgafael, Yrhag Caer Lwytgoed, neus dug Morfael...'

The sky was entirely black now, except for a dusting of early stars, and the braziers glowed sullen red.

"'I shall mourn until I enter the fastness of the earth,'" Gabriel said in English.

She thought his right hand moved and then there was a burst of flame as the nearest fire blazed up, making those nearest it recoil, dazzling the dark-adjusted eyes of all of them. From the far end where the staff had gathered there was a scream of alarm. When, blinking, Caroline could see properly again the dais was empty and the robed figure had vanished.

'My dear Knighton!' The men clustered around her father, full of congratulations. 'Magnificent! The atmosphere, the voice, the drama!' That was Lord Calderbeck, uncharacteristically animated. The others echoed him, only Woodruffe hung back, his hand on the back of his chair.

Caroline kept an eye on him as she directed the servants to clear the terrace of its chairs and props, watched him follow listlessly as the other guests trooped back into the drawing room.

'Damn good show, Knighton,' he roused himself to say. 'If you'll forgive me, I'm for my bed. Don't feel quite the thing, you know...'

The others barely spared him a glance. Caroline, assessing the heavy eyes and barely stifled yawns, hurried to his side in a display of feminine concern. 'Are you unwell, Lord Woodruffe? Should we send for a doctor?'

'No, no. Just a trifle weary for some reason. The night air, I have no doubt.' He smiled at her, a knowing smirk that had her fighting the urge to step back. 'You're a good girl to make a fuss of me. Make a wonderful wife for some lucky man, eh?' His chuckle was lost in another jaw-cracking yawn and he wandered off towards the door, leaving Caroline to struggle with the expression on her own face.

'Send a footman to keep an eye on Lord Woodruffe,' she said to Blackstone. 'We wouldn't want any accidents on the stairs.'

Now what? Is Gabriel watching from the darkness, waiting for us to go to bed, or is he already in the house, perhaps in Woodruffe's room? But her part was done. The men drifted towards the card tables and Caroline took herself to bed, still half-lost in the swirling mists of ancient legend.

Her maid was agog with the excitements of the evening. 'Ooh, my lady, when there was that great flame and he vanished I almost fainted with the terror of it. Witchcraft it was.'

'I'm sorry you were frightened, Jenny.' Caroline un-hooked her earrings and sat at the dressing table for the maid to unpin her hair. 'It was only the kind of tricks they play on stage.'

'I wasn't really scared, my lady—it was lovely, like a novel. I've got shivers up and down my spine just think-ing about it.'

'Well, I have shivers, too. Go and close the doors on to the balcony, please, before the moths get in.'

It seemed to take for ever to get ready for bed and even longer to send Jenny, still bubbling with excitement, on her way. Caroline left the little oil lamp by her bed burn-ing while she lay back, knowing she was not going to be able to sleep, not for a long while.

Part of her was braced for the shouts that would mark Gabriel's discovery, but there was only the distant sound of men's voices from the drawing room, the occasional burst of laughter and, out in the park, the sharp bark of a vixen.

The voices had stilled by the time the sound of fin-gernails on the glass of the balcony door brought her up-right in bed, one hand clapped over her mouth to stifle the shriek of alarm. They carried on their light tapping as she scrambled up and pulled on her wrapper. When she warily pushed back the curtains she almost did shriek in earnest at the sight of a dark figure on the narrow space between door and balustrade.

'Oh, it is you!'

Gabriel in breeches, boots and a dark coat slid into the room and jerked the curtains back again. 'Who did you expect?'

'Not you outside dressed like that,' she said irrationally, then gasped. 'How long have you been out there?'

'Long enough to be almost sent over the edge by your

maid closing the doors. And what did you expect me to be wearing? I can hardly climb the wisteria in a robe.' Her agitation finally seemed to register. 'Yes, I was out there all the time you were preparing for bed, and, yes, the curtains were tightly drawn and even if they had not been, I have no need to lurk outside maidens' bedchambers like a Peeping Tom, hoping for a glimpse of bare ankle.'

'Because you find it all too easy to be inside bedchambers, I suppose.' Gabriel gave a low hum of agreement. 'I do wish you were not constantly putting me to the blush,' she snapped, cross with herself. 'I was surprised, that was all. I thought you would have been inside the house long ago.'

'When everyone was still up and about and I had no idea which room was Woodruffe's?'

He spoke softly and she came close. To whisper back, she told herself. 'It is in the other wing. You'll need to cross the head of the stairs and go straight ahead, take the first right. His is the first door up the little flight of steps.'

'Stairs, across, right, steps. First door. Got it. Did you manage to drug him?'

'I gave him a light dose of laudanum, enough to make him sleepy. I didn't dare use more,' she confessed. 'I suppose murder is a rather extreme solution to the problem,' she added, then had to bite her lip to keep back the totally inappropriate giggles. *I am becoming hysterical with nerves*, she thought and then lost all desire to laugh when she saw the expression on Gabriel's face.

'It is,' he said grimly.

Something in his expression… 'I didn't mean it.' Her voice quavered.

Gabriel pulled her into his arms, her face against his coat. 'I know you did not.'

'That beard looks ridiculous with those clothes,' she

muttered, saying the first thing that came into her head. 'It is tickling my ear.'

'It is driving me insane,' he confessed, his voice a low rumble. 'I wish I could shave it off.'

'Why? Does it itch?' Caroline leaned back a little to examine it at close quarters.

'That, and I suspect that you will not like it when I do this.'

The kiss took her totally by surprise. It seemed to take Gabriel by surprise, too, judging from the sound he made as he gathered her in to the curve of his arm. The beard was soft, but wiry, she discovered, though not as soft as the dark springing hair on his head as she slid her fingers into it, curved them around his head.

My second kiss ever. And it was very different from that first, brief meeting of lips. *It must be the beard,* she thought, trying to stay rational and controlled. Gabriel smelled of cold air and lake water and, she supposed, of man. His mouth on hers was decidedly more active than it had been that first time. More assertive. More… *Oh!* His tongue found hers, then explored the tender inside of her mouth, then his teeth were nipping lightly at her lower lip and she found she was pressed against him, very conscious of his body.

Gabriel stepped back until he held her by the shoulders at arm's length. 'Damn. I had no intention of doing that.'

Her lower lip quivered and she bit it. Gabriel's gaze shifted to her mouth. 'It wasn't *that* bad.'

'I never said it was.' He smiled at her ruefully. 'The *damn* was for me. I apologise for both my presumption and the scratchy whiskers.'

'They are quite soft, actually.' She controlled the urge to pet them and gave herself a little shake. This was merely the release of tension, nothing more. Gabriel certainly did not appear much stirred by the experience and he should know. 'You'll need a lamp, you can take the little oil one from beside my bed.' She watched Gabriel check the wick. 'I think I will come with you to keep watch outside the door.'

'And if anyone comes? How are you going to explain what you are doing at this hour, flitting about a house full of men?'

'Um… Overcome by desire for Woodruffe? My father would approve of that.'

'Your father would have you married to him by special licence ten minutes after he manages to locate a bishop to provide one if he thought you had committed that sort of indiscretion in front of witnesses.'

'I suppose you are right. I could say I heard a sound like breaking glass so I went to investigate?'

'Without calling for help?'

'I am just a poor air-headed female.' She widened her eyes at Gabriel and the corner of his mouth kicked up. 'It never occurred to me it might be anything other than the wind on an unlatched casement that I ought to close.'

'You are not air-headed, Caroline. You are a positive menace. But come if you must.'

She followed him out the door, resisting the temptation to clutch at his coat tails. The house was as silent as it ever was, alive with the creaks and groans of its old timbers, the whistle of the wind in the chimneys, the tap of the branches of the elm on the east parlour side. Gabriel moved, soft-footed as a housebreaker, drifting down the corridors, across the stairhead with a glance down at the hooded chair by the front door where the footman on duty was asleep, a lamp turned down low beside him.

At Woodruffe's door Gabriel put his ear to the panels. 'He's asleep,' he murmured in Caroline's ear as he eased the door open and slid through the gap. Then she was alone on the landing with only the shivery sensation of his warm breath on her cheek to tell her that this was not some fevered dream.

Woodruffe was sprawled snoring across the bed, still in his shirt. Gabriel averted his gaze from the white hairy legs, the slack-mouthed face, and scanned the rest of the bedchamber.

Imagining this man in bed with Caroline did nothing for his concentration. He had been fighting the urge to kiss her, to toss her on to the nearest flat surface—piano, *chaise*, bed, hearthrug—and plunder that innocence until they were both exhausted. So far at least he had managed to behave like the gentleman he was supposed to be and not the rake he actually was, and keep his hands off her body.

Knight-errantry was supposed to bring its own rewards, not acute frustration, he thought bitterly as he studied Woodruffe's belongings. He should have thrown Caroline out the moment he found her in his drawing room, now he could not help himself trying to right her wrongs, not now he knew she had been hurt, not knowing what he did about Woodruffe. He was a man now, not a desperate child, and he had the power to thwart both men who threatened her. But once he had done something about this he was going to take himself off to Paris and plunge into mindless, hedonistic pleasure because virtue was, most certainly, overvalued.

A dressing case sat on the table, the lid pushed up by the paper that had been jammed inside it. Gabriel set the lamp down so the light was shielded from the sleeper and lifted out the contents. Bills, most of them third or fourth demands, a letter from Woodruffe's steward and a bulky, folded, piece of parchment that weighed heavy in his hand.

Gabriel opened it, wincing as the stiff folds crackled like gunshot. The weight was explained by the red seal that swung free at the bottom. A marriage licence and, by the size of it, a special licence at that. He did not risk unfolding the thing, knowing it would be the size of the table top, but set it aside and checked the rest of the box.

The collection of prints secreted at the bottom were certainly obscene. Gabriel was no prude, but he found he was handling these with the tips of his fingers as though the smut would rub off. Woodruffe had an unpleasant predilection for images of helpless women tied up, or in chains—and none of them appeared to be enjoying the experience. Certainly not the whips and canes the leering men in the prints were wielding.

He packed it all away, then took the lamp and searched the drawers in the dresser, the clothes press and finally, as Woodruffe snored on, the books on his bedside table.

Feeling he was in need of a bath, Gabriel eased his way out of the door and closed it silently behind him.

'Did you find anything?' Caroline whispered.

Too much. He studied her in the simple white nightgown that reached to her bare toes, her hair in a plait over one shoulder. She looked worryingly like the innocent victims in Woodruffe's pornographic prints. The thought of the man laying his sweaty hands on her, let alone anything else, almost made Gabriel shudder.

'Not here, back to your bedchamber.'

Once they were inside, the door locked, he picked up her robe from the foot of the bed and handed it to her. 'Put that on.'

'I am not cold. Tell me what you found.'

'Put it on. Please.' He sat down in one of the armchairs and studied the toe of his boot while he sought for some control.

'Oh, very well.' She shrugged into it and came to perch on the edge of the stool opposite. 'What did you find?'

Gabriel resisted the urge to lean over to tighten the sash and pull the edges of her robe together. 'Nothing actually illegal.' He was certainly not going to describe those prints to her. He recrossed his legs and contemplated the other toe. 'How eager is your father to get his hands on that land of Woodruffe's? Is it valuable?'

'No, just pasture. Not even good rich water meadow. I don't think it is worth much.'

'Woodruffe is in debt, by the look of it. You come with a good dowry, I assume? More than that land is worth on the open market?'

'Goodness, yes. Father might regard daughters as an irrelevance in the greater scheme of things, but he would be mortified to have it known my dowry was anything but generous. The value of the land is irrelevant, it is the enlargement of the estate that matters to my father.'

'Damn. I'd hoped that there might be a let-out there. In that case you need to know that the two of them must be quite determined on this match. Woodruffe has a special licence in his possession.'

'A *special* licence? That means he can marry without delay, wherever he wants, doesn't it?'

'It does.'

'I can keep saying no.' A thread of uncertainty ran through the statement.

Gabriel looked up, then leaned forward and caught her hand, pushed back the sleeve. The bruises had quite gone now. 'They have a clean slate to begin again. If your father hit you once, he will do it again if you anger him. And Woodruffe...' How the devil did one explain such tendencies to an innocent? 'Woodruffe is aroused by violence. Your resistance will only encourage him.'

Caroline met his eyes and shuddered. 'I don't think I want to know what you mean by that or how you discovered it.' She squared her shoulders and pulled her hand free from his lax grip. 'I will have to run away then. I've been hoping against hope that I wouldn't have to, but at least Anthony is at school much of the time and old enough to go to friends in the holidays. He is in no danger of anything but neglect from our father.

'I don't suppose you are any good at safe breaking? Mama's own jewellery is locked up in the study along with the things my godmother left me. I don't want to sell it, but I will need to part with some of it to live on until I find work.'

'I can pick a lock. Some locks,' Gabriel qualified. He hadn't needed to since his childhood. 'It all depends on how good it is.'

'You really are unscrupulous, aren't you?' Caroline's expression had turned from anxious but determined to something close to judgemental. 'Not that I am criticising, you understand.'

It sounded like that to him and, amazingly, her words hurt. 'You are not?' he enquired, unable to prevent the hint of ice in the question. What the devil was the matter with him if one young woman's opinion had the power to pierce his armour and wound? He was becoming vulnerable and he had never felt so before. Not mentally, at least.

'I know you are only trying to help me and I am very grateful, but subterfuge over who you are in order to become the hermit, searching Woodruffe's things with a view to blackmail and now lock-picking...'

She was right, this was over the thin line and into illegality, even if the jewellery was Caroline's. He should walk away. Now.

Chapter Eight

Walk away, for her own good. For mine. I have never become emotionally involved with a woman before and that is what this is.

Women wanted a man's thoughts, his secrets, his soul. His mother had uncovered her husband's soul and what she found had blighted her entire marriage, had driven her to the drug bottle and to her death. Gabriel had done what he had promised her, but taking responsibility for another person was like a heavy chain around the neck. His brothers had needed his protection and he had given them that at the cost of pain and loneliness and, almost, his freedom, if not his life. But a woman would want emotion.

Emotion is dangerous. Someone is going to get hurt. Stop now before this has gone beyond the point of no return and find some other way to help her. Gabriel found it was easier to decide to walk away than to do it. He sighed inwardly at his own unfamiliar indecision and tried to work things through logically.

Caroline was learning caution fast, it seemed. At first, seized with the desperate need to retrieve those deeds, she had almost innocently offered herself in order to save her brother's land and future. Now she was regarding the man who had been a stranger, perhaps almost an unreal figure, with speculation. There were questions in the clear blue gaze, questions and doubts that had not been there before he had kissed her.

'You think I should not do these things and ignore a lady in distress in order to preserve my own moral purity?' he asked when she did not speak. *And when did you ever have morals, let alone pure ones? Get down off your high horse, Edenbridge.* 'And now we are in deep you wonder just who you are involved with? You knew I was a sinner, not a saint, when you first came to me. I might break the law here and there, but are you telling me that your father and Woodruffe do not deserve to be thwarted?'

'No. No, of course not.' He could see the thoughts chasing each other, the anxiety and the doubt, the desire to snatch at help and the growing awareness that she was getting into very dangerous waters with a man she did not know. 'And I was the one who suggested you pick the lock,' Caroline added, obviously striving to be fair.

'Look, you can stay here, pretend none of this ever happened, marry Woodruffe.' Her shudder was an adequate answer to that suggestion. 'Or you can stay here, but refuse to marry him.' She shook her head. And he did not miss the betraying way one hand went to her cheek, cradling it. So the swine had hit her in the face as well as bruising her arms. Gabriel thought longingly of having Knighton at his mercy at the card tables again, a sure and legal way to ruin the man. But hell, the thought of killing him was tempting. Far more tempting. *Murder solves nothing*, he reminded himself. But it was so easy to do, the human frame was so vulnerable. He saw his father's broken body at his feet, all that power and vigour rendered impotent in a moment.

Gabriel clenched his fists until the nails bit into his palms and breathed deeply until the swirling memories were back under control. 'Or you can flee, with my help or without it. I assume as you have put it off this long that there is no one you can run to?'

How had he got himself into this? One step at a time, of course. He had let himself care, allowed himself to feel responsible for someone for the first time since his father's death, and now he had no more choice but to help Caroline than if he had found her drowning.

'There is no one.' Gabriel saw the conscious effort she was making to gather her courage and cope. 'I can go without your help, or with it, as you say. I had thought to find some cheap lodgings while I looked for work, but I really have no idea how to go about that. The risks to me are far greater if I try it alone—' She caught the involuntary twist of his lips and smiled, although it was not with much warmth. 'I have realised that you have no desire to take me up on my foolish IOU, so that makes me feel even safer.'

'I kissed you. Twice.' Where was this scrupulous urge to point out all the facts coming from? And he wanted to do far more than kiss her. He forced himself to plan how he was going to get her away, what he was going to do when he had.

Caroline shrugged. 'Men do tend to try to kiss women, I have observed. It doesn't mean anything.'

So his kisses were to be dismissed, were they? Gabriel got a grip on what remained of his sense of humour after this evening's events and waited for her to work her way through to a decision before he told her the results of his rapid planning.

'I will be safer with you, whether or not we can retrieve my jewels. But,' she added as he drew breath to suggest that, if she had made up her mind, they should get on with things, 'it has decided disadvantages for you.'

'It has?' Perhaps she was not so innocent after all.

'I am asking you to commit a criminal act, even if they are my own jewels, because the safe is not mine. And I will be putting you to considerable inconvenience and, I rather fear, expense. At least until I can sell or pawn some jewellery and pay you back.'

'This much entertainment is cheap at the price,' he drawled, hoping to lighten her mood, or at least make her cross enough to carry her through the night. Cost, if she only realised it, was the least of their problems.

'We will get to London and I will take you to one of the wives of my best friends. They are all married to women of...' he groped for the words to encompass the three and compromised with '...independent thought. It will not disconcert them in the slightest to harbour a runaway and we can rely absolutely on their discretion. Pack what you will need for about four days in your smallest valise. Then we will take the jewellery and be on our way. The fewer trips back and forth inside this house tonight, the better.'

'Oh, yes, thank you, that would be wonderful. The thought of some female support is, I must confess, very welcome.'

Gabriel braced himself for a long wait and then a tussle over a bulging valise and a hatbox or two. Caroline surprised him by removing a few items from drawers and bringing an oilskin bag and a hairbrush from her dressing room. Finally she lifted the lid of the window seat, rummaged inside and produced a large purse that clinked. 'I have been hoarding my pin money,' she explained when she saw his attention on the bag.

It all fitted into a small case. She scooped up the trinkets from the dressing table and swept them in on top, then draped a woollen pelisse over her arm. 'That is all I need.'

'You would make a good wife for a soldier,' Gabriel commented.

'I have been planning this for days,' Caroline countered. 'I hoped I would not have to do it, but now I do not think I have a choice.' He saw her cast a lingering look around her bedchamber which probably represented sanctuary and privacy, certainly comfort, but she did not hesitate. His respect for her increased another notch.

The night had begun to feel like a dream. Her surroundings were familiar, yet her behaviour was not. Things that she took for granted suddenly loomed terrifying and strange—the grotesque carvings on the newel posts, the suits of armour in the Long Gallery, the grinding sound the long-case clock in the hallway made as it readied itself to strike, all were exaggerated.

The man beside her was a stranger, too. He was not the softly spoken Welsh hermit, nor the dishevelled rake she had caught on his way to bed that first morning. Neither was he the elegant, if careless, nobleman who occasionally spared social events an hour or two of his time. This man was a creature of the dark, moving through the shadows like a cat, prepared to break the law to help her and quite confident about his ability to do so. This was the man who had kissed her with careless expertise, leaving her wanting more, even as she shocked herself with that wanting.

What would his friends be like? At least they were all married, although the idea of the women of *independent thought* was rather more alarming than the prospect of meeting three more rakish gentlemen. What if the wives all despised or disliked her? Or worse, pitied her.

She was worrying so hard that she almost walked past the study. 'In here,' she breathed.

The door was unlocked and well oiled. Once inside Gabriel drew the curtains tightly closed before he turned up the wick of the lamp. 'Where is the safe?' With light on him she could see the tension in his body, the alertness. He looked ready to fight.

'Here.' She lifted down a landscape in a gilt frame to reveal a small door set flush into the wall.

'I can force this easily enough.'

'It is iron painted to look like wood,' she warned.

'Damn.' Gabriel produced the two hairpins that she had seen him lift from her dressing table. 'Hold the light to shine on the lock.' He straightened the first pin, slid it into the keyhole and began to manipulate it.

Ten minutes passed. Caroline shifted the lamp to the other hand and propped her arm against the wall to ease the ache. Gabriel's eyes were narrowed, his lips compressed. He had two pins, bent at odd angles, in the lock now.

'It must be fifteen years since I tried this,' he muttered.

'If it is too difficult—' she began. The clock made its grinding noise and they both froze, then relaxed as it chimed three.

Gabriel closed his eyes as something went *click*. 'Got it.'

It was almost an anticlimax to have the door swing open to reveal nothing more than some folded documents, a bag of coin and a stack of jewellery boxes. In the almost Gothic atmosphere of flickering lamplight and tension the least the safe should have contained was a skull and a vial of poison. Caroline did not feel this was the moment to be sharing such fancies with Gabriel.

She sorted out her own jewels from the family gems, which were to be passed down to the eldest son for his wife, and nodded to Gabriel. He closed the door, manipulated the picks until, much faster this time, the lock clicked home, and then lifted the picture back into place.

'What do we do now?' she asked as she stuffed the valuables deep into her valise.

'We go to the hermitage until I can make arrangements.

Is it possible to get out of the house without leaving a trace?
I'd like to delay pursuit as long as possible.'

'The side entrance to the garden. There's a trick to jig-
gling the lock.'

Gabriel cracked open the door. 'Hell.' He pushed her
back into the study. 'Someone is coming.'

'There's nothing beyond this room. It must be my father.'

Gabriel cast a swift look around, then fell to his knees,
dragging her with him as he blew out the lamp. 'Under
the desk.'

It was a double-depth partners' desk, designed for two
men to face each other as they worked. The kneehole might
give them both enough space to remain hidden, provided
no one sat down and extended their legs. Crushed under
there against Gabriel, the valise jammed under her raised
knees, Caroline held her breath until coloured dots began
to swirl in the blackness.

As the door opened she drew in a shallow breath. Surely
her heartbeat must be audible? Beside her Gabriel was utterly still, then she felt his finger begin a slow movement
against the back of her hand. *I am here*, it seemed to say.
Don't be afraid.

She closed her fingers around his, holding on as the tension grew. Her father put down his lamp and began to sort
through the papers on the desk above them, muttering irritably as if he could not locate what he wanted.

Her body was hot and cold. Cold with fear, hot where it
touched Gabriel's. Beneath the broadcloth she could feel
his strength, the muscles tensed for action, the total control. His confidence seeped into her, allowing her to relax
just a little, to breathe more easily, and as the panic ebbed
something else flowed in to replace it, an aching physical awareness, the need for Gabriel's arms around her, his

mouth on hers. She lowered her head until her parted lips touched the back of his hand and then she stilled, breathing in the smell of his skin, letting the taste of him seep into her mouth. His fingers tensed in hers.

Finally her father gave a grunt of satisfaction and moved towards the door. The light vanished and the sound of his footsteps dwindled away. Gabriel backed out of the tight space, pulled out the valise and finally Caroline, unresisting and shivering, into his arms. His kiss was hard, almost angry, over in a second, a wordless acknowledgement of their narrow escape.

'Hurry.' He let her lead the way to the garden door and watched the passageway behind them as she lifted the handle, wiggled it up and down and then pressed on the door panels. The lock opened with a scrape, then, as she pulled it closed behind them, it dropped back into place.

The tall hedges that led from the house to the ha-ha made deep shadows and Gabriel set a fast pace, the sharp scent of the yew drifting back as he brushed the edges.

He vaulted down from the lawn into the ditch and she sat on the edge, then jumped into his upheld hands, gripping his shoulders to steady herself. His mouth sought hers again, with fierce and fleeting heat, then he set her on her feet and turned to climb the gentle slope of the other bank.

Panting with fear and relief and desire, Caroline gathered up her skirts and followed across the pasture, hurrying in the wake of Gabriel's long stride.

As they reached mid-slope Gabriel stopped, turned and looked back at the house. 'No lights. We're clear away for now.'

She tried not to puff. She should be flattered, she supposed, that he had assumed she could keep up, that she would not need treating as though she was some fragile little flower who required cosseting. She was going to need all the strength she had to make good her escape, however much help she had. She would not think about those kisses. Not yet.

'Are you all right?' He might have read her mind, or perhaps her breathing was not as controlled as she had thought. It was impossible to read his face by starlight.

'I…I don't know,' she said as he caught her hand and began to stride on up the hill. *Know what?*

When they reached the chapel Gabriel slammed the door, caught her to him and locked his mouth on hers. When he finally lifted his head he seemed as breathless as she was. 'Yes?'

'Yes.' *This. Now. We're safe, we're alive and we did it together.*

His lips captured hers again, his hands moved over her clothes, things fell away, cool air touched her skin. *Bare skin.* Gabriel was still fully dressed.

Caroline scrabbled between their bodies, found buttons, pulled and tugged and now he was helping her. His shirt was gone, her breasts were crushed against his bare chest and he was still except for his hands caressing down over her shoulders, his thumb tracing her spine, his breath hot on her neck.

She wriggled, not knowing what she wanted, only knowing that she needed him.

'Shh.' Gabriel's voice was a breath in her ear, a shiver that followed his fingers on her backbone. He set her slightly away from him and she protested, then stilled as the space gave room for the crisp hair on his chest to tease her breasts, for him to slide one hand up between their bodies to capture a nipple between thumb and forefinger, his palm cupping the breast as he rolled the sensitive nub until she was gasping, her forehead dropped on his shoulder for support, her hands clutching at his upper arms.

He moved, pulling her with him, and she was sprawled in his lap as he sat on the edge of the bed, one hand still tormenting her breast, his mouth on the other nipple, sucking and licking as the waves of sensation rippled through her, down to her belly, down between her legs. There was pressure, a building, aching pressure down there and she arched up, needing something to ease it, to end it, to make it last for ever.

As though he understood, Gabriel's hand slid from under her and he touched her *there* where she needed him. His fingers slipped into the swollen, wet, intimate folds as she bowed up to him, he bit gently on the nipple he was sucking and a shudder of some electric, terrifying sensation ran through her, then he slipped one finger, two, into her and she heard her own voice in an incoherent cry as the pleasure swept her away. Impossible to withstand, terrifying, wonderful.

He moved. She found herself alone on the narrow bed and whimpered, reaching blindly for him, for his heat, then Gabriel's weight was over her.

'Caroline.'

'Yes,' she panted. 'Gabriel. Please.'

He kissed her again, his lips travelling softly over her jaw, down her neck…

She smiled to herself, wrapped in the warmth of the pleasure he was giving her. She ran her fingers through his hair and gasped as his tongue met her breast again.

'Are you finally claiming my IOU?' she murmured, trailing her fingers down the solid muscles of his back.

He stilled.

Under her splayed fingers she could feel the shift of muscle, the tension that shivered under his skin. Then he rolled off her, down the floor and sat, back to the bed, his head on his raised knees.

'Gabriel?'

'I am sorry, Caroline. That should not have happened.'

Not? The pleasure still rippled through her, wonderful, transforming, but something inside her shrivelled like a rosebud in the frost. 'I want you. I am a grown woman, I can make my own decisions.' *I will not feel shame.* 'And you want me.' Which was the truth.

He stood up. Tall, beautiful, arrogantly male, half-naked. She wanted him to come back so she could touch him, explore that loose-limbed body, but she was too proud, too hurt, to ask.

'That was a mistake. The result of shared danger, suspense and too-close proximity.' Gabriel scooped up his shirt from the floor and pulled it over his head, his back turned to her. 'I have never... *Damn it*, I do not sleep with virgins. I should never have taken that idiotic IOU.'

He gathered up her scattered clothing, heaped it on a chair close by her, still without looking, and went to the fire.

'I do not regard it,' she said. She dragged on her clothes, fingers fumbling with laces and hooks.

'You are good to forgive it. Now it is better forgotten.'

What was there to say to that? *But that was the start of something wonderful? Please come back to me?* Presumably he thought verbal cold water worked as well as the real thing for quenching desire.

The silence seemed to fill the room like fog. Someone had to find a way through it. Be practical.

'Gabriel, where is there to hide here? The first thing Father is going to do is search all the buildings on the estate.'

He took a breath as though she had jerked him back from far away, but his voice was perfectly normal when he spoke. 'When I arrived here I looked for a cache for the things I brought with me that would have revealed my identity.' He had stopped frowning, no doubt because he could now stop thinking about what had just happened. 'You might say I've discovered a priest's hole. It is certainly large enough to hide you in.'

He bent over the hearth, raked the embers into a heap at the back and ducked under the piece of timber that had been nailed across the opening to make a shelf. 'Come and see.'

There was just room to stand beside him on the hot stone. Gabriel took the candle, put his foot into a crack in the masonry and began to climb. She saw the light dim as he seemed to thrust the candle into the wall, then with a heave he vanished, too. 'Can you follow me?' His head emerged, apparently out of solid stone.

'I'll try.' Caroline tucked up her skirts and got her toe into the first foothold.

It was a scramble, but with Gabriel's strong arm to haul on she found herself level with a hole that opened into a small chamber. 'What is this?' It smelled, not unpleasantly, of wood smoke.

'They built the tower as a hollow sham. Then your father wanted the place made habitable and told the builders to make a hearth. They created a shaft inside the tower with the chimney poking out below the crenulations, roofed over the top and sealed the opening at ground level. They could have filled in the tower completely, but that would have wasted stone and taken time, so they simply put in this intermediate level, I assume for support.

'I worked out what they had done, moved a stone or two to see if there was a possible hiding place and found this space. You can't see it from below and I doubt your father even realises it is here. I only found it because I was expecting makeshift construction—the whole place is no more than a stage set.'

Caroline looked around. There was a pair of valises stacked in the corner and when she lifted the candle she could see the roof high above her head. 'There's room to lie down and sleep.'

'I'll bring you up blankets.'

'Not yet. We have to talk.'

'In the morning.' Gabriel backed out of the hole and vanished. She heard him moving around below, then he reappeared with two blankets and her valise, went down again and brought up a jug. 'Drinking water.'

'I am coming down for a minute.' Caroline clambered down, which was considerably less easy than climbing up. 'I'll be back shortly,' she said as she went outside and headed for the edge of the clearing. There was a nice non-brambly clump of bushes just there, she recalled, and there were limits to how long she could be expected to sit in a tower trying not to think about running water. Although that was less uncomfortable than thinking about facing the man who had just brought her that shattering pleasure and almost relieved her of her maidenhood.

When she came back Gabriel was remaking the fire at the front edge of the hearth. 'I'll light it when you are up and keep it in all night, I've checked and the draw on the chimney is so good the smoke hardly gets into the chamber at all. When your father turns up I want the hearth to look as normal as possible.'

'You think of everything.' She paused beside him, laid her hand on his arm. 'Thank you so much. No one else would help me like this.'

'You have nothing to thank me for. I have nothing to lose by it and I was bored.'

She tried to disregard the cynicism which she suspected masked a very real anger over their almost-lovemaking. 'But if he discovers you helped me, my father might call you out.' Under her fingers she could feel the strength of his forearm, a swordsman's arm.

'And I would refuse to fight a man old enough to be my father, a perfectly honourable course.'

'Lucas, then!'

'I'd put him on his back with a neat rapier hole in his shoulder. Much less dangerous to his health than pistols.'

'You are exasperatingly calm about all this.' Caroline sat down on the simple wooden chair, her legs refusing to tolerate any more.

'I'm sorry.' Gabriel hitched one hip on the table and folded his arms. He had an edge to him that was new to her, the sense that he was operating at a different level of concentration and awareness than anyone else. Perhaps this was what made him the successful gambler that he was. Or perhaps that was what a frustrating, almost sexual encounter did to a man.

'Would you rather we had high drama?' he asked. 'I find that sort of thing distracting. Tomorrow I will send a letter and arrange a rendezvous. The hermit will vanish and your father has no means of finding him because every step of the process in London was under false names. My eminently sensible and well-connected friends will put their heads together with us and we will decide on how you can vanish and begin a new life.'

'I have been incredibly lucky, haven't I? And hopelessly naive.' The awareness swept through her along with the weariness. 'I was so worried about Anthony's lands that I came up with a quite shocking solution and I did not deserve your forbearance. And now you rescue me again at the risk of scandal.'

'Scandal does not concern me.'

'Why not?' She was almost asleep where she sat now, drowsy with reaction and a strange mixture of tension and relief. And awareness. The room seemed to be full of man… This man who now knew her body intimately, while she knew him not at all.

'There's a Scottish proverb I have always held by. *They say! What say they? Let them say.* I concern myself with the good opinion of those I respect, everyone else can go to the devil. And you, my lady, are asleep where you sit. Bed for you.'

That seemed such a good idea. He was pulling her to her feet and his arms were around her and he smelt of warmth and yew trees, smoke and man, and something musky. Mingled, it made a very excellent scent. 'Bottle it,' Caroline murmured, holding on to as much of Gabriel as she could get her arms around. Yes, bed was a wonderful idea. Bed with Gabriel.

'Asleep and dreaming,' he murmured in her ear. 'Come on, one foot in front of the other, and duck…and this foot up and there you go.'

A large hand was under her backside and she was heaved unceremoniously up and into the secret chamber. Her searching fingers found rough wool and Caroline had enough strength to roll on to one blanket and pull the other over her. Then she fell asleep.

Chapter Nine

Caroline woke to the scent of wood smoke mingling with coffee and bacon. A faint red glow marked the entrance to the chamber and she realised that Gabriel must have stirred up the fire and was making breakfast. She stretched, blushing as she remembered last night.

She crawled to the entrance and called down, 'Gabriel?' before she could think about being shy.

His voice echoed up the chimney. 'Stay there and I'll scout around.'

'But I need—'

'Stay!'

He was back within moments. 'Someone is coming. Keep back, keep silent.'

All thoughts of coffee, of embarrassment, of a convenient bush or of warm water vanished. Caroline retreated into the corner with the valises, pulling the blankets with her, and heard what had alerted Gabriel, the hoofbeats of horses moving fast.

'My lord?' That was Gabriel, his voice carrying from outside. He must have left the door open.

'My daughter. Have you seen her?'

'Lady Caroline? Not since last night, my lord. Is something amiss?' Gabriel had remembered his Welsh accent.

'Of course there's something damn well amiss, you idiot! She is missing.' That was Woodruffe.

'Search the place.' Her father again. There was the sound of booted feet on the stone flags.

'My lord, I protest!'

'You are in my employ and this is my property. I'll search what and where I please.' Her father was in the room now, his angry voice carrying clearly up the chimney. Caroline froze into immobility as the scraping of furniture being dragged over the flagged floor drowned out the sound of voices.

There's virtually nothing to search once they've overturned the bed. A loud thud suggested they had just done that.

'The chimney.'

'But the fire, my lord. It's alight.' That was one of the grooms.

'Step round it and look up, you dolt. Take the lantern.'

'I can see the sky, my lord,' the man said after a moment. A flicker of light hit the wall opposite the opening, but from below she knew the entrance was invisible. 'There's no one up there, that's for sure. And there's no ladder or rope or anything.'

'All right, come out, take that path there. You, go down that ride. Look for tracks.'

'My lord, I may be in your employ, but that does not mean I have to accept accusations of assisting in—what? A kidnap? Abduction? Elopement?' Gabriel had found just the right note of angered innocence.

'You, and every man in this place, will accept what I say,' her father snapped. 'And you spent time with her. Enough time for her to wind you round her finger.'

'And why should Lady Caroline do that, my lord?'

'Mind your own business and keep your place, damn you.'

Her nails were digging into her palms at the threat in her father's voice. She had seen him use his whip once on a hedger who had answered back. If he struck Gabriel she had no idea what the reaction would be. Murder, probably.

She had moved to the opening when Gabriel, sounding like an affronted Welsh solicitor's clerk, said, 'Then I must reconsider my employment here.'

Caroline stuffed her knuckles into her mouth to stifle the sudden urge to laugh. He was a loss to the stage, her father's hermit.

'Don't be a fool. Who else will pay you for sitting on a stump writing poetry? Stay here and keep watch. If you see anything, send to the house. If you can lay hands on her, lock her in the chapel.'

There was the sound of horses moving off, of shouts becoming fainter.

'Stay put a little longer,' Gabriel said quietly from below. 'I'll climb the hill and locate them all.'

It seemed like an hour before he came back, but she supposed, counting her own pounding pulse in the darkness, that it was only a few minutes.

'You can come down now.' When she arrived in front of him, rumpled and dusty and sneezing from the soot, he checked from the door again. 'You're safe to go out for a few minutes now, I'll heat you some water.'

When she returned Gabriel was busy at the fireside. 'Here, have some coffee. I have seen them all at a good distance. The guests are out with your father on horseback. There were three grooms, also mounted, they've gone down towards the lake away from here. I could see people searching on foot, but they're nearer the house. I think you can wash and we can safely have breakfast, then I'll go to the village and leave a letter at the posting house.'

Caroline sat down with more of a bump than she had intended. 'Don't go yet.' Her voice wavered and she took a moment to steady it. 'The post boy doesn't get to the inn until past ten.'

Gabriel put a mug on the table beside her and hunkered down to look into her face. 'Are you about to cry?' He sounded less than happy at the thought.

'No, of course not.' She wished she felt as confident of that as she sounded. 'I am just rather...shaken, I suppose.'

'Is this about last night?' He jerked his head towards the bed. 'Do you want to go back home?'

'No!'

'I wouldn't let you if you did.' Gabriel got to his feet with a swish of brown robes. 'I would assume you'd lost your wits. Look, last night must have been...fraught. You are tired. You are anxious and uncertain and you have no idea what is going to happen to you. And you have lost control of the situation to me. That's a combination calculated to make you weepy or angry or stupidly docile. Any one of those would be perfectly natural, but we have no time for any of them.'

'I can certainly manage anger,' she said and sat up straight to glare at him. 'Do you talk to every lady of your acquaintance like this? That must explain your reputation as a lover.'

'Sarcasm does not become you. And, no, I do not usually talk to a lady like that.' Gabriel smiled. The slow, reminiscent curl of his lips made something shift inside her, distracted her for a moment, dismayed her as she recognised both desire and jealousy in the jumble of emotions. 'I am speaking to you frankly as I would to a man because we do not have the luxury of soft words and end-less discussion here.'

Gabriel had not treated her as another man last night. He must have seen the kindling light of indignation in her eyes because he threw up his hands, palm out in the fencer's sign of surrender. 'Wash and eat your breakfast while I write the letter outside where I can keep an eye on things, then back up the chimney with you and I'll go to the village.'

Irritation with the entire male sex got her through bacon and eggs. Caroline cleaned the plate and mug in the bucket of warm water by the fire and put them away, leaving the remains of Gabriel's own breakfast where they lay. He could do his own washing up and besides, it emphasised to anyone who looked in that there was only one person there.

She scrambled up the chimney by herself, still determined to show him that she was not some weak and clinging female, subject to weeping. Show him that those moments in his bed had meant nothing. It was only as she rolled herself into the blanket and tried to catch up on her sleep that she realised he had probably been deliberately provoking her into just this spirit of militant determination. 'Wretch,' she muttered, despite the tinge of admiration for his tactics.

The day passed somehow. She slept, woke to find Gabriel had returned from the village and came down to eat, then retreated back to her cave. Life was beginning to take on an unreal, dreamlike quality. Perhaps she would spend for ever in this safe, smoky little chamber, venturing out at night like some woodland creature. Behind the unreality was the awareness that Gabriel was there, standing between her and whatever lurked in the darkness beyond the fire.

She worried about Anthony and how she would be able to write to him now. Would she find some way to see him when he was at school? How would she know if he was ill or unhappy? She had done the best she could for him, but she fretted that it was not enough. Her only consolation was that if she was married to Woodruffe she would not be with her brother either.

There was another visitation, this time by some of the guests, although they did not enter the chapel. The lurch of fear at the sound of their shouts shattered her dreaming state and she lay, gripping the edge of the blanket, as tense as a leveret hearing the fox stalking towards it through the grass.

When they had gone Gabriel stayed outside and she supposed he was presenting an innocent face to anyone who might be secretly observing. Eventually, stupefied by a mixture of boredom and anxiety, Caroline slept again.

She woke at the sound of someone inside the chimney, grabbed the water jug and raised it to throw as the pale oval of a face, eerily lit, rose above the edge of the opening.

'It's me,' Gabriel said, sharply.

'You frightened the life out of me. What happened to your beard?'

'Shaved it off. The relief is immense.' He boosted himself into the tiny room and pulled a candle and flint from his pocket. When he struck a light she could see that he was in breeches and shirtsleeves, his hair tied back.

'Oh.' Caroline grounded the jug and sat down again in her nest of blankets. 'But if anyone sees you they will guess something is wrong.'

'Petrus the Hermit has evaporated. We are about to leave.'

'Already?'

'It is almost dawn. The letter will have reached London by the evening post and one of my friends will be on his way with some sort of vehicle by now. I wrote to the two of them who are in London at the moment.'

'You are sure someone will come? What if they were engaged yesterday evening?'

'The letter had my seal with a certain mark we all use beside it. Our servants know to deliver messages immediately if they see that. Cris de Feaux once left a royal *levée* to bail Alex out of gaol when his footman smuggled that in to him.'

'The Marquess of Avenmore? But no one leaves a *levée* before the king. What did he do?'

'Fainted dramatically. Full length—which you have to agree is considerable—in front of the princesses. They had a lovely time fussing over him.'

'I have never spoken to him, but the Marquess of Avenmore looks so chilly and correct. I can't believe he would do such a thing.'

'Neither did anyone else. Therefore it could only have been genuine, so he got away with it. Cris has got away with a lot behind that façade of perfection.'

'And he would drive through the night for me?'

'No, for me. Although that's not to say he wouldn't rescue you if he knew you needed it. It might be Cris who comes or it might be Alex Tempest, who is Viscount Weybourn. The third of my closest friends, Grant Rivers, the Earl of Allundale, is at home in Northumberland. Come to think of it, Cris is probably still engrossed with the smuggler's widow, his new wife, so my money would be on Alex.'

Smuggler's widow? No, do not ask, just be thankful for rescue, although it was a shock to discover that three noblemen whom she had always assumed were upstanding members of society were, apparently, as ramshackle as Gabriel.

'There's hot water below and tea. You come down and get ready, I'll keep watch.' Gabriel vanished down the chimney, then called up, 'Hand down the valises first.'

An all-over wash in a bucket in front of the embers of the fire was bliss. Caroline had not realised how sticky and sooty she had become until she was clean again. She put on the fresh underwear she had packed, braided her hair tightly out of the way and found Gabriel outside checking over the clearing in the gathering light.

'Just making certain it all looks normal out here. I'll build the fire up, so there will be smoke from the chimney for a time, and we'll leave the interior as though I was coming back. It might just win us an advantage if they come by and assume I'm down at the lake or communing with nature in the woods.'

'Do you often commune with nature?' Caroline found she was feeling a trifle tipsy. The sense of unreality had returned.

Gabriel gave a snort of amusement. 'I wouldn't know how.'

No, she supposed he spent far too much time in smoky gaming hells. *When he isn't entertaining ladies in their luxurious silk-hung bedchambers.* 'This Spartan life must have been uncomfortable for you, in that case.' It came out more tartly than she had intended and she saw the sidelong look he sent her.

'I am capable of roughing it,' Gabriel said mildly. 'I do occasionally set foot outside, you know, but I am not used to spending so much time simply existing in one spot in the countryside.' He slung a leather satchel over his shoulder and picked up the valises. 'It is curiously restful. At least, it might be if I wasn't trying to remember my Welsh accent and using far too much energy keeping my temper with your father. Ready?'

'Ready.' She managed a smile as she fell into step beside him. What on earth was she doing? She was running away from home with a man she barely knew other than as a hardened gambler and a skilful deceiver. Just by leaving Knighton Park she had compromised herself and, after just one night alone with a man, had almost ruined herself. Not that Gabriel appeared to have been very affected by those hectic moments on his bed, Caroline thought ruefully, all too aware of the rangy body moving easily beside her, the wicked gypsy-dark looks of the man she was trusting with her life.

I might as well be hanged for a sheep as a lamb. If I am ruined it is a pity not to do it properly, not that he shows any interest in actually making love to me. He must be right and it was simply reaction, heat of the moment.

She stumbled over a tree root and Gabriel caught her arm, steadied her and then walked on, apparently as untroubled by the contact as he had been untouched by nearly making love to her last night.

Caroline resisted the urge to rub her arm where those long fingers had curled and held her, tried to ignore the shiver of heat that ran to her fingertips. *He doesn't want me.* He touched her with a careless efficiency that somehow underlined how unimportant those moments of contact were to him and was now acting like a totally impersonal escort through the woods.

She would do better to stop entertaining immodest thoughts about the Earl of Edenbridge and think instead about what she was going to do when she reached London. She had no money, no references and no skills to market. She doubted whether she'd even make a halfway competent housemaid. It was one thing knowing how a house-

hold should be run, another to have the knack of polishing
metalwork, getting stains out of carpets or black-leading
grates. She could speak French competently, Italian a little, play the piano and add up accounts, so she supposed
she might be employable as a governess in a not-very-
demanding household. But who would entrust their children to an unknown young woman with no recommen-
dations?

Perhaps Gabriel was a forger as well as a lock-picking,
play-acting, potential blackmailer... Her thoughts came to
a crashing stop as she walked into his exceedingly solid
back. *'Ough!'*

He had stopped behind a large oak by the opening into
the lane that led to the turnpike road. 'All clear.' He turned
towards the highway.

'The village is that way.' Caroline pointed to the foot-
path that led away across the meadows.

'I said in the note to meet us at the junction where the
gibbet is. With any luck no one will see the carriage and
they certainly would if it were to drive into the village to
collect us. If we keep to the wheel ruts we will avoid leaving tracks in the dewy grass.'

Caroline hitched up her skirts, jumped the shallow ditch
and followed. 'They gibbeted Black Sam Baggins the highwayman there last year and they haven't taken the remains
down yet. It's disgusting.'

'All the more reason for no one to suspect you'd be
hanging around there—if you'll pardon the expression—
waiting for a passing vehicle.'

When they reached the sinister black gallows with the
dangling iron cage Gabriel contemplated the revolting object while Caroline studiously counted how many varieties
of wild flower she could see in the opposite hedge.

'There's not a lot left of him,' Gabriel remarked.

'Some of the local people stole his clothes very early on, before he began to…you know. And now the superstitious ones have been taking bits as they drop off—finger and toe bones and so forth. They grind them up and put them in medicines. Apparently fragments of highwaymen aren't as efficacious as murderers, but we haven't had any of those for many years, thank goodness.'

'What on earth are deceased highwayman's toes supposed to cure?' Gabriel sounded more intrigued than disgusted. 'There's a fallen tree over there you can sit on while we wait. It looks dry, it is shielded from the road and you won't have to contemplate the remains of Black Sam.'

Caroline sat down. 'I think the bones are a cure for toothache and sore throats.'

'I'd rather have the sore throat. You stay here.' Gabriel melted away into the undergrowth.

By straining her eyes she could just make him out, still and watchful, his attention on the road. For a man who said he spent little time communing with nature, he certainly knew how to take advantage of it when he needed to. His russet greatcoat with its modest double cape and the conker-brown leather of his boots merged into the mottled foliage of the hedgerow and his dark head was hidden in the shade as the sun at last began to penetrate the trees.

As she stared she was able to make out one ungloved hand resting on the low bough of a young oak, then the sunlight sparked a glint of light off something metallic and she realised he was holding a pistol. If her father came, or Lucas, would he fire? Would she want him to? Of course not. But he wouldn't, she told herself. He would threaten, that was all. Gabriel wasn't reckless, nor really a criminal. He simply had a rather broader view of acceptable behaviour for an earl than she was used to.

There was the thud of hooves, felt through the soles of her boots before she heard it, then the jingle of a harness and an elegant carriage, glossy black and driven by a team of fine bays, appeared around the corner and drew up opposite her. The horses sidled and snorted, sensing perhaps the horrid thing hanging from the gibbet, and the coachman soothed them with a murmured word.

They stilled and for a moment nothing moved. Then Gabriel stepped out into the road, the hand that had held the pistol empty at his side. 'Good morning to you, Thomas.'

The coachman touched the brim of his hat. 'Good morning, my lord.'

The door on the far side from Caroline swung open and a man got out. 'This is a damnably early hour for anything but a duel, Gabe,' he remarked, his voice a pleasant drawl. 'Have you any idea what time I had to get out of my bed?'

'Did you bother to go to it?' Gabriel enquired. Caroline caught a glimpse of him across the backs of the horses as he strode forward and took the other man by the shoulders in a brief, fierce embrace.

'Oh, yes,' his friend said with a chuckle as he returned the gesture with a buffet to Gabriel's arm. 'My lady wife expects me to act in a husbandly manner these days.' Despite the laughter in his voice it was obvious to Caroline that this was one husband who was not bored with his marital bed.

'And how is Lady Weybourn?' Gabriel led his friend around the carriage.

'Blooming, now the queasiness has left her. But why the devil am I summoned to this particularly gruesome spot at the crack of dawn?'

'To rescue a lady in distress. Caroline, come and meet Alex Tempest.'

She emerged from her hiding place and walked towards

them, smiling slightly at the contrast between Gabriel's wild looks and the careless way he wore his plain and practical clothing and the elegant gentleman with the quizzical brows and the fashionable crop.

'Oh, well done, Gabe,' Viscount Weybourn said as she emerged. 'And about time, too.'

Chapter Ten

'No,' Gabriel said. 'No, no, and absolutely no. You have the wrong end of the stick, Alex.' Caroline was staring at him as though he was talking complete nonsense. Alex was within a whisker of a smirk. And of receiving a right hook to the chin.

'Lady Caroline, may I present Alex Tempest, Viscount Weybourn. Alex, Lady Caroline Holm, the daughter of Lord Knighton. Lady Caroline finds it necessary to leave her home clandestinely. Alone.'

'Alone?' Alex's infuriatingly expressive eyebrows rose. 'Then this is not an elo—'

'Absolutely not.' Caroline, thankfully, was still looking mystified. Gabriel contemplated kicking Alex on the ankle, then settled for saying, 'I am merely helping Lady Caroline remove herself from her father's house.'

'Where to?'

'London to start with. What happens after that is still to be decided.'

'Urgent, I gather?' Alex offered Caroline his arm and began to walk back to the carriage. 'I believe we have danced together at Almack's before now, Lady Caroline.'

'Just Caroline, please. And, yes, I recall that with pleasure, Lord Weybourn.'

'Before we begin a delightful reminiscence of every time the pair of you have met socially, could we get on our way, do you think?' Gabriel retrieved the bags and handed them up to the coachman. 'There is a certain urgency.'

'Why? An infuriated father with a shotgun on your trail?' Alex helped Caroline into a forward-facing seat and sat down beside her, leaving Gabriel to sit with his back to the horses. He lounged back into a corner and propped his boots up on the other end of the bench, enjoying Alex's wince at the insult to the plush upholstery.

'That and the prospect of a trip to the altar with Woodruffe.'

'Lord Woodruffe? Edgar Parfit?' Alex's eyes narrowed. 'No, really, Caroline, you don't want to go marrying him. A sad dog, that one.'

'No, of course I don't, which is why I am leaving home and Lord Edenbridge is helping me.'

'Your father is not open to reason on the subject?'

'No.'

There was a tremor in her voice and Gabriel glared at Alex, even as he saw the other man's face harden as he heard it, too. He knew about Woodruffe's proclivities, too, it appeared.

'Nothing for it but to take a bolt to town, I see,' Alex said easily. 'You've nothing to worry about now. Gabe's a scape-gallows, but I am thoroughly reliable and exceedingly respectable.'

'If you are respectable it is only because of Tess's influence.'

'The love of a good woman,' Alex said smugly.

Was that why Alex was so eager to assume this was an elopement—he was in love and therefore Gabriel's actions must stem from the same source? He liked Caroline. Very much, he realised as he watched her making the effort to be calm and pleasant with Alex. He admired her. He desired her physically, which was hardly a surprise to him. And he would fight anyone who tried to hurt her. But then any gentleman with a shred of honour was duty-bound to protect a lady. The uncomfortable feeling of possessiveness was simply because this was the lady whose safety had fallen to him to defend.

'Now, are you hungry, Caroline?' Alex said. 'We have a breakfast hamper under Gabriel's seat. Dig it out, there's a good fellow.'

'Food that someone else has cooked?' Gabriel swung his feet down and bent to explore the wicker basket. He was hungry. That was probably why he was brooding on his emotional state, of all things. 'Heaven.'

'Do I deduce that you have been fending for yourself?' Alex caught the packet of bacon-filled rolls that Gabriel tossed at him. 'That I should like to see.'

'Lord Edenbridge has been acting as a hermit, part of my father's landscaped park.' Caroline took the roll Alex passed to her and a napkin that Gabriel unearthed from the hamper. 'The kitchen sent him down supplies, but he has been cooking for himself in the hermitage.'

'One snigger from you, Tempest, and you will regret it,' Gabriel warned.

'Dressed how?' Alex demanded, filling beakers from a flask of cold tea. 'Not in robes, surely?'

'Oh, yes, with an enormous beard and a beautiful Welsh accent.' Caroline was recovering her spirits along with the food, Gabriel was glad to see. 'He was very convincing.'

'Of course I saw the beard.' Alex chuckled. 'He was able to fool even Tess with such a disguise. But why—?' Under Gabriel's fulminating stare Alex snapped his mouth shut, but there was more speculation than amusement in the sharp hazel gaze that met his.

'Later,' Gabriel said. 'I am only going to explain this once and I have no doubt there will be an audience awaiting us. Where are we going?'

'Half Moon Street. My house. I sent a note to Cris and told him I would fetch you, but you are right, it is certain we'll find him there with Tamsyn when we arrive.'

'The Marquess of Avenmore? I have never met him, but I know his reputation. He is not going to approve of me, is he?' Caroline sounded anxious again.

'Cris is a pussy cat since his smuggler's widow got her hands on him,' Gabriel said, contemplating the choice between a raised pork pie or a slice of cheese flan and deciding on both.

'He'll fillet you if he hears you describing Tamsyn in those terms.' Alex poured Caroline some more tea and settled to explaining that the new marchioness was a perfectly respectable lady who had committed the minor indiscretion of a first marriage to the leader of a gang of smugglers.

She was relaxing now, even laughing at Alex's irreverent remarks. He had an indecent amount of charm when he chose to exert it. Before his marriage he had been wary of directing it at unmarried ladies and since his marriage he was probably in danger of grievous bodily harm from his adoring wife if he flirted, but Gabriel could tell he could not resist trying to put Caroline at her ease.

He should be glad of it. The last thing they wanted on their hands was a frightened woman, too nervous to make a decision about her own future. On the other hand, his idiocy last night had probably given her plenty to think about. Thank heavens he'd the self-control to stop. But what had he been thinking about? *With my damn boots on, too.* He could only account for it as the release of tension after the dangers of the night.

'What are you glowering about?' Alex enquired.

'Is anything wrong, Gabriel?'

The last thing he needed was anxious sympathy and a pair of worried blue eyes gazing at him, to feel this strange pang under his breastbone because she was looking weary and that lovely blonde hair was bedraggled, with just one lock coming loose to her collar. He wanted to kiss the shadows under those periwinkle eyes…

'Tired, that's all. If Alex would only be quiet for five minutes together, I'd go to sleep.' He stretched his legs out along the seat again, tipped his hat over his eyes and pre-pared to feign slumber. It came immediately, taking him by surprise, whirling him down into soft darkness and strange dreams, soothed by a soft, unfamiliar chuckle. *I've never heard her laugh, not like that…* Gabriel slept.

'We have arrived. Do you have a veil?'

Alex's words, the first in over an hour, jerked Caroline out of the trance state she had entered as the effects of food, warmth and safety took effect. She had been watch-ing Gabriel as he slept, his long body loose and beautiful in its unconsidered sprawl. He should have seemed vul-nerable, but she had seen the sudden tensing of his hands as they had slowed for a turnpike, then the instant relax-ation as the familiar bustle of the gate registered with his sleeping brain. In a crisis he would have been awake and dangerous in seconds.

'A veil? No, I am sorry.' Of course, the viscount would not want his neighbours recognising the crumpled and unchaperoned female stumbling out of his carriage. This was a fashionable street and at least a few residents would know her by sight.

'No need to worry, Tess made me bring one.' Alex produced a handful of black gauze from his pocket and she swathed it over head and face as Gabriel sat up, got his feet on the floor and his hat straight.

'What time is it?'

'Gone twelve. Later than I'd planned, but Caroline would not let me spring the horses, said it would wake you up.'

Alex got out as the front door opened and Caroline made a business of ordering her skirts, grateful that the veil obscured her blush at the look Gabriel sent her. No doubt he was as surprised over her concern as Alex had been.

'Have you got them safe?' A lady was in the hall, flushed from Alex's enthusiastic kiss. Caroline's immediate impression was of softness—soft brown hair, soft curves on a slender frame, soft voice. 'Oh, yes, there you are, Gabriel, and this must be— Oh!' Caroline pushed back the folds of her veil. 'But you are Lady Caroline Holm, I recognise you, although we have never met.' She turned to the open door behind her. 'Cris, Tamsyn, they are here safe.'

The tall, intimidating figure of the Marquess of Avenmore appeared in the doorway and, in front of him, a young woman who said, 'But I've seen you before. In the corridor at Lady Ancaster's soirée, with Gabriel.'

'At Lady Ancaster's…' That must have been when Gabriel had just kissed her, had told her that he had never meant to act on the IOU for her virtue, had dismissed her, leaving her feeling naive and gauche and unwanted. This young woman had come up behind Gabriel. Had she overheard what Caroline had said? *A promise is a promise, but if you do not want me—*

It could have meant anything, she told herself desper-

ately. *If you do not want me to dance with you next week.*
If you do not want me to give you one of the kittens...

'Kittens,' she said out loud, wondering if she was about
to faint.

'For goodness sake, the poor dear is on the point of collapse.' It was the brunette again. 'Make room, all of you,
and let her come into the drawing room.'

Hands propelled her through the door before she had
the opportunity to make her curtsy to the marquess, which
suddenly seemed important. She found herself seated on a
chaise in front of a small fire that was comforting, despite
the warmth of the day.

'Tea is coming. Now put up your feet and we will send
these men out.' The brunette made vague flapping gestures as though shooing chickens and the three large males
obediently took themselves off, leaving the room sooth-
ingly quiet.

'Now do not feel you have to explain anything just yet,'
the lady from the soirée said. 'If you have been with Gabriel for several days you probably just want to lie down
with a cold compress on your head and sip camomile tea.
That man manages to be utterly exhausting, even when
he is simply standing still.'

'It is because he looks as though he is thinking wicked
thoughts all the time,' the soft-voiced one said. 'Really *very*
wicked thoughts, even when he has a perfectly straight
face. And I get intrigued and wonder about them and how
wicked they are…and then I catch his eye and I am convinced he knows I am imagining such things so I blush and
he smiles and then—' She laughed. 'And here I am, very
happily married, passionately in love with my husband,
pregnant, and the very last thing I want is to be doing anything even mildly naughty with Gabriel Stone. I'm Tess,

by the way. Teresa Tempest, which is a ridiculous name. And this is Tamsyn de Feaux.'

'Lady Weybourn, Lady Avenmore.' Caroline dragged her tumbling thoughts back from contemplating Gabriel and wickedness and tried to remember her manners. 'I am Caroline Holm, Lord Knighton's daughter.'

'And you are very welcome to my house,' Tess said warmly. 'Gabriel's note simply said you needed rescuing. May we ask what from?'

'Edgar Parfit, Lord Woodruffe. And, I suppose, from my father.'

'He wants you to marry that slug? Well then, certainly you must be rescued!' Tess turned to Tamsyn. 'Have you met him? He's a nasty, unhealthy, pale colour with fat hands and thick lips and a beastly habit of ogling any female who is not well protected. Even when you are, he tries to stand too close, or brush against you by *accident*. I stood on his toes with my new French heels the other evening—quite by accident, of course. He had tried to pinch my *derrière*. And he must need money because he is wildly extravagant.'

'Fortunately I haven't been out in London society long enough to have encountered him.' Tamsyn regarded Caroline, head on one side. Caroline made an effort to sit up straighter and not look as feeble as she felt, just at this moment. This woman, the smuggler's widow, looked as though she would take a musket to Lord Woodruffe if provoked, not run away. 'I suppose that just refusing to marry him didn't work?'

'No.' Caroline took a deep breath. 'You will probably think I am exaggerating the problem. I had better tell you everything.' *Not about my IOU, bartering my virginity for the deeds, but everything else. They need to understand.*

* * *

There was silence when she finished, then Tamsyn, her faint Devon accent heightened by emotion. said, 'Your father is somewhat obsessional, is he not? And in the grip of a strong compulsion to gamble. I can understand how dangerous that can be. My cousin Franklin, Lord Chelford, got himself in over his head with gambling debts, then moneylenders, and ended with vandalism, murder and an attempt to frame me for the crime.'

'And he almost managed to murder you,' Tess said with a shudder. 'It is all a secret, of course. People think he went slightly insane and died after an unfortunate encounter with a Bow Street Runner.

'Anyway, we understand that people do act in these extreme ways and that you aren't exaggerating in the slightest. Besides anything else, if your father is going to use force, then nothing else matters. And Gabriel is just the person to help, he was wonderful with Tamsyn's problem.'

'Once he stopped lecturing Cris on how unsuitable I was for a marquess,' Tamsyn said with a grimace. 'He was quite right, of course, but it did not endear him to me at the time!'

'There are four of them, close friends.' Caroline tried to pick her way through the relationships. 'Gabriel, your husbands and someone else? Gabriel did tell me, but I'm afraid I have forgotten.'

'Grant Rivers, Earl of Allundale. He and his wife Kate live up in Northumberland with their two children. I wish they would come down to London for a while, but Kate is shy of society. So, you have five of us on hand to help, although if you need to flee the area, I am sure Grant and Kate would give you sanctuary.'

'I can't just run away and hide for ever. I do not have any money, just a little jewellery, so I must earn my living somehow. I suppose I could become a nursery governess, or a companion to a reclusive old lady, if you wouldn't mind providing me with references? I am very reliable, despite appearances.'

And horribly afraid, and ridiculously homesick, despite everything. And Anthony. Could I have looked after him any better by staying?

'It would not be as bad as marriage to the Egregious Edgar, but a pretty grim existence nevertheless,' Tess said. 'I almost ended up like that, only in my case it was that or become a nun.'

A nun? 'I can see that marriage to Lord Weybourn was preferable,' Caroline said, finding her spirits rising as she finished her second cup of tea. She still could see no easy way out of her problems, but at least she felt confident her new friends would not desert her. She need not feel afraid now and married to Woodruffe she would have been just as cut off from Anthony.

There was a tap on the door and a maid came in. 'The bath is ready, my lady. And Miss Perkins is brushing and pressing your gowns, ma'am,' she added with a bob of a curtsy to Caroline.

'A bath would be heaven,' Caroline said as the door closed behind the maid. 'I have spent a day and a night up a chimney.'

'I would have thought that Gabriel would look after a lady better than that,' Tamsyn said with a chuckle. 'On the other hand, he is the only man I know who would think of hiding someone in such a place, so, on balance, it was probably for the best.'

'Are you ready to get out now, ma'am? Or should I top up the hot water?'

'Oh, top it up, please. I'll lie here for a while longer.'

134   *The Unexpected Marriage of Gabriel Stone*

Caroline slid under the scented water once more, rubbing at her scalp until she was convinced that every last piece of grit, soot and dead spider was out of it.

'I'll be back in a while then, ma'am.' The maid heaped towels on a chair and went out.

After ten minutes the water began to cool and there was no sign of the maid. Or of a bell pull. Caroline climbed out and wrapped herself in a large bath sheet, towelled her hair and began to explore. She tried one door and found herself in a large bedchamber, the dressing table littered with perfume sprays, hair brushes and ribbons. She rather suspected that this was Tess's own room.

She could hardly rummage in the clothes presses for a robe. Caroline tied her damp hair up into a turban with a small towel and cracked open the door on to the corridor. Still no sign of the maid, so she ventured out, her bare toes curling into the deep pile of the carpet runner over the polished boards. What had happened to the girl?

The door opposite her opened, she took a hasty step backwards, trod on the trailing edge of the towel and sat down with a thud as one of the Roman emperors appeared on the threshold.

'Caroline? What the devil are you doing?' Not a Roman emperor, just Gabriel, swathed as she was in linen.

'Looking for the maid.' She scrabbled at the fabric, too embarrassed to look down and see just how much of her wet body was exposed. Even if there was no bare flesh, then damp linen was surely clinging to every curve. She tried to hold Gabriel's gaze to stop it moving down below her face. 'She vanished and I've no robe.'

'Nor have I and Alex's valet is nowhere to be seen.' He grinned, but behind the amusement was something she had never seen in his face before, the thing that had been piquing her feminine pride ever since her first reckless

proposal to him. There was heat in his eyes, and awareness, and he was not the rake who had made the agreement,
not the man who had kissed her at the soirée. And he was
most certainly not the hermit who had been focused on
knight-errantry and rescuing her from her father's ploys.

This Gabriel was looking at her as a man looks at a
woman he wants, with all his attention, and she had no idea
whether she was terrified or thrilled. It had meant something to him, after all. *He is remembering what nearly happened in the chapel, he desires me.* The blood was singing
in her veins and her breath was coming in short gasps and
the sight of his naked shoulders and arms was enough to
make her want to drag him back into the dressing room
and— He stepped back and closed the door sharply just
before she, too, heard the hurrying footsteps.

'Oh, miss, I'm ever so sorry, I was bringing your robe
from the laundry and then Prue knocked a pile of my
lady's lace on to the floor, so I bent to pick it up before
it got soiled and tripped up his lordship's valet who was
bringing Lord Edenbridge's robe and…'

'Not a problem. Just shut the door.' Caroline got to her
feet, careless of dignity. Those eyes, dark and intense and
locked with hers. She looked down at herself and was
faintly surprised not to see steam rising.

'Yes, miss. Sorry, miss.'

Caroline put on the robe and let the maid deal with her
hair, then dressed, scolding herself all the while.

*Focus. This is not about Gabriel. This is about making
a new life for myself, about staying safe. About not ending
up starving in the gutter or in some brothel. The man is a
rake and whatever he wants, even if it is me again for five
minutes, it will not last. So stop daydreaming. And anyway, he doesn't really want* me, *he's just a typical man.
That night we were so wound up it is a miracle we didn't*

combust from tension and just now I was sprawled at his feet, nearly naked. He would have reacted like that whoever it was.

'Her ladyship says, she can send up luncheon on a tray, or you are very welcome to come down. Whatever you wish, miss.'

'I'll go down.' Caroline put her shoulders back, her chin up and made for the stairs. This was the start of her new life as an independent woman and she was going to take control, with the help of her new friends and allies.

Chapter Eleven

'What is this? A Board of Inquiry, or a jury?' Gabriel entered the drawing room to find a semicircle of his friends facing him. 'I deny everything, on principle.'

The habit of self-protection, of hiding his feelings and his vulnerabilities, came back to help him. Then it had been a shelter from his father's savage temper, the act that had allowed him to be strong enough to protect his brothers, the locked door behind which he could trap his own fear and vulnerability, his own guilt that somehow he could have prevented his mother's suicide.

It had become his gambler's mask and now he was using it to conceal emotions from his closest friends. He did not understand what he was feeling himself and, if he was not careful, he was going to entangle an innocent woman, a woman who had to be protected from all the darkness in his soul, just as she must be protected from Woodruffe's cruelty.

'We are concerned, that is all.' Cris de Feaux sat back and crossed his legs, the gleam on his Hessians a reproach to every other pair of boots in the room.

'For both of you,' Tess said, a crease of worry between her finely drawn brown brows.

'You must admit, this affair is not going to be easy to carry off without scandal,' Alex said. 'Sherry?'

'Loathe the stuff. Scandal is out of the question. We need to get Caroline out of this with as little gossip as possible.' He slouched in the one remaining armchair, the one facing the jury, and concentrated on keeping the tension out of his expression. 'Woodruffe must not find out where she is, let alone her father. The man beat her.'

'Bastard,' Tamsyn said, with feeling. 'Men like that need a good flogging themselves.'

Caroline's slender shoulders as she sat there on the floor draped in that bath sheet, the pale, soft skin. The delicate bones under his hands on the narrow bed... He could not get the image out of his head. And that swine had struck her. He was going to pay for that.

'But I do not see how we can avoid scandal,' Tess said. 'Caroline is of age, of course, and that helps. But you can't marry her under a false name and even though you can obviously protect her physically, you can't hide her. This is not a novel with secret wives hidden in some tower in the forest. Knighton and Woodruffe will raise every kind of storm. Lady Caroline will never be received at Court.'

'Or, given your reputation already, Gabe, anywhere else,' Alex commented.

'Marriage?' Gabriel stared at them, jolted right out of his normal control. 'Are you mad? Whatever gave you the idea I want to *marry* the chit?' *Damnation, this was what came of brooding about* feelings, *I let my guard down and overreact.*

'The fact that you eloped with her?' Cris said.

'Lord Edenbridge did not elope with me. He helped me escape.' The voice from the doorway was cool and polite and, Gabriel could tell after days spent in her company, the speaker was furious.

The other men got to their feet and Gabriel followed, more slowly. Caroline was standing behind him, her hair in ringlets on top of her head, her creased gown restored to order, her expression completely unreadable.

'I have no intention of marrying Lord Edenbridge and he has no desire to marry me, which is an agreeable co-incidence, is it not?'

She passed him, close enough to touch, close enough for him to have reached out and twitched a pin or two out of that provoking coiffure to see her hair tumble free. Gabriel kept his hands by his side and worked on restoring his expression to one of amused calm.

'I am very grateful to you, my lord,' she said earnestly, stopping just in front of him. 'But if you call me a chit again I will have you kidnapped and force-fed sherry for a week.'

'You were eavesdropping,' he drawled, still fighting the tumbling curls fantasy. 'No one ever hears good of themselves by listening at doors.'

'A fortnight,' Caroline amended with a sweet smile.

Cris gave a crack of laughter. 'Please, take my chair, Lady Caroline.'

'Thank you, Lord Avenmore.'

She sat with perfect decorum, while Gabriel's memory provided a series of images of anything but ladylike behaviour—Caroline scrambling up the chimney, Caroline in a tangle of wet towels, Caroline standing on his hearth rug making him an outrageous proposition. Caroline under him in the split second before he got control of himself. He knew which version he preferred. He lowered his lids and sent her the smouldering look that was guaranteed to send innocent young debutantes fleeing to their mamas like a flock of panicking chickens. The one that should send her to safety from a man who was thoroughly unsuited for matrimony.

She looked down her nose at him, perfectly composed, then turned towards Tess. 'I do not expect ever to regain the place in society I once had,' she explained. 'I am hoping for something respectable, but retired, like a companion's post. I might pass muster as a nursery governess, I suppose. Or I could keep house, I have done that for my father for years.'

'You would need references,' Tamsyn pointed out. 'Although we could supply those.'

'You are ridiculously young to be a housekeeper,' Gabriel said, sharply enough for the others to turn and look at him.

'It is the most respectable option,' Tamsyn pointed out with annoying reasonableness. 'And the safest. Housekeepers have some status in the establishment so they are less at the mercy of predatory males in the household than governesses are and companions are very likely to become general dogsbodies.'

'Even so.' Gabriel waved a hand to encompass Caroline's face, hairstyle, figure. 'She looks far too young.' *And vulnerable. And tempting.* And she should be kept away from men like him. Men who had no model of a decent marriage, men whose very blood was tainted. *Blood.* The picture swirled back from behind the locked door. His father's broken body, the blood on the marble. His father dead, the death itself the scandal of the area because Gabriel had failed in his duty to those who depended on him.

'A cap, a pair of spectacles with plain glass and a severe manner,' suggested Tess, her head on one side, eyes narrowed, as she studied Caroline. 'Add a sensible wardrobe, a chatelaine... There is nothing like a bunch of keys rattling at the waist to give an impression of gravitas. I made Alex an admirable housekeeper.'

Her husband snorted. 'I would be interested to see the slightest evidence of gravitas, my lady.'

'I still do not like it,' Gabriel said, attempting to ignore their exchange of adoring looks. What the devil was he doing? He had brought Caroline here so his friends could help her and they were. It was not as though he had any brilliant ideas himself. They would help protect her from Woodruffe and her father and they would protect her from him, the man who wanted to taste that innocence at the same time as he wanted to guard it.

All three women sent him exasperated looks, Alex regarded the ceiling and pursed his lips in a silent whistle and Cris observed, 'If you do not marry Lady Caroline, her options are very limited.'

'Lord Edenbridge's wishes in the matter are irrelevant,' Caroline said, very pink in the face. 'I have no intention of marrying *him*. Grateful as I am to him for rescuing me, he is not, I am sure you would agree, suitable husband material.'

'I never suggested that I was,' Gabriel retorted. *But if I was, would I be courting you, Caroline? Would I want that smile and those lips, that loyalty and that passion, for myself? Oh, yes.*

'Luncheon is served, my lady.'

'I'm sure we'll all be in a much better frame of mind for planning when we have eaten,' Tess said, getting to her feet and leading the way to the dining room.

'How did you meet?' Cris enquired once they were all seated with food in front of them.

'My father lost an estate in Hertfordshire to Lord Edenbridge. It should have gone to my younger brother. I explained the situation and Lord Edenbridge kindly agreed to keep Springbourne in trust for Anthony until he is of age.'

The words *He did what?* hung unspoken in the air.

'Remarkably generous of you, Gabriel,' Cris eventually remarked.

'Remarkably unlike you,' Alex added.

'I am not in the business of robbing innocent striplings of their inheritance simply because their parent is a fool,' Gabriel retorted. 'I would never have accepted the stake if I had known. Lady Caroline saved me from an unwitting blunder.'

'It was brave of you to approach someone with such a wild reputation as Gabriel, Caroline,' Tamsyn said. 'That would have been at Lady Ancaster's soirée, I imagine.'

'No, I went to his house before then,' Caroline admitted calmly.

Surely she was not going to tell them about that outrageous offer? His conscience, unused to scrutiny in the harsh light of day, was still tender on that subject.

'I explained the circumstances frankly and Lord Edenbridge was very...accommodating.'

'I am still not clear when Gabriel realised you had a further problem, or quite what he was doing in Hertfordshire,' Cris said as he buttered a roll. 'From a fleeting allusion he made when he was down in Devon, I gather you had met some time in June, yet here we are in early August.'

'We had some limited correspondence about the estate,' Gabriel said, choosing his words with care. 'I suspected something was wrong and when I discovered that Lord Knighton was looking for a hermit for his park I thought it would be amusing to see if I could fool him and check on Lady Caroline's well-being at the same time.'

'A hermit?' For once he had the satisfaction of seeing

Cris's jaw drop. He made a quick recovery. 'Hence the appalling length of your hair, I assume,' he drawled.

'It went beautifully with the beard,' Caroline remarked demurely. 'Lord Edenbridge grewa most impressive one and spoke with a Welsh accent.'

'Yes, and please do not do it again.' Alex gave an exaggerated shudder. 'My dear fellow, one must make every effort to assist a lady, but really, there are limits.'

'I doubt you could produce a beard that would cover your features in under a month, Tempest,' Gabriel retorted.

'I'd advise a severe and fashionable crop as well,' Cris said. 'Just in case Knighton comes storming up to town and recognises his missing hermit. I'll get my valet to cut it for you.'

'The things I do for you, Lady Caroline,' Gabriel said, trying to recall the last time he had had a haircut that might have been thought *severe and fashionable*.

'I am exceedingly grateful, my lord.' She dimpled prettily at him across the table, looking so much like some airheaded miss, and so unlike the young woman he had come to know, that he almost choked on his ale.

'I have an idea,' Tess said suddenly. 'We'll go down and talk to Mrs Sanders, our housekeeper. She'll soon transform you into a convincing candidate.'

'She transforms me into a nervous jelly,' Alex admitted. 'Fearsome woman.'

'And Tamsyn and I will write you references, and I'll get in touch with Kate in Northumberland and ask her for one as well, and then you'll be ready to approach the domestic agencies. Unless we can come up with someone who needs a housekeeper before then.'

Needs a housekeeper... Really, his brain must have been atrophied by the country air. Why on earth had he not thought of it before? 'There is no need for references, although the training might be a good thing.' Gabriel put down his knife and fork and swept a glance around the table. 'May I present to you the new housekeeper of Springbourne?'

'Oh, how clever of you, Gabriel!' Caroline beamed at him across the table, all dignity forgotten, and he caught the swift exchange of glances between the other women at her use of his name. 'Why didn't I think of that? I'll be safe there until Anthony comes of age in five years' time. Father thinks it is yours, so he will have no reason to go anywhere near it. Then, when Anthony can legally control it, I can continue living with him.'

'Are there staff there now?' Tess asked.

'Just a few, I think, more for security than anything else,' she said, suddenly serious. 'They certainly do not know me by sight.'

'I sent my man of business down to report,' Gabriel said. 'He found a tenant at the Home Farm who had only been there a year and who seemed competent enough. The house is virtually shut up, as Caroline says, with an elderly housekeeper and a trio of indoor servants. He suggested I pension off the housekeeper, who is anxious to go and live with her sister in Worthing, and keep the other staff. I haven't had time to reply to him yet.'

'It is the perfect solution.' Caroline was glowing at him again, which was good for his self-esteem, but fatal for his detachment. Gabriel thought about scratchy beards, porridge and Edgar Parfit and shifted in his seat when all of those failed to stop most of his blood supply heading southwards. It was lust, simply lust, that he felt and the sooner she was away, the better.

'I will be working for my brother, so I can draw a wage and living expenses from the estate with a good conscience and I will make certain it is in perfect order for him when he can finally claim it.'

'What will you tell him?' Tamsyn asked. 'Does he know your father has lost the estate?'

'No. I thought it best not to say anything unless Father told Anthony, in case he reacted in a way that betrayed the secret. But I am sure my father has simply put it out of his mind. Water under the bridge.' She bit her lip. 'Anthony will be wondering why I haven't written, I always do every week while he is at school. Normally he'd be home now, but he is staying with a friend in Buckinghamshire. I miss him.' She smiled bleakly. 'I wonder when I will see him again.'

'We will discuss the details now if you have finished your luncheon.' Gabriel stood. 'I'll find my notes. There is no need to trouble the rest of you. We can use your breakfast room, I suppose, Tess?' There was a limit to how long he was prepared to stay the focus of his friends' fascinated scrutiny, or to endure Caroline looking at him in public as though he was her hero again. The sooner they had this sorted out and she was in safe seclusion in the country, the better.

'I'll come now, if you will excuse me?' She stood up, smiling at the others, and he wondered just how well that smile would stay fixed if she knew the lascivious thoughts that would not get themselves out of his head, the urge to seize her and snarl *Mine!* at every man who looked at her.

He picked up his portfolio from the luggage in the hall and led the way to the little breakfast room. Caroline sat on the sofa, folded her hands neatly in her lap and appeared ready to give him her full attention, much as if he was addressing a public meeting.

Nettled, Gabriel sat at his ease in the chair opposite her, fished out the correspondence from his agent and ran a finger down it. 'I'll get him to pension off the old house-keeper and tell the staff I will send them a new one.

'Now, money. Wilkins is already managing the staff salaries. I'll have him add you to the list, but pay you a year in advance, and I'll authorise you to draw on an account for everything you need for the household and for yourself.'

'Will he not be surprised at the payment in advance?' She yawned, hastily hiding it behind her hand.

'He'll assume you are one of my light-skirts that I am paying off,' Gabriel said with deliberate crudity as he studied the papers again. He had no idea what was motivating him, which was worrying in itself. Perhaps he wanted to prove to himself that he was the same old rakehell he had always, so comfortably, been. Or perhaps he simply wanted to provoke some reaction, even if it was only a delightful blush.

There was no response. He looked up, anticipating one of Caroline's frosty stares, which were stimulating in their own way, and found that she was asleep, slumped sideways on to the sofa cushions. The piled curls were already surrendering to the forces of gravity, the pins sliding free from the glossy, newly washed hair, and her mouth was very slightly open, the parted pink lips wreaking havoc with his pulse rate. When he got silently to his feet and bent over her he saw the dark curl of lashes on her cheek, the soft vulnerability of her skin, the shadows of worry and exhaustion beneath her eyes.

Gabriel thought about lifting her feet on to the sofa, of loosening her bodice, her stays, so she could be more comfortable… *No.* But he leaned down, touched her cheek with the back of his fingers, watched as she smiled in her sleep at his touch and felt something turn over in his chest. Innocence and trust were enough to touch even the most cynical of hearts, it seemed.

He went out into the hall, closing the door softly behind him and met Tess. 'Caroline is asleep.'

'I am not surprised, she must be exhausted. I don't suppose it occurred to you to allow for a little feminine weakness in planning your adventure?'

'If I had, she'd be back in her father's hands by now. Or I'd have shot him. She's tougher than she looks, is Caroline Holm.'

Tess shook her head at him. 'Idiot man. She is brave and stoical and she will obviously do anything for her little brother.' Her penetrating stare had him wanting to shift uncomfortably. He resisted the weakness and smiled back, his lazy wolf smile. Tess's glare hardened. 'She is not strong, Gabriel, simply courageous. Do not try her too hard. I was brought up in a nunnery, in cold rooms, on plain food and hard work. Tamsyn has been acting as an estate manager for years, out in all weathers on that harsh Devon coast. But Caroline is like Kate, a lady—and raised as one.' She moved as though to leave him, then added, 'And don't you dare ruin her.'

'You believe I haven't already?' The way she was sniping at him, he would not be surprised if she had not guessed at the temptation that racked him.

'Do you honestly think I would have you in this house if I suspected you would do that? Friend of Alex's or not, your sorry carcase wouldn't cross the threshold, believe me.'

The dangerous silence that followed that remark hung between them for a full half-minute, then Tess laughed. 'It is such fun to tease you.'

He laughed, too, as he followed her back to the drawing room, telling himself that he had absolutely nothing to worry about. Caroline would be safely, respectably, hidden and his life could return to normal, mercifully free of female interference. Perfect. He wondered why he did not feel happier about it.

Cris strolled in. 'If you've nothing better to do, my valet will cut your hair now.'

Gabriel hauled himself to his feet and went upstairs to his fate.

Chapter Twelve

'It is a very extravagant carriage for a housekeeper.' Caroline stood on the front steps of Tess's house and studied the chaise and four that stood at the kerb while the footmen loaded on her new trunk. 'Will it not cause gossip if I do not travel on the stage?'

'You are a very superior housekeeper and I am a top-lofty employer who would not dream of his upper servants being seen on the common coach.' Gabriel said. He seemed distant somehow, with his fashionable cropped hair, and he was more smartly dressed than she had ever seen him. He had a cool detachment that she guessed was the manner he adopted when he was playing cards. It certainly succeeded in hiding his feelings from her.

Not that they had been very apparent for the past four days in any case. While she had remained secluded in Half Moon Street he had communicated by politely formal notes, recounting his agent's progress in despatching the elderly Mrs Buckley to her retirement and setting up funds for Caroline to draw on. Yesterday evening the man himself had arrived, fresh from the country, bringing the account books for Caroline to go through with him.

Tess's housekeeper had chosen her new wardrobe of

respectable plain gowns and caps and Dollands in Bond Street had sent two pairs of spectacles with plain lenses. She had gone, heavily veiled, to the domestic agency to interview for her own maid who would be picked up from there on the way so there was nothing to connect her with the Weybourns' house. The address of Reddish's Hotel in Jermyn Street had completely satisfied the agency.

'You look the part and we have left no kind of trail anywhere.' Gabriel seemed relaxed, standing on the step beside her, but she could tell he was watching the street.

'And you look different,' she said without thinking.

'It is the hair.' He glanced down at her, a formal stranger.

'No, it is more than that. You look positively respect...' *Oh, goodness, that was not tactful.* 'I mean...'

'Respectable,' he agreed with a shrug. 'Wrestling with your brother's estate has prompted an unusual desire to be about the business of my own properties. I have the haircut so I thought I would further unnerve my various solicitors, bankers and agents by looking like the sort of earl they normally have to deal with. My brother Louis is in town, so I'll drag him round, too. Hopefully he won't decide that estate management is the last thing he wants to do and bolt on me.'

'That will be pleasant, being with your brother.' The footmen were still struggling to secure the trunk to the chaise. 'Is he very like you?'

Gabriel gave a snort of amusement. 'Hardly. Louis is a serious soul with my head for figures, which you need to be a good card player, but I doubt he's ever played more than whist for sixpenny stakes. He's a cautious lawyer to the bone, although where he inherited that from, I have no idea. When he's finished his final year at university I hope he will take control of the estates for me. He could go to the Inns of Court and eat his dinners, qualify fully, but I think he wants to get down to work.'

'He is not your only brother, is he?'

'He is the youngest. Ben's in the army and George is a vicar. I haven't seen them for over a year, I suppose. We're not a close family and they don't seem to have wanted money recently. Not so much they needed to turn up to ask for it in person, anyway. Oh, for goodness sake! Haven't you two the slightest idea of how to tie a rope?' He strode across to the chaise and snatched the rope from the flustered footmen, flicking it into place and tying off the ends with a complex, rapid knot.

How sad that he was not close to his brothers, Caroline thought. She adored Anthony and even Lucas was good company when he wasn't pandering to their father's latest whims. A soldier, a vicar, a lawyer and a gambler. In most families the gambler would be the youngest son, not the oldest. Gabriel was intelligent, decisive, gallant and…*isolated,* she thought. Despite his friends, despite his title and rank, he seemed to be a wolf walking in the wild, fierce and independent and alone.

'Ready,' Gabriel said, and opened the chaise door for her. 'You have everything you need?'

'I will miss you.' The words were unconsidered, true. Unwise.

Gabriel's expression had been neutral, now it became even more shuttered. 'You should be glad to see the back of me.'

'You gave up a valuable estate for me. You understood that I was in trouble, so you rescued me. You have made a future possible for both Anthony and for me. It all took time and money and effort and risk. I am very grateful.'

'I am easily bored, it was a diversion,' Gabriel said with a shrug. 'Do not have any delusions, Caroline. I take what

I want for as long as it is amusing and no longer. You have my lawyer's address for any correspondence.' He closed the door and walked away as the others appeared on the steps.

'Gabriel?' Tess called, then shrugged and came to where Caroline still stood on the step of the chaise. 'Men! Now, take care and don't forget to write. Let us know if there is anything that you need.'

'You have been so very kind, thank you.' *Of course* her lip was trembling and her vision was blurred. Tess and Tamsyn had become friends in these past few days and it was a wrench to leave them. Nothing to do with insensitive, amoral, hard-hearted men. Nothing. She had been a distraction for a while, now he no longer wanted her. She was no longer *amusing*. Fair enough. She did not want him. Not at all.

Caroline blew her nose briskly as the chaise rattled away over the cobbles and into Piccadilly. By the time it drew up in front of Wellings and Arbuthott, Suppliers of Domestic Staff to the Nobility, her new spectacles were firmly in place, her face composed and her spine straight. She had been snubbed, but that was her own fault for attempting to get close to a rake. The lesson was learned and she wouldn't make that mistake again if she ever saw Gabriel Stone in the future, which was reassuringly unlikely.

'There is a young gentleman to see you, my lord.'

Gabriel turned with relief from Louis's lecture on the desirable length for agricultural leases. He was never certain whether his youngest brother was naturally earnest or whether it was a shield he erected when they were together. For the thousandth time he wondered if Louis was actually afraid of him, then dismissed the thought. He was unconscious that night when their father…died. He could remember nothing of it, surely?

He realised that Hampshire was waiting for him to collect his thoughts. 'No card?'

'He is too young a gentleman to have one, I believe, my lord.' Hampshire cleared his throat. 'He is very much on his dignity and, if I may be so bold, I would advise caution. I sense repressed emotion about him. Some instability.'

'I'll stay. It sounds as though you might need a lawyer,' Louis said with rather too much enthusiasm.

'Show him in, Hampshire. And you,' he added as the butler closed the door, 'you remember that you aren't a lawyer yet and keep quiet.'

'Breach of promise, do you think?' Louis speculated, for once acting his age. 'You wouldn't gamble with a stripling, so that's all I can think of. So, outraged younger brother come to defend his spurned sister. George says it is about time you—'

'Louis. Shut up if you value your allowance.'

'Mr Holm, my lord.'

Oh, Satan's toenails. Her baby brother. 'Mr Holm. I am Edenbridge. This is my brother, Mr Louis Stone. How may I assist you?'

The young man standing in front of him was obviously Caroline's brother, with his blue eyes and blond hair and handsome, open countenance. Anthony swallowed once, hard, but made a very proper bow. 'My lord. Mr Stone. I have come about a property.'

'I see.' No mention of Caroline yet. 'Will you sit down, Mr Holm? A glass of brandy, perhaps?'

He could see in the boy's expression the desire to appear a man of the world warring with the knowledge that he was not going to be able to drink strong spirits at five in the afternoon and carry on a discussion at the same time.

'Thank you, no, my lord,' he said, winning points with Gabriel. He sat down, crossed his gangling legs with a fair assumption of ease, and then looked anxious when Gabriel sat, too, but remained silent. 'Er… Springbourne, my lord.'

'Call me Edenbridge. I won a Hertfordshire estate called Springbourne from your father some time ago.'

'I need to buy it back. I can't pay you now, of course, but if you tell me how much, then I will start to make re-payments just as soon as I am able. You will expect interest and I realise it will take some time…'

'What is your allowance?' Gabriel enquired.

'Twenty-five pounds a quarter.'

'And you are how old?'

'Sixteen, sir. My lor… Edenbridge.'

'Louis, how much is Springbourne worth?' His brother whipped open a file and produced a neat summary paper. Gabriel handed it to Anthony. 'At compound interest of even a modest four percent, can you work out how long it would take you to pay it back?'

'Yes.' For a moment his chin wobbled, then he got it under control. Gabriel had a vivid recollection of Caroline firming her own jaw before launching into an explanation of why she had come to him that first morning. 'I can see it is impossible. But that was my future, you see. I had to try. However, I quite understand. I will not trouble you further, my lord. Good day.'

He was on his feet, but Gabriel did not move. 'Sit down. You give up very easily, Mr Holm. How did you find out that your father had lost the estate to me?'

The boy sat. 'He told me two days ago when I said I wanted to spend some of the summer there.'

'I imagine he was not conciliatory.'

'No.' Anthony tightened his lips and, for a moment, his shoulders hunched.

The bastard hit him, Gabriel realised with a surge of anger. Boys expected to be beaten for misdemeanours, but not for enquiring about property they thought would be theirs. And not thrashed. Involuntarily his hand reached for Louis, then he jerked it back.

'He's not in a good temper at the moment because of my sis…I mean… Oh, drat, I shouldn't have said that. You'll forget it?'

'Forget what? Mr Holm, I am not in the habit of gaming for property that has been promised to someone other than the person staking it. I discovered the facts about that estate and it is now being held in trust for you without your father's knowledge. The income will be invested and the whole, less running costs, will revert to you on your twenty-first birthday.'

Suddenly, appallingly, the boy burst into tears. After a moment he dragged a bedraggled handkerchief out of his pocket, blew his nose and peered wetly over the top at Gabriel. 'I'm sorry, sir. But are you serious? You aren't jesting with me?'

'Look at my brother. I'm a frivolous sort, but Louis never jests, certainly not about money, do you, Louis?' He had told his brother the bare outlines of the story, without telling him how he had discovered that the estate was destined for Anthony Holm and certainly without mentioning Caroline.

'Of course not.' Louis, all of three years older than Anthony, sent Gabriel his best lawyerly reproving look, the one Gabriel suspected he practised in front of the mirror. 'You may scrutinise the books at any time, Mr Holm. We realise that you are not able to employ anyone to audit them, but if you nominate someone we can set that against the estate income.'

'I should not advise any son to deceive his father, but in

this case might I suggest that you do not reveal this conversation to Lord Knighton? You had best pretend that Springbourne is lost to you for five years,' Gabriel said.

'Yes. Yes of course. Thank you, my… Edenbridge.' He set his jaw. 'I was going to join the navy. Or I would have done if only I'd known where Ca… Anyway, I won't need to now.'

'Have that brandy.' Gabriel stood up and poured three glasses. Had Caroline written to her brother yet? He waited until Anthony had taken a huge swallow of the spirit, choked, been thumped on the back by Louis and then settled down, rather red-eyed, but happier. 'It is some time since I had the pleasure of speaking to your sister. I trust she is well.'

'Er… Yes. Yes, she is quite safe.' It seemed to occur to him that this was odd phrasing. 'I mean, she is quite *well*. Resting, you know, somewhere…I mean elsewhere. Rather a trying Season, I believe, but she writes to me. I'll tell her you were asking.'

'You do that,' Gabriel said with a smile. *Just never apply for the diplomatic service or any occupation where you have to deviate from the truth, young man. You are the worst liar I have ever come across.*

'Where does your father think you are now?'

'Staying with a school friend in Chelsea. Which I am, actually. I went home a few days ago, Papa told me about Springbourne and then I remembered Percy had invited me to stay with him, so I came down here.'

'You'll need some ready money if you are to enjoy London.' Gabriel opened a drawer and peeled fifty pounds off a roll of banknotes. 'Louis, enter that in the ledger as an advance to Mr Holm. Don't go near women, cards, drinking dens or friendly older men who offer to show you a good time.'

'No, sir! Thank you very much, my... Edenbridge.' Anthony's grin threatened to reach his ears. He got to his feet, only slightly unsteady, and bowed. 'I'll never forget this. Never.'

'Was that wise?' Louis enquired as the door shut behind young Mr Holm. 'He's off the leash in London, goodness knows what he will get up to.'

'Speaking from experience, Louis?'

'Certainly not.'

Gabriel grinned at the offended expression, but it was Anthony who gave him pause. His father had been reminded about Springbourne and that could be dangerous. Might it occur to him that Caroline had gone there? Gabriel doubted Lord Knighton had actually told Caroline about the loss of the estate—in fact, he seemed to recall her saying she had discovered its loss by overhearing him talking about it, so he might think she'd see it as a refuge.

He should write and warn her. Or go and see her? He really ought to inspect the estate after all. It wasn't right to leave it entirely to agents, however reliable.

'I'm going to Hertfordshire, look at this place for myself,' he said abruptly.

'Fine. I'll pack.' Louis got to his feet.

'No need to trouble yourself.' Gabriel said it with regret. It gave him unexpected pleasure that Louis wanted his company, but the last thing he needed was an encounter with Caroline with his little brother looking on. 'I only want to familiarise myself with it. I'll go first thing tomorrow and be back the day after.' A brisk conversation with Caroline, just to put her on her guard, a rapid look at the place and then he would put up at the Red Lion in Hemel Hempstead for the night. All done and dusted.

Gabriel recalled the last glimpse he'd had of her, her bounty of blonde curls wrenched back into submission, her blue eyes wide with hurt behind those ridiculous spectacles, the shock on her face at his snubbing words. It had been for the best, of course. Women became...attached and she had no experience of men like him. She saw him as a rescuer, not as what he was, jaded and amoral and severely tempted to take what he should not.

She needed a nice young man, a countryman, perhaps the son of a local gentry family. She'd be safe with a man like that, someone straightforward who wouldn't hurt her, who wouldn't become bored with innocence and trust as he assuredly would. The ache in his chest at the thought was presumably his damnable new conscience again.

'George and I were wondering,' Louis began.

Words to put fear into any older brother. 'Yes?' Gabriel said warily, half his thoughts still on a suitable husband for Caroline.

'Are you intending to get married? Because, he's a good chap of course, but Ben's in the army, which doesn't seem very safe for the heir, and George really wants to be a bishop.'

'I was not planning on needing an heir in the near future,' Gabriel said, all his concentration jerked back to his brother. It was very unlike Louis to venture into such personal territory. 'What on earth is this about, anyway?'

'We wondered, that's all. You taking an interest in the land now. And your three closest friends marrying. You are getting on, after all.'

'I am twenty-nine,' Gabriel snapped. 'Hardly in my dotage.'

'You ought to think about it,' Louis persisted. 'I've been reading up on marriage settlements and entails and all that recently, so I'm completely on top of the subject for when you need advice.'

'Louis.' His brother raised short-sighted green eyes and

squinted at him. 'Pay attention. I do not require lectures on marriage and the production of heirs from my spotty little brother.' He got up and left the room, followed by Louis's indignant protests.

'I am not spotty!'

'Hampshire, my travelling carriage for eight tomorrow morning. Breakfast for seven and tell Corbridge I'll not be needing him, just an overnight bag.'

'My lord.'

Gabriel took his hat from the hall stand and let himself out of the front door. There was a new hell off Hill Street that was as informal as the stakes were high. It was one place he was quite certain he'd be safe from prosing brothers, well-meaning friends, matchmaking mothers and respectable damsels with big blue eyes and that was where he would be until midnight.

Chapter Thirteen

It had never occurred to her that a housekeeper's life would be a lonely one. In a large household there was a butler, a steward, a cook and a mature lady's maid for the mistress of the house, a little inner circle of upper servants. But here, with no family in residence, the housekeeper reigned in an isolated state.

Caroline set the flower arrangement on a table in the hall and looked out through the open door, down the carriage drive between the high yew hedges that were receiving their first good cut in years and on to the green haze of the Vale of Aylesbury in the August sunlight. Behind the house the beech woods rose like a blanket over the swell of the Chiltern Hills, nestling it into the tiny valley of the Spring Bourne, the seasonal stream that rose from the chalk after heavy rain, then vanished in summer.

This was a lovely spot, the house was charming and soon it would become a home for Anthony and for herself. But meanwhile, although there was a lot to do and even more to be thankful for, the loneliness pressed in on her. *And it has only been three weeks.*

'I've finished the panelling in the dining room, Mrs Crabtree.' Jane, the housemaid, came into the hall carrying a basket of jars of beeswax and polishing cloths. 'It'll take a few more goes to get the shine up proper, though.'

'Once a week and not too much wax, more elbow grease,' Caroline said. That was what was advised in *Mrs Pomfrett's Household Management*, the thick tome that was her night-time reading. 'Too much wax builds up and dulls the shine.'

'Yes, ma'am. I'll lay the table in your room, Mrs Crabtree. Almost time for luncheon.'

That was another thing. Every meal had to be taken alone in the housekeeper's parlour while the cheerful sounds of chatter from the servants' hall echoed down the flagged passageway. She'd been tempted to prop a book up in front of her, but that was a bad example to the maids, so must be resisted. They relied on the training they received here for their next post, perhaps promotion to a bigger household, or cook-housekeeper to a widow or single gentleman. It all left far too much time to be thinking about a certain brown-eyed gentleman.

'There's a rider coming up the drive, Mrs Crabtree.'

'Who can that be?' Caroline squinted against the sunlight, heart pounding. A boyish rider on a chestnut hack with a rather shambling gait. Not a tall man on a fine piece of bloodstock. Of course not.

'Close the front door, alert William that someone is coming. Possibly they are lost and want directions.'

She followed the scurrying maid towards the back of the hall and waited in the shadows while the footman emerged, tugged down his waistcoat and went to open the door.

'Good morning, sir. I regret that none of the family is in residence.'

'Well, I am now.' The light, cheerful voice cracked midsentence, betraying the speaker's nerves as well as his age. 'I am Mr Anthony Holm and this is my house.'

William's gulp was audible. 'Perhaps you would come through to the drawing room, sir, and I'll fetch the house-keeper.'

Caroline hardly caught a glimpse of her brother before William had him shut in the front room. She met the foot-man halfway across the hall.

'Mrs Crabtree, ma'am, I didn't know where to put my-self! The poor young gentleman can't know his father's sold the estate to Lord Edenbridge.' That was the story she had told the staff, not wanting to expose her father's folly at gambling it away.

'I'll go and speak to him. Don't bring refreshments until I ring.' She went in and closed the door behind herself. 'Anthony,' she said quietly. 'This is a surprise.'

'Caro!' He spun round from his contemplation of the view from the window, his face a mixture of pleasure, sur-prise and then, when he took in her costume, bafflement. 'What on earth are you doing here dressed like that?'

She hugged him fiercely, shaken by how much his gan-gling frame had grown since the last time she had held him. He was not her little brother any longer. 'Oh, how I have missed you! Sit down and I'll tell you everything— and then you must tell me how you got here.'

She left out the offer to exchange her virginity for the deeds, saying instead that she had explained the situation to Gabriel and he had immediately returned them. When it came to her reasons for fleeing she told him only that Woodruffe had an unsavoury reputation. Even so, Anthony was clearly old enough to guess it was worse than she said.

'The old devil,' he gasped when he heard that their fa-ther had beaten her. His horror became fascination at the story of Gabriel's imposture and he was boy enough to be vastly amused at the thought of an earl disguised as a hermit.

'So here I am, guarding your inheritance and staying safe myself,' Caroline finished.

'He's a great gun, isn't he? Lord Edenbridge, I mean.' Anthony's face glowed with hero worship. 'Father told me, just in passing, about losing Springbourne. I said what I thought, pretty loudly, and got a thrashing for my pains.' He shrugged off her hands when she would have caught him to her for a hug and stuck out his chin pugnaciously. 'I'd got an invitation to stay with Percy—you know, Herrick's younger brother?—near London, so I went there. Father didn't mind.

'Then I called on Lord Edenbridge and he told me he was looking after the estate for me. His youngest brother was there, a bit of a stuffed shirt, I thought.' His blue gaze slid round to her. 'Edenbridge didn't say anything about you.' When she did not comment he shrugged. 'Anyway, he advanced me some money from the estate, so I thought I'd come and have a look. May I stay?'

'Of *course* you may.' She just wanted to hold him and not let go. 'But you must remember that you are here as a guest of Lord Edenbridge and I'll let the staff know you were upset because of the estate being sold, but that the earl has allowed you to visit for a while. And you must call me Mrs Crabtree and treat me like the housekeeper. We can say that I knew you when you were a little boy, which is true and that will explain any familiarity.'

'*Crabtree?*'

'I realised I hadn't thought of a name and when I arrived that was the first thing I saw,' Caroline said defensively. 'I think it sounds suitable for a housekeeper.'

'Gnarled and vinegary,' Anthony teased.

'I'll ring for luncheon. You'll have to eat it in solitary splendour because it wouldn't do for the housekeeper to sit down with you.' As she stood up she glimpsed movement at the end of the drive. 'A carriage is coming. Of all the bad timing! You had best stay out of sight. I do hope it isn't Father.'

Anthony leapt to his feet with an oath that had her scolding him.

'Not in front of ladies, you brat! Look, it is a team of greys.' She relaxed. Her father always drove bays. It was irrational, of course, this fear. There was not the slightest clue to bring him here, but even so, she kept waking in the night in a cold sweat of dread, fighting a nightmare of being dragged back to Knighton Park and Lord Woodruff's grasping hands.

'And very nice, too,' Anthony said with a sigh of envy. 'Real high-steppers. I'll go into the back garden.'

Caroline followed him out, called for William and retreated to the back of the hall again. She had not seen a single visitor all the time she had been at Springbourne except tradesmen and local people and now someone had to turn up hot on Anthony's heels. This was like one of those farces with everyone diving behind sofas or into cupboards as more and more people arrived at inconvenient or compromising moments. It would make Gabriel laugh, she thought as William, peering through the glass at the side of the door, opened it before the caller could knock.

'Good afternoon,' said a very familiar voice. 'I am Edenbridge.'

'My lord.' William sounded even more flustered than he had at Anthony's arrival. She could hardly blame him: she was totally confused herself. And, she realised, very happy.

'Might I come in?' Gabriel enquired mildly.

'Yes, of course, my lord. I do apologise, my lord, keeping you standing on your own doorstep.' His ears and the back of his neck were crimson as he took Gabriel's hat and gloves. 'I'll...er... Should I have luncheon sent up, my lord?'

'Please do. This is the drawing room? Ask the house-keeper if she could join me at her convenience.'

'Yes, my lord. Certainly, my lord.' The footman closed the door and scurried to the back of the hall. 'It's Lord Edenbridge, Mrs Crabtree.'

'Ask Cook to prepare luncheon for three and I will join the gentlemen. Go to Mr Holm and give him my compli-ments and tell him I will be with him as soon as possible.' The staff would think it strange, but now the two of them were here she simply had to talk to them together. But Ga-briel first. And alone.

'Caroline.' He came across the room to her, his hand stretched out, and it took her a second to realise he intended to shake hers, not gather her into his arms.

Of course, you idiot. She smiled and offered her own hand and asked him to be seated with commendable com-posure. His hair had grown out of its strict crop since she had seen him last and his breeches, boots and riding coat were as carelessly thrown on as always, even though he had come in a carriage and not on horseback.

'How are you managing?' he asked, studying her as she sat there looking, she was very aware, like a neat, dowdy housekeeper.

'Very well, thank you, my lord. It is quiet, but there is plenty to keep me occupied. Might I ask what brings you here? Not a problem, I trust. Or perhaps you have become bored and fancied a change of scenery?' That was bitter and she regretted the words as soon as she spoke them. They betrayed how much his parting words had hurt her. She had her pride.

Gabriel did not make the mistake of apologising, which was sensible of him as well as preserving what dignity she had left. 'Your brother Anthony arrived on my doorstep proposing to buy back Springbourne. It was necessary to explain the true circumstances to him. Your father had told him he had lost it and it occurred to me that he had not told *you*. For all Knighton knows you still believe this to be a family property, one where he never visits and somewhere you might think of as a sanctuary. I wanted to warn you and discuss how to mitigate the danger.'

So her night-time fears were not so far-fetched after all if Gabriel shared them. 'Thank you, I appreciate you taking the trouble to come in person.' It sounded stilted, but perhaps she should be making the effort to distance herself with formality. It was too easy to yearn for the closeness that had been between them when Gabriel had been the hermit and she a fugitive.

Caroline kept her gaze on her own hands, folded neatly in her lap, and not on his long, expressive fingers. 'Anthony is here. He arrived very shortly before you did.'

'The little devil! I advanced him some money, but I thought he was staying with a school friend. What is he doing here?'

'Heaving a huge sigh of relief that it is his again, I suspect. He was taken aback to discover that the housekeeper, Mrs Crabtree, knew him very well.'

'I am not surprised, *Mrs Crabtree*. We had better have a council of war, the three of us.'

'That is what I thought. I told him about Woodruffe.'

There was a tap on the door. 'Luncheon is served, Mrs Crabtree.'

'Thank you, William. Please ask Mr Holm to join us in the dining room.'

Anthony came in, looking wary. 'I heard your voice in the hall, Edenbridge. You're wondering what I am doing here, I suppose?'

'You may go where you please.' Gabriel held the chair for Caroline, then took his own place opposite her. 'I am not your guardian.'

'I know, sir, but you gave me money and I let you think I was staying in London.'

'I advanced you your own money. It is of no matter. Let us eat and think how best to handle the situation. I came because I was uneasy that your father might search here for Lady Caroline. We're mired in a tangle of deceptions: I'm pretending to own this place, you are pretending you do not know it is now yours again and that your sister is hiding from her own father and posing as the housekeeper. I just hope you are a good actor, Anthony, because you are going to have to face your father and play the role of the disappointed son well enough to convince him that you are pining for Springbourne. And you're a poor liar, I've noticed.'

'I'm a good actor, though,' Anthony said, reaching for a slice of cold beef. 'I've acted at school and got some pretty enthusiastic reviews. And this is important, really important. It isn't as though it is some little white lie I might forget about. I'll sulk a bit and keep out of Father's way, that's what he'd expect.'

'And what about you, Mrs Crabtree?' He seemed to find the name as amusing as Anthony did.

'I never answer the front door, of course. If my father does come, then I will leave by the back and hide in the woods. He could search for a year and not find me there.'

'I suppose it will have to do.' Gabriel looked unsatisfied, although it did not seem to be impairing his appetite.

Caroline wondered whether to ring and tell Cook to send up the apple pie along with the cheese. She helped herself to the game pie before the two hungry males demolished it. 'It gives me bad dreams, imagining he has found me,' she confessed. 'But I really do not think it is a serious risk. He is very self-centred and I don't believe he thinks much about other people's motives.'

As she spoke the doorbell rang, followed by the thump of the knocker. 'Who now? Really, after weeks of perfect peace the place is like the White Horse Cellar when the mails come in!'

Then there was the sound of William opening the door and the voice of the caller and the footman's agitated protests. Caroline dropped her knife with a clatter on her plate and Anthony jumped to his feet as the door swung open.

'So you *are* here, boy, you impudent whelp.'

Chapter Fourteen

Her father strode into the room, brushing past her as she froze, her back to the door. 'I thought you were too meek when I told you about this place so I decided I had better check that you hadn't sneaked off here. What in Hades do you think you're doing? And who the devil are you?' He moved closer to Gabriel, who stood up with leisurely, dangerous grace. Caroline edged her chair backwards. A few more inches and she could slide from her seat and tiptoe out.

She stood, turned, and came face to face with Lucas.

'Caroline!'

'What?' Her father swung round his face choleric with a mixture of surprise, temper and triumph. 'You are both here? You plotted the whole thing, you disobedient little slut. What is Edenbridge going to do when he finds the pair of you skulking here?'

Gabriel moved to stand between him and Caroline. 'If you use language of that kind to Lady Caroline again I'll floor you, Knighton, even if you are old enough to be my father.'

'Edenbridge.' Her father finally recognised who was standing in front of him. 'What the blazes do you think you are playing at?' His gaze swung back and forth between the three of them and then fixed back on Gabriel with dawning recognition. '*You*. You're the hermit. Lucas, tell me I'm right. It's that cursed Welsh hermit.'

Lucas pushed past Caroline to stand at his father's shoulder. 'Yes, you are right. Take away that beard and change the voice and it's the same man. But what is going on?'

It was a nightmare, and when Gabriel swung round and cursed Anthony, it seemed to Caroline simply part of it.

'You stupid brat, coming here with your idiotic pleas for her to go home. You led them here.' He grabbed Anthony by the neckcloth and began to shake him, his face pressed close to the boy's.

Suddenly Anthony began to fight back. 'I knew I had to when I found her here! It isn't right, what you are doing, of course she should come home with me.'

Gabriel made a sound of disgust and pushed him into his father's arms. 'Have the little prig. He turns up here whining that he wants just one more look at the place, finds us and reads us a fine sermon.'

'You were trying to make her come back?' Her father held Anthony away from him so he could look into his face.

'Yes, sir. Of course. I was upset about the estate, and I shouldn't have come here, but Caroline and that man...'

He really can act, she thought. *And Gabriel has saved him from total disgrace with my father and a beating, thank Heavens. But what am I going to do?* Lucas had moved to block the door and it was too far to reach the window and scramble through, even if Gabriel held back her father and brother. They were two to his one and if they attacked him she knew she could never leave him and run. He might overcome them—he was strong and courageous—but her father always carried a knife in his boot and she knew he'd use it without scruple.

'Good boy,' he said now, pushing Anthony towards Lucas. 'And as for you, my girl, I'll have to sweeten the pot now to get Woodruffe to take you, damn it. Used goods.'

'I will not warn you again, Knighton,' Gabriel said. 'I am marrying Lady Caroline and no one threatens or abuses my fiancée.'

'Marry her? You? Her reputation will be in the dirt after this.'

Marry me?

'Mine is not that wonderful,' Gabriel said with a smile that was guaranteed to infuriate. 'But as I will procure a special licence from my cousin, the Archbishop of Canterbury, that should help. Even better if he'll marry us. I believe he's at Lambeth Palace at the moment, which is convenient.'

Her father expressed an opinion on what the archbishop could do with his crozier. 'I refuse my consent.'

'Lady Caroline is of age,' Gabriel pointed out. He seemed perfectly calm, contemptuous even, her father's rage breaking against him like a wave against a rock, with as much effect.

'You'll not see a penny piece of dowry from me.' Her father was puce with frustrated rage now.

'I do not need your money, Knighton, although that reminds me, you owe me a week's wages for my stint as your hermit.'

'Under false pretences! You inveigle your way into my home, you seduce my daughter—'

Caroline finally found her voice. 'Lord Edenbridge came to help because you were forcing me to marry Lord Woodruffe.'

'Woodruffe will call you out,' her father threatened Gabriel.

'That lump of perverted lard is welcome to do so. I would enjoy puncturing him.'

'And you, Lucas. What kind of brother are you? Why aren't *you* calling him out?'

'I imagine Lord Whiston has more common sense than to make the situation worse than it already is. Besides, I am not prepared to meet the man who is about to become my brother-in-law.'

'Father, it has gone too far to stop. He's an earl, he's perfectly eligible, and she's of age.' Lucas stood his ground, perhaps given strength by the appeal to his reasonableness. 'He's an earl, a better match than Woodruffe, after all.'

'Not for the family, he isn't. He won't bring me land.' He switched his attention back to Gabriel. 'What about settlements?'

'I will settle property and investments on Lady Caroline in consultation with lawyers of her choice. It is, Knighton, no longer your affair.'

'You'll be sorry, Edenbridge. And as for you, my girl, you've made your bed, you may lie in it. Don't expect to come crawling home when you discover what kind of man you've married. A Captain Sharp, a charlatan, that is what he is and I will make certain the whole world knows it.' He snapped his fingers at his sons. 'Come on, both of you.'

Anthony trailed behind, rather white around the mouth, but he turned at the last minute to wink at Caroline. She managed a quick smile for him, then turned all her focus on Gabriel as he stood at the window watching the carriage drive away.

'They've gone,' he said finally.

Caroline sat down with a bump in the nearest chair and

said the first thing that came into her head. 'Are you really the Archbishop of Canterbury's cousin?'

'Third, once removed. I won't have any difficulty getting a licence, but I don't think I will ask him to marry us.' He turned and, for the first time in what seemed like a hundred years, smiled. 'Unless you have set your heart on it?'

'Don't jest about this, Gabriel. You do not want to marry me, I know that perfectly well. And I will not marry you.'

'You will not? I am deeply wounded, my lady.' The smile had become thinner.

'Of course I will not. What kind of marriage would it be? You have been put in a position where you have had to do the honourable thing, but I have no wish to take a martyr for a husband.'

Gabriel shrugged, that mocking smile still in place. 'I am an earl, I need a wife, as my so-sensible youngest brother informs me. You are the daughter of an earl and perfectly eligible. There may be a scandal, but I do not care about that.'

'I do.' As soon as the words were out she knew she meant them. The talk, the turned shoulders, the whispers, the cuts… She had seen it happen to other people, now she would be responsible for putting them both in that position. If they had a chance of making a happy marriage she would be very tempted to wed this man. But like this? *Never.*

'Is this the woman who came and offered me her virginity? Who plotted to shock her husband on her wedding night? Is this the woman who broke into her father's safe to purloin her own jewels and ran away from home with a man of dubious reputation? And *now* you quibble about scandal?'

'It is not a quibble and everything has changed. I would have done whatever it took to get this estate back for Anthony—except something that put you in such an invidious position. And I was naive before to think I could escape that marriage by shocking my suitors.

'This is my responsibility to resolve. I will ask Tessa and Tamsyn for references. Perhaps your friends in Northumberland know of someone who needs a housekeeper.' *I do not want to be married to you with a cauldron of anger seething just below that smile that isn't a smile. I do not want to be responsible for you losing your good name because, rogue you may be, you are received everywhere. Now.*

'You would rather be a domestic servant than my countess? What did I do that made you dislike me so much?'

'Nothing.' She found she was wringing her hands and stilled them. *I like you too well, that is the problem.* 'You have done nothing except treat me better than I deserve, be concerned about me, rescue me. You do not have to do this, Gabriel. Let me be and I will vanish.'

'Leaving me with the reputation of a seducer, a man who abducts an earl's daughter and then abandons her? Or worse. If you disappear I have no doubt your father will put it about that I've disposed of you. Once the story of my hermit imposture gets around this will all seem a very dubious plot indeed. Now that really would be a scandal.'

'So I must marry you for the sake of *your* reputation?' He was right, of course, her father's spite would whip up a storm of vicious talk.

'Ironic, isn't it? I cannot force you, Caroline. I may be a scoundrel, but I do draw the line at that. I just want you to see that it is no help at all, you being noble and refusing me.'

'But you hope my sense of honour is at least as well developed as yours.' She rather feared it was.

Gabriel stopped prowling around the room, sat down on the other side of the table and rested his forearms on the cloth. It should have been better because he was no longer looming over her, but his focused, unsmiling gaze was no more comfortable. He looked weary, she thought, seeing the shadows under the dark eyes, the tightness of his mouth.

'I hope that you will see that, unsatisfactory though this is, it is the only way for us both to deal with the situation,' he said with the control of a man hanging on to his patience by a thread. When she did not reply he flung himself back in the chair. 'Surely I have to be better than Woodruffe?'

'Of course you are. But I do not want to be married to anyone. Not my father's choice, not someone who has been trapped into it.' It sounded mulish, but it was the truth. The thought of perhaps fifty years of marriage to a man who resented her, tolerated her, was repellent.

'Waiting for hearts and flowers and a meeting of soul-mates?' Gabriel enquired perceptively. 'You've more patience than I have and more romance in your soul than is good for you.'

Caroline gritted her teeth at the mockery. 'Your three friends married for love, did they not? I heard how you tried to stop Tamsyn marrying the marquess because you thought she was unsuitable, but you have accepted it now, because they are made for each other and even you can see it. What are they going to say about you settling for *this*?' She waved her hands to encompass the whole impossible situation.

'You are neither the illegitimate offspring of a bigamous marriage, nor the mother of a child out of wedlock nor the widow of a man who was almost hanged as a smuggler, which between ourselves, describes the brides my friends have taken. You are an eminently suitable match, if one ignores your father, which I devoutly intend to do. My friends have no right to dictate my emotional life—'

'Or lack of it,' Caroline flung back. 'What if we marry and then you fall in love with someone else? Or I do?'

'We do what aristocrats down the ages have always done, we cope with it. An heir and spare is non-negotiable. After that, provided you don't fall for a short redhead there is no problem.'

'How can you be so cold-blooded? You wouldn't be if the situation did arise—you would be shooting my lover at dawn.'

'Why do you think my brother Louis is half a head shorter than his older brothers, has green eyes and sandy hair?'

'No! Did your father know?'

'Of course.' Gabriel's expression was bleak. Then he shrugged. 'So does Louis. He took one look at Lord Belmond and announced it was a relief to finally know who his father was. No one in the family treats him any differently.'

'Poor boy. As if I could do that to a child of mine. If I married you I would be faithful and I would expect you to be faithful, too.'

'The rules require me to be discreet.'

'The vows demand rather more,' she snapped, more shaken by his cynicism than she would have thought possible.

Gabriel shrugged. 'I am a sinner. You knew that from the very first.' There was a knock at the door. 'Come in, damn it!'

'Mrs Crabtree, should we clear now, or bring tea, or what, ma'am?' Jane hesitated on the threshold, the wooden tray clutched to her skinny chest like a shield.

'Tea, in the drawing room please, Jane.'

Gabriel followed her through in silence that persisted while she poured and drank two cups of tea. That did something for the raging thirst that had suddenly gripped her, but not a great deal for the confused misery inside.

He left his own cup untouched, waiting with a controlled patience that frayed at her nerves more than ranting and temper would have done. *I suppose I am used to ranting,* she thought miserably. *No one is ever in any doubt about my father's mood or desires. I cannot read Gabriel's.*

'Is there no other way than marriage?'

'No. Not to escape without a major scandal and ensure your future. It will be a nine-day wonder, but everyone knows how eccentric and difficult your father is, so there will be sympathy for your desire to flee his roof. And I may not be society's darling, but there are not many who hold much of a brief for Woodruffe.' He picked up the cup and drained the cold tea, then smiled at her. 'Caroline, we get on well enough.' He reached out, touched the back of his hand gently to her cheek. 'We will be good in bed, I think, even if we have not had the best of beginnings in that respect. Now what are you blushing about?'

'I am not used to such frankness.'

'This from the woman who tried to barter her virginity for this estate? And I still have that IOU. Your marriage has been announced and I intend to call it in.'

Of course she expected that this would be a full marriage, a man in need of an heir did not propose a union in name only. But surely he did not mean… 'You mean *before* we are married?' *I need time.* 'We have not fixed the date.'

'Five days' time should be perfect. We'll go up to London tomorrow. Then there are three days for you, Tess and Tamsyn to shop for all the things you'll need. I'll sort out the licence and the legal details and find a clergyman. I'm hoping that Cris will let us use his house in St James's Square. That will prevent any hint of the hole-and-corner about the marriage.'

'It certainly will,' Caroline said hollowly. The thought of Crispin de Feaux's cool blue regard simply made her want to curl up into a ball and seek out every hole and corner she could find.

'So, are we agreed?'

There was the sensation of holding her breath, as though she was about to jump into icy water or walk out along a narrow ledge. 'Yes,' Caroline said. There was a guilty relief in surrender that she tried not to analyse too closely.

'Then I think we should summon the staff, who are probably all agog about this morning's incidents and making up the most lurid tales. We will tell them who you are and that we are to be married. There's no disguising the clandestine nature of all of this, so let us hope they are both loyal and idiotically romantic.'

Idiotically romantic, like me. And I am also idiotically loyal, Gabriel Stone. Vows mean something to me.

The staff had been embarrassingly excited to be part of what they obviously saw as a Great Romance. Caroline promised to send them a new housekeeper as soon as possible and spent the afternoon immersed in practical details, which at least had the advantage of keeping her mind distracted.

Gabriel appeared to have employed the time creating a stack of letters which he sent off with the groom to the nearest receiving office. Dinner was formal and polite with only an exchange of the most trivial chitchat. Caroline made her excuses and retired immediately afterwards, frankly retreating from the domestic intimacy of tea in the drawing room.

At least Harriet, the personal maid who had been recruited in London, was sufficiently down to earth to ask questions. 'Will you still be requiring me when you go back to London, ma'am? My lady, I should say.'

Caroline sat at her dressing table as the young woman unpinned her hair before brushing it out. 'I need a lady's maid, Harriet, and you've done very well. But can you manage elaborate hair styles and the care of fine fabrics? I will be a countess and that will mean a considerable social life and the clothes and jewels to go with it.' *Provided we are not completely shunned by decent society.* 'I quite understand if you think it will be too much and I would give you an excellent reference.'

'Oh, no, my lady. I can do it.' Her face broke into a happy smile. 'I might have to learn a few things, but if you tell me when I go wrong, I learn ever so fast, truly I do.'

This is really happening. I have my affianced husband in the house, I have a lady's maid, I have a wedding date. And I very much fear that the man in question is going to come to my door tonight. And then... Will I open it?

Chapter Fifteen

The knock on the door came at midnight. It was nicely judged, Caroline thought as she got up from the chair where she had been curled up with an unread book. Not a demanding thump, not a wary tap, not a secretive scratch. Just a mannerly light knock.

She opened it, and stepped back so that Gabriel could enter. He came in far enough to close the door behind him, then studied her as she stood there in her sensible flannel wrapper, suitable for any night-time emergencies that might call a housekeeper from her lonely bed. It took an effort not to clutch the lapels closed or fold her arms defensively across her well-shrouded bosom.

'I have been thinking. We need a very frank discussion.' He gestured to the ottoman atthe foot of the bed and raised an interrogative eyebrow.

'Yes?' Caroline retreated to her chair, tossing Byron, who was less than helpful under the circumstances, to the floor. Gabriel sat down and regarded her from beneath heavy lids. She did not make the mistake of thinking him sleepy.

'You raised any number of objections to this match, as I recall. I am also aware that I have two, shall we say, stick-

ing points, which have become stickier the more I considered them. I am not prepared to make a marriage in name
only, but on the other hand I am not prepared to force an
unwilling woman. I was wrong to try to pressure you by
referring to my own reputation suffering.' He shrugged.
'I thought it might work, but I can't blackmail you, Caroline. Just because we cannot see a way out of this now does
not mean there is not some other solution if we think hard
enough. But answer me this. If I had asked you to marry
me in June, what would you have said?'

The question took her completely off balance. 'Yes,' she
said, surprised at herself. 'I would have said yes, I think.'

'Why?'

'Because...' Caroline swallowed and studied her bare
toes. 'Because I found—find—you physically attractive.
You know that.' She fixed her gaze on the point where Gabriel's robe formed a vee exposing bare skin and a curl of
dark hair and tried to stop gibbering. 'I found you intelligent and interesting. And although you were shocking
you were also kind to me. Much kinder than my impetu-
osity deserved. And you did the right thing for Anthony
when it meant a significant financial loss and you had no
reason to want to help him.'

'So, a mixture of gratitude and sexual attraction.' She
could not tell without looking at his face whether he was
amused or annoyed.

'And you were much better than the alternatives,' she
added frankly and found herself looking at him. That curl.
Would it feel silky if she twined her fingers around it?

Now his expression was definitely sardonic. 'Have any
of those opinions changed?'

Caroline shook her head.

'So your objections are because you feel my hand has

been forced, not because you object to marriage to me as such?'

'I suppose so. Yes.' Strangely she was beyond embarrassment, driven by an instinct that only the truth would serve them now.

'You are very frank, Caroline. I would expect any sheltered young lady to faint dead away before admitting to physical attraction.'

'I must be honest with you. With myself. Coyness and misunderstandings are not going to help us, are they? If I had not already seen you, found you attractive, then I would never have made the proposal that I did. Which puts my so-called sacrifice for my brother in a different light, I suppose. It would hardly have *been* a sacrifice. Young women have to pretend that we have no idea about physical matters when of course we do. We certainly do not keep our gaze fixed above a man's waist level.' Gabriel's lips twitched. 'I was attracted by the way you moved,' she confessed. 'So it would be hypocritical of me to pretend I am shocked at the prospect of sharing a bed with you. Nervous and shy, yes. Shocked, no. But it would be very wrong to expect you to marry me.'

'I find I am becoming strangely reconciled to the prospect, my lady.'

Caroline realised it was her turn to be taken aback. Gabriel was smiling in a way that brought the blood to her cheeks, which must be why her heart was beating so erratically. 'Are you certain?' she demanded. 'Why?' *And why do I know you are telling me the truth?* Perhaps it was simply desperation or exhaustion and she was delusional, but she trusted Gabriel.

'Possibly because I've never had to work so hard to get a woman into bed as I have today. If it had been anyone else I'd have given up hours ago.' She frowned at his levity and he smiled. 'I am teasing you. Marry me, Caroline. I admire your courage and your sense of honour. I think you're beautiful. And I am driven to distraction by that garment.'

He admires me, thinks I'm beautiful? Can I believe him? 'This?' She plucked at the wrapper which was a discouraging shade of grey.

'Any right-thinking man would want to burn it, which means taking it off first.'

I want him. He apparently wants me again. He is being scrupulous about this. And that put all the onus for a decision on her. Caroline took a deep breath. *I ought to say no. But I am at least an eligible wife for him in rank and I know I will do my best to make the marriage work.* 'Yes.'

'Yes, you will marry me knowing me as you do, having heard me warning you that I will not be the sort of husband you dreamed of?' She nodded. 'Yes to tonight?'

'Yes to both.' She got to her feet and walked past him, turned the key in the lock and then came to stand in front of the ottoman. It gave her the illusion, at least, of being in control.

'You are nervous,' Gabriel said, looking down to where the sagging hem was quivering just above her bare insteps.

'I told you I was and I would wager so were you when you lost your virginity,' she retorted. She had admitted that she desired him and he was probably far too experienced not to have realised it anyway, but instinct told her to hide how he made her feel, hide just how much she wanted *him*, not simply that rangy body. Somehow she had to retain some strength in this relationship.

His hands came to rest lightly either side of her waist, warm even through the flannel, then, when she stayed where she was, he tugged the ends of the sash so the robe fell open to reveal her equally chaste white cotton nightgown.

'As for my virginity, the second time, yes, I was nervous. The first time I was so excited that I wasn't thinking about anything. Not coherently. My father took me to a high-class brothel to be initiated into lovemaking, just as he selected the right tutors for us, bought us the right horses to learn on, sent us to the right teachers for fencing and shooting. Everything had to be perfect for his sons.' She thought his voice took on a bitter edge. Then it was gone. 'After he died I did the same for my brothers.' He slid his hands under the robe to caress the curve of her hips through the cotton. 'You are a very lovely shape. Classical.'

Caroline sorted her breathing out. 'I am appalled at your father. How old were you?'

'Fifteen.' Gabriel pulled her a little closer, leant in to kiss the slight swell of her stomach.

'That's younger than Anthony! And you took your own brothers.'

'We will worry about your baby brother's education later.' Gabriel was on his feet and her wrapper, somehow, was on the floor and so was his robe.

Under it he was naked.

There was silence, broken only by the sound of her breathing, which was not even, and his, which was not either. That was comforting. Slightly. They were standing so close that she could feel her nightgown brushing against his legs, the warmth of his bare flesh. And so close that it was surely safe to drop her gaze.

Or not. Bare chest, dark curling hair that did not conceal his nipples and that arrowed down over a flat, muscled stomach to his navel and…

Caroline had no idea what to do. But talking, especially

when one was nervous, was easy. 'I know about the mechanics of the act, of course. No young lady with access to a library, some knowledge of basic Latin, an enquiring mind and eyes to see men in tight evening breeches need be ignorant, exactly. And there was the night in the hermitage, of course. Only I was not quite prepared for…*that.*'

She made a wildly sweeping gesture and found her hand resting on Gabriel's chest, her fingers in that intriguing hair. 'Oh, it is soft. I wondered.'

'Feel free,' he said. 'Explore. And don't worry about *that.* We'll get to him later. We have time now.' He was amused, but not laughing at her, more inviting her to share a joke. Could lovemaking be *fun* then? He seemed so relaxed with her, as though he truly liked *her,* not just her body.

'Him?' She teased her fingertips into the curls, trailed a pattern into them, brushed his right nipple accidentally and stopped, fascinated as it hardened and puckered. She rolled it gently between her fingertips. 'Yours do that, too?'

'As you see.'

'And *him*?'

'It is definitely male. It has a mind of its own and is inclined to be unruly at the most awkward moments.' Again she was aware that Gabriel's breathing was not quite under control. 'You may carry on exploring, you know.'

Above the waist was safe. That unruly male object could definitely be left for later. Much later. 'You are very warm. And I did not expect your skin to be smooth.' She tried to circle her fingers around his upper arm and realised just how muscled he was. 'So hard underneath. And I can see the muscles. I've got some, I think that is from riding, but mine are smooth.' She traced a finger down the arrow of hair and Gabriel sucked in his breath as she dipped her finger into his navel. 'Am I talking too much?'

'There are absolutely no rules, although you are wearing altogether too much clothing.'

'I am shy. I told you that, too.'

Gabriel pulled her gently forward until her forehead rested on his chest. 'You are beautiful and you are even more beautiful naked in my arms. How long is your hair, Lady Godiva? I have never seen it out of its plait and it will veil your blushes.' His fingers were busy in it as he spoke, then he combed it out over her shoulders until it hung around her. 'We may safely undo some of these buttons now.'

'You are very good at undressing,' Caroline said after a moment as the fiddly buttons yielded, one after another.

'I am handy with corset strings, too. There, almost unveiled.' Her nightgown slipped down, clinging precariously to her hips. Gabriel smoothed her hair down, the palms of his hands brushed her nipples, then stilled as she made a faint, involuntary sound. He bent his head and blew gently on the strands, parting them so he could seek her left nipple with his mouth. His hands held her steady by the waist as she stiffened, then softened into his embrace.

It was bliss, and frightening, and delicious all at once. She could feel every movement of his lips, the tiny nip of his teeth, the soothing stroke of his tongue, not only at her breast but deep in her belly and between her thighs. Before had been wonderful, but so fast she had hardly been aware of anything but the urgency of their desire, the shock of that violent pleasure building. Him leaving her at that crucial moment.

Gabriel moved to the other breast, his hands sliding up to cup her, then down to give the nightgown the one last touch it needed to send it pooling around her feet.

Caroline caught at his shoulders, off balance with desire, confusion, the need to touch him. She found herself swept off her feet and deposited on the bed, wrapped in Gabriel's arms, his leg thrown over her hips, her whole body gathered in against his heat and hardness, all at once both safe and overwhelmed, swept up in the sheer masculine power of him.

Her body remembered, responded with enthusiasm as she burrowed against him, her hands running over the powerful shoulders, down to the narrow waist, the hard swell of his buttocks. She should be ashamed of her eagerness, her upbringing warned her, but she did not care. Everything throbbed and ached and wanted more. 'Tell me what to do,' she managed when he lifted his mouth from hers.

'Whatever you want, or just leave it to me.' His hand slid between her thighs as he spoke and she parted her legs instinctively, then almost arched off the bed with the pleasure of it and the embarrassing discovery that she was wet and aching there and that his fingers were sliding inside and she *liked* it.

They were more than sliding. They were stroking into the folds of flesh that seemed swollen and more sensitive than she could ever have imagined, then he focused his attention on one spot, teasing and caressing and everything, the entire universe, her whole needy, pleasure-filled body, was focused on that single point and the sensation became unbearable and then impossible and suddenly everything fell apart into something that was more than just pleasure.

She was vaguely conscious of being on her back, of a weight over her, of Gabriel's lips on hers again and then... 'Ow!' Indignant at the discomfort that shattered her bliss, she dug her fingernails into his shoulders. She had forgotten it might be painful, and he was very large and she was very new to this.

'I'm sorry.' His voice was husky. Caroline opened her

eyes to find herself almost nose to nose with him, the points of her nipples fretted by the hair on his chest, his hips tight against hers, and realised his body was deep within hers. 'It will get better in a moment, I promise. Trust me.'

She was not so sure, not when the pleasure and the tingling and the heat were ebbing in the face of this male intrusion. Why couldn't he be fast, so she didn't need to think? She could push him away, resist it, or she could trust him, she realised as he began to move again, rocking slowly into her, edging deeper. She closed her eyes, unable to cope with sight as well as touch and sound and the scent of their passion, musky and heady. Gabriel had never let her down yet, she realised as her body began to soften, embrace his hardness, open to him like a flower worshipping to the sun. And the pleasure flooded back, different from before, better than before.

'Come for me, Caroline,' he said and she opened her eyes to meet his, dark and deep and utterly focused on her. She did not understand what he meant, but he slid his hand between them, touched her in that magic place, and she spun out of control, out of herself again. She was conscious of Gabriel surging deeper, of his hoarse cry, of heat deep in her core and then she was lost in the strange bliss their two bodies had created.

Caroline came to herself with her head on Gabriel's chest, knowing exactly where she was, who she was with. *I love him.* She knew that as a certainty, too, and she knew not to say the words. Not yet. *I will show him if he will only give me the chance.*

She raised her head and discovered that Gabriel was asleep. Infinitely slowly she wriggled and slid until she could prop herself up on the pillow next to him and study him. The clever, cynical face was relaxed and off guard.

Vulnerable. He looked younger with the dark lashes on his cheeks, the wayward hair tousled over his brow, the mocking mouth softened and curved into a half-smile. She could imagine him as a wild, eager youth and wondered at the process that had turned him into the self-sufficient man behind the gambler's mask.

She reached down to pull the sheet up over their bodies, left the candles to burn themselves out, then snuggled back against him. *I will be sleeping with this man for the rest of my life now. If I can keep him. If we can make this work.* Her lids drooped and she fell asleep to the beat of his heart beneath her cheek.

Gabriel woke to dawn light and a feeling of bodily well-being. Except for cold feet. There was a definite warm draught stirring the hairs on his chest. He turned his head on the pillow and found Caroline curled up against him, her nose buried just under his collarbone, her hair veiling her face.

He had taken her virginity before marriage, yet he could feel no guilt. *We've done it, there's no way back from this, she cannot change her mind now.*

Her honesty about her physical desires had taken his breath away. Caroline, it seemed, was not good at prevaricating, not with herself and not, apparently, with him. That could be refreshing, it could be perilous. The little white lies and hypocrisies of everyday life kept the wheels of society moving smoothly and they probably kept marriages running smoothly as well, at least on the surface.

The nights, it seemed, would be pleasurable if Caroline's sensual enthusiasm was anything to judge by. Which should mean she would be with child soon and that, surely, would content her. He supposed he would have to modify his life a trifle. Now he was about to take a wife he could hardly act the rackety bachelor every night. He wanted her to be happy, to enjoy being a countess. She deserved that. *Dinner parties*, he thought vaguely. *She'll want escorting around to balls and so forth when the Season starts. Almack's, even.* He grimaced. Alex and Cris would be taking their wives, Caroline could join their parties.

But that aside, his life wouldn't change that much. He'd give her a good allowance, let her loose on the London house to start with. When a child was on the way she could move down to Edenvale and amuse herself with making that over as she wanted. The more she changed it, the happier he would be. There was no need to worry about emotions, about breaking her heart. This had been a marriage of necessity and he had been frank from the start. She was an intelligent woman who could have few illusions about him.

He found he cared that she was happy, an uncomfortable, unwelcome burden. *Keep her at a distance*, his head warned him even as he felt that warm, contented, sensation in his chest. *You'll only let her down sooner or later if she comes to believe this is more than it is.*

Caroline stirred, stretched, and her hand began to move slowly across his stomach. Yes, this was going to work.

'Good morning.' He slid up against the pillows with the result that her hand slipped southwards in a most delightful manner.

'Oh!' To his regret Caroline let go of his enthusiastically awakening wedding tackle and sat up in a swirl of sheets. Her eyes were sultry with sleep, her mouth was swollen with kisses and her cheeks were pink. 'Gabriel.'

'Which is who you were expecting, I trust. Did you sleep well?'

'So well.' She stretched with her arms above her head, presenting him with a ravishing picture of perfect small breasts, the movement of skin and muscle over her rib cage and stomach and a glimpse of her secret triangle of dark-blonde hair.

There was no artifice in the gesture, no calculation. Caroline was waking up, she needed to stretch and she was comfortable enough with him to do so without hesitation or self-consciousness. He was not used to that and it was, 'Delicious,' Gabriel murmured and pounced, rolling her on to her back and leaning on one elbow to look down at her. 'Are you sore?'

That did make her blush. She wriggled experimentally, causing his heart rate to kick up several beats. 'A little.'

He tossed the sheet on to the floor, slid down the bed and worked his way between her legs, pushing her thighs apart with his shoulders.

'Gabriel?'

'Shh. Relax. Go back to sleep if you like.' *As though I would let you.*

'Gabriel!' His name broke in the middle and Caroline gave a faint shriek as he lowered his mouth to her.

He put his hands firmly on either side of her hips to hold her still and licked into the core of her, exploring her secrets, relentlessly gentle and persistent until her gasps of protest turned into sighs and she began to lift her hips to meet his questing lips and tongue. He took her over once, then again, then came up her body to slide into the soft wet heat that was so ready for him. She came for him again, crying his name as she convulsed around him, sending him over the edge, all technique and restraint forgotten.

'Are you still reconciled?' she asked a little later, her eyelashes tickling as she leaned over to kiss his throat.

'Oh, yes, I think so, although I believe we will have to repeat the exercise frequently to make certain.'

She laughed softly as he pulled her tight against his side

and Gabriel relaxed. Caroline was a darling. This marriage business would be no trouble at all, provided he kept it at the level of sex and friendship.

Chapter Sixteen

'Lord Edenbridge. Good morning, my lord.' The Aven-more butler regarded Gabriel with a more kindly eye than he deserved, given that they had arrived on the doorstep of the St James's Square house at the outrageous hour of nine o'clock. 'My lord and lady are at breakfast, but if you would care to wait in the drawing room, I will apprise them of your arrival.'

'We'll join them, Benson. Just send in two more place settings.'

'Yes, my lord.' The butler did not quite roll his eyes, but Gabriel suspected it was a close-run thing. 'Should I announce you? The lady—'

'No need.' He took Caroline's arm and ushered her through to the dining room. 'Good morning.'

'What have you done now?' Cris enquired, folding *The Times* and setting it beside hisplate as he got to his feet. 'Good morning, Lady Caroline.'

'Cris!' Tamsyn scolded, getting to her feet, too, and hurrying around the table to hug Caroline. She released her, regarded Gabriel with her head on one side for a moment, grinned and hugged him, too. 'You are going to get married, aren't you? Sit down and have some breakfast and tell us all about it. I'll just ring for— Oh, thank you, Benson.'

Gabriel waited until he had served both himself and Caroline from the buffet. 'Yes. I am almost afraid to ask how you know. Some form of Devon witchcraft, I assume.'

Tamsyn shook her head at him. 'A woman's instinct. I only had to look at the pair of you.'

'What happened?' Cris, with his usual uncanny nose for trouble, knew this was more than a sudden attack of romance.

'My father found me,' Caroline said. She was wary of Cris, he knew, but he could only admire the calm way she gave him back blue-eyed stare for stare. 'And Gabriel was there.'

'So Caroline gallantly saved my honour, and what remains of my good name, by consenting to marry me.' He saw her fingers tighten on the knife and fork as he spoke. *You must get used to it, my dear. Life with me is no romantic bed of roses.*

'You are a fortunate man,' Cris said. 'I felicitate you. Caroline, tell me what we can do to help you. We are entirely at your disposal.'

'I hardly like to ask it, but Gabriel suggested that you might allow us to marry here.' She was perfectly calm, perfectly composed. For a moment Gabriel was lulled into thinking that everything was all right, that Caroline was placidly accepting things as they were, as they had to be. Then he realised that she had learned this calm acceptance as a defence against her father's tempers, his moods, his blows. And now she was using it as a defence against him.

'Gabriel?'

He looked up at the whisper to see Tamsyn's concerned expression, then down to where the fragile coffee cup had cracked in his hand. *Unthinking violence. Hell, what is happening to me?*

'Lord, I'm a clumsy oaf,' he said lightly. 'I'm sorry, Tamsyn. I'll replace it.' He glanced around and found Cris was still talking to Caroline.

'Please, don't worry about it. I bought them in Mr Wedgwood's showroom across the Square only a few days ago. It is no trouble to find another.' She passed him another cup and murmured, 'Gabriel, is everything all right?'

'Yes, of course it is. Unpleasant for Caroline, of course, her father ranting and raving and then finding herself landed with me as a husband. But for myself, I couldn't be happier.'

'No. Of course not.' Her expression was a trifle quizzical. 'As the daughter of an earl she must be considered most eligible, which we know is of paramount importance to you.'

'Are you ever going to forgive me for opposing your match with Cris?' he asked.

'Certainly I will.' Her slanting smile carried promises and threats. 'Provided you make Caroline a good husband.'

'I have every intention of doing so.'

'I am sure you have. But is your definition of a good husband the same as mine, I wonder?'

Gabriel had told himself he was not going to be riled by her, that her wariness of him was more than understandable, so it was a surprise to find himself snapping back. 'As we all know Cris is a paragon of all the virtues, so I doubt anyone else can reach his level of perfection as a husband.'

He deserved a snub for that remark, he knew, not to provoke Tamsyn into laughter. He assumed an expression of mild enquiry, accompanied by one of his better sardonic smiles, as Cris said, 'Now what is amusing you, my love?'

'Gabriel considers that you are a paragon of all the virtues and must be making me an absolutely perfect husband.' Tamsyn was mopping her eyes with her napkin.

'And am I not?' Gabriel had never seen that tender look in the ice-blue eyes before.

'You are coming along very nicely, my lord,' Tamsyn said primly. 'Constant practice is, of course, required.'

'As with everything,' Cris observed. 'I must confess myself deeply flattered by your opinion, Gabriel. On the other hand, if I was certain you would know a virtue when you saw one, I might be more complacent.'

'Gabriel has many virtues,' Caroline said hotly. 'I beg your pardon, Lord Avenmore, but I will not sit by and have him abused.'

'He is teasing me,' Gabriel said, and then, when she still looked unconvinced, added, 'Male friends do, you know.'

'It is true,' Tamsyn put in. 'You must have observed it. The fonder they are of each other, the more objectionable they become. Men are not good at showing their emotions. Look at them—they both look thoroughly uncomfortable now.'

'As Gabriel appears to have finished his breakfast he and I can go and be uncomfortable together and leave you two to the full and frank exchange of your emotional states while you discuss arrangements for the wedding.' Cris got to his feet. 'Bring the coffee pot, Gabe, and we will retreat to the library to lick our wounds.'

'I have known you for years, yet when you look like that I still cannot read you,' Cris observed as they settled into the chairs facing each other on either side of the library fireplace. 'I have no idea whether you are delighted that your hand has been forced or appalled that you have to do the honourable thing.' He took a mouthful of coffee. 'Which is why I never play cards with you except for coppers.'

'I am neither,' Gabriel said. Strange that he did not resent Cris's probing, but then he and his three friends had never had secrets, not about the things that really mattered. Certainly not about the wounds they all carried from long ago. Except the one thing that he never, ever, talked about. 'I am simply content with the arrangement. I should marry because of the title and Caroline is perfectly eligible if one discounts her appalling father. I like and admire her. There is a certain basic mutual attraction.'

'Yes, one can see that.' Cris's lips twitched.

'I believe her reluctance is because she knows my hand is being forced. I made the mistake of attempting moral blackmail when I was desperate for her to agree. However, she is now resigned because I am, apparently, considerably better than the alternatives on offer.'

The twitch became one of his friend's rare grins. 'The more I see of Lady Caroline the more I approve of her.' He filled his cup and watched Gabriel over the rim. 'So why are you merely content, given that you are definitely attracted?'

'You think I will make any kind of a decent husband? Leaving aside this scandal, my reputation is not going to be any help to her. If we're received I'll squire her about, of course, but I'm hoping she'll be happier in the country bringing up the children.'

'This is not really about your reputation, is it?'

'I always thought you were a loss to the legal profession. You should be making some poor soul's life hell on the witness stand, not interrogating me.' Gabriel leaned across to take the coffee pot and stayed silent until he had drunk the fresh cupful. 'But, yes, you are right, of course. Damn it, Cris, I have no idea how to be a decent husband.

I'll be kind to her, look after her—that goes without saying. But neither of us were brought up to know what a happy family looks like. Her father is a self-centred obsessive, you know that. And then he hit her.'

'Does she realise how much you have in common?' Cris asked.

Gabriel shook his head. 'And she won't.'

'She will when she sees your back. Or has she already?'

'Not yet.' He moved uneasily as though the pressure of the chair back might chafe the old scars into active life again and shifted the subject. 'How do you do it, you and Alex and Grant? You all make your wives happy.'

'Love,' Cris said simply. 'It is a novelty for men raised as we were. For most aristocrats, I suppose. But we married women who understood about love and family and *warmth*, I suppose. Do you love Caroline?'

'No.' Gabriel was certain about that. He had no idea what loving a woman in the emotional sense would feel like, but he was very certain he would know it if it happened to him. It had changed his friends and he was the same man that he had been before Caroline had erupted into his life. Absolutely the same.

'Does she love you?'

Lord, I hope not. The thought of hurting Caroline appalled him. He would try his best, but he felt he was embarking on a journey with no road maps, no compass. 'I told you. She's resigned to marrying me, but that is all.'

'If you want my advice, and you probably do not, tell her about your family.'

'You mean so she can conclude that I will turn out like my father and flee screaming?' Gabriel enquired.

'You never would. You wouldn't be worrying about it if there was any danger of that.'

'What a comfort you are,' Gabriel retorted to cover the

fact that, yes, it *was* a comforting thought. 'I hardly recognise you.'

'I know it. It must be the effects of marriage. What do you say, shall we see if Alex can join us and we'll have a bachelor night out on the town?'

'Perfect. I'll call in on him on my way home.' He got to his feet, but stopped at the door. 'Did I tell you I found a new hell just off Hill Street?'

'I am not playing cards with you! Have you any idea how expensive wives are?'

Gabriel was still smiling when he collected his hat from Benson. *Thank heavens for my friends.* 'Would you give my compliments to Lady Caroline and tell her I will call tomorrow? I imagine she is closeted with Lady Avenmore at the moment.'

He tipped his hat to a rakish angle, pulled on his gloves and sauntered along King Street, passing Almack's with a faint shudder. Yes, thank heavens for his friends. There was no one else he could talk freely about his demons to, no one else he would admit weakness or anxiety to either. Certainly none of those things were to be discussed with a wife, a woman who needed only his strength and his protection, not his doubts and fears and secret nightmares.

'Madame Fleur, this may be a quiet wedding, but I can assure you it will be an important one,' Tamsyn said with a steely determination that sent a shiver down Caroline's spine. It looked as though it was having a similar effect on the modiste who stood in the middle of Tamsyn's bedroom surrounded by what appeared to be the entire stock of her shop, a number of half-finished gowns and several twittering assistants.

'You are being given the opportunity not only to provide the wedding gown for the new Countess of Edenbridge, but her entire wardrobe. And to demonstrate that I was right to select you to dress me exclusively,' Tamsyn continued.

The calculation was plain on the dressmaker's face: upset a number of clients who were waiting for gowns or seriously displease the Marchioness of Avenmore *and* lose the publicity surrounding what might well be the most talked-of wedding of the summer.

'But of course, my lady.' Madame rose to the occasion, gathered up her tape measure. 'My hesitation was merely while I acquainted myself with Lady Caroline's colouring and style. If you would condescend to disrobe and to stand here, my lady, we will begin. The entire wardrobe, you say?'

'Everything except a court dress. That can wait,' Tamsyn said, brushing lightly past the fact that one might never be needed.

Two hours later Tamsyn was still talking of lists as they descended the stairs. 'Millinery, shoes, stockings, corsets, lingerie, ribbons, hairdresser…I need more paper. I will go and jot all this down while I think of it. Why don't you go and have a rest in the drawing room for a while? Do ring for the tea tray.' She swept on, leaving Caroline feeling like a wilted nosegay in her wake.

'Never mind tea, I need brandy,' she murmured as she walked into the front reception room.

A young man clutching a leather portfolio rose to his feet. 'Lady Caroline? Benson said I might wait for you in here.'

Sandy hair, green eyes, half a head shorter than Gabriel and not yet twenty. 'Are you by any chance Mr Louis Stone?' she enquired, holding out her hand to him. *At last, a glimpse into Gabriel's home life.*

'Yes, I am.' He peered at her myopically. 'We haven't met, have we?'

'No, Gabriel described you. I was just about to take tea. Will you join me, Mr Stone?' She rang the bell, then gestured to the sofa and sat down beside him so that he did not have to squint across the room at her. 'I am delighted to meet one of Gabriel's family at last. Are you in London permanently?'

'No, just for the vacation. I go back to Cambridge at the beginning of October for the Michaelmas term,' he explained. 'But I am staying with Gabriel for the moment and helping him as much as possible.' He was flushed with earnest enthusiasm and Caroline was reminded painfully of Anthony, even though Lucas was almost a young man. 'I finished today's tasks, so I have come to see if I could be of any assistance to you, Lady Caroline.'

'Caroline, please.' She smiled at him, liking his earnest manner. The contrast with Gabriel was almost amusing. 'We will be brother and sister very soon.' He grinned at her, suddenly a student and no longer the earnest man he was trying to be. 'Tell me how you assist Gabriel.'

He talked readily, even when the tea tray had been brought and he had to juggle cup, saucer and a plate of cakes.

Why, he worships his brother. This was far from the distant relationship that Gabriel's few references to his family had left her imagining. 'Do you see much of your brothers?' she asked. 'I have not yet been to Edenvale and I am looking forward to that very much. I imagine you all get together there as often as possible.'

It was as though he had brought a shutter down over his face. Louis said stiffly, 'No, not often. Ben is with his regiment, of course, and George has his parish and Gabriel avoids the place like...I mean, he prefers London. I usually visit friends during vacations, but this summer Gabriel has started teaching me about the estates so I have seen much more of him.'

'Tell me more about Edenvale,' she encouraged him. 'Gabriel has hardly mentioned it. It must hold wonderful childhood memories for you.'

This time the shutters positively slammed down. 'I was never very fond of it. I have written to Ben and George and I have every expectation that they will be able to come to the wedding. Can I help with anything here? Place cards, perhaps? I have a good hand.'

So what on earth was wrong with Gabriel's country house that he avoided it? And it certainly seemed to hold no good memories for Louis either. Yet Gabriel had made no mention of any problems to her and she assumed that was where they would go after the wedding. It occurred to her abruptly that the subject had never even been discussed.

There was no point in pressing Louis, nor should she. 'I am certain Lady Avenmore would be delighted if someone took on that task. The marquess's secretary is already loaded down with all the work we are finding for him. Ah, here she is. Lady Avenmore, may I present Mr Louis Stone, Gabriel's youngest brother. Louis, the Marchioness of Avenmore.'

Louis made a very proper bow and shook hands and they all sat again while Caroline explained about his offer of help and Tamsyn accepted gratefully.

'Lord Edenbridge, my lady.' Benson ushered Gabriel in.

'Tamsyn, Caroline.' He stopped halfway across the carpet. 'Louis? What are you doing here?'

'I came to offer my assistance as I have completed everything you left me.'

'Have you indeed? And you have made yourself right at

home, I see.' Gabriel cast a jaundiced eye over his brother's crumb-strewn plate.

'We are very glad to see him, and I am delighted to make his acquaintance,' Caroline said. 'We were just talking about Edenvale.'

In the silence that followed she thought she could hear her own heart beating.

'What about it, exactly?'

'I was just saying that I couldn't tell Caroline much because I hardly ever go there,' Louis said.

'I don't even know where it is,' she added in an effort to ease the strained atmosphere. 'I am looking forward to seeing it very much.'

'We will drive over when we are in Brighton,' Gabriel said with no marked enthusiasm.

'We are not going there for our honeymoon, then?'

'Brighton, yes. Edenvale, no. It needs work doing to it,' he added. 'I thought you would like Brighton. Have you been before?'

'No, never.' *And I know a* No Trespassing *sign when I see one.* 'I am sure it will be delightful if this weather holds.'

'It looks set fair. Excuse me, I must go and discuss wine with Cris. Make yourself useful here, Louis, and I will see you for dinner at Mount Street.' He paused with one hand on the door. 'I have asked Cris to be my best man. I wondered if you would like Alex to give you away, Caroline.'

'Oh, yes, I would.' He nodded and went out as she said to Tamsyn, 'I cannot think of anyone better qualified to soothe a nervous bride's nerves.'

'Are you nervous?' Louis asked, then blushed violently. 'I do beg your pardon, I am sure that is the sort of thing one does not ask.'

He was so charmingly dismayed that she laughed. 'It is merely the scandal, that is all.'

'The scandal? You know about...?' His voice trailed away. 'Oh, you mean the scandal about the elopement. If you will excuse me, I will go and find Lord Avenmore's secretary and offer to help with the place cards.'

'And what was that about?' Caroline asked Tamsyn whose bemused expression must be a match for her own. 'What scandal?'

'I have no idea. You will have to ask Gabriel.'

'No, Gabriel has enough to worry about. If he wants me to know, he will tell me.'

'You are very trusting. Anyone would think you were in love with the man,' Tamsyn said slyly. 'Have another cake.'

Chapter Seventeen

'Deep breath, chin up.' Alex said, settling her hand more firmly in the crook of his elbow. 'You look ravishing, you'll bring Gabriel to his knees, every man in the place, including the vicar, will want to run off with you and all the ladies will be green with envy over your gown.'

If the laugh that escaped her was shaky it did release some of the tension, which was presumably why Alex was laying on the flattery with a trowel. 'Thank you,' Caroline said, answering the intent, not the words.

'Off we go then.' Alex set off at a slow walk for the head of the stairs, then paused for her to lift the hem of her skirt a little and get a grip on the spray of cream-and-pink roses and ferns she carried.

At the foot of the great sweep of staircase the household staff were arrayed in formal ranks and, as she came down the final curve, Caroline could see heads turning in the drawing room. Goodness knew what strings Cris and Alex had pulled, what wiles Tess and Tamsyn had employed, to get such a number of guests there. And such influential ones, too. Two Patronesses of Almack's, the Swedish ambassador and his wife, one ancient duke, a marquess, a scattering of countesses, an archdeacon…

Tess had briefed her about each and every guest and it had all fled what passed for her brain now the wedding was actually happening. She had hardly slept last night, tossing and turning with nightmare visions of everything that might happen to stop it—her father appearing with a shotgun, the archbishop refusing the licence, Gabriel coming to his senses. And when she had fought all those phantoms down she was racked with worry that it *would* happen and that the marriage would be a disaster and—

'Breathe,' Alex murmured as they entered the drawing room. For a second her knees turned to jelly and then she looked up through the gauzy veil and saw Gabriel standing at the far end of the room. He was a stranger, a well-groomed gentleman in a beautiful tail coat and silk breeches, his hair fashionably cropped, his expression severe. And then he saw her and everything was all right. She had no idea what tomorrow might bring, but here, now, the man she loved was smiling at her, was, against all convention, holding out his hand to her, and she was conscious of nothing more than his voice speaking the vows, the warmth of his grip, the caress of his lips as he put back her veil and kissed her.

'You make a very lovely countess,' Gabriel said as they processed back between the rows of guests.

'It is this gown.' She was walking on air now in her pretty French kid slippers, ready to believe he thought her *lovely* as the cream silk whispered behind her, as the tiny crystals and pearls caught the light and sparkled like snow in summer, as the diamonds he had given her flashed defiant fire at her ears and throat, wrist and in her hair.

'It is you, my lady. You would have this room at your feet even if you were wearing sackcloth. You make me proud to be your husband.'

Hold this moment a little voice inside her urged. *You will need this memory, you will need its strength.*

'How married do you feel?' Gabriel asked as the chaise rattled over the cobbles past Brixton church and Caroline took off her bonnet and sat back with a sigh. They had a six-hour journey ahead of them, it was already well past noon and his bride was a trifle wan. She was still beautiful, but pale now and her smiles were beginning to look artificial. She would regain her spirits, he had confidence in her resilience, but for now he would try and keep things light.

'I feel very married. But I am not certain about being a countess,' Caroline confessed, with a dimple appearing that looked perfectly natural. 'I will have to get Harriet to address me as Lady Edenbridge with every sentence until I become accustomed. How married do *you* feel?'

'Exceedingly. The sight of my beautiful bride might have been a dream, but I have been comprehensively lectured by Cris and Alex on the subject, I have signed numerous legal papers, much to Louis's delight, and I have seen an alarming amount of luggage loaded on the coach this morning. That all feels very real.' So did the pleasure he felt when he looked at her, caught one of her smiles. It was almost easy to believe that he could make her happy. That she could make him happy.

'Wait until the bills arrive, then you'll most definitely know you have a wife,' she said darkly. 'Tamsyn and Tess insisted that you had given them *carte blanche* to buy whatever they felt was necessary, but it seems like a great deal to me.' Glancing down, he saw that the dimple had vanished. 'I wish my father would release my dowry, I do not like coming to you empty-handed.'

'You bring yourself. That is all I need. I am a rich man, Caroline. I can well support a wife in style.'

She slipped her hand into his. 'Thank you.' Caroline was silent almost as far as Streatham village and he was wondering if she had fallen asleep. Then she said, 'I do like your brothers.'

'You do?' He had kept a wary eye on them, as far as he was able amidst the demands of an early wedding breakfast.

'Ben is a good officer, I imagine. He has that same knack of leadership that you do, but allied to military discipline. And I imagine that he takes good care of his men, for all his seeming rather abrupt. That is like you, too.'

'Me? I lead no one anywhere except into trouble and I have no one to take care of. Except you now.' A sweet duty.

'And your brothers. And your friends. But if you are going to be foolishly modest I will tell you that I also liked George and I consider him quite indecently good looking for a clergyman. The poor man will spend his entire career evading heart-struck spinsters in the vestry. He will make a very beautiful bishop, which Louis informs me he intends to become.'

'I am prepared to admit that he resembles me in looks,' Gabriel said, fishing to see just how truthful she would be.

'George is better looking than you are. His nose is straighter and he has a very engaging smile.'

'That puts me in my place. And what about Louis?'

'Oh, Louis is a darling. He is anxious to do well in his studies so that when he graduates he can be of the greatest use to you. He hero-worships you, of course.'

'Nonsense. They all avoid me like the plague unless they need money. Or, in Louis's case, employment.'

'They are in awe of you,' Caroline said, tipping back her head to frown at him. 'They look up to you. I never spoke to them all together, but they all said the same thing, that they owe you so much. They love you, you know.'

Gabriel shifted on the seat, the plush upholstery suddenly as hard as planks. They could only have been referring to their childhood, but none of them knew just what lengths he had gone to in order to protect them. And none of them had witnessed that final crisis, only Louis, for whom the memory had been blanked out by shock.

He had sneered at Caroline's devotion to Anthony, her total commitment to putting his welfare above her own. But he knew now why it had made him so uneasy and defensive. He had felt the same, had made his own sacrifices. But all this flummery about love... No. Even if his brothers did know, all he had done was his duty to them. He was the eldest and they were his responsibility.

'You will invite them to stay, won't you?' Caroline rested her head on his shoulder. 'There is room for guests at Mount Street and I imagine Edenvale is large enough for proper house parties. Now what have I said?' She sat up again. 'You have gone all stiff.'

'None of us likes Edenvale.'

'Then we must fix whatever is wrong with it. It is a wicked waste to have a large house uninhabited. It should be giving employment to the entire district, for one thing.'

She sank back against his shoulder and Gabriel wondered why that gesture was quite as pleasing as it was. This was his wedding day, he should want kisses and caresses from his wife, not confiding snuggling. Then she nudged him in the ribs. 'Ouch!'

'What about Edenvale? What is wrong with it?'

'You are quite right about the employment. And I had meant to open it up for you as I imagine you would be happier down there when the children come along.' Now it was her turn to stiffen, but he judged it unwise to ask why. 'We did not have very happy childhoods there, that is all. A familiar enough tale, I suppose. Our mother died when I was fourteen. Ben was eleven, George ten and Louis only four. Our father was not an easy man.' And that was all he was going to say on the subject.

'And I suppose it is entailed, so you cannot sell it,' Caroline mused as they entered Croydon. 'But as I assume you did not intend depositing me, and our hopeful family, down there and never visiting, we must change it enough to reconcile you to it.'

'As you say,' he temporised, choosing to ignore the soft snort that produced. 'Tell me why you have never been to Brighton. I would have thought your father was entranced by the Pavilion.'

'Oh, yes, he much admires it. But he did not believe in taking the family on holidays when we had a perfectly good country house for fresh air and recreation. Tell me all about it. Where will we stay and what is there to do?'

'I have taken a house overlooking the Steine. We were lucky to get it at this date, but apparently Lady Maltravers, who was renting it, had a violent quarrel with her bosom friend Lady Feldrake over a young man and has flounced off to Weymouth, declaring that the company there is far less vulgar.'

Gabriel talked about assemblies and libraries, drives and public breakfasts, the dubious aesthetics of the Pavilion and, of course, the opportunities for sea-bathing, until Crawley was behind them. 'This is Pease Pottage,' he said, expecting a murmur of amusement at the name. 'We will change horses at the Black Swan.' A soft, lady-like snore greeted this intelligence so he made no move to get out, instead settling Caroline more comfortably against his shoulder and gesturing away the landlord who came busting out while the grooms changed the horses and the postilions vanished into the taproom for a hasty pint of ale.

She was exhausted, and no wonder, he thought, surprising himself when he realised he was feeling no impatience at being trapped in the chaise instead of being able to get out, stretch his legs and take refreshment. It was a novelty to have a woman to take care of, one that he was discovering an unexpected tenderness for.

Caroline woke with a start and found they had drawn up abruptly because a young man was struggling to turn his gig and half-blocking the road. 'I am so sorry.' She sat up, uncomfortably aware that the shoulder of Gabriel's coat was creased where her head must have rested, that her hair was in disorder and that she had slept at a time when any other bride would have been wide awake and paying close attention to her new husband. 'Where are we?'

She had expected Gabriel to be irritable with her, but his smile was the rare one that reached his eyes and made her want to hug him. The smile she had seen at the altar. 'Hand Cross, thirty-three miles from London. We'll stop at the Red Lion, I expect you would like some tea.'

'I would, definitely. I am sorry I went to sleep.'

'Why be sorry? You are tired, which is no surprise, given what has transpired over the past few days.'

'It is not very wifely behaviour,' she said primly, which made him burst out laughing as the chaise turned into the inn yard.

'And what do you know about wifely behaviour?'

'About as much as you, I imagine. Or were you in the habit of driving down to Brighton with young ladies in the guise of Mr and Mrs Smith of Scandal on Thames?'

'*Ladies?* One at a time, Lady Edenbridge, please. You have a flattering notion of my stamina.' When she shook her head at him he smiled. 'I am not in the habit of travelling with females.'

'Are you not?' she quizzed him, but he got down from

the chaise and helped her out. She did not like to tease when there was the chance they might be overheard.

To Caroline's surprise, Gabriel returned to the subject when she joined him in the private parlour after seeking out what the landlady coyly referred to as, 'The amenities, ma'am.'

'Did you think I travelled with a bevy of light-skirts and opera dancers?' he enquired as she poured tea.

'I have no idea.' Caroline passed him his cup and surveyed the assortment of dainties that had been brought in with the tea. 'I have no knowledge of that sort of thing, but you *do* have a reputation.'

'For a sequence of *chères amis*, all of whom were, shall we say, ladies rather than professionals. And note I did say sequence. One at a time is quite adequate.'

Caroline digested this along with a cake that was turning to sawdust in her mouth. 'Who is the current one?'

Gabriel choked on his tea. 'No one!' He recovered himself and added with his old, mocking half-smile, 'Terribly bad *ton* for a newly married man.'

'So you gave the lady her *congé*?' She tried to gain some comfort from this, although the implication of his words only confirmed his earlier remarks about the likelihood he would stray from his vows.

'I did. All very amicable, I assure you.'

Caroline almost believed him, but she was beginning to be able to read Gabriel, just a little, and there had been a betraying tightness about his mouth for a moment. So, the mistress of the moment had not been pleased. She repressed a little shiver, then assured herself that pride, if nothing else, would prevent whoever it was from making an unpleasant scene when she next encountered Gabriel in public. All the scandals about this marriage were going to be the ones she was responsible for bringing with her.

I will be a good wife, she promised herself. *I will make him happy if it kills me. And I will not give him any excuse to chase other women,* she added grimly. *If he does then I will not be a complacent wife, even if Gabriel thinks that would make me a good one. I love him and I do not intend to share.*

'This is an excellent inn,' Gabriel observed, looking round at the warm glow of the polished panelling. 'It has been a long day. Shall we ask if they have a decent room available to go with this parlour? We could break our journey here.'

'But we are only about twenty miles from Brighton, surely?'

'Yes, but that is another two hours and there will be all the business of arriving at a hired house which is never straightforward, however early one sends down the staff. We could rest and then have dinner and go to bed early.' His eyes had the heavy-lidded look she had seen before, the one that sent an answering *frisson* of desire through her.

'*Rest*, my lord?' Caroline pushed away the niggling little doubt that it was talking about his former lovers that had made Gabriel think about bed now.

'A convenient euphemism I have learned from my married friends. It is amazing how weary marriage makes some couples. It is, after all, our wedding night.'

'Then, yes, let us take a bedchamber. You have warned me, after all, not to overestimate your stamina.' She widened her eyes at him in mock-innocence and felt a certain return of confidence when he got immediately to his feet and strode from the room.

There *was* a chamber, charming and old-fashioned with a great oaken four-poster bed, a thick Turkey carpet on the uneven floor and a ceiling that bulged and dipped so that Gabriel banged his head as he straightened up after dragging the curtains part-way across the window. Caroline bit her lip with sympathetic amusement, then felt the laughter die as she saw his face, recognised the heat and the desire. He wanted her and she wanted him, wanted him with a fever that had consumed her for days, ever since he had shown her what they could be together.

'No, leave it all,' he said as she lifted her hands to open the catch on her necklace, a fine double string of pearls left to her by her mother. They lay warm and comforting against her skin, now she arched her neck so he could lift her hair away from the nape and manipulate the delicate fastening.

Gabriel seemed in no hurry. His fingers played along her hairline, making the fine hairs stand up in response to his touch, then he bent and kissed her nape, his lips slightly open so she felt the heat of his breath, the tiny touches of his tongue.

The pearls curled on to the dressing table, then he unhooked her earrings, kissing behind each ear. Caroline leant into the delicious, teasing caress as he nibbled his way down the tendon at the side of her neck and gasped as he closed his teeth over it and bit down gently.

'Mine,' Gabriel murmured, his voice possessive. 'My bride to unwrap like a particularly delicious parcel.'

She had changed into a walking dress of deep sapphire, worn under a pelisse of paler blue that she had removed when they sat down to tea. Now Gabriel had unobstructed access to the row of tiny enamelled buttons down the back, which had taken Harriet her maid minutes to fasten, but which seemed to evaporate under his touch. The gown vanished, so did her petticoats, chemise and shoes, which left her in a corset, stockings and garters.

Gabriel stepped back from the bed and surveyed the result, like some pasha viewing the latest slave girl brought from his harem, she thought with mingled excitement and indignation.

She reached for her garters and he growled, 'Leave them.'

'But this feels more indecent than when I was wearing nothing,' she protested, flustered.

'I know.' The growl became the purr of a large cat. 'That's because it is. Very arousing. Look.' He tipped the glass on the dressing-table mirror so she could see herself sprawled on the pale-rose coverlet, her breasts pushed up by the tight lacing, her legs looking longer with the white stockings and the blue of the garters drawing the eye…

Caroline closed her legs abruptly and curled up against the headboard. 'You are still wearing all your clothes.'

Gabriel sat down, hauled off his boots and stockings together, shed his coat, waistcoat and neckcloth, unbuttoned his shirt and then his falls. The breeches slid down his long flanks, taking his smallclothes with them. 'Better?'

His shirt, open for the first ten inches, showed a tantalising amount of chest and hid a tantalising amount of everything else. Without troubling to remove it he sat on the edge of the bed and pulled her towards him.

She wanted to say, *No, take it off, let me look at you in daylight,* but the words stuck to the roof of her very dry mouth and then Gabriel was running his finger along the top edge of the corset, teasing her nipples in their tight confinement. He pushed at the edge until they were free, then bent to blow gently on the tips.

'Like cherries on a plate being offered up for me to nibble,' he said, and did.

The corset was tight, the pressure seeming to tip both her pelvis and her breasts towards Gabriel, into his clever hands and wicked mouth. She was breathless, racked with tension and delicious, terrifying sensation, desperate to touch him, to have his skin against hers. She tugged at the hem of his shirt, but it was crushed between them, then her hands found the neck opening and she jerked the sides apart, heard the fabric rip, then burrowed down to fasten with lips and teeth on to his right nipple.

Everything happened very quickly then. Gabriel was inside her and her body remembered him, responded without her having to think or do more than cling to him as he swept her up into the storm of his own powerful urgency. Her fingers knotted into the shirt over his shoulders, her heels locked into the small of his back, she heard her own voice gasping his name, heard the sound of their bodies meeting in hot, wet, desperation and then he reared up on his knees, lifting her with him so that he sank impossibly deep and she buried her face against his neck as the pleasure exploded, spinning her into fragments and she was lost in him.

Chapter Eighteen

Gabriel woke her by trailing deliberately sloppy kisses and licks around her right ear.

'Beast!' Caroline sat up, batting him off.

'It was the only bit of you I could get at,' he grumbled, falling back on to the pillows. 'You were curled up like a hedgehog.'

He was still wearing the ripped shirt and nothing else. When she leaned over and ran her fingers into the dark curls on his chest he caught her hand and pressed it flat until she could feel the beat of his heart under her palm. 'Caroline.' She looked up to meet his gaze and saw he was suddenly serious. 'Did I hurt you? I was too rough, I forgot that this is still new for you.'

'No, you didn't hurt me, although, frankly I doubt I would have noticed. And I was rough, too, I ripped your shirt.'

'That was exciting, my little hellcat. No one has ever done that to me before.'

She turned her fingers into claws beneath his hand and raked gently down his chest, following the trail of silky hair. When his eyes narrowed she whispered, 'Do you know what I want to do now?'

Gabriel shook his head, his gaze as intent as a hawk watching a vole.

'Get out of these stays and have a bath. Oh, no—we haven't any luggage!'

'Yes, we have. Look.' In the corner were three valises and her dressing case. 'I thought it was unwise to send everything ahead of us.'

'Yes, but it has only just occurred to me, Harriet and your valet will be wondering what has become of us. They will be so worried.'

'I expect they will guess we have been held up on the road.' He was looking so innocent as he straightened up from the bags with their robes in his hands that Caroline was immediately suspicious.

'You planned this, didn't you? You told them we wouldn't be in Brighton tonight.'

'I thought you might like something more spontaneous, more like a scandalous elopement,' Gabriel said as he shrugged on a heavy amber silk banyan over the tattered shirt. 'Let me untie that tight lacing before we ring for baths.'

'Why, I do declare you are a romantic, Gabriel Stone,' she said on a sigh of relief as her stays tumbled to the floor.

He held the peignoir for her. 'No, I am not, merely a rake. That's why we are so dangerous to innocents.'

Caroline blinked hard as he crossed the room to tug on the bell pull. *That's what you get for being romantic yourself, you fool. He doesn't love you, he is merely displaying his usual repertoire of seduction and lovemaking. And he is very good at it. The benefit of experience as he says.*

Caroline had her smile stitched firmly in place as her husband turned back. He had spoken in jest with no intention of hurting her, she was certain, for he would have to know that she loved him for that comment to have been meant to wound. She'd had no illusions about who and what she was marrying and she was not going to start their life together with tears and reproaches.

The cheerful expression was still intact as the maid came in and Gabriel gave orders for baths, shaving water, dinner. *The years of practice hiding my feelings from my father are bearing fruit now,* she thought and then had to turn away abruptly as the tears slid down her cheeks. Of all the bitter ironies, to have to use the deceit learned in her early life in order to hide her true feelings from the man who had rescued her from it.

'I am so enjoying Brighton.' Caroline tightened her grip on Gabriel's arm for a second and he glanced down at her, his expression amused.

'You haven't exhausted all the entertainments in a week?'

'Of course not. After all, this is the first time we have been swimming.' She gave him a sidelong look from under her lashes. 'It is the first morning I have been able to drag you out of bed in time.'

'You were not so unwilling to stay there,' he murmured, lowering his voice because Harriet and Corbridge were walking behind them, the valet carrying towels and the maid with Caroline's swimming outfit and hairbrushes.

It was true that she was easily persuaded to stay in bed for just one more kiss, which usually led to more than kissing. On the other hand Gabriel appeared to consider any time of the day or night suitable for lovemaking, so getting up on such a glorious morning as this would hardly deprive either of them.

'Mrs Wilberforce is waving from her carriage,' she said, drawing Gabriel's attention to the passing matron and her daughters. He lifted his hat, Caroline exchanged slight bows with the other ladies and they walked on, passing several new acquaintances and others whom Caroline or Gabriel knew from London.

'Everyone is so friendly,' she said. 'I did not expect it. We eloped, so I thought many of the matrons would poker up and that they would not welcome me associating with their daughters.'

'I suspect our friends have been busy on our behalf, although I must admit to being pleasantly surprised. Probably your father's eccentricities are so well known that no one blames you for escaping. And we did come to London and marry at once from a most respectable address. You are a countess now and although I have got a reputation, as you very well know, I have always been received.' He doffed his hat to a handsome lady in an open carriage who dimpled back at him.

'Stop flirting,' Caroline said lightly. She might as well tell a cat to stop chasing mice. Gabriel noticed pretty women, looked at pretty women and smiled at them, too. *And* he had spent two evenings at the Castle Inn assembly rooms deep in card play. But there was no sign that he went any further than smiling and as for the cards, he kept an eye on her and tossed in his hand the moment he noticed her looking tired.

'I am male, I have a pulse and I am under ninety and given that I caught you in Donaldson's circulating library using the telescope to study the west beach, I have to tell you, my lady, that was a case of the pot calling the kettle black.'

'I was not studying it! I only happened to swing the telescope in that direction. How was I to know it was the men's bathing area?' *Or that they all bathe stark naked?* None of the Brighton machines had the all-enveloping hoods that she had read about. It made her blush all over again just thinking of it.

'I will bespeak two bathing machines, mine at the eastern edge of the men's beach and yours at the western edge of the ladies' beach and then I can keep myself between you and any more assaults on your modesty.'

They were approaching the bathing house where those wishing to be 'dipped' booked their machine. Down on the beach the mules were trundling up and down the shingle, dragging the bathing machines and from the water came faint shrieks as ladies were ducked by the muscular female dippers.

'I do not want to be dipped, Gabriel.'

'A dipper is a fixture with the ladies' machines, I'm afraid. Besides, if you haven't been in the sea before then it is easy to be swept off your feet. I do not want you drowned, my dear. Just tell her you want to keep your head above water.'

He thinks I am nervous of being forced under the surface. I never told him I can swim, she realised, almost blurting it out, then thinking again. It might be fun to surprise Gabriel if he really was going to be close enough to reach without the risk of encountering any of the other men. Her mother, hearing of a tragedy where an entire family had been drowned on a boating trip, had insisted that her daughter as well as her sons were taught to swim before they were allowed to row on the lake. Lucas had taught her, surprisingly patient as she doggy-paddled around in the shallows in a voluminous shift over a pair of his old breeches.

She was still smiling at the memory as Gabriel paid the one shilling and three pence for her and the one shilling for himself without a dipper.

'There are two machines free now, just where I wanted

them. Apparently the ladies prefer not to be so close to the men and the gentlemen are inhibited by the thought of appearing to spy on the ladies.'

Caroline went down the ladies' steps to the beach with Harriet to be met by a woman with her sleeves rolled up over brawny arms. Her stout form was clad in a voluminous and soaking wet black-bombazine gown with numerous flannel petticoats dripping below the hem.

'I am Mrs 'Uggins, marm, and I'll be your dipper. No need for any alarm, marm, I've dipped them all from dairy maids to duchesses and never lost one yet. If you and your woman just step along and climb aboard, 'Uggins will take you down to the briny, smooth as silk.'

They clambered up the steps, through the door and into a narrow box with wooden benches on either side, a door at the far end and louvered slats letting in some light and the sound of the sea.

'It is a good thing I spoke to Mrs Chamberlain's maid yesterday and got some advice,' Harriet said as she began to unfasten Caroline's walking dress. 'It would be far too difficult getting fully dressed and undressed in this, my lady.'

She had the simple gown and one petticoat off without any trouble and was just attacking the strings of the pair of short stays that was all the corsetry Caroline was wearing when the machine gave a lurch and began to move. Harriet sat down with a thump on one bench and Caroline on the other.

She was still giggling when she emerged through the door on to the steps into the sea to find Mrs Huggins at the foot of them, the waves rising and falling around her vast hips, her impressive bosom emerging like sea cliffs from the foam.

'Down you come, marm. Lovely and warm it is. We'll have you dipped three times before you can say Neptune!'

Caroline took advantage of the dipper's bulk as a screen as she descended the steps, stifling a shriek as the water hit her stomach. Then she was in, her Bathing Preserver, as invented by the modiste Mrs Bell and widely advertised, shrouding her in its folds. The weighted hem kept it from billowing up and once she had arranged it evenly around her she felt quite decently covered and surprisingly unhampered.

'I do not require dipping, Mrs Huggins. I can swim quite well.' And in fact it was quite difficult to keep her feet on the bottom in the buoyant salty water.

'It's more healthful to be dipped,' said the bathing woman doubtfully. 'Not many ladies swim. Are you used to the waves, marm?'

'I am perfectly confident, thank you. I can see my husband over there.' And sure enough Gabriel's dark head was visible as he swam powerfully out to sea from the next bathing machine. He dived under and re-emerged to swim back towards the hut and when he reached the steps he rolled on to his back and began to float.

Caroline struck out, put her head under, blinked at the salt, then, suddenly confident, dived and swam submerged towards him. Being beneath the sea was different from the still cloudiness of the lake and clouds of bubbles released by the breakers and the swirls of sand disorientated her for a moment. Then she saw Gabriel's legs and surfaced close behind his back, ready to splash and startle him.

The sunshine was directly on him, gilding the water on his skin, emphasising the muscles, the beautiful masculine taper from shoulders to waist, the dip of his spine. *The scars.*

Gabriel turned at her gasp and his face, for once unguarded, was stark with shock and anger in equal parts. 'Get back over there,' he snarled. 'Are you mad? If anyone saw you behaving like a hoyden the word would be around Brighton before you have dried your hair.'

Blindly she dived back under the water and came up within the shadow of her own hut. Mrs Huggins was calling across to one of the other dippers and seemed not to have seen her and she realised that the incident had been over in seconds. No one was looking across from the men's swimming area, the ladies were too preoccupied with their own rigorous dippings to peer through saltwater-laden lashes in her direction and as far as she could see the few telescopes in evidence on the promenade were trained at the horizon.

She had not been seen, and if someone had spotted one head popping up too close to the invisible dividing line, then there was no reason to suppose she could have been recognised. And Gabriel knew that. His anger had been because of what she had seen, not what she had done.

Those scars. In the unforgiving light his back had been a tracery of thin silvery lines, dead straight, criss-crossing like intricate lace created by some demon. He had been whipped, often and often, and he had tried to hide the fact from her. When they made love the curtains were always at least partly drawn, or the candles away from the bedside. When he got out of bed he reached for his robe, or his shirt, before turning his back to her and always took his bath behind a screen. She had thought it simply a courtesy to preserve any modesty she might feel once the intimacy of lovemaking was over.

But he could not have thought he could hide them from her for ever, surely? As her confidence grew she felt an increasing desire to sometimes take the lead in bed, to explore Gabriel's body, to push the robe from his shoulders or to see what erotic games might be played in a bath. And in the day-to-day intimacy of married life, surely he might expect her to walk in on him unclothed and unaware?

Unless he did not expect their intimacy to extend much beyond this honeymoon trip. Unless domestic closeness was the last thing he intended.

'Marm, are you all right? You've gone all white-like. Knew you should have had a good dipping and then got out.' Mrs Huggins surged towards her like some amiable sea monster. 'Up you go now, your girl's waiting for you with a nice big towel.'

Her legs were tired which must be why she was so clumsy. Stumbling up the rough wooden steps, she stubbed her big toe painfully enough to bring tears to her eyes. Harriet, anxiously fussed over the bruised toe, worrying as she swathed Caroline in towels and did her best to get her dressed in the gloom.

'Oh, my lady, that must hurt so much. I can't see if there are splinters. We must send for a doctor directly, you might have broken it, for you to cry so.'

'I'm not...' *Yes, I am.* With an effort she pulled herself together, scrubbed at her eyes with the edge of the towel, and did her best to get her clothing in order over her damp skin. 'It was the shock. You know how things always hurt more when you are cold? I'll just slip my foot into the slipper and not fit it right on.'

Harriet was down the beachside steps before her when they finally jolted to a halt. She ran over the shingle to where Gabriel waited, his face once more his impassive card-player's mask. Caroline, hobbling down the steps with the assistance of Mrs Huggins, could hear her talking.

'...broken toe, my lord...doctor...'

Gabriel came striding down the beach and scooped her up from the bottom step with a curt nod to the dipper.

'Harriet, find a coin in your mistress's reticule for this good woman.'

He took the steps up to the bathing house without pausing, passing an interested group of ladies at the top. 'My wife has a slight injury to her foot, that is all. Thank you for your concern, Lady Oxenford. Mrs Hughes, too kind, I am sure it is nothing serious. If there is a retiring room where she can rest while we wait for a doctor to come—'

Through sore eyes Caroline could see that no one was looking censorious as the manager ushered them through to a small room with a *chaise longue* and assured them a doctor would be with them directly. Her *hoydonish* prank had not been observed.

'No one saw me,' she said the moment the door was closed.

'What did you do to your foot?' Gabriel was stripping off her stocking, ignoring her words.

'I stubbed my toe on the steps.'

'It is beginning to bruise. It might be broken.' He looked up. 'Your eyes are red.' It sounded like an accusation.

'They were watering with the pain. I rubbed them too hard, that is all. Gabriel—' The knock on the door silenced her.

'Lady Edenbridge? My lord. I am Dr Foster, I was with one of my patients using the warm baths, so I am most conveniently on hand, am I not? Now, ma'am, what seems to be the trouble?'

'The trouble *seems* to be a severely stubbed toe and possibly a broken bone,' Gabriel said. He set an upright chair by the head of the *chaise* and took Caroline's hand in his.

It should have been an affectionate gesture but, glancing up at his set jaw, Caroline wondered if it was simply to prevent her babbling out any more indiscretions. She was glad of it for support when the doctor, keeping up a constant flow of inane chatter presumably intended to soothe her, manipulated the toe, announced that it was not broken and bandaged it.

Gabriel thanked him punctiliously, handed him his card and invited him to send in his account to the London address. He walked out with him and came back with the information that he had a sedan chair for her. 'Should I carry you to it? There is a throng of interested ladies outside.'

'Then I see no reason to give them any more opportunity to gawp at you displaying your muscles,' Caroline snapped. She had no wish to find herself carried, to lie back and revel in the romantic thrill of being carried by her strong husband. Not now, with him so angry at her.

Chapter Nineteen

Gabriel escorted her back to the house on the Steine, striding beside the chair in total silence. He gave her his arm to hobble into the hall and up the stairs and instructed Harriet curtly to look after her mistress.

'Where are you going, my lord?' Caroline enquired as he turned to the door.

'Out.'

'Harriet, please leave us.' She waited until the maid had gone, then got up from the chair where Gabriel had deposited her. 'You are not running away from me until you tell me what you are so angry about. And do not tell me it was because I approached the men's part of the beach. No one saw me and they would have had a hard time recognising me if they had.'

'Madam, I do not require your permission to come and go in my own house.' But he stayed where he was.

Caroline drew in a silent breath of relief for that small mercy at least. 'You were never a common soldier. You were never a criminal. And if you have a desire for pain along with your sexual pleasure, then you are hiding the fact exceedingly well. Therefore those scars on your back were put there by your father when you were under his control. And that means he was a vicious man who should have been ashamed of himself. It does not explain why you feel you have to hide them from *me*.'

'Marriage does not mean I have to confide every detail of my past to my wife.'

'*Detail?* You call receiving savage whippings a *detail*, Gabriel?'

'I call it the past and I have avoided this because I knew it would end up with you becoming ridiculously over-emotional about it.'

'I am not over-emotional,' she snapped.

'Then what are you crying about?'

'You, you idiot.' She threw up her hands in frustration, wising she could pace up and down the room, or thump the man to get some reaction from him. 'The boy you were, because those scars are not recent. And you now, because it is plain they still hurt as much as they ever did.'

'My father was subject to uncontrollable rages and the conviction that his word was law. He demanded perfection. That made him demanding and difficult to live with. You can no doubt understand that from your own experience. I did not want to remind you of what you had suffered, that is all.' As though realising that his very rigidity betrayed his feelings Gabriel moved away from the door with his habitual relaxed prowl. Anyone who did not know him well—*anyone who does not love him*—would have seen nothing amiss.

'My father is a deeply selfish man with a number of eccentricities who loses his temper when he is thwarted. He lashed out at me and that was very wrong of him.' She paused while she got her breathing back under control. 'But he had never done it before and, although I know he has chastised Lucas and Anthony, just as every schoolboy in the country must have been punished, it was never the kind of systematic whipping that produces scars like those. And you were the eldest. What on earth did he do to your three younger brothers?' She thought of Ben, big and bluff, George, scholarly and ambitious, and Louis. Earnest, studious Louis.

'Very little. He rarely found them at fault,' Gabriel said with his mocking smile. 'I was the flawed one, the wicked, provoking one.' When she opened her mouth to protest he said, 'You wanted to know where I was going? To Edenvale. You may come, too, if you wish, provided I am not subjected to any more maudlin tears about the past.'

'You can be quite hateful when you choose, Gabriel Stone.' And it was a deliberate choice to be so, she was certain of that. He wanted to push her away. Or perhaps the word was *needed*.

'Are you only just discovering that, my dear?' He paused at the door, as cool as she was heated. 'You had best change if you are coming with me, I have hired a curricle.'

His mood was communicating itself to the hired pair who fidgeted and sidled as he kept them waiting for Caroline to emerge from the house. Gabriel forced himself to relax his hands, to speak to the horses until they calmed. He only wished he could exert the same soothing influence over his knotted guts. The memories of the past were bad enough. Not the pain, that he had learned to lock away, but the flashbacks to his father's body at his feet, strangely pathetic in death, all that power and fury reduced to nothing but flesh and bone and expensive tailoring. He had been glad he had died, he had to bear the guilt of that as well.

The images flooded in as he fought them. Louis, a white-faced child, mercifully unconscious; Ben and George, just boys themselves, stammering questions; and further back, his mother as white as the sheet she lay upon and the doctor sweeping a bottle into his case with one hasty brush of his hand. *A tragic accident*, he had said, and fourteen-year-old Gabriel, shivering with dread behind the curtains, had known with absolute certainty that he lied.

But that was the past and he had learned to live with it, contain it. His marriage was the present and he had allowed the poison to leak from that sealed room in his mind to hurt Caroline. And what had he done this for, this marriage, if it were not to save her from hurt?

She came down the steps using her parasol as a cane, her weight on her heel, waving away the footman. 'Thank you, Robert. I can manage.' But she let the man help her into the curricle and settled herself with perfect composure beside Gabriel.

His wife was a lady through and through, he told himself as the pair moved sedately out into the traffic bordering the Steine. Whatever had passed between them, whatever hurts she had, mental or physical, she would not sulk and she would not show anything but a pleasant face in public. His mood softened, he felt himself grow calmer, just because she was beside him.

'I had expected a high-perch curricle,' she said as he gave a wide berth to the fishermen drying their nets on the end of the greensward nearest the beach and then turned eastwards along the seafront.

Play the cards as they were dealt, he reminded himself. You didn't win at cards by cursing every poor hand that came your way, but by working with what you had. And just now he had a wife who was apparently forgiving enough to drive out with him.

'The roads around Edenvale are more lanes than anything. One needs a carriage built with substance rather than style. I had no wish to deposit you in a ditch when an axle broke.'

'Then you had planned for us to make this expedition today?' Unspoken was the question of why he had not mentioned it before.

Cowardice was probably the correct answer, but he left that unspoken also. 'Yes. It is less than an hour's drive.' Which was no answer at all.

Caroline maintained a flow of intelligent conversation as they drove, commenting on the landscape, the boats to be seen along the coast, the state of the tide, the occasional picturesque cottage or view. None of it was taxing, none required an answer beyond the occasional monosyllable. Gabriel decided he was probably being managed and that he deserved it. That he welcomed it. He did not want to be at odds with his wife.

He turned inland when they reached Saltdene, wending his way through narrow lanes up on to the rolling downland. 'Access is better from the north, but this is a more attractive route,' he added as he made the sharp turn into the park through the gate to the Home Farm.

She was silent as they drove across the parkland, past the famous herd of fallow deer, past the lake and the great stable block and, finally, to the front of the house.

'Queen Anne,' Gabriel offered when she was still silent. 'Not over-large and the rose-red brickwork is considered rather fine.'

'It is beautiful and seems very well kept up.'

'I have excellent staff here.'

As he spoke the front doors were opened. Two footmen appeared and a groom came running from the stables. Gabriel helped Caroline down and offered his arm as she limped across to the steps. 'Does it pain you very much?'

'Just the bruising coming out. If I did not have to wear a shoe it would be trivial.'

'My lord.' Hoskins, the butler, stood waiting, permitting himself one of his rare smiles. 'Welcome home, my lord. And, my lady?'

'Indeed yes. My dear, this is Hoskins, who has been with me for ten years. Hoskins, Lady Edenbridge, your new mistress.'

Caroline smiled warmly at the man and then looked around the great double-height hall. 'I see you manage the house in fine style, Hoskins. What a magnificent staircase!'

'It is one of the showpieces of the house, my lady. That double sweep, the ornately carved newel posts, the painted ceiling—students of architecture frequently call just to admire it.'

She stood at the foot where the two arms of the stairs came together on the pure white stone and Gabriel could see, beneath her feet, the pool of crimson slowly spreading, spreading... Then he blinked and all was clean marble again.

'Refreshments for her ladyship in the Chinese Drawing Room, Hoskins. And no doubt Mrs Hoskins will make certain the countess's suite is in readiness should she wish to rest.'

'Thank you, but I feel the need for tea more than anything else.'

'You have the butler charmed, which is a good start,' Gabriel observed as they seated themselves in the drawing room. It was in good order, but then it should be: he had written before they had set off to Brighton to tell Hoskins that he would be opening up the house again.

'A good start for when you leave me here by myself, you mean?'

'There is little to entertain you in London just now, I would have thought. Naturally you will want to return when the Season starts, but in the meantime I assumed you would want to order this place as you see fit.'

'While *you* will have plenty to entertain you in London?'

'Probably. My clubs… It is pretty much a bachelor society at this time of year. And then when hunting starts I expect to receive invitations to various people's boxes in the shires.' *The clubs, the hells, the safe, solitary evenings.* The loneliness that had seemed like peace before he had become used to Caroline's presence.

'I see. You no longer require my company?' Caroline's colour was up. 'Or my presence in your—' She broke off as a footman came in with a tea tray and thanked him as he set it at her side. 'Bed,' she finished when the door closed again. 'I cannot say you did not warn me. But I also warned you, Gabriel, that I take marriage vows seriously. I am not prepared to simply acquiesce to this. I will not nag, I will do everything in my power not to mention it again, but I will not be closeted in the depths of the country while you commit adultery all over London.'

'Adultery?' It took him so much aback that he stared at her. 'Who said anything about adultery?'

'You did. Before we were married. You said you would not keep your vows, you as good as instructed me to take a lover once I had provided you with the requisite number of sons. Well, Gabriel Stone, I am not prepared to be stabled down here in the country like a brood mare awaiting the attentions of the stallion. I will be faithful to you because *I* take vows seriously, but I will live in London or here or visit friends as I wish.'

He could not deny what he had said, fool that he was. 'I have no desire to be with another woman.' *When had that happened?* 'Nor would I force myself on you. If you allow me to your bed then I would be…honoured. There will be no other women in my life.'

'Then why do you want me away from you?' Caroline attempted to pour tea, sloshed it into the saucer, said a word he had no idea she knew and banged the teapot back down again.

'Because I thought you would want your freedom to do the things that interest you. I want… I am not used to this intimacy, of living with someone, sharing thoughts.'

'The day you share a thought with me, an intimate, important thought, without it being forced from you, will be a first, Gabriel.' Caroline lifted the teapot again and this time managed to pour two cups. 'I do not want to pry, I do not expect you to share every passing thought, every private contemplation with me. I do not want to force your secrets out of you. But I do not want to spend the rest of my life alone and I find it hard that you seem to want loneliness. Aloneness.'

'Everyone is different,' Gabriel said harshly.

'Your brothers love you. Your friends and their wives love you. What are you afraid of, Gabriel? That I might love you, too?'

'You love far too many people for your own safety, Caroline. That is your nature and I cannot prevent you including me in the band that you take to your so-loyal heart. But to fall *in love* with me? You have far more sense than that. It would be a tragedy, would it not?'

He could accept love now, he was learning that. The changes in the lives of his three closest friends had made those friendships richer. His brothers, rallying round at the wedding, welcoming Caroline without hesitation, had stirred something deep inside him. He was their older brother and it had always been his duty to protect them as well as he could, and, at the end, he had so nearly failed.

Caroline was a woman who had turned to him for help and it was his duty to give that, whatever it took.

But he had always known there was something lacking in him, some spark that some other men seemed to have, the willingness to expose himself to the risk of pain that love, accepted and returned, brought. Had brought. He *would not* think of his mother. 'I fear hurting you,' he said now, as gently as he knew.

'Deliberately?' she asked, watching him with a frown line between her brows as though he was a puzzle to be solved.

'No. Never that.'

'Then do not shut me away. This is a lovely house and I would like to spend time here with you. But not now. We will go back to Brighton, finish our honeymoon, learn to co-exist a little better, if you can bear that. Then we will decide what each of us does next and discuss it.'

Caroline was making plans. He was beginning to recognise that when she was under pressure she felt better for having a strategy. 'Very well. Shall I show you around now we are here?' He could manage that, surely? He had the courage to face a duel, wade into a street fight. Take a beating. He could summon up the guts to show his wife around a house.

They drove back to Brighton in a state of wary truce. Something had gone very wrong in that house, Caroline knew that for a certainty, and she felt as certain that Gabriel had built high walls around the memories. But the poison was seeping out like the miasma from a vault. She shivered convulsively, appalled at the ghoulish image that conjured up. She was becoming emotional lately and every little feeling seemed heightened.

'Are you cold?'

'No. Just a goose walking over my grave.' *Stop thinking about graves.*

'I have upset you. I am sorry for my temper and my secrets. I want whatever compromise is best for the both of us, whatever will work for us.'

'Compromise is a word that does not come often to your lips, I think.' She ventured a teasing note and, glancing up, was rewarded with a smile.

'Not often enough, I am sure.'

Reassured by the smile, Caroline tucked her gloved hand under Gabriel's elbow and was not repulsed. *We must look the perfect just-married couple,* she thought as they reached the Parade and passed the grassy length of Marine Square, its new houses sparkling white in the sunshine. 'There is Lady Carmichael. She was so pleasant when I spoke to her in Donaldson's the other day.' Caroline waved. 'Oh! Gabriel, she *cut* me.'

'You are imagining things. She must not have seen who we were.'

'But she did, I saw her recognise me and then she just went blank. Gabriel, slow down, there is Mrs Wilberforce, walking with her daughters.' As the curricle drew level she smiled and waved. 'Good afternoon, Mrs Wilberforce.'

The matron who had beamed at her only that morning gathered her three girls closer as though to shield them from contagion and hurried on.

'Stop!' Caroline made a grab for the reins and when Gabriel brought the pair to a halt she half-scrambled, half-jumped down, gasping in pain as she jarred her sore toe. 'Mrs Wilberforce, wait, please.'

The older woman turned. 'Lady Edenbridge, I will thank you not to accost me, or my daughters, again.'

'Why not?' Caroline demanded, keeping her voice moderate with an effort. Even so, heads were turning. 'You acknowledged me this morning.'

'I was prepared to make every allowance for you, given your blameless record since your come-out and the fact that, despite your shocking elopement, you married immediately and with such distinguished sponsors. But I am not prepared to give countenance to the wife of a murderer. A *patricide*.' She turned on her heel. 'Come, girls.'

'No, you will not turn your back on me after making such an accusation.' Caroline caught at her sleeve, jerking her to a stop. 'Where did you hear such lies?'

'Why, today's *Morning Post* and a letter from London from my good friend the Duchess of Brancaster. Now, unhand me, Lady Edenbridge.'

She marched away and Caroline turned, aghast. People were slowing, someone pointed and just in front of where Gabriel was backing the team, a couple crossed the road to the other side, heads averted.

'What the devil?' he demanded as the curricle drew level with her.

'She said…she says the newspapers say…that you are a *murderer*.'

Chapter Twenty

'Get in.' Gabriel held out a hand to help her. 'Smile. Don't cry.'

'I am not crying,' Caroline said between gritted teeth. 'I am furious. How dare she? How dare the *Morning Post?* It is libel, you must sue them. Who are you supposed to have murdered, for goodness sake?'

'My father, I assume,' Gabriel said as he drew rein outside their rented house. 'Can you manage to get down? Go straight inside and wait while I return this to the mews.'

That was enough to knock the anger clean out of her. Caroline limped up the steps, back straight, chin up, and the door swung open before she could knock. James, the footman, closed it, virtually on her heels.

'My lady, the newspapers—is his lordship coming back soon?'

'Yes.' Ebbing fury left her sick and weak and it took a conscious effort to speak calmly. 'Take the decanters to the drawing room. Is there any post?'

'Yes, my lady.' He hurried after her with half a dozen letters on a silver salver and three folded newspapers.

Most of the letters were for Gabriel, but she recognised Tess's neat black handwriting and broke the seal without sitting down.

> *My dearest Caroline,*
> *I hope this reaches you before the news is abroad in Brighton, but I doubt it. Your father has descended on London telling all who will listen that he had the man who 'abducted' his daughter investigated and has found a witness who swears that Gabriel murdered his own father twelve years ago.*
>
> *Cris tells me that he knows about the accident and that it cannot have been anything else, and of course we, and all your friends, are countering the rumours wherever we hear them.*
>
> *Cris is writing and will do nothing more until he hears from Gabriel whether he wants him to secure the services of the best lawyers or whether he is coming back to London himself. He says to tell you, 'Courage!' and to do your best to stop Gabriel committing murder in reality.*
>
> *Tamsyn and I stand ready to come to you, if that would help, or to do whatever you ask.*
> *Your loving friend,*
> *Tess*

'It was my father,' she said the moment Gabriel walked into the room. 'He is telling everyone that he has a witness who says you murdered your father.' She thrust the letters into his hands. 'Cris has written and I think that one is from Alex.' When he took them she went and poured brandy into two glasses and brought one to him. Then she sat and waited, fighting the churning panic. This was her father's revenge, she had brought this down on the man she loved.

Gabriel put the letters down unopened and ignored the brandy. 'Are you not going to ask me if I did it?' His eyes were dark and steady as he watched her face, but lines bracketed his mouth and his voice was harsh.

'Of course you did not.' But a tiny worm of doubt stirred. Something dreadful had happened at Edenvale, something that had made the place hateful to Gabriel and his father had whipped him unmercifully. Surely not...

'It was brought in at the inquest as an accident. There were no witnesses. He fell down the stairs, smashed in his head on the marble, broke his neck, but no one could account for why,' Gabriel said. He had his composure again and his voice was devoid of emotion. 'Your father's investigator has turned up the old case.'

'Was he drunk?' she managed.

'At four in the afternoon? No. Stone-cold sober. None of the servants would admit to being in the hall or near the head of the stairs. By the sound of it there must have been someone after all and your father's money has loosened their tongue.'

She wanted to ask whether he meant that someone's tongue had been loosened to tell lies, or the truth, but she could not bring herself to show such disloyalty. 'But there was no one you know about?'

'Louis,' Gabriel said as though the name was being dragged out of him. 'But he had fallen at the top of the stairs and knocked himself out. He could remember nothing, not then, not to this day. You saw those carved newel posts. It was a bad blow and it made his sight worse.'

'There must have been some conclusions drawn, surely?'

'Oh, yes. The jurors found that my father had tripped over the riding whip he was carrying, that Louis had seen him begin to fall, rushed forward to help, tripped himself and hit his head. When the butler came on the scene I was at the foot of the stairs standing in a pool of blood, the broken whip in my hands. The coroner was prepared to accept that I had heard the fall, rushed to the scene from the study on the ground floor and automatically picked up the whip in my shock.'

'Then there is nothing to it but wicked fantasies created by my father. A good lawyer will sort this out, force him to retract under threat of legal action. The original coroner's report can be republished. I will never forgive him for this, never.'

'The slight problem is, my dear, that it did not happen as the coroner stated. I was not downstairs when my father fell, I was on the stairs. And there was a slash on his cheek from the whip that was never accounted for.' Finally Gabriel picked up the glass. He drained it in one swallow and sat down. 'The coroner concluded that somehow the whip had hit him as he fell.' Caroline pushed her own untouched brandy glass towards him, but he shook his head. 'It would only take one servant who did in fact see me going down those stairs with the whip in my hand and I will discover whether the old tale about silken nooses for peers is true.'

The whip, Gabriel's back. How many vicious thrashings did it take before a young man snapped, hit back? Killed his tormentor? No. But Gabriel had not denied it.

'Stop trying to make light of this,' Caroline said, amazed that her voice was steady. 'There is more to it than you told me, certainly more than you told the coroner's court. If they found it was an accident, then that was what it was and you cannot have been responsible.'

'You believe that? I saw your expression when you heard what I said about the whip and his face. You were thinking about the scars on my back, weren't you?'

'Yes.' She would not lie to him. 'I do not understand it

all and I do not know what you are hiding, although I think you are protecting Louis in some way, but I do not believe you could kill in cold blood, nor hot blood either. Not and intend it. And unless my father withdraws this accusation and publically apologises, then I will stand up in court and swear that he is mentally incompetent.'

'You will *not* get involved.' Gabriel slapped one hand down on the table, making her jump, then stood up and began to pace, as though movement helped him think. 'Murder is not treason, therefore the title and the estate are safe for Ben, whatever they find. I can make provision for you. The problem is the damage this will do to your reputation, but the lapse of time from the death is in our favour there. Everyone will assume you were taken in by me, that you are simply a victim in all this.' He sounded perfectly calm, as though working through a problem that his steward had brought to him.

'I will surrender myself to whoever is the chief magistrate here, not wait to be dragged out of the house. That will create a better impression and may allow me a little more freedom to manage my affairs. It will certainly make less of a scene here and may divert any sensation-seekers from the house and from you.'

'Gabriel, stop it.' Caroline found she was on her feet, too. 'You are frightening me. You must fight this, prove your innocence.'

'I cannot. I am very sorry, Caroline, but I cannot. I was a fool to believe that I actually had a chance of real happiness with you.' He caught her by the shoulders and kissed her, taking her mouth with a savage desperation that stole her breath and filled her with fear. 'Now, stay here. Order the servants not to answer the door to anyone. Write to Cris, tell him to come and fetch you, send you to Grant in Northumberland. You'll be away from the public eye there.' He released her as suddenly as he had seized her, leaving her to stagger back into a chair, her hand to her mouth. His smile as he turned back from the door was gentle. 'Goodbye, my love.'

'No. Gabriel, I must tell you, I am— *No!*' But he was gone. *A chance of real happiness with you. He called me my love.*

Caroline jumped to her feet and yanked the bell pull. When James entered, so quickly that he must have been lurking outside, she snapped, 'Answer the door to no one but the Marquess of Avenmore or Lord Weybourn. Be ready to take letters to the receiving office in a minute and send Corbridge to me.'

The valet came in as she was addressing the first letter to Cris. 'Corbridge, I must write to his lordship's brothers, most particularly Mr Louis. Have you their directions?'

'Yes, my lady.'

'Were you with my husband when his father died?' she asked as she scribbled the next note.

'I was a footman at Edenvale, my lady.' There was something in his tone that made her glance up sharply. The valet tightened his lips as if on some outburst, then said in his normal, quiet voice, 'It was an accident, my lady. I have seen the newspapers, but nothing will make me believe otherwise.'

'Could anyone have witnessed the fall who has not come forward before now?' She wrote Louis's name on the next letter and reached for a fresh sheet of paper.

'I cannot think so. Let me address those, my lady.' He gathered up the letters as she finished them. 'They will catch the post to London and be with the marquess, and Major Stone, tomorrow morning. Mr Louis may receive his in the evening, I believe.'

'Thank you, Corbridge. Then come back, please.'

He was away perhaps two minutes, long enough for
Caroline to take a small mouthful of brandy and to wipe
all trace of tears from her eyes. She had suspicions, she
also had, if not a plan, at least the outlines of a strategy
and she would not give way to despair. Besides, there had
been that smile, those words. *He loves me, even if he does
not quite believe it, even if there is some other loyalty that
is stopping him from telling me the truth.*

'Corbridge, your master has gone to seek out the chief
magistrate of the town and intends to surrender himself
to him for the investigation of these accusations.' Perhaps
it was only shock that allowed her to sound so calm and
collected, but if it was, then she would use whatever advantage it gave her. 'I want you to find him. I have no idea
what that will involve, but I need to know where my husband is and what he needs.'

Waiting was the worst thing. Or perhaps uncertainty,
she could not decide which. Caroline moved into the back
parlour when people began to walk slowly past the house,
staring, and waited there as James answered the door time
and again with the same message. 'My lady is not at home.
My lord is not at home.'

She hated the wallpaper in that room. She hated the
pattern of the carpet. She absolutely loathed all the novels she picked up and tossed aside in the two hours it took
for Corbridge to return.

'I have seen his lordship. The magistrate, Sir Humphrey Potter, feels it is best if he remains at his house for
the moment because of the interest the matter is arousing,
my lady. As his guest, Sir Humphrey asked me to assure
you.' Corbridge brushed at a smear of green on his sleeve.
'Forgive my appearance, my lady, but it was necessary for
me to climb over several garden walls and to enter through

the back garden. James has already evicted one man who climbed in through the coal hole and was attempting to bribe the kitchen maid for information.'

'Will the magistrate allow you to stay with his lordship, Corbridge? No? Then I trust he will accept it if we pack a valise for him. Come.'

While Corbridge laid out a change of linen and Gabriel's shaving gear, Caroline fetched her new travelling case and took one of the razors to its lining. Under the leather she slid thirty guinea coins, all she could find in the safe, and six hairpins, tied in a handkerchief. Corbridge set out a pair of evening shoes and she wrapped the little pistol from the safe in the stockings and tucked that into the toe of one of the shoes. It would all come right, she had to make herself believe it, but just in case…

'Please tell his lordship that this is my newest valise and to be particularly careful of it. He can be so careless.'

'As you say, my lady.' Corbridge took the bag and Caroline was left with nothing to do but wait and try to find some comfort in the fact that Gabriel was not languishing in Brighton's lock-up.

Cris and Tamsyn reached Brighton at ten the next night, bringing with them a second coach containing four burly men. 'Some of my grooms,' Cris said as he straightened up from kissing her cheek. 'I guessed you might need the barricades manned.'

'People are such vultures,' Tamsyn said as she hugged Caroline. 'Tess and Alex send their love and they are staying in London to do anything needed at that end. Where is Gabriel?'

Caroline told them everything while they ate supper. 'Do you know what happened?' she asked Cris. 'Gabriel is hiding something, but I cannot believe he would kill his own father.'

'You have seen his back, of course,' Cris said. 'A court might well feel that evidence of such harsh treatment shows motive enough, especially as he was holding a whip when the body was discovered. But I do not know the truth. What he told me is what he told you. Like you I do not believe he did it and also that he is withholding something.'

'I have sent for Louis,' Caroline said and took a sip of the port she and Tamsyn were sharing with Cris.

'Yes? Then you share my instincts about this. But I have always understood he remembered nothing of the accident.'

'I cannot think of anyone other than his brothers whom Gabriel would shield at the hazard of his own life,' Caroline said. 'But we cannot expect to see Louis until late tomorrow at the earliest.' The doorbell rang. 'Oh, for goodness sake! Who is that at this hour? People have no decency.'

'Major Stone, Mr George Stone, Mr Louis Stone, my lady.' James opened the door wide and Gabriel's three brothers walked in, heavy-eyed and travel-worn.

'Where is Gabriel?' Ben demanded the moment they were inside.

'Residing with the magistrate,' Caroline said. 'How did you all get here? I am so glad to see you, but I only wrote to Louis yesterday. Come in, sit down. James, fetch food and wine.'

'I never got your letter. I saw the papers and left Cambridge immediately.' Louis was pale and behind the lenses of his spectacles his eyes were red with exhaustion. 'I found the others in London at Lord Weybourn's house.'

The brothers ate while they listened to the news, but Caroline noticed that Louis soon put down his knife and fork. He looked as though he might be sick at any moment.

'So, either someone saw something at the time that

seems incriminating and have only just come forward in response to my father's probing for scandal in Gabriel's life, or he is making bricks without straw. But Gabriel is not telling me the entire truth, of that I am certain. If only someone we can trust actually saw what happened.'

There was an aching silence, then Ben put down his cutlery with a clatter. 'I saw and George, too. Gabriel doesn't know.' He looked across the table at his brother sitting beside Louis. George's face as was white as his clerical bands. 'He would be furious if he knew we had spoken.'

'Gabriel can kick you from here to London for all I care,' Caroline snapped. 'I only want him alive to be able to do it.'

Louis snatched up his glass, gulped the contents and banged it down again. 'I did it. I killed Father.'

Chapter Twenty-One

'Lady Edenbridge has sent this valise by your valet, my lord.' The magistrate's man set the bag down on the ottoman at the foot of the bed. 'He asked me to pass on her message to please be careful of the leather as it is her ladyship's new case.' He passed a professional hand over the surface and nodded approval of its quality. 'Sir Humphrey is dining alone this evening and requests the pleasure of your company at dinner, my lord. I will come up to assist you at seven o'clock, if that is convenient.'

Such a polite gaoler. 'Thank you, yes. Please convey my thanks to Sir Humphrey.' Gabriel waited until the valet had bowed himself out then opened the valise.

It was not like Caroline to fuss over her possessions, let alone send chiding messages at a time like this, which meant she was up to something. He lifted out the carefully packed clothes, then almost dropped one evening shoe in surprise at its weight. The little pistol designed to be carried in a pocket gleamed up at him dangerously. Gabriel shook his head, checked that it was loaded and uncocked and slid it into the breast of his coat. What else had she done?

Even empty the bag was heavy. It did not take him long

to find the money and the hairpins. He sat on the edge of the bed, the little twists of wire on one palm, wondering at the strange tightness around his heart and the absurd, inappropriate urge to laugh. He was hysterical... *No, I am happy. Oh, Caroline, you will never give up, will you?* Presumably she imagined him in some dank cell, picking the locks, fighting his way to freedom, and she would give him the tools to escape whatever the cost to herself. 'I love you, you brave, loyal, beautiful woman.'

How long had he felt like this and not recognised it for what it was? Those unguarded words as he had left her had come from somewhere deep inside, a blinding revelation that the way he felt when he was with her, when he thought about her, was *love*.

The urge to laugh left him as suddenly as it had come, but the grip around his heart did not ease. Of all the times to discover that he could fall in love—and with his own wife, the most unlikely of miracles. Gabriel stamped down on the hope that Caroline might one day come to love him, too. She was as open as she was loyal and honest. She had admitted her physical attraction to him, a daring thing for a young lady to do, so it seemed impossible that she would be reticent about the much more respectable emotion of love.

Better that she never did, given that all he could look forward to was disgrace at the best and death at the worst. He could not, would not, tell the truth about what had happened. Of all the times to find his loyalties stretched on the rack. He could hear his mother's voice in his head as clearly as he had that day when he had been fourteen and had found her weeping in her bedchamber. *Promise me you will look after your brothers, Gabriel. Swear to me.* And he had sworn, not understanding. Not then.

* * *

Dinner with the magistrate was surprisingly civilised. Sir Humphrey was a widower in his early sixties, a burly, down-to-earth man.

'You're better off here,' he remarked as he gestured to Gabriel to refill his wine glass with the good Burgundy they had drunk with the beef. 'It will do no harm for it to be known that you surrendered to me of your own free will the moment you heard the rumours. Makes a good impression, that sort of thing. Lady Edenbridge will be safe in that house with all your servants around her, I have no doubt.'

Nor had Gabriel. He would not have left her otherwise, but Corbridge had his orders, and Gabriel's pistols, and he would lose a large wager with himself if Cris de Feaux wasn't on her doorstep by tomorrow.

'Sunday tomorrow,' Sir Humphrey observed. 'We won't see the coroner before Monday, I imagine. He lives in Lewes, of course, you'll recall from the original inquest, it being the nearest town to the house. You'll not want to go to church tomorrow, I presume?'

'I have no desire to disrupt a service, which is no doubt what would happen.'

'Quite. Should I ask the vicar to call in? Perhaps you would welcome some quiet contemplation and prayer with him.'

'Thank you, no.' The last thing he needed was quiet contemplation. What he *needed* was to be alone with Caroline, a large bed and a *Not Guilty* verdict. What he *wanted* was his hands around her father's throat. Neither of those ambitions could be confessed to the vicar. 'The use of your library would be much appreciated.' If nothing else the sight of his unwilling guest calmly reading might help convince the magistrate that he had no bloody crimes on his conscience. It was likely to be a long day.

* * *

'Who the devil?' Sir Humphrey enquired the next morning as the sound of the knocker reached the breakfast room. 'We have hardly finished our meal. This is no time to be making calls.'

'The coroner, perhaps?' Gabriel suggested, moving aside the London Sunday papers that the footman had placed between the two men. Time enough for the first stagecoach to bring Monday's budget of gossip, speculation and lies. He was not going to ruin his breakfast with yesterday's.

'He'll still be at his own table. Yes, who is it?'

The footman looked decidedly flustered. 'The Marquess of Avenmore, Sir Humphrey. And a lady, a clergyman, an army major and a young gentleman and they all say they want to speak to you. I told them you would not be available yet and they said they would wait.'

'They want to speak to me, you mean,' Gabriel interrupted. His brothers as well? And he had thought things could not get much worse.

'No, my lord. They were very definite, it is Sir Humphrey they want to see.'

'Put them in the study, fetch them refreshments and tell them I will be with them shortly.' He waited until the man went out and turned to Gabriel. 'Well? What is this delegation?'

'A close friend, my wife and my brothers, I assume.'

'With evidence?'

Gabriel shrugged. 'I very much doubt it. As I have said all along, there were no witnesses to my father's fall.'

'Then if it is not evidence I do not need to wait for the coroner and I see no harm in you joining me. I haven't had so much excitement since the last time Prinny's entourage kicked up a riot in town.'

The party waiting for them in the magistrate's study was certainly more tastefully dressed, and considerably more sober, than the new king's cronies. Caroline, thank heavens, was pale but perfectly composed, the fine veil thrown back over her bonnet apparently her only concession to the fact that her husband was under house arrest and their name a byword over the nation's breakfast tables. She was wearing the newest and most fashionable of her London walking dresses and smiled at him in a way that made him catch his breath.

At her side Cris, as elegant and cool as ever, stood to exchange bows with the magistrate. 'Sir Humphrey? I am Avenmore. May I introduce Lady Edenbridge. Major Stone, the Reverend Mr Stone, Mr Louis Stone. I apologise for this early interruption to your morning, but we have evidence in the matter of the late Earl of Edenbridge's death.'

'Evidence? In that case I feel I should wait for the coroner.' The magistrate looked none too happy.

'There is none. There can be none,' Gabriel said. Louis was white and he saw Caroline reach out and touch his hand for a moment.

'Excuse me, Sir Humphrey.' It was the nervous footman again.

'Yes? What now?'

'Mr Barton, the coroner from Lewes, sir.'

'Already? Well, send him in, this cannot become much more irregular than it is already.'

Gabriel barely recognised the coroner, but then it had been ten years since the inquest and the man must have been in his fifties then. He stalked in like a dyspeptic heron, peered around and snapped, 'I've come on the Edenbridge matter, Sir Humphrey. What is this? Trying the case already?'

'Certainly not. Allow me to introduce you.' The magistrate made the introductions and everyone sat down again, making the study feel uncomfortably small. 'Apparently Lord Avenmore believes that some of those present have evidence to present.'

'Do you indeed?' Barton seemed unintimidated by the presence of a marquess, even Cris at his most arctic. Gabriel felt an unwilling twinge of admiration and an equally unpleasant lurch of apprehension. This old bird was going to show neither fear nor favour.

'I wish to speak to my brothers in private.'

'Collusion? I think not, my lord. If they wish to address me, they may do so.'

Louis stood up and Ben, magnificent in full scarlet regimentals, waved him back to his seat. 'Let me. Lord Knighton has a grudge against my brother because of Gabriel's elopement with his daughter. He has spread it about that his investigations have revealed a witness to my father's death, but I know who did witness it and I can attest to the fact that none of those present that day have spoken to any investigator. In other words, he is inventing evidence.'

'And who were those witnesses?'

Witnesses, plural? Gabriel looked at Louis again and saw that Caroline had put her hand on his forearm.

'My eldest brother, the present Lord Edenbridge, you know about, sir. There were also myself and my other two brothers.'

'You were not there,' Gabriel interrupted. 'And Louis was unconscious.'

'Allow Major Stone to finish, if you please. Where were the servants? As I recall, we were told they were all below stairs or in various rooms not within sight of the hall and landing.'

'Yes, sir. There was to be a dinner party that evening. The staff were either in the kitchens, or in the dining room or preparing the drawing room. My brother George and I were in the room where we studied because our tutor had left us an exercise in Latin translation before he went into Lewes. We heard a loud crash.'

'Yes, I knocked over a valuable Chinese vase that stood at the head of the stairs,' Gabriel stated. 'You were no-where in sight.' He felt Caroline's gaze on him as though she had prodded him with her finger, but he did not look in her direction. He wasn't under oath, not yet.

'That is not true,' Louis said and all eyes turned to him. 'I knocked it over and I was trying to hide the pieces, which was stupid of me. But I knew if I didn't then Gabriel would take the blame like he always did and he would be the one who was whipped.'

'Louis—'

'No. We should have spoken up long ago, right from the beginning, but we were all too afraid. We let you pre-tend you were the clumsy one, or the one who had done something out of mischief. Father soon believed you were wicked—you didn't have to try very hard to fake the evi-dence and protect us.'

'Damn it, Louis! *Will you be quiet?*'

George, Ben and Sir Humphrey all began to speak at once.

'No, Gabriel,' Caroline said, her quiet voice stilling the noise like one chime of a bell. 'No, Louis will not be quiet. He is going to tell the truth and so, finally, are you.'

At a stroke she was going to uncover all the wounds he had spent such pain and misery covering up, would shat-ter his brothers' memories of their childhood, would make him break his vow to his mother. He knew why—she had a passion for truth, she had a fierce loyalty to him as her husband. But his loyalties were older than their marriage and he could not allow how he felt about her to shake them.

'You are my wife and you will do as I tell you. Now, be silent.' He had never spoken to Caroline like that before, had never thought he would. In his own voice he heard echoes of his father, of hers, and he saw her go white even as he felt the stab of nausea in his gut.

'No,' she said again. 'We are all going to disobey you. Your wife, your brothers and your friend. We have made a conspiracy against your secrets. The truth matters and, besides, our child is not going to grow up believing she or he had a murderer for a father. Go on, Louis.'

It took perhaps two seconds for her words to hit home, then the rest of the room vanished from his consciousness. *Our child? Caroline is expecting our child? But that is impossible.*

He came back to himself to find everyone, his wife included, had their attention fixed on Louis, who must have simply carried on with his story. '...it was idiotic to try to hide the damage, but I was in a panic. Then I heard Father coming. He had heard the crash, of course, and he had his whip. I expect he thought it was Gabriel again. He rushed towards me, shouting.'

'We'd heard the noise and we were just coming out of the corridor when we saw you running up the stairs, Gabriel,' Ben said. He stood at attention as though he was making a report to his commanding officer.

'Father slashed at Louis, who grabbed at the whip. Father jerked it back and Louis let go, so it flew back and it hit Father's face. Louis crashed into the newel post and Father tripped over his body—he was going too fast and was off balance because of the blow to his face. He went down the stairs, hit the banisters on the curve—I think that was what broke his neck—tumbled past you, Gabriel, and hit the floor. I saw you run back down to him, then all hell broke loose. George started retching and I dragged him away so he couldn't see. By the time I came out again you were telling people the story you told at the inquest. I couldn't contradict you, and besides, there was all the fuss over Louis.'

He turned to the Coroner. 'If there had been any danger of Gabriel being blamed I would have spoken at the inquest, sir. But George and I were frightened for Louis. He was only a child and when he came round he couldn't recall anything about it. Provided Gabriel was safe, we thought it was best to say nothing.'

'And now you conveniently recall it all, young man?' the Coroner said to Louis.

'Now, yes. For years I just had nightmares, flashes of memory that I thought were a kind of waking dream. Then it all began to get worse about six months ago when I started working closely with Gabriel.' He looked round at Ben and George. 'When I read the newspaper accounts, I suspected it was real memories and went to talk to my brothers. I suppose you'll want to arrest me now, Sir Humphrey.'

'And me,' Ben said, making to draw his sabre from his belt in formal surrender.

'For what?' Sir Humphrey enquired. 'No perjury was involved. Neither of you was called to give evidence and you were both schoolboys. It is up to my colleague, of course, but I can see no legal reason to reopen the inquest. No new evidence has been brought forward that would make the verdict of Accidental Death unsafe in my opinion.'

'Nor mine,' Barton said. He looked at George. 'Reverend Stone, can you confirm what has been said?'

'Yes, sir. Every word.'

'Then Sir Humphrey and I will issue a report stating that we have interviewed three new witnesses to the death of the late earl and that their evidence supports the original verdict of accidental death. The newspapers will get their teeth into that, I have no doubt. I suggest, my lord, that you take legal advice and issue your father-in-law with a strongly worded warning of what will happen if he does not withdraw his slanders. Major, Reverend, Mr Stone, I will take down your evidence with Sir Humphrey as witness. I see no reason to detain you, my lady, my lords. Good day.'

Gabriel found himself outside a firmly closed door. 'I can't leave my brothers.'

'They are grown men.' Cris gave him a decidedly unfriendly shove towards the front door. 'I would suggest you cannot leave your wife.'

There was a considerable crowd in the street outside, far more than could be explained by the sight of Cris's magnificent coach and team of matched bays. 'Get in.'

'Cris—' Gabriel realised that he was confused, relieved and, quite simply, furious.

'Damn you, accept some help from your family for once. The last time you were this aggravating I knocked you on your backside and I swear if you do not get in that carriage with Caroline in the next twenty seconds I'll do it again.'

Gabriel offered his hand to Caroline and she got into the carriage. She had put down her veil and he could not see her face, but her chin was up, he could tell.

Cris slammed the door on them. 'Now go home. I'm walking.'

'Gabriel?'

'How could you?' he asked, hearing his own voice cold and hard. 'How could you do that without asking me? All my life I have protected my brothers and you tossed them to the wolves.'

'They told the truth, finally, and everything is all right.' Caroline threw back the veil. 'You are safe, they are safe, my father's horrible scheme has been checkmated. Can't you be happy about that?'

'Not when you lie to me in front of a room full of people, try to manipulate sympathy by telling falsehoods. You cannot know that you are pregnant, it is barely a month since that first night.'

Chapter Twenty-Two

So, this is what you get for loving a rake. Accusations and ingratitude and anger. Caroline took a deep breath and saw they were drawing up at their own front door where there was another, smaller, crowd with Cris's grooms holding them at bay. This was not the time to lose all control and scream at the man, tell him how much he hurt her, how much she cared for him.

'I may not have to tell our child his father is a murderer,' she said as she lowered her veil. 'But I *am* going to have to explain to the poor little soul that he is an ungrateful idiot.'

The groom holding the door for her lost his composure for a moment, then got his face under control as Caroline swept out of the carriage and up the steps to the front door that, thankfully, opened as she reached it.

'*I* am an idiot?' Gabriel slammed the door behind him, shaking the silver tray on the hall table. 'I was not the one smuggling hairpins and firearms and sovereigns into a magistrate's house. Why not go the whole nine yards and bake a cake with a file in it?'

'I didn't think of that.' She paused on the bottom step of the stairs and swung round. 'Perhaps because I am a poor feeble woman with my brain turned to porridge by pregnancy. Or perhaps because I knew there were no bars, but that you might need to get out of the house and bribe a boatman to take you across to France. For some reason, which is escaping me now, I did not want you to hang.'

Caroline stalked upstairs, ignoring the throbbing in her toe, and found a little comfort in the fact that she could close the bedchamber door without slamming it. She turned the key and sat down at her dressing table. Men were the very devil, all of them. But she loved one, was married to one and she was carrying his child, whatever the stubborn creature believed.

She had expected Gabriel to come to the door and ask her to open it. She had half-expected him to kick it down, but when the tap came half an hour later it was Tamsyn.

'May I come in?' When Caroline opened the door Tamsyn caught her in a hug, then held her at arm's length. 'Cris says we are to pack and go back to London straight away. He says, and I quote, "Gabriel always was the one with the brains, if he could only be brought to realise it. Let him work this out, because it is beyond me."'

'Oh. If Cris is abandoning us…'

'I think he is simply putting a safe distance between himself and the urge to hit Gabriel. Personally I think it would be an excellent idea to punch him, but men are strange.' She cocked her head on one side. 'This isn't just about his father, is it?'

'I told him I was expecting his baby.'

She could see Tamsyn doing some mental arithmetic. 'Er…'

'It is very, very early. But it is his. I am certain, but he thinks that I lied to the magistrate just to get sympathy.'

'Oh, so you…before the wedding?'

'Yes, not long before. The night my father found me,

after we agreed to marry. I don't understand why he is so upset, I thought he wanted children.'

'Don't be a cloth-head,' Tamsyn said inelegantly. 'You blurted it out in the middle of that meeting, in front of his brothers and the magistrate and the coroner? My dear, that might not be the best time and place to tell a man he is going to be a father.'

'I was becoming angry with him,' Caroline confessed miserably. 'And frustrated that he would not tell the simple truth. He is so protective of his brothers, he seems to feel that he has total responsibility for them, whatever they have done.'

'He is protective of you, too. Look what he did for you,' Tamsyn pointed out.

She didn't need reminding. 'But his oldest loyalty is to them. He actually worked it all out, how if they hanged him I would be looked after and how Ben would get the title. He is angry with me because I acted without telling him, exposed Louis's part in their father's death.'

Tamsyn shivered. 'So cold blooded.'

'He is a gambler. And I think that being like that helps him cope. He has pushed all his emotions right down so they can't hurt him.'

'Are you going to leave him? You can come back with us.'

'Would you have left Cris?'

'Yes. I did.' Tamsyn looked bleak. 'I thought it was the best thing for him. It was horrible. But he didn't agree with me and came and got me, thank heavens.'

'You were not married then?' The other woman shook her head. 'Well, I am. For better, for worse. I promised.'

'When he calms down he'll want to do the right thing because of the baby,' Tamsyn suggested.

'I don't want him doing the right thing because that is

his duty. I want him to trust me and to love me. And, yes, I know I am wishing for the moon.'

'Good luck.' Tamsyn got up and pressed a kiss on Caroline's cheek. 'I would offer to stay, but I think you two need to work this one out for yourselves.'

Caroline clung for a moment. 'Thank you. You have been such a good friend. And Cris and Alex and Tess. Give them my love.'

A carriage pulled up outside, then away again. *Cris and Tamsyn.* The sound of voices in the street ebbed to its normal level and when Caroline tilted the dressing-table mirror to reflect the view outside she saw the crowd beginning to disperse across the Steine. They had heard the news about Gabriel's innocence and were off to discuss the whole intriguing scandal over the tea cups, she assumed. The house was quiet, the servants were tiptoeing about while their master brooded behind closed doors.

She could go down, insist that he listen to her and then he would accept that she was telling the truth about the baby, that it wasn't simply a ploy to attract sympathy from the Coroner and that would be that. She could forgive him being angry to have that sprung on him in public, he'd had a lot on his mind, to put it mildly.

'But I love him,' Caroline said into the silence.

And I want him to love me. I want a real marriage, a love match, a family. I want him to be happy, not just content with an arrangement.

But how? If she marched in and explained and then announced she loved him Gabriel might very well be feeling guilty enough to pretend he loved her, too, and that would be...awful. She would have to think and hope her instincts would guide her, because just at the moment her brain was not helping in the slightest.

The front door slammed and she jumped to her feet

and went to the window. Gabriel, hatless, gloveless, was striding across the grassy expanse of the Steine towards the sea, anger in every uncoordinated, jerky step. She had never seen him move like this, without elegant, careless grace. He was hurting.

Well, so am I, Gabriel Stone. So am I.

The wind had got up and the clouds, a ragged grey threat of rain, scudded across the sky. The sea was already showing white horses in a vicious chop of small waves and the last bathers were being towed up the beach towards warmth, dry clothes and their luncheons.

A few brave souls were promenading along Marine Parade, but the ladies were furling their pretty parasols and clutching the arms of their escorts who were hurrying towards their lodgings before the rain fell, free hands clamped to the top of their hats.

Gabriel went down the steps on to the beach, his feet sinking into the shingle, walked almost to the water's edge and then began to follow it. The tide was on the ebb and he was walking in sodden pebbles, his boots already wet. He hunched his shoulders, thrust cold hands into his pockets, the wind whipping his hair into his eyes, stinging with the salt-laden air.

He walked on, the loose footing, making each step as much effort as ten on hard sand, walked until he lost track of time and found himself beyond even the newest developments that were spreading Brighton along the coast. There were dinghies pulled up clear of the high-water mark, like so many turtles, and he sat down on one with his back to the town and tried not to think.

Not that his mind would clear, that was the problem. His brothers, his parents, Caroline, his friends. *A baby.* Everything was churned up and nothing made sense.

The threatened rain came in a sudden, spiteful shower that whipped against him like handfuls of thrown grit. It was gone in moments, leaving him damp and cold, but at least it had shocked him into vaguely rational thought.

It must have been that very first time, that night at Springbourne when all that had seemed to matter had been persuading her to marry him and finally losing himself in her. The time before he realised he loved her, the time when he had complacently thought of children as some theoretical, abstract outcome of their marriage. But they were not an abstract. They were real, important, and he had thrown the miraculous news that he was to be a father back in her face along with his anger and ingratitude at being saved from the gallows.

He got to his feet, raked the wet hair off his forehead and turned to walk back. Apologise. Thank her. Try to understand his own feelings about his past, about their future. Hope against hope that somehow he could understand hers, because Caroline was his wife and he loved her. Somehow, with no model of how to do it right, he was going to have a family to look after. For the first time in his adult life he felt fear, gut-clenching, knee-weakening fear. *What if I can't do it? Can't be a decent father and husband? What if...?* The doubts raged in his head like the wind that was battering the coast now.

It seemed like a hundred miles back along the shore, the shifting pebbles dragging at his feet until his legs began to feel like lead. He should cut up towards the coast road. Gabriel stopped and assessed the ways up the low, crumbling cliffs and saw, in the distance, a figure coming towards him, laboriously battling wildly blowing skirts and hampering shingle. As he watched her bonnet whipped off her head and out to sea and her hair broke loose as she clutched for the ribbons, the blonde streamers in the wind like a flag. *Caroline.*

Gabriel began to run, heedless of the strain on his tired legs. It was like a nightmare where every step seems to be mired in mud. She was carrying a child, she shouldn't be struggling along this damned beach. She was coming to him.

He realised the moment she saw him and recognised who it was, because she stopped walking and bent over, hands on her knees, out of breath. When he reached her, breathless himself, she had straightened up and only the high colour in her cheeks and the rise and fall of her bosom revealed the speed she must have been walking at.

'Caroline. You shouldn't be out here, not exerting yourself like this.'

'I am pregnant, not sick.'

'Why did you follow me?' He took her arm and steered her, unresisting, up the beach to where a fisherman had constructed a rough shelter out of driftwood and old planks. 'Sit down, it is going to rain again in a moment.'

'I saw you leave, so angry you could hardly walk straight. And I saw where you were heading and I thought...'

'That I was going to throw myself in the sea?'

'No.' She smiled faintly. 'But I thought you might need me.'

'If I did, why should you care? This is the man who is so damned thoughtless and insensitive that a shock is enough to make him cruel and ungrateful.'

'You are my husband.'

'And you take your vows very seriously,' he said, feeling the weight of despair on his shoulders. He was a duty to her and she was going to do her duty if it killed her.

'So do you. To whom did you make a promise to always look after your brothers? Your mother, I suppose.'

He nodded, unable to find the words. When she did not press him he managed to say it. 'She killed herself. Took poison. I'll never know whether my father beat her or whether it was the unkindness of words or neglect. I was fourteen, too young to really understand. Such a good little boy.'

'Were you?' That little smile had deepened, made soft dimples in her cheeks. He wanted to kiss them.

'I was the heir. It was my duty to be good,' he said, mocking the earnest child he had once been.

'And then you turned into a miniature hellion to deflect your father's anger on to you.'

'Yes.'

'Clever, as well as brave. Your mother would have been very proud of you.' When he shrugged, embarrassed by the praise, appalled to find it mattered so much, she asked, 'But why did you become so remote from them that they were unable to come to you and tell you what they had seen?'

'If I had shown I was fond of them then he would have suspected.'

'So you made yourself be alone with no one to love you.' To his horror Caroline burst into tears, just as another squall hit, lashing them with icy rain. Gabriel curled himself around her, sheltering her, and let her sob on his shoulder until the squall and the tears ceased together. 'Oh, I am sorry. I feel so weepy at the moment. Harriet says it is because of the baby and her sister was a complete watering pot for months.'

He found a handkerchief and mopped her eyes, but she took it from him and blew her nose briskly. 'I am too stunned to add up.'

'I have only just missed my courses, but I am always so regular and I am absolutely convinced that something has changed.' Caroline took a deep breath. 'It is far too early to have said anything. Many pregnancies don't go beyond the first month or two. But somehow…'

'Somehow you are sure.' He stood up and held out his hand to help her to her feet. 'Shall we start out before the next rain squall comes?' When she nodded and slipped her hand into his he felt a shock of fierce protectiveness. 'I'll do my level best to be a good father, Caroline. At least I've plenty of experience of what makes a bad one.' She said nothing, but tightened her grip for a moment. 'I'll do my best to be a good husband, too. I'm not good at emotion, Caroline.'

'I noticed.' She was teasing him, he thought. Hoped. 'I understand. It has never been very safe for you to feel, has it?'

He thought that was all she was going to say. They walked back slowly in silence, then, as they reached their own front door, she said, 'Promise me something?'

'Anything.'

'Rash!' She was serious again in a moment. 'Promise never to lie to me. I won't probe your secrets, I won't expect you to open your heart to me. But do not lie to me, Gabriel. Not about how you feel. You told me you do not obey vows, but you do, don't you?'

'I do when they are to you. Yes, I promise.' It felt very serious, very heavy, that promise, but her smile was suddenly light and gay.

He insisted on walking her upstairs. 'Call Harriet, lie down and rest.'

'I will.' Caroline stood in the bedchamber, her hand on the edge of the half-open door. 'I love you, Gabriel.' Then, softly, she closed it, leaving him on the far side. Alone.

* * *

Half an hour later Gabriel was sitting in the drawing room nursing a glass of brandy he was not drinking and trying to remember what his life had been like on the first day of June at eleven in the morning. He had been single, heart-free and with no responsibilities in the world other than three brothers who were either independent of him or on the verge of being so. He owned estates that were run efficiently by excellent employees, a house full of memories that he could close the door on and walk away from and three close friends whose own lives had recently been turned upside down in a way that he had been certain would change their relationship with him for ever.

He'd been comfortable, self-indulgent, vaguely uneasy and…bored.

Now those locked doors had been flung wide open and it had been his brothers who had come to stand shoulder to shoulder with him. His friends had rallied to guard his back just as they always had. He had a wife, a child on the way and a secret lifted off his neck.

He had a wife who loved him. That promise she had extracted from him made sense now. She was afraid that he would take pity on her and mouth the words in response, pretend a depth of emotion he did not truly feel. Clever Caroline. She knew he would lie *for* her, but now, not *to* her.

There was a bang on the door and Gabriel put down the untouched brandy, cursing under his breath and got to his feet. *What now?* His brothers came in, filling the room with their energy and their excitement.

'It is all over town.' Louis, grinning like an idiot, threw his arms around Gabriel and hugged him fiercely. Startled, he found himself hugging back, then both Ben and George piled in to.

When they finally broke apart Ben picked up the brandy glass and knocked it back in one gulp. 'The gossip mill is in full swing and your father-in-law's name is mud. The ladies are swooning with the romantic delights of the elopement and you rescuing Caroline from what was some sort of Gothic house of horrors and the gentlemen are assuring each other that they always knew Knighton was queer in the attic and that you are as good a man as our grandfather.'

'And they got all this from the statement that witnesses had been examined and the fact of an accident has been confirmed?' Gabriel asked, suspicious.

'We have been elucidating the situation,' George pronounced, looking pious. 'Naturally we did not want anyone to retain the wrong impression.'

'And we've done a damn good job,' Louis said, straightening his spectacles. 'Ben stuck his chest out, rattled his sabre and looked manful while commending your honourable reluctance to call out your father-in-law. George has been murmuring about the chivalrous rescue of a lady in terms which, frankly, were fairly sickening when he got round to comparing you to Lancelot, although it did make Lady Hesslethwaite weep. And I've been muttering about having my advice about suing for slander turned down. In fact, Brother, you are probably not safe to go out alone or you'll be mobbed by the ladies and have your hand shaken off by the men.'

Gabriel stared round at them. Ben was smirking, George was smug and Louis was grinning and suddenly they were all laughing and he was, too, and they were just his brothers. Not responsibilities to sacrifice himself for, not a constant aching worry. Simply his brothers whom he loved and, startlingly, appeared to love him. Not that a gentleman talked about such things, so, still gasping with laughter, Gabriel filled four glasses and raised his own in a toast.

'The Brothers Stone.'

Chapter Twenty-Three

The bed dipped and warm lips began to kiss their way down the back of her neck. It was a dream…but did dream lovers rasp their stubbled chins on your more delicate areas of skin and did they smell of brandy?

'Gabriel?' Carolyn wriggled back and there was a moment of tugging and flapping before there was a male body under the covers for her to snuggle into. Definitely not a dream. Dream lovers did not have to fight the bedding.

'No, the Archbishop of Canterbury. Who were you expecting?'

'Are you drunk?'

'Surprisingly not.' He wrapped an arm firmly around her waist and Caroline realised that he was as naked as she was. 'Did we sound as though we were carousing downstairs? I'm sorry if we disturbed you.'

'You sounded happy. That was good to go to sleep hearing.' She twisted round until she could burrow her head under his chin and pressed her lips to his collarbone.

'I sincerely hope I usually sound happy when we finally do go to sleep,' Gabriel grumbled into her hair.

'You don't laugh then. I have never heard you laugh before.'

'Never?' He bent back and pushed up her chin so he could frown at her, their noses almost touching.

'Never. Not a proper, letting-everything-go laugh because you are happy rather than because something amuses you.'

Gabriel tucked her head down against his shoulder again. 'I must be a misery to live with.'

'No, merely rather intense sometimes.'

There was silence and she was content to lie there against his warmth, feeling his heart beating close to hers, his breath stirring her hair.

'I have no idea how to be a father,' Gabriel said abruptly.

'And I have no idea how to be a mother, so we will just have to work it out as we go along. You know what makes a bad father.'

'That's true.' By some miracle he sounded amused. 'And you already know how to be a wife.'

'I do? I suspect I am rather a disobedient one.'

'Dreadfully so,' he agreed. Caroline felt him take a deep breath and the long body cradling hers became tense. 'Not letting yourself feel emotion is like taking laudanum when you've got a broken leg. You know there is a vast amount of pain out there somewhere, but it is behind shutters, quite safe unless you are foolish enough to let it out by stopping the dose. But you have to stop the dose because otherwise you become addicted to the medicine.'

'You have to want to stop,' Caroline suggested.

'Yes. You caught me at just the right moment.'

'I caught you? That makes me sound like a designing hussy.'

'You are a hussy.' She could hear the laughter in his voice. 'You proposition notorious rakes, you drug unwanted suitors, you hide up chimneys, you order marquesses about and invade the homes of respectable magistrates. No wonder I love you. Such a rakehell as I am needs a wicked wife to love.'

'You…' Her heart seemed to have stilled to a slow, almost painful, thud. 'Gabriel, I know you desire me—' Just at the moment there was absolutely no ignoring the physical evidence of that.

'Have you such little faith in my promises?' Gabriel rolled over on to his back as though to stop himself clouding her thoughts with his touch. 'I had no idea that was what I was feeling and I didn't want to dig and find out, coward that I am. I have always controlled risk. People think gamblers are reckless, but successful ones are the exact opposite. We calculate risk, we know just what we can afford to lose. Loving gives a hostage to fortune, doesn't it? I did not dare to hazard my heart on you. How have you so much more courage than I do?'

Caroline turned to rest on her elbow and smiled at him. 'I have been practising loving all my life. My mother, my brothers. I even worked hard at loving my father. And I suspect women find it natural to take the risk, because if we have children then every moment we could be in fear for them and if we couldn't face that, then the human race would die out.'

She loved Gabriel's face when he was thinking hard. Every ounce of intelligence, every scrap of ferocious concentration showed in those dark eyes, in the set of the sensual lips, in the line that formed between his brows. He was so good at putting on the mask that hid his feelings that she knew it was only absolute trust that let him relax so in front of her.

'I can't promise I'll always get it right.'

'Nor me. How dull if we did,' Caroline teased. 'No arguments, no drama, no lovely making it up afterwards.'

'Hmm.' Gabriel's eyes had lost their brooding intensity. 'Are you tired still?

'No,' Caroline said demurely. 'I am wide awake. Oh!'

Gabriel tossed back the covers and began to smooth his hands down over her body. 'Nothing shows yet.' He sounded ridiculously disappointed.

'Of course not! It will soon enough and then I'll be lumbering about like a whale.'

'More lovely curves.' Gabriel's tongue drew a lingering trail of liquid fire down over the swell of one breast, into the valley between them and up over the other. He explored her body as though it were new to him, murmuring with appreciation over the curve of her hip, the dimple beside her knee, the elegance of the curl of her ear until he almost had her believing herself that she was the most beautiful woman in the world. *Perhaps I am to him,* Caroline thought in wonder. *I think he is the most handsome man. And the kindest and the...*

'Wickedest!' she gasped as Gabriel slid down the bed and began to do outrageous things with his tongue.

'You called?' He lifted his head and looked at her with such an innocent expression that she laughed and was still laughing, joyously, as he came up the bed and abandoned gentle teasing for a passionate possession that sent her spinning from laughter into blind ecstasy in moments.

'You are thinking,' Caroline said much later, as she lay with Gabriel watching the light fade out of the sky. 'I can hear the wheels turning.'

'So are you. A guinea for them?'

'You may have them for free. I was wondering what you wanted to do with Edenvale.'

'Turn it into a home,' Gabriel said without hesitation. 'I won't let my life be ruled by memories and secrets any more and I certainly won't allow my father's ghost to drive me out of what should be our family home. And we'll have my brothers and yours to stay, often, and Alex, Cris and Grant and their children and make so much noise that not a single spectre dare linger.'

'I do like the idea of ghosts and ghouls fleeing gibbering in the face of a house full of happiness. And what was on your mind?'

'What you wanted to do about your father. Louis wants to sue the boots off him, I favour leaving him to stew in his own juice.'

'I will write to Lucas. I do not want to be estranged from him and I suspect if he and Anthony encourage my father to start a new building project he will soon retreat from reality into that. And perhaps one day he will be… stable enough to want to see his grandchild.'

'So we have put the world to rights between us.' Gabriel stretched, languorous as a big cat.

'We have put our corner of it to rights at least,' Caroline leant over to kiss his smiling lips.

'Our new world,' her husband said. 'And it will take us a lifetime to explore it, my love. Beginning now.'

Epilogue

Half Moon Street, London—February 14th, 1821

'We are definitely going to have to move house. We cannot even hold a christening party without it resembling the crush at a royal Drawing Room and Alex's valet is becoming fretful over the dressing room becoming a nursery.'

Tess sank down on the end of the sofa in the window alcove, the only available seat left in the drawing room, and tucked Dominic Alexander Hugh Tempest and all his yards of christening robe snuggly into the crook of her arm.

'Perhaps this fashion for huge skirts and ridiculous puffed sleeves will subside.' Kate, the Countess of Allundale, squashed her own skirts up to make more room. 'Although that will only help with parties, not bedchambers. I worry that our new house in Brook Street isn't big enough.' She laid one hand over the spot where a myriad of heaped ruffles concealed the third of the Rivers' brood, due to make an appearance in July. 'Grant has become so enthusiastic over suffrage reform that he keeps throwing political receptions and dinners so the downstairs guest bedchamber must be sacrificed to extend the drawing room.'

'You don't mind London life and parties any more? No, don't move, I'll just slide round and prop myself up on the back of the sofa which is inelegant, but does wonders for my back.' Caroline sighed with relief. 'Don't say anything, but I have just taken off my slippers.'

'*What* a good idea,' Kate said. There was some surreptitious rustling and two more sighs. 'How we suffer for fashion. And parties. But, no, I enjoy them now. I've even become used to being a countess. Almost. I still keep thinking people are going to point at me and cry "Imposter", but it hasn't happened yet. I can hardly believe how much my life has changed. Do you know, I even found myself arguing with the Prime Minister about married women's property rights the other evening?'

'Goodness. What did he say?' Tamsyn arrived, set a footstool in front of the sofa and sank down in a cloud of amber silk and blonde gauze, careless of what anyone might think of a marchioness virtually sitting on the floor.

'He huffed and puffed and called me *dear lady* and escaped as soon as he could, but I'll corner him yet. We've all taken our slippers off,' she added in a whisper to Tamsyn who promptly did the same.

'My ankles are swelling,' she grumbled. 'No one tells you these things.'

'You— You're not expecting, too?' Caroline managed to keep her voice down to a muted shriek.

'Shh! Yes, but I haven't told Cris yet. I saw how Alex fussed and Gabriel and Grant seem almost as bad. But today is St Valentine's Day, so I have ordered a special supper and I am going to tell him then.'

'You are looking smug,' Kate observed. 'I assume a new negligée is to hand?'

'Definitely. Sea-green silk. That should keep his mind off fussing.'

'So the four Lords of Disgrace are going to be the proud and respectable fathers of four babies within a year,' Tess mused. 'Just think, if one of you has a boy and two have girls, perhaps in twenty years' time we could be sitting down and planning two weddings.'

'Tess, you are a hopeless romantic,' Caroline teased. 'But what a wonderful thought. We all had such a rocky path to finding our true love and the men were there for each other…'

'Here they are.' Tamsyn waved to Cris, who stood with his friends, the four of them making the room seem crowded with masculine energy.

'And so beautiful, all of them,' Kate said with a sigh as their husbands crossed the room to them. 'And not looking in the slightest bit respectable, thank goodness.'

'What are up to, my ladies?' Cris asked, stooping to kiss his wife.

'We were just saying how handsome you all were.' Kate batted her eyelashes at Grant as he stretched out a hand to her.

'And what else?' Alex demanded. 'You are scheming, I can tell. I've come to claim my son for five minutes,' he added as he took the sleeping baby from Tess.

'Yes, we are,' Caroline agreed. 'But you can all relax. You will not need to worry for, oh…twenty years at least.'

Gabriel looked from his wife to his friends. 'Gentlemen, I suggest we retreat to the study and take young Dominic with us. I have no idea what our wives are up to, but he is going to need all the advice we can give him if he is to end up as happy as we are.'

* * * * *

LET'S TALK
Romance

For exclusive extracts, competitions
and special offers, find us online: